Burn Notice

CARI BLAKE

ISBN (Amazon): 9798277972007

ISBN (IngramSpark): 9798998947537

chapter
one

THE ALARM SHATTERED the relative quiet of Station 2 at 0347 hours, and I was moving before my brain fully processed the dispatcher's words.

"Structure fire, Sunset Manor Retirement Community, 1247 Oak Street. Engine 18, Truck 12, Battalion 3, respond."

Structure fire. The two words that made every firefighter's pulse spike, no matter how many times it turned out to be burnt toast or malfunctioning smoke detectors.

I was already moving, my crew falling into our practiced rhythm without a word needed. At five-foot-seven and lean from years of hauling equipment, I wasn't the most physically imposing lieutenant in the department, but I'd learned early that presence wasn't about size. It was about certainty.

And I was certain.

Martinez headed for the driver's seat while Thompson and Benny moved to their positions. This was muscle memory, built from hundreds of calls. We were almost at the end of our 48 hour shift, and B-shift was still moving sharp. That's what separated us from the others — we didn't slack off on day two.

Around me, the station exploded into controlled chaos. Each of us hit our designated gear rack. I stepped into my boots — bunker pants pre-positioned around them, suspenders hanging ready on the outside. Step, pull up pants, suspenders over shoulders, tighten.

Radio strap went under the coat first, adjusting it slightly to sit flat against my sports bra — a lesson I'd learned the hard way as a rookie when I'd trapped my radio under my gear. The department had finally gotten women's cut turnout gear two years ago, but the radio straps were still designed for someone without curves.

Antenna positioned along my back. Hood around my neck. Turnout coat on and zipped, radio mic clipped to the tab where I could find it blind. Gloves in their usual spot on my belt.

Fifty-four seconds. Not my best time, but respectable, especially for oh-dark-thirty. Benny was already in the driver's seat, doing his mental checklist, Martinez climbing into the back.

"Thompson, don't forget your irons," I called out, catching his eye. Thompson — forty-six, built like a fire hydrant and prematurely gray hair he claimed was from raising two daughters — flipped me off good-naturedly while securing his Halligan bar.

"One time, L.T. I forgot them *one* time..."

"Engine 18 responding," I radioed as Martinez fired up the diesel engine, air brakes hissing as we rolled out into the pre-dawn darkness.

"Engine 18. Be advised, caller reports heavy smoke visible from Building C, possible occupants still inside."

My stomach tightened. Sunset Manor housed over two hundred elderly residents, many with mobility issues. If this was real — if we had an actual working fire with potential entrapments — this could go bad fast.

"Thompson, start thinking water supply," I called over the engine noise. "There's a hydrant half a block south of the main entrance. Martinez, position us just past the building — leave room for Truck 12 to set up their aerial."

"Copy that, L.T."

I keyed my radio again. "Dispatch, Engine 18. Do we have confirmation on occupants?"

"Engine 18, be advised, facility staff is conducting headcount now. Battalion 3 is responding from quarters, ETA four minutes."

No confirmation. Which meant we had to assume the worst and hope for the best. I ran through the building layout in my head — single-story structure, decent egress, but filled with people who couldn't move quickly. We'd done walkthroughs here during day shifts.

I tried to picture Building C specifically. Corner unit, if I remembered right.

"Thirty seconds out," Benny announced, his voice steady as always. Twenty-three years on the job, and he still drove like every run mattered. He'd been my father's driver back in the day — probably the only reason my application to Station 2 hadn't hit any mysterious roadblocks when I'd transferred in as a rookie.

The red brick buildings of Sunset Manor came into view, emergency lighting casting everything in harsh relief. I scanned for smoke, flame, any sign of actual fire. Building C sat dark and quiet, no visible smoke from the exterior.

"Engine 18 on scene," I radioed. "Three-story residential facility, nothing showing from the Alpha side. Investigating Building C."

We positioned the engine and I was out before Martinez had fully stopped, grabbing my SCBA and helmet. Chin strap secured, mask hanging ready around my neck — we only masked up when we had confirmed smoke conditions. Thompson stood ready at the crosslay, hand on the loops, waiting for my size-up. No point pulling two hundred feet of hose for burnt toast.

"Thompson, Martinez, grab the water can and come with me. Benny, stand by at the panel."

A facility supervisor in pajamas and a bathrobe rushed over, looking frazzled but not panicked. "Lieutenant, I'm so sorry. Mrs. Jones in C-Wing tried to make popcorn in the microwave at three a.m. The bag caught fire, set off the smoke detector. We thought we had it out, but protocol says — "

"You did exactly right calling us," I assured her, though internally I was already deflating. Another false alarm. But we'd run it exactly like the real thing, because that's what you do. The day you assume it's nothing is the day someone dies. "Let me just confirm it's fully extinguished. Which unit?"

"C-4, just down this hallway and to the right."

The supervisor led us through the main entrance and down a short corridor that smelled like industrial disinfectant mixed with that faint nursing home scent — medications and cafeteria food and something indefinably institutional. The burnt-popcorn-and-melted-plastic smell hit as soon as we rounded the corner.

Mrs. Jones' kitchenette was exactly what I expected. The microwave door hung open, interior blackened but contained. Smoke detector chirped overhead, reset but still sensitive to the lingering haze. A pressurized water extinguisher sat on the counter — someone had made an attempt before we arrived.

"Mrs. Jones thought she'd set it for sixty seconds but hit six minutes," the supervisor explained. "She's mortified. We've moved her to the common area."

"These things happen," I said, pulling out my thermal imaging camera and doing a quick scan. No hot spots, no extension into the walls or cabinets. "You might want to review microwave safety with residents, but no harm done."

I keyed my radio. "Battalion 3, Engine 18. We have a light smoke condition, confined to the microwave unit. Building secure, no extension, no injuries. Power secured to the appliance."

"Copy, Engine 18. Battalion 3 is pulling up now. Need any additional resources?"

"Negative. We'll ventilate and return to service."

Thompson was already setting up the positive pressure fan in the doorway while Martinez opened windows. Within minutes, we'd cleared most of the smoke. Back outside, Truck 12 was just arriving, Captain Miller climbing down from the officer's seat with a knowing look.

"Let me guess," he called out. "Microwave casualty?"

"Popcorn," I confirmed, pulling off my helmet and loosening my coat. The pre-dawn air felt good against my sweat-dampened hair.

"That's the third time this month," Martinez muttered, helping Thompson load the fan back onto the engine. "Someone needs to hide the microwave popcorn."

"Or teach a basic cooking class," Thompson added, his voice dripping with his signature dry delivery. "I love being a firefighter at four in the morning."

Rodriguez from Truck 12 wandered over, grinning. "Hey, at least you got to stretch your legs. We didn't even get to take the stick out of bed."

"Yeah, well, at least you know which end of the ladder goes up,"

Thompson shot back automatically. "That's more than most truckies can manage."

"Big talk from a guy who probably needed help finding the front door," Rodriguez countered.

The familiar banter washed over me as I did a final walk-around of the engine, checking that all equipment was secured. A few years ago, I might have felt obligated to jump in with my own comeback, to prove I could hang with their humor. Now I just let it roll past like background noise — I had nothing to prove to anyone who still thought "that's what *she* said" jokes were peak comedy.

This was the reality of the job — ninety percent routine calls, ten percent life-and-death emergencies, and you never knew which was which until you arrived.

"All right, let's wrap it up," I said. "Martinez, get the water can back on the engine. Thompson, make sure the fan's secured. We don't get sloppy just because it was a nothing call."

"Roger that, L.T."

Battalion Chief Evans appeared from his SUV, coffee somehow already in hand despite the hour. "Good response time, Delgado."

"Thank you, sir."

"How's the crew holding up? You're, what, thirty-seven hours in?"

"Thirty-eight, sir. They're solid." I glanced at my crew loading equipment with the same precision they'd show at hour one. "B-shift doesn't do tired."

He nodded approvingly. "Captain O'Sullivan trained you all well. Speaking of which, how's he doing?"

The question hit me square in the chest, but I kept my expression neutral. "Hanging in there, sir. Has a treatment this afternoon."

"Good man. Give him my best." Evans headed back to his vehicle, already pulling out his phone to probably update the duty chief.

Twenty minutes later, Engine 18 was backing into the bay at Station 2. The sky was starting to lighten in the east, that gray pre-dawn that meant the overnight was almost done. Ten more hours until shift change. Ten hours until I could pick up Cap for his appointment at the cancer center.

As we climbed down from the rig, Martinez shook his head. "False alarm number forty-seven this month. I swear, if I have to respond to one more burnt dinner..."

"You'll respond professionally and treat it like the real thing," I finished for him. "Because the day we start assuming it's nothing is the day someone dies while we're rolling our eyes."

He had the grace to look sheepish. "Yes, ma'am."

"Besides," Benny added, running his hand along the pump panel one last time, "keeps us sharp. I'd rather run a hundred false alarms than miss the one real one because we got complacent."

Smart man. It's why he'd lasted twenty-three years and counting.

"L.T., I'm gonna hit the shower before someone else uses all the hot water," Thompson announced.

"Or all the shampoo," Martinez added darkly. "Assuming A-shift left us any."

I headed for the office to complete the incident report, but paused at the apparatus bay door. My crew moved with quiet efficiency, each handling their post-call tasks without needing direction. Thompson was already wiping down his tools. Martinez double-checked the medical bag supplies. Benny ran his hand along the engine's pump panel like he was petting a faithful dog.

This was why Station 2 had the best response times in the county. This was why other departments requested us for mutual aid. And this was why I couldn't afford to show weakness, even for a second.

My phone buzzed. A text from Cap. Up early this morning, although after his diagnosis, he'd been sleeping less. "Gonna be sleeping forever soon," he'd told me darkly, "why sleep now?"

CAP

Still good for the 1430 appointment?
Margaret's making me eat actual breakfast
first. Says coffee doesn't count.

I typed back:

I'll be there. And she's right about the coffee.

CAP

Don't you start too, kiddo.

I smiled despite myself, then locked the phone and focused on the paperwork. Incident report: food on the stove, no injuries, no property damage beyond one microwave. Straightforward.

But as I filled out the forms, listening to my crew's voices drift in from the apparatus bay — Thompson complaining about A-shift, Martinez defending his shower schedule, Benny mediating with his quiet humor — I let myself feel grateful for the nothing call.

In ten hours, I'd be sitting in a different kind of uncomfortable chair, watching poison drip into the veins of the man who'd helped raise me. But right now, my crew was safe, the residents of Sunset Manor were safe, and we had ten more hours to be ready for whatever came next.

Even if it was just another bag of popcorn.

chapter
two

Jimmy

THERE ARE two fundamental truths about the night shift in the Metro General ER. The first is that the laws of space and time cease to apply somewhere around 3 a.m. The second is that you either learn to ride the chaotic, caffeine-fueled wave, or you have a complete nervous breakdown.

"It's only a half-joke," I told Chloe, my new orientee, as we cleared the last suture-removal kit from the Fast Track bay. It was just past eleven, the hour when we officially shut down the minor care area and the real night began. From now until sunrise, every cough, cut, and chest pain would come through the main ER doors.

"So ... breakdown it is, then," she muttered, her eyes already wide with the signature terror of a nurse new to the nocturnal chaos. She was barely a month in, still carrying the shine of nursing school theory that hadn't yet been scuffed off by the gritty reality of emergency medicine.

"Nah, you'll be fine," I said, steering her toward the breakroom. "The secret is carbs. And denial."

"Night shift is different," I continued. "Day shift has every resource imaginable. Cafeteria's open, case managers in the ER, dedicated pharmacist, administrators checking on things every hour. We get vending machines, one case manager for the entire hospital, and pharmacy calls from whoever's covering upstairs. But you know what we also get? Freedom. No suits parading through at 2 a.m. checking if your scrub top is regulation navy blue."

I placed a comically large Tupperware container on the counter and popped the lid. The rich scent of brown butter, chocolate, and vanilla immediately filled the small room, a more effective beacon than any pager. The reaction was instantaneous. From various corners of the room, where tired staff were documenting notes or chugging questionable-looking energy drinks, heads popped up. It was like a scene from a nature documentary, if the apex predators wore scrubs and responded to the crinkle of a plastic container.

"Plus," I said, lowering my voice conspiratorially, "night shift has to be tight-knit. We don't have a choice. Day shift leaves us notes about things they 'didn't have time to fix' because night shift is supposedly 'slower.' Which is sometimes true, but not nearly as much as they'd like you to believe. Meanwhile, the inpatient nurses act like we're personally attacking them when we try to send up an admission at 3 a.m. because we're interrupting their Netflix time."

Chloe looked alarmed. "Is there really that much tension between shifts?"

"Nah, not really. A few years back, management tried swapping people between day and night to 'build understanding.' Went over like a lead balloon — turns out everyone likes their own brand of chaos. It's like dogs barking at each other through a fence. All noise until you open the gate, then everyone gets along fine."

"Dalton, you beautiful bastard," Doug, another night nurse, said, materializing as if out of thin air at the prospect of cookies. "Did you bring the good stuff?"

"Only the best."

I make the cookies by the gross. The recipe is a Frankenstein's monster of a dozen others I've tweaked over the years — European butter, three times the vanilla the original recipe calls for, and just enough instant pudding mix to keep them soft for days. The real trick is letting the dough rest in the fridge for at least twenty-four hours to let the flavors get to know each other. I can't eat that many myself (I'd discover Type III diabetes if I tried to, anyway), and bringing them here is better than any team-building exercise HR could dream up.

You could leave a tray of E. coli-tainted deli meat on the breakroom counter and it would vanish if it was free, but even I'm impressed by how fast the cookies disappear. Chloe took one, biting into it tentatively. Her eyes widened in reverence.

"Oh my God."

"See? You'll make it through the night." I grabbed one for myself. "Alright, let's go get our assignment from the boss."

We walked back into the main department, the relative quiet of Fast Track giving way to the steady beeps and alarms of the acute side. Carly, our night-shift charge nurse, was standing at the main station, her back to us, on the phone with Admitting.

"...I don't care if you don't have a tele bed," she said, her voice tight with frustration. "This one's a ticking time bomb. Find one." She hung up with a sharp click and turned, her eyes landing on us. She was a phenomenal nurse — sharp, quick, and technically skilled — but as charge, she wore her stress like armor, often coming across as prickly and dismissive.

"Finally," she said. "I've got a real winner for you in Room 5. Fifty-two-year-old male, came in drunker than a lord — "

"Hold that thought," I interrupted, holding up the Tupperware container like a peace offering. "Cookie?"

Carly's eyes narrowed, then darted to the container. A flicker of something other than stress crossed her face. Her shoulders slumped just a fraction.

"Dalton," she sighed, a hint of a smile finally breaking through her tough exterior. She took a cookie, her eyes brightening as she took a bite. "I knew I loved you for a reason." She leaned in and gave me a quick, one-armed hug before turning her attention to my shadow.

She sized up Chloe with a practiced, critical eye. "You must be the new meat. Chloe, right?" Chloe nodded, looking terrified.

Carly's expression softened. "Well, if you have to be with a nurse preceptor, you could do a lot worse than Jimmy here," she said, then turned back to me, a mischievous glint in her eyes. "Although, Jimmy, I'm surprised they let you precept again, after what happened to the last orientee. Oof."

Chloe's jaw practically hit the floor. I just laughed. "Does that joke ever get old?"

Carly put a hand on her chest in mock offense. "Absolutely not, how dare you ruin it early! You're supposed to at least pretend for a little bit!" She shook her head, then handed me the chart for Bay 5. "Now go deal with your drunken ankle pain so I can figure out where to put this chest pain. And save me another cookie for my 3 a.m. crisis."

"You got it, boss."

As Carly marched off to fight her next battle with the bed board, Chloe whispered, "What ... what happened to the last orientee?"

I laughed. "Nothing, that's just a joke that was old back when the old-timers used it on *us*," I said, leading her toward Bay 5. "Nobody comes up with new jokes here, we just recycle the old ones until everyone who knows them is gone."

The man in Bay 5 was exactly as advertised: loud, belligerent, and smelling faintly of stale beer and regret. For the next hour, I navigated the delicate art of de-escalation, a skill they don't teach you in nursing school. It involved a lot of patient listening, a little bit of firm boundary-setting, and a well-timed offering of a turkey sandwich. By the time we discharged him, he was calling me his best friend and promising to name his firstborn son after me.

"How did you do that?" Chloe asked, looking bewildered as she cleaned the room. "He was threatening to sue us ten minutes ago."

"Most people, even the angry ones, just want to be heard," I said, stripping off my gloves. "And never underestimate the persuasive power of a warm blanket and a free sandwich."

That was the rhythm of the night shift. It wasn't always dramatic life-or-death situations. More often than not, it was this: small acts of kindness, the quiet untangling of human messes, one patient at a time. It was holding the hand of a scared grandmother, explaining a diagnosis for the fifth time to a worried spouse, or just sitting with someone in the dark until the turkey sandwich worked its magic.

I settled in at the nurses' station to chart, the vast, quiet hours of the night stretching before us. This was my world — predictably unpre-dictable. And for now, it was enough. I had my crew, my cookies, and the steady, quiet satisfaction of knowing that, in this little pocket of fluorescent-lit chaos, I was making a difference.

chapter
three

Izzy

THE MORNING EQUIPMENT check was a sacred ritual at Station 2, and I ran mine like a military inspection. Every piece of gear had to be spotless, every tool in its designated place, every system tested and logged. We were forty-two hours into our shift now, but standards didn't slip on B-shift.

"Martinez, when's the last time that SCBA was decontaminated?" I asked, running my hand along the air bottle's housing.

"Last week after that garage fire on Maple, L.T.," he replied, pulling up the maintenance log on his tablet. "Full wash-down, dried, and inspected. Greco checked all the bottle dates this morning — we're all current through next quarter."

I nodded, checking the regulator connections myself. *Trust but verify*. "Thompson, how's that hose bed looking?"

"Like a work of art," Thompson called from the back of Engine 18, his voice dripping with pride. "Minuteman load, packed tight enough to bounce a quarter off. A-shift left us their usual triple-layer disaster, but we fixed that before coffee."

"Before coffee?" Martinez looked impressed. "That's dedication."

"That's survival," Thompson corrected. "You think I'm going into a fire with their spaghetti special? I choose life."

I climbed up to inspect his work. The hose lay in perfect folds, each section positioned for rapid deployment without snags. Thompson might be salty as hell, but when it came to the technical work, he was flawless.

"Outstanding. Benny, pump panel?"

"All green, Lieutenant. Pressure tested, foam proportioner calibrated, deck gun checked and secured." Benny Carter's voice carried the quiet confidence of twenty-three years on the job. "Running smoother than A-shift's bald heads."

"Hey now," Rodriguez called over from Truck 12, "leave Santoro's chrome dome out of this. That thing's a safety hazard — blinds pilots on approach to the airport."

My phone buzzed. Cap's ringtone, the one I'd chosen just for him. *Simple Man*. The joking died away immediately.

Everyone knew that ringtone.

"Excuse me," I told the crew, stepping into the apparatus bay where the engine noise would mask the conversation.

"Morning, Cap."

"Izzy." His voice sounded tired but steady. These days, I cataloged every conversation, noted every cough, every pause. "Just confirming today's appointment. Three thirty pickup still work for you?"

"Of course. Regular treatment?"

"Yeah, just the usual poison drip," he said with dark humor that didn't quite mask the fear underneath. "Margaret's coming, too. Says I need supervision."

"She's not wrong."

"Et tu, kiddo?" But I could hear the smile in his voice. "How's the shift going?"

"Quiet morning. Nothing big."

"Always nice." He paused, and I heard him take a careful breath. "Alright. Stay safe."

"I will. See you at three thirty."

Cap's medical retirement had been processed two months ago, pancreatic cancer listed as having come from a line-of-duty exposure. After thirty-two years of breathing smoke and chemicals, his body had finally said enough. The treatments were buying time, nothing more, but we'd take every day we could get.

I hung up and rejoined the crew, pushing down the familiar knot in my stomach. Six more hours until shift change, then straight to pick up Cap. Focus on what you can control, Delgado.

"Alright, let's finish checks," I said. "Rodriguez, how's that ladder truck running?"

From across the bay, Rodriguez looked up from Truck 12's equipment compartment. "All systems green, Lieutenant. Hydraulics tested, stabilizers functioning, aerial smooth as butter. Checked and double-checked."

"Good. Make sure your crew's following decon protocols."

Rodriguez nodded seriously. The younger guys thought I was being paranoid about gear contamination, but they hadn't watched what thirty-two years of "just doing the job" could do to the best man you'd ever known.

"Hey, L.T.," Martinez called out, "you seeing this?"

I turned to find most of the crew gathered around the TV in the day room, staring at the screen with expressions of absolute horror. On screen, actors in firefighter gear were standing in what appeared to be a kitchen, their SCBA masks dangling casually from their necks while smoke rolled past them.

"What the hell are they doing?" Thompson demanded, pointing at the TV.

"*Milwaukee Fire*," Benny said grimly. "Rodriguez put it on during breakfast."

"I didn't know it would be this bad," Rodriguez protested from Truck 12's bay.

On screen, one of the actors was leaning against a kitchen counter, his mask resting on the same surface where food was being prepared. The entire crew recoiled as if they were watching someone juggle live grenades.

"Turn it off," O'Malley called from the truck. "I can't watch anymore."

"No, wait," Thompson said, his voice filled with morbid fascination. "I want to see how much worse it gets."

The actor picked up his mask and put it directly on his face without any cleaning, having just had it sitting on a contaminated surface next to someone's lunch.

"JESUS CHRIST!" Martinez yelped, actually stepping back from the TV. "That thing's never been cleaned! Ever!"

"It's like they're trying to give themselves cancer," Rodriguez muttered.

"*Ope, sorry there rook, but lemme tell ya how we do things in Milwaukee,*" the actor playing the seasoned veteran was telling his "probie" with theatrical wisdom, "*When that bell rings, you grab your gear and you run into that fire like you're headed to a fish fry on Friday.*"

"Did he just say 'ope'?" Benny asked. "Do people actually say that?"

"Alright, enough torture," I said, though I'll admit I was transfixed by the horror show, too. "Turn it off before someone has a stroke."

"But L.T., they're about to eat food that was sitting next to the dirty gear," Thompson protested. "This is like watching a snuff film."

"Off. Now. That's an order."

Rodriguez grabbed the remote and switched to a cooking show. The visible tension in the room decreased immediately, though Martinez was still muttering about "criminal negligence" and "lawsuit waiting to happen."

"How do they expect people to take us seriously when that's what they put on TV?" Martinez asked, still looking genuinely shaken.

"Because most people don't know any better," Benny said. "They think it's just soot, not carcinogens. They see the hero shots, not the guys dying at fifty from throat cancer."

"Speaking of soot," Thompson said, breaking the silence with forced energy, "when's the last time you truckies actually cleaned your gear instead of just posing for calendar photos?"

"We follow protocol," Rodriguez shot back, grateful for the return to normal. "Unlike you water fairies who think soap is optional."

"Soap? We use industrial degreaser. You need it when you actually work for a living."

"Work? You mean standing around pointing a hose while we do all the thinking?"

"Thinking? Is that what you call it when you spend twenty minutes figuring out which end of the ladder goes up?"

"At least we don't treat nozzle time like foreplay. Maybe if you finished faster, we wouldn't have to ventilate so much."

"Hah! Makes perfect sense, 'cause teaching a truckie is like having sex with a rock. It's really fucking hard."

"Your wife tell you that?" Rodriguez grinned. "Makes sense, she's been looking for something hard — "

"Alright, *children*," I interrupted before Thompson could launch himself across the day room. "Save it for the training ground."

Battalion Chief Evans appeared in the bay doorway, coffee in hand like always. The man had a sixth sense for showing up right when the crew was getting rowdy. "Morning, Delgado. Equipment checks going well?"

"Yes, sir. All apparatus ready for service."

"Good." He glanced toward the day room where Thompson and Rodriguez were still trading glares. "Crew seems... spirited this morning."

"Just the usual engine-truck rivalry, sir. Keeps them sharp."

"Right." Evans shifted awkwardly, doing that thing where he wanted to say something but couldn't quite get there. "Listen, how's Captain O'Sullivan doing? Heard he's got another treatment scheduled."

"He's hanging in there. Stays positive. The whole department's been supportive."

"Good man. Thirty-two years of service, and half the department still calls him for advice." Evans nodded approvingly. "Hell, I called him last week about that hazmat incident on the south side. You tell him the battalion's thinking of him."

"I will, sir."

After Evans left, Thompson appeared at my elbow. "BC's not wrong about Cap. Man's got more friends in this department than anyone else. Did you know he showed up at Rodriguez's wedding? Kid didn't even work under him, but Cap heard his folks couldn't make it from Puerto Rico, so he stood in."

"That's Cap," I said. He had a way of knowing exactly when someone needed a quiet word or a firm push. He'd pulled me out of more than one dark moment over the years, especially after my dad died.

The alarm tones cut through our conversation. "*Engine 18, Truck 12, Medic 402, respond to vehicle accident with possible entrapment, Highway 45 northbound at Montrose Road.*"

The world snapped into focus. The banter died. The crew moved as one.

"Engine 18 responding," I said into my shoulder mic, already swinging into the officer's seat. Behind me, I heard Truck 12's diesel roar to life.

The ride out was all business, Benny navigating traffic while I pulled up the location on our mobile data terminal. Highway 45 at Montrose — that was a bad stretch, a curve where people always took the bend too fast.

"Truck 12, Engine 18," Captain Miller's voice came over the radio. "We'll set up for stabilization. You guys handle fire suppression if needed."

"Copy that, Truck 12."

This was the dance — ego and rivalry vanished the second the tones dropped. Out here, we were one team with one goal.

We were first on scene by thirty seconds. A sedan lay on its passenger side against the guardrail, roof crumpled where it had made contact. Fluids leaking, that sharp smell of coolant and oil mixing with morning dew.

My training took over. "Benny, position us for a block. Thompson, Martinez, grab the water can and stand by. Truck 12's gonna need room to work."

Miller's crew was already pulling up, their movements efficient and purposeful. I saw O'Malley grabbing the combi tool while Rodriguez set up cribbing. My crew positioned for fire watch — with fluids leaking and a potential ignition source, we couldn't be too careful.

I made my way to the vehicle for patient contact. Inside, a young woman with wide, terrified eyes, suspended by her seatbelt, driver's side door crushed inward.

"Hi, I'm Lieutenant Delgado with the fire department," I said, my voice calm and steady. "We're going to get you out of here. What's your name?"

"Ashley," she whispered, her voice trembling. "I can't... I can't feel my legs."

"Okay, Ashley. Sometimes that happens when you're in this position. We're going to move very carefully. The truck company's the best in the city — they'll have you out in just a few minutes. Can you wiggle your fingers for me?"

She could. Good sign. I kept talking to her, maintaining that calm presence while Miller's crew worked the hydraulics. The sound of tearing metal and breaking glass filled the air, but Ashley's eyes stayed locked on mine.

Jack McKenzie from Medic 402 appeared at my shoulder, his trauma bag in hand. We exchanged a quick, professional nod — I'd been maintaining c-spine stabilization without even thinking about it.

"Patient is conscious and alert, Jack. Complaining of numbness in lower extremities, but that could be positional. Airway's clear. We'll have her out for you in three."

"Copy that, L.T."

In four minutes and thirty seconds, Miller's crew had the door off and the dash rolled. Jack slipped in with a c-collar while I maintained stabilization. Together, we got Ashley on a backboard and into Jack's care. As they loaded her into the ambulance, she grabbed my hand.

"Thank you," she whispered.

"You did great, Ashley. They're going to take good care of you."

It was a clean, efficient operation. Textbook. Engine and truck working together like we'd never exchanged a harsh word. That's what mattered out here.

Back in the engine, the adrenaline began to fade, leaving that familiar post-call quiet. We'd controlled the chaos. We'd fixed the problem. Miller's crew had already left — truck companies always cleared first, the glory boys — but there'd be a case of beer from them in our fridge tomorrow. That was the way it worked. We talked shit, but we took care of each other.

"Good stabilization, L.T.," Thompson said quietly. "That girl was lucky you kept her calm."

"That's the job," I said, but I was thinking about Ashley's eyes, that terror slowly replaced by trust. This was why we did it. This was what made all the false alarms and politics worth it.

But as we drove back to the station, the knot in my stomach returned, tighter than before. In four hours, I'd be sitting in a different kind of chair, watching a different kind of professional try to save someone. I could cut a person out of twisted metal, keep them calm in their worst moment, coordinate a rescue with precision.

But I couldn't cut the cancer out of the man who was more of a father to me than my own had ever been.

And for that problem, there was no tool, no training, no textbook solution. There was only being there, the same way he'd always been there for me.

Three thirty couldn't come fast enough.

chapter
four

THE WITCHING HOUR in the ER isn't midnight; it's the dead space between two and four in the morning. It's when the city's fever finally breaks, leaving behind a strange, quiet stillness punctuated by the rhythmic beeping of monitors and the occasional soft groan from a curtained-off bay. It's when the exhaustion really settles into your bones.

"How are you holding up?" I asked Chloe, keeping my voice low. We were catching up on charting at the main nurses' station, the glow of the computer monitors painting our faces.

"I think the edge is wearing off," she whispered, her eyes wide. "Everything feels ... weirdly quiet. It's creeping me out."

"That's just the night shift settling in," I said. "Don't worry, it never lasts."

As if on cue, the triage doors slid open and a young man, probably early twenties, shuffled in, holding a bloody rag to his upper arm. He was doing a poor job of acting casual, his eyes darting around the empty waiting room as if he expected a SWAT team to rappel from the ceiling.

"I'll take him," I said, nodding to Chloe to follow me.

I led him back to an empty bay, the scent of iron from the blood already sharp in the air. "What's going on tonight?" I asked, my voice calm and neutral as I pulled on a fresh pair of gloves.

"Uh, roofing injury," he mumbled, not quite meeting my eyes.

"Roofing injury?" I kept my tone conversational, reaching for gauze. "What kind of roofing injury?"

He shifted on the gurney, wincing slightly. "It was, uh... a roofing nailer."

I carefully pulled the rag away from his arm. It was a clean, circular wound. A through-and-through. "A roofing nailer," I said, my tone perfectly even. I glanced at the clock on the wall. It was 2:15 a.m. "At two in the morning?"

"Yeah," he said, a little too quickly. "Night job. Construction deadline."

"I see." I cleaned the wound, my movements efficient. "That's an interesting diameter for a roofing nail."

The kid just shrugged, his jaw tight.

I dressed the wound. It was superficial, clean, and wouldn't require much more than a good cleaning and some antibiotics. But we both knew what it was. Chloe, standing behind me, knew what it was. The kid knew we knew. But the word "gunshot" was never spoken. Because if he said "gunshot," I'd have to call the cops. The unspoken agreement hung in the air between us: *I'll let you call it a roofing nail if you let us stitch you up and keep you from getting a nasty infection.*

After he left, with a prescription for antibiotics and strict instructions for wound care, Chloe turned to me, her expression a mixture of confusion and frustration.

"That was a bullet wound," she said, her voice a hushed accusation. "We should have called the police."

I led her to a quiet corner of the nurses' station. "You're right, it was. Looked like a 9mm to me. And you saw how he was looking over his shoulder. He's scared. He's probably in trouble. But our job isn't to be detectives, Chloe. Our job is to treat the patient in front of us."

"But he lied to us!"

"Probably. Maybe he *was* roofing; heck, we don't know. But if he lied, it was because he was afraid," I countered gently. "Gun violence in this city is endemic. Guns are everywhere. But if we start pushing people, if we make them feel like this isn't a safe place, they won't come. He'll go home, pour some whiskey on that wound, and show up here in a week with a raging infection, septic or worse. We have to be a sanctuary. By our very nature, the ER has to make itself vulnerable to be a place people aren't afraid to come to in their most desperate moments. We treat the wound, not the story."

Chloe was quiet for a moment, processing this. I could see her wrestling with the ethical complexity of what we did here — the gray areas that nursing school never quite prepared you for.

"Come on," I said, gesturing toward the supply room. "Let's restock while it's quiet. Night shift rule number one: always be ready for the next wave."

We spent the next twenty minutes refilling the crash carts and checking expiration dates on medications. It was the kind of mundane task that gave your mind time to process what you'd just seen, to file it away in that mental compartment marked "things that happened but we don't talk about."

Around 3 a.m., we got a straightforward case — a middle-aged woman with a kidney stone, writhing in pain. I walked Chloe through starting the IV, drawing labs, and administering pain medication. Within thirty minutes, the woman was resting comfortably, tears of relief streaming down her face.

"Thank you," she whispered, grabbing my hand. "Thank you so much. That was worse than when I had my son."

"Just doing our job," I said, but Chloe caught my eye and I saw her understanding something — that sometimes our job was about more than medical care. Sometimes it was about witnessing someone's pain and making it stop.

We were back at the nurses' station, Chloe practicing her documentation while I reviewed lab results, when Carly appeared looking harried.

"I need a coffee," she announced. "This shift is testing me. Mrs. Patterson in Bay 6 has asked me four times if we can call her psychic to consult on her diagnosis."

"Did you?" I asked, deadpan.

"I was tempted. The psychic probably has better availability than cardiology." She rubbed her eyes. "How's the new kid doing?"

"She's got good instincts," I said, glancing at Chloe, who was pretending not to listen while clearly hanging on every word.

"Good. We need more nurses who can handle the weird stuff without losing their minds." Carly started to walk away, then paused. "Oh, heads up — Bay 3 just got interesting. Might need you in a few minutes."

"Interesting how?" I asked, but she was already heading toward the medication room.

I turned to Chloe. "In ER speak, 'interesting' is never good."

Sure enough, ten minutes later, the charge phone rang. Carly's voice was strained. "Jimmy, can you and your new shadow come give me a hand in Bay 3?"

We walked in to find a man in his late forties on the gurney, his face a mask of pain and profound embarrassment. He was curled on his side, clutching a pillow to his abdomen.

"Mr. Smith here had an accident," Carly said, her face a perfect, professional blank. "He tells me he ... fell in the shower."

"On a bottle of shampoo," the man added, his voice a pained squeak.

I looked at the X-ray pulled up on the monitor screen. A full-sized bottle of shampoo was lodged, impossibly, in his rectum.

"I see," I said, my voice betraying nothing. "Well, let's see what we can do to help you get fixed up, Mr. Smith."

Chloe stood frozen by the door, her mouth slightly agape. I gave her a look that said, *Not. A. Word.*

Later, after we had successfully assisted the doctor with the, ahh ... *extraction*, and Mr. Smith was resting comfortably, Chloe finally spoke.

"There is no way," she whispered, shaking her head in disbelief. "There is no way he just fell on that."

"The physics alone are staggering," I agreed quietly. "The aim required would get him into the Guinness Book of World Records. But you know what we do here, Chloe?"

She looked at me, the lesson from the "roofing nail" incident starting to sink in.

"We don't judge," I said. "We don't laugh. We don't share the story in the breakroom. Because we want Mr. Smith, and every other Mr. Smith out there, to feel safe enough to come to us when they've made a mistake, or done something they're ashamed of, or just found them-selves in a situation they can't get out of alone. Our job is to fix the problem, no questions asked."

I could see the understanding dawning in her eyes. This was the real work of the night shift. It wasn't just about medicine. It was about creating a small, brightly-lit island of non-judgment in the middle of a dark and complicated world.

"Does this happen a lot?" Chloe asked as we headed back to the nurses' station.

"More than you'd think. People are creative, and sometimes creativity meets poor judgment. Our job isn't to figure out how they got into these situations. It's to get them out safely."

The rest of the shift settled into a more predictable rhythm. A woman with chest pain that turned out to be anxiety. She was convinced she was dying, tears streaming down her face as she clutched at her hospital gown.

"My heart won't stop racing," she gasped. "Something's wrong. Something's really wrong."

I pulled up a chair beside her bed — not standing over her, not hovering by the door, but sitting at her eye level. "What's your name?"

"Patty."

"Patty, I want you to breathe with me. In through your nose, hold it, out through your mouth." I demonstrated, exaggerating the slowness. "Your body thinks you're in danger, but you're safe. We're going to remind it together."

For twenty minutes, we sat there breathing together. I told her about the physiology of panic — how her body was doing exactly what it was supposed to do, just at the wrong time. By the end, her heart rate had dropped from 140 to 85, and she was managing a shaky smile.

"Thank you for not making me feel crazy," she said.

"You're not crazy," I told her. "You're human. There's a difference."

A teenager with what his mother was convinced was appendicitis but was actually gas. The relief on both their faces when the CT came back clear was worth the radiation exposure.

At 5:03 a.m., right on schedule, the charge desk phone rang. I happened to be passing by, so I answered it.

"Metro General ER, this is Jimmy."

"Hi, this is Sandra from Sunset Gardens. We're calling EMS, but I just wanted to give you report. We've got an 82-year-old female, ground-level fall, found down by her bed about twenty minutes ago. She's alert and oriented but complaining of hip pain..."

I took the report, hung up, and then turned to Chloe. "And there it is. 5 a.m. Right on time."

"What?"

"Someone just went to check on grandma and found her down on the floor. Gravity. It's not just a good idea, it's the law."

Chloe looked confused. "Is that... normal?"

"Like clockwork. The 5 a.m. nursing home calls are as predictable as the sunrise. Poor lady probably got up to use the bathroom, got a little dizzy, down she went. We'll get her sorted out."

As the ambulance pulled up outside, I felt the familiar satisfaction of another night shift drawing to a close. We'd handled gunshot wounds disguised as construction accidents, embarrassing injuries that required delicate care, and now we'd help an elderly woman who'd had an unlucky encounter with gravity.

This was the job: meeting people in their worst moments and somehow making them better, one patient at a time. No judgment, no questions they didn't want to answer, just care.

And in a few hours, day shift would take over, and we'd do it all again tomorrow night.

chapter
five

Izzy

THE FIRST DAY off after a forty-eight-hour shift was always a disorienting limbo. My body, still humming with the ghost vibrations of the engine and the phantom shrill of alarm tones, didn't know what to do with stillness. My apartment, a small but meticulously clean one-bedroom in a quiet part of the city, felt like an alien planet compared to the controlled chaos of Station 2. Here, there were no checklists, no urgent calls, no crew to manage. There was only me.

I spent the first few hours in a ritual of decontamination, both physical and mental. My dirty station uniform went straight into the washing machine on the sanitary cycle, a habit ingrained so deeply it was second nature. I stood under the spray of a scalding hot shower for a solid twenty minutes, methodically scrubbing away the grime and the lingering smell of smoke that seemed to seep into my pores. It wasn't just about being clean; it was about washing away the shift, shedding the skin of Lieutenant Delgado to find the woman underneath.

The woman underneath, I reflected as I pulled on a pair of worn-out sweatpants and a threadbare academy t-shirt, was a lot less sure of herself.

At the station, I was in command. My orders were followed without question because my crew trusted my judgment. My world was a series of problems with tactical solutions: a fire required water, an entrapment required hydraulics, a medical emergency required a clear protocol. I knew the steps. I knew the rules.

Here, in the quiet of my own living room, the problems were messier. There was the ever-growing stack of paperwork for my Captain's promotion exam, a mountain of policies and procedures I had to memorize. And, of course, the low-grade hum of anxiety about BC Evans and the political games being played by Lieutenant Santoro.

The car incident still burned, three months later. Not because of what happened (which was objectively *hilarious*), but because of how Santoro had weaponized it.

I'd dealt with Santoro's brand of bullshit before. The way he'd talk over me in officer meetings. The backhanded compliments—"Pretty good stop for a crew your size" or "Impressive you got that line stretched so fast, considering." The jokes that weren't quite jokes, delivered with a smile that dared you to take offense. Deniable. Always deniable.

But that had been generic asshole behavior. The ambient misogyny of a guy who resented sharing space with women but knew better than to say it out loud. The car incident had made it personal. Like a bully who'd always been looking for an excuse, and now he had one. *Look what you made me do.*

It had been a nothing call. Automatic fire alarm at a dentist's office, probably a contractor setting off dust. But when the tones dropped, Santoro's pristine white Dodge Charger was parked directly in front of Engine 18's bay door. He'd been at Station 2 for some battalion meeting, supposedly "just running in for a minute."

I'd gone looking for him. Day room, empty. Kitchen, empty. I was checking the back hallway when I heard the diesel engine fire up behind me.

By the time I got back to the apparatus bay, the Charger was sitting on the grass strip next to the parking lot, and Engine 18 was rolling out. Thompson was climbing into his seat with the expression of a man who had done nothing wrong and would swear to it in court. Benny's face was carefully neutral, which was how I knew he'd helped.

I didn't order it. I didn't do it. But God help me, I laughed my ass off.

Santoro emerged from the bathroom ninety seconds later, still tucking in his shirt, to find his car decorating the lawn like a misplaced garden ornament. By the time we got back from the false alarm, he'd already been on the phone with someone — I never found out who.

If Thompson's crew had done that to Martinez's Honda, it would've been a legend. They'd still be telling the story at retirement parties twenty years from now. But when my crew did it to Santoro's Charger, suddenly it was "evidence of a hostile work environment" and "questions about Lieutenant Delgado's command presence."

Evans had called me into his office the next week. "Look, I know Santoro can be... particular," he'd said, not meeting my eyes. "But you've got to keep your guys in line. This kind of thing doesn't look good for someone up for promotion."

"My guys cleared an obstructed bay door so we could respond to a call," I'd said. "They didn't damage anything. They didn't touch him. They moved a car that shouldn't have been there."

"I know, I know. But perception matters, Delgado. You've got to think about how things look."

How things look. The unofficial motto of every old boys' club since the dawn of time. It doesn't matter what actually happened. It matters how the people in power choose to describe it.

My crew had done what any crew would do. They just didn't have to think about how it would be twisted — they'd never had to. That was a weight they didn't carry. I didn't blame them for it.

And honestly? If it hadn't been the car, it would have been something else. A call I ran that made him look slow. A commendation that should have been his. The way I answered a question in an officer's meeting. Men like Santoro didn't need real reasons. They just needed excuses — something to point to when they did what they were always going to do anyway.

The car just made it convenient.

Even so, those were problems I could at least fight, even if the deck was stacked. But the biggest problem — the most unsolvable problem of all — was Cap.

I sank onto my couch, the worn leather sighing under my weight. I picked up my phone, my thumb hovering over his contact. I'd seen him yesterday for his treatment, and he'd looked ... *tired*. More than tired. The strength that had always seemed to radiate from him, the quiet confidence that had mentored half the department, was fading, eroded by the relentless poison of his illness and the equally toxic poison they pumped into his veins to fight it.

My job was to run into burning buildings. To face down chaos and wrestle it into submission. But I couldn't fight this. I couldn't command the cancer to stand down. I couldn't force a solution. All I could do was drive him to his appointments, sit with him in sterile waiting rooms, and pretend I wasn't watching the best man I'd ever known slowly disappear before my eyes. The helplessness was a physical weight, a crushing pressure in my chest that no amount of training could prepare me for.

I forced myself up, busying my hands to quiet my mind. I cleaned my already-clean kitchen. I organized my bookshelf by color, then by author, then back by color. I did a brutal HIIT workout in my living room until my muscles screamed and my lungs burned, the physical pain a welcome distraction from the emotional kind. By the time I finally collapsed back onto the couch, exhaustion had won. I fell into a deep, dreamless sleep, the kind that only comes after forty-eight hours on duty.

I woke up three hours later, still restless, my body refusing to accept true rest. The afternoon sun streamed through my windows, highlighting the sterile functionality of my living space. No photos on the walls, no personal touches that might reveal who I was beneath the uniform. Just clean lines and practical furniture.

Unable to sit still, I grabbed my keys and headed down to the parking lot.

My father's 1995 Ford F-150 sat in my assigned space like a shrine to everything I'd lost and everything I was trying to become. Miguel Delgado had restored this truck with his own hands, teaching me to hold a wrench before I could properly hold a pencil. The forest green paint still gleamed despite its age, the chrome bumper reflecting the afternoon light.

I popped the hood and began my ritual inspection. Oil levels, coolant, belts, hoses — everything Miguel had taught me to check. The mechanical precision of the engine was soothing in a way that promotion study materials never could be. Here was something I could understand completely, something I could fix if it broke.

"That's a beautiful truck."

I looked up to find Mrs. Park from apartment 3B standing nearby with her small dog, both of them watching me with friendly curiosity.

"Thank you," I said, wiping my hands on an old rag. "It was my father's."

"Was he a mechanic?"

"Firefighter. But he liked to tinker." I closed the hood, signaling the end of the conversation. Mrs. Park meant well, but I wasn't looking for neighborhood friendships.

"Well, he did beautiful work. Have a nice day, dear."

I watched her walk away, feeling the familiar pang of guilt that came with keeping people at arm's length. But letting people in meant letting them see your vulnerabilities, and in my line of work, vulnerabilities could cost lives.

Back in my apartment, I made a simple dinner — grilled chicken, steamed vegetables, brown rice. Fuel, not pleasure. As I ate, my phone rang with a number I recognized but dreaded.

"Hi, Mom."

"Mija," Carmen's voice carried that particular mix of love and disappointment that only mothers could perfect. "How are you? You sound tired."

"Just got off shift. I'm fine."

"Are you eating enough? Taking care of yourself?"

"I'm fine, Mom." I could hear the edge creeping into my voice.

A pause. "I heard about Captain O'Sullivan. Ramona Martinez's daughter works at the hospital. She said he's been in for treatments."

Ramona Martinez. Of course. The Latino community in our city was small enough that everyone knew everyone's business.

"He's fighting it," I said carefully.

"Ay, mija. This job ..." Another pause, heavier this time. "Maybe this is a sign. You could go back to school, get your nursing degree like you always talked about. David has connections at the hospital where he works."

David. Her new husband, the accountant. Safe, stable, everything my father hadn't been.

"I'm already in school, Mom. For my Captain's exam."

"That's not what I meant, and you know it." Her voice softened. "I just worry. First your father, now Captain O'Sullivan. This job takes the good ones, Izzy. It takes them young."

The conversation we'd been dancing around for years finally lay bare between us. Carmen had loved my father, but she'd also spent every shift terrified that he wouldn't come home. When the structure fire took him — when that burning roof collapsed — it had confirmed every one of her worst fears about the job. Now, watching Cap waste away from cancer caused by decades of breathing smoke and chemicals, it felt like the job was claiming its victims in every way possible.

"I know you worry," I said quietly. "But this is who I am, Mom. This is what I'm meant to do."

"You're meant to be happy, mija. You're meant to have a family, a life outside of that station."

"I have a life."

"You have a job. There's a difference."

The conversation ended the way it always did — with careful "I love yous" and the unspoken understanding that we'd never see eye to eye on this. After I hung up, I sat in my kitchen feeling the weight of her words. Maybe she was right. Maybe I didn't have a life so much as a series of duties and obligations.

But it was my choice to make.

I spent the evening reviewing promotion materials, memorizing policy numbers and command structures until my eyes burned. By nine p.m., I was ready for sleep, grateful for the exhaustion that would keep my mind from wandering to darker places.

The shrill ring of my phone jolted me awake. The room was pitch black, the glowing numbers on the cable box reading 1:17 a.m. My heart hammered against my ribs, my body instantly flooded with adrenaline. A call at this hour meant one thing: something was wrong.

It was Margaret, Cap's wife. Her voice was thin, stretched tight with panic.

"Izzy? I'm so sorry to call so late, but it's Michael. He's in so much pain, and ... oh, God, Izzy, he's yellow."

The floor dropped out from under me. Jaundice. That meant his liver was failing.

"I'm on my way," I said, my voice all business, the calm, commanding tone of Lieutenant Delgado taking over. "Don't try to move him. Just keep him comfortable. I'll be there in fifteen minutes. We're going to Metro General."

I was dressed and out the door in under three minutes, my mind a blur of tactical assessment. Abdominal pain, jaundice, pancreatic cancer — it was a straight line to the worst-case scenario. As I sped through the deserted city streets, the familiar route to Cap's house felt different, fraught with a new and terrible urgency.

When Margaret opened the door, her face was pale and tear-streaked. I gave her a quick, firm squeeze on the shoulder. "Where is he?"

"In the bathroom."

I found him kneeling on the floor, leaning over the toilet, his body wracked with tremors. The bathroom light was unforgiving. His skin, normally weathered and tan from years of outdoor work, was a ghastly, sallow yellow. His eyes, when he looked up at me, were the same awful color. The pain was etched into every line on his face.

"Hey, Cap," I said softly, my professional calm a thin shield over the terror clawing at my throat.

"Izzy," he rasped. "This is ... this one's bad."

"I know," I said, my hand instinctively going to his wrist to check his pulse. It was thready and weak. "We're going to get you some help. Can you stand?"

With my help and Margaret's, we got him to his feet. Every movement was a fresh wave of agony for him. Leaning heavily on me, we shuffled slowly out to my car. The fifteen-minute drive to Metro General was the longest of my life. Cap was quiet, his breathing shallow, his focus turned inward on the pain. I kept one hand on the wheel and the other on my phone, ready to call 911 if he crashed on the way.

The emergency bay at Metro General was an oasis of bright, fluorescent light in the dark of the night. I pulled up to the ambulance entrance, a place I'd been a thousand times in the engine, but never like this. Never as the terrified loved one.

I helped him out of the car while Margaret went to the triage desk. A nurse in dark blue scrubs met us at the door with a wheelchair. He was tall — six feet or more — with sandy brown hair and the kind of lean build that suggested he'd been an athlete in another life. But it was his face that registered through my panic: kind, open, with green eyes that held steady on mine as he assessed the situation.

There was an air of calm about him that seemed to soak up some of the panic radiating from me.

"What's going on?" he asked, his voice steady as he helped me ease Cap into the chair.

"This is Michael O'Sullivan," I said, the words catching in my throat. "History of pancreatic cancer. Acute onset of severe abdominal pain and jaundice."

The nurse's eyes met mine, and in them, I saw an immediate, professional understanding. He wasn't just looking at another sick patient; he was seeing the whole picture. He was seeing Cap, and he was seeing me.

"Alright, Michael," he said, his voice gentle but firm. "Let's get you inside and get you some help. My name is Jimmy. You're in the right place."

chapter six

THE MOMENT I SAW THEM, my brain triaged the scene in a fraction of a second. Patient: male, late fifties, profound jaundice, diaphoretic, obvious distress. That was the medical problem. Then there were the two women. One, older, her face a mask of pale, frantic worry — the wife. The other, younger, with dark, intense eyes and a ramrod-straight posture that radiated coiled, controlled energy — the daughter, but something more.

She was a professional rescuer. Even if the "Summit County Fire Rescue" shirt she was wearing didn't give it away, I'd seen that look a thousand times on nurses, doctors, and firefighters who found themselves suddenly on the other side of the stretcher; it was the look of someone used to being in charge, now thrust into a situation they couldn't control. And it was terrifying to them.

"Alright, Michael," I said, keeping my voice gentle but firm as I helped him into the wheelchair. "Let's get you inside and get you some help. My name is Jimmy. You're in the right place."

I pushed the chair through the double doors, the daughter — Izzy, I thought the wife had called her — walking so close beside us she was practically a shadow. I led them straight back to Bay 4, one of our critical care rooms.

"Chloe, can you grab me a full set of vitals and get him on the monitor?" I asked, my voice calm. "Let's get a gown on him, too."

Chloe nodded and moved to the bedside with a new, quiet confidence I hadn't seen earlier in the shift. She'd been learning a lot over the past few shifts. I was proud of how well she was getting along.

I turned my attention to Michael — or Cap, as Izzy had called him in the car. His breathing was shallow, his teeth clenched against a wave of pain. "Cap, I need to get an IV started, draw some blood. Is one arm better than the other?"

He just shook his head, his eyes squeezed shut.

"Okay." I gently took his arm. His veins were good — strong and easy to find, a product of a life of hard work. I slid an 18-gauge needle in with practiced ease, the dark flash of blood confirming I was in. I drew a rainbow of blood tubes for the lab — a CBC, CMP, lipase, coagulation panel — everything the docs would need.

"Alright, we're in," I said, securing the line. "The doctor will be in to see you in just a minute. In the meantime, let's talk about getting some medicine for that pain."

"No," he rasped, his voice surprisingly firm. "No narcotics. I can handle it."

I stopped what I was doing and looked at him. It was a line I'd heard a hundred times, usually from men who equated pain with weakness. Standing by the gurney, Izzy's posture stiffened even more. She knew this argument, had probably had it before.

"Sir," I said, my voice soft but clear, meeting his pained, yellowed eyes. "With all due respect, I have no doubt you can handle it. I'm looking at a man who has probably handled more tough situations than I can imagine. But you don't have to. There are no medals for suffering in here. Your body is already fighting a war; letting the pain win is just giving the enemy ground. Let us help you."

He stared at me, his breathing still shallow. I saw a flicker of something in his eyes — not defeat, but a weary kind of understanding.

"He's right, Michael," his wife, Margaret, said, her voice trembling as she stroked his hand.

He let out a long, slow breath that was half sigh, half groan. "Okay," he whispered.

"Alright." I turned to the medication station. "I'm going to get you a small dose of Dilaudid. It'll take the edge off while we wait for the lab work to come back."

I drew up the medication, my movements precise. As I pushed it slowly into his IV line, I watched the cardiac monitor. His heart rate, which had been racing at 130, slowly began to drift down. The tense lines around his eyes softened, the rigid set of his jaw relaxed. His breathing deepened. For the first time since he'd arrived, he looked comfortable.

I glanced over at Izzy. She was watching me, her expression unreadable, but the rigid, military bearing had eased. The sentinel was still at her post, but she was no longer braced for impact. Whatever her relationship to this patient — daughter, maybe, or someone equally important — the relief on her face as his pain subsided was unmistakable.

The next hour was a whirlwind of controlled activity. The doctor came and went, orders were placed, and Michael was scheduled for a CT scan. Through it all, Izzy stood her silent watch.

Finally, after the tech had wheeled him off to imaging, she and I were left alone in the quiet of the bay.

"Thank you," she said, her voice low. She was looking at the empty gurney, not at me.

"Just doing my job," I said.

"No," she said, finally turning to look at me. Her dark eyes were exhausted, but they held a fierce intelligence. "You spoke to him like a person, not just a patient. Not everyone does that."

"He deserves that respect," I said simply.

We stood in a comfortable silence for a moment. I could see the wheels turning in her head, the tactical mind trying to process a new, unfamiliar situation.

"This is going to be a long night," I said, breaking the silence. "A lot of waiting, a lot of information that might not make sense at first." I thought for a second, and then grabbed a pen and a blank patient label, scribbling my name and number on it. "Look, I know this is a lot to process, and hospital-speak can be confusing. If you have questions later, or just need to vent ... seriously, I'm awake this time of day anyway. It's no problem. Us first responders have to look out for one another."

She took the label, her calloused fingertips brushing against mine. She looked at the number, then back at me, a flicker of surprise in her eyes. "Thank you," she said again, her voice softer this time. She tucked the label carefully into the pocket of her jeans.

Just then, Carly poked her head into the room. "Jimmy, Admitting just called. They've got a bed for him upstairs."

And just like that, the moment was over. I went back to my duties, and Izzy went to be with her family.

An hour later, as I was charting at the nurses' station, Carly sidled up next to me, a fresh cookie in her hand. "So," she said, her voice full of mischief. "The tough-as-nails fire lieutenant. That was smooth, Dalton. Real smooth."

I looked at her, genuinely confused. "What are you talking about?"

"Giving her your number," she said, nudging me with her elbow. "Playing the sensitive, caring nurse card. I see you."

"What? No," I said, shaking my head. "That's not ... her family member is dying, Carly. I was just trying to be helpful."

"Uh-huh," she said, not believing a word of it. "A big-booty firefighter who looks like she could bench press *me* shows up looking terrified, and you just happened to offer up your number out of the goodness of your heart. I didn't know you had it in you! I'm proud, honestly."

I opened my mouth to protest again, but then I stopped. I replayed the scene in my head. Izzy standing there, her fierce loyalty a tangible thing in the air. The way her dark eyes had locked with mine. The feeling of her fingertips brushing against my hand.

And suddenly, I was *acutely* aware of my worn-out scrubs with the "Cookie Monster" sticker I'd let a pediatric patient affix to my breast pocket as a bribe for letting me swab them for strep throat, the fact that my hair was probably a ridiculous mess, and the deep, unshakable exhaustion that was part of the night-shift uniform.

Oh, I thought, a slow heat creeping up my neck.

Oh.

chapter
seven

Izzy

THE WAITING room on the fourth floor was a study in institutional beige — uncomfortable chairs arranged in precise rows, fluorescent lights that hummed with a frequency designed to make you want to leave, and motivational posters that felt like insults when you were sitting there in the pre-dawn darkness watching someone you love disappear by degrees.

Margaret had gone home around midnight to get some sleep and feed the cat. "You should go too, *mija*," she'd said, using the endearment that always made my chest tight. "Get some rest."

But I couldn't leave. Not when Cap was upstairs in a bed that looked too small for him, hooked up to monitors that beeped and flashed like some kind of medical Christmas tree. Not when I could still see the awful yellow of his skin under the harsh hospital lights.

The doctor had come by an hour ago — Dr. Patel, I think, though the names were starting to blur together. He'd rattled off a string of words that might as well have been a foreign language: "The CT confirms our suspicions. Elevated bilirubin and alkaline phosphatase suggest cholestasis, likely due to a biliary obstruction. We need to rule out cholangitis and determine if this is related to tumor progression or a separate issue entirely."

I'd nodded like I understood, the way I always did. Lieutenant Isabel Delgado was supposed to have answers, was supposed to be in control. But sitting there in that waiting room, I felt like I was drowning in medical terminology and acronyms that everyone else seemed to speak fluently.

At the station, I knew everything. I could tell you the flow rate on any piece of equipment, the best approach for any type of structure, the exact protocol for any emergency. I could make life-and-death decisions without hesitation because I understood the variables, the risks, the tools at my disposal.

Here, I was just another family member, sitting in a plastic chair, waiting for someone else to tell me whether the person I loved most in the world was going to live or die.

The exhaustion was starting to hit me now that the adrenaline had worn off. My eyes burned from the fluorescent lights and too many hours without sleep. My hands, which never shook on a fire scene, were trembling slightly as I held my phone.

I pulled the patient label from my pocket for the third time in an hour. *Jimmy Dalton* was written in neat handwriting, followed by his number. *Us first responders have to look out for one another.*

The internal argument started immediately.

Don't be a burden. He was just being nice. He's probably busy with other patients.

But then I thought about the way he'd spoken to Cap — gentle but authoritative, treating him like a person instead of just another case. The way he'd convinced Cap to take the pain medication when I'd have been trying for hours. The way he'd looked at me when he handed me that paper, like he actually meant it.

I don't understand what's happening. I need to know.

He said to call.

First responders look out for each other.

That was the permission I needed. This wasn't about being weak or needy. This was professional courtesy. One first responder helping another navigate unfamiliar territory.

I crafted the text carefully, reading it over three times before hitting send:

> Hey, this is Izzy Delgado, from the ER earlier. Sorry to bother you, but the doctor mentioned 'biliary obstruction.' Can you explain what that means in plain English? Don't feel obligated to answer, I know you're busy.

I hit send before I could change my mind, then immediately regretted it. It was almost 4 a.m. He was probably with other patients, or finally getting a break, or —

My phone buzzed.

JIMMY

> No bother at all. It basically means there's a blockage in one of the tubes that drains fluid from his liver. It's what's causing the jaundice and the pain. The CT scan should tell us where and what it is. It's a common complication, and we can usually treat it.

I read the message twice, feeling some of the tension in my shoulders ease. That made sense. A blockage was something concrete, something that could be fixed. I was formulating a reply when another message came through.

JIMMY

> The more important question is, how are YOU holding up? That was a tough night.

I stared at the screen. When was the last time someone had asked me that question? When was the last time someone had looked past Lieutenant Delgado to see the person underneath?

My fingers hovered over the keyboard. The professional response would be to say I was fine, thank him for the information, and end the conversation. That's what I always did. That's what was expected.

Instead, I found myself typing:

> I'm okay. Just tired. Thanks for explaining.

The response came quickly:

Tired is an understatement. Get some coffee
if you can. And try to breathe. He's in the
best place he can be right now. Let us do
the worrying for a bit.

Let us do the worrying for a bit.

I read that line over and over. When was the last time someone had
offered to carry part of the load? When was the last time someone had
told me it was okay to not be strong for a minute?

I looked around the empty waiting room, with its bad coffee and
worse lighting, and for the first time since Margaret called me, the
crushing weight on my chest felt a little lighter. Not gone — it would
never be gone while Cap was fighting for his life — but manageable.

I typed back:

Thank you. Really.

JIMMY

Anytime. I mean that.

I tucked the phone back into my pocket, but not before saving his
number properly in my contacts. Jimmy Dalton. The night shift nurse
who'd treated Cap like he mattered, who'd taken the time to explain
things in words I could understand, who'd asked how I was holding up
like the answer actually mattered to him.

For the first time all night, I allowed myself a small, weary smile. The
professional connection had shifted into something else, something I
wasn't quite ready to name. But sitting there in that sterile waiting
room, watching the sunrise creep through the windows, I felt something
I hadn't felt in a long time.

I felt seen. Not as Lieutenant Delgado, not as the woman who had
to have all the answers, but as Izzy. Just Izzy, who was scared and tired
and grateful for a kind voice in the dark.

And maybe that was enough to get me through whatever came next.

chapter
eight

SEVEN A.M. WAS the cruelest hour for night shift workers. Not because it marked the end of twelve hours of controlled chaos — that was actually the good part. No, seven a.m. was cruel because it was the exact moment when the rest of the world was starting their day with fresh coffee and optimism, while you were stumbling out into the morning light feeling like you'd been hit by a truck, craving nothing more than a greasy burger and the sweet embrace of blackout curtains.

"See you tonight, Jimmy," Chloe called as I gathered my things from the nurses' station. She'd made it through her first full week on night shift, and despite the challenges we'd thrown at her — roofing nails that weren't roofing nails, shampoo bottles in places shampoo bottles had no business being, and one very sick firefighter — she'd handled it all with grace.

"You did good tonight," I told her. "Get some sleep."

"You too. Thanks for everything."

I nodded and headed for the parking garage, my body already anticipating the ritual of sleep preparation. But as I walked, my mind kept drifting back to the text exchange with Izzy. Three messages. That was it. But something about the way she'd said "*Thank you. Really.*" had stuck with me.

The drive home was a study in frustration. Every restaurant I passed was advertising breakfast — pancakes, eggs Benedict, fresh-baked muffins. All I wanted was a double cheeseburger with fries, the kind of comfort food that made sense after a night of dealing with humanity at its most vulnerable. But noooooooo, society had decided that 7:30 a.m. was pancake time, not burger time.

I settled for a gas station diet lemonade and a sad-looking breakfast sandwich, cursing the tyranny of normal people's schedules.

My apartment building was quiet when I pulled into the parking lot. Mrs. Peters from 2B was already in her garden, probably wondering why the nice young man from 3A looked like he'd been through a blender. I gave her a tired wave and headed upstairs.

My one-bedroom apartment was a study in carefully cultivated comfort. Plants lined the windowsills — pothos and snake plants that could survive my erratic schedule. Cookbooks were stacked on every available surface, dog-eared and splattered with evidence of my experiments. The kitchen counters were clean but lived-in, with a sourdough starter I'd been babying for two years sitting in its place of honor next to the coffee maker.

It was the polar opposite of what I imagined a first responder's place might look like. No minimalist efficiency, no tactical gear laid out with military precision. Just warmth and life and the accumulated comfort of someone who'd learned to find joy in small, controllable things.

I went through my post-shift routine with practiced efficiency. Shower to wash off the hospital smell and the weight of the night. Change into soft clothes that had never seen the inside of an ER. Brush my teeth while my brain finally started to wind down from the hypervigilance that twelve hours of emergency nursing required.

But as I pulled the blackout curtains closed and climbed into bed, I found myself reaching for my phone. I'd already checked it twice on the drive home, which was stupid. Izzy was probably sleeping, or dealing with whatever came next with Cap's treatment, or just getting on with her life.

I set the phone on my nightstand and closed my eyes, willing my body to embrace the sleep it desperately needed. I had another twelve-hour shift starting at 7 p.m. Eight hours of sleep was sacred. Non-negotiable.

I lasted about ten minutes before I was reaching for the phone again.

No new messages. Of course not. What had I been expecting?

This was ridiculous. I helped families navigate medical crises all the time. It was part of the job. The fact that this particular family member happened to be a competent, beautiful firefighter with tired eyes and calloused hands was irrelevant.

Except it wasn't irrelevant, was it? Because I couldn't stop thinking about the way she'd looked when Cap's pain finally eased. The careful control she'd maintained even when she was clearly terrified. The surprise in her eyes when I'd given her my number, like kindness was something unexpected.

I put the phone back on the nightstand and rolled over, burying my face in the pillow. Sleep. I needed sleep.

But five minutes later, I was staring at the ceiling, thinking about whether she'd gotten any rest, whether the doctors had given her more information, whether she was sitting in that waiting room feeling as lost as she'd looked at 4 a.m.

This was insane. I barely knew her. Three text messages and one emergency room encounter did not constitute a relationship. I was probably just projecting, reading meaning into professional courtesy.

My phone buzzed.

I grabbed it so fast I nearly knocked over the water glass on my nightstand, my heart doing something completely unprofessional at the sight of her name on the screen.

> IZZY
>
> How's your sleep schedule? Do you work tonight?

I stared at the message for a long moment, trying to decode it. Was she checking on my wellbeing? Did she need something? Was there a problem with Cap?

> Working tonight, trying to sleep now. Everything okay?

The response came quickly:

IZZY

Cap's doing better this morning. Doctor says the stent placement went well. I just wanted to thank you again for last night. And to say if you need anything, coffee, food, whatever, let me know. I owe you.

I read the message twice, a slow warmth spreading through my chest that had nothing to do with the morning sunlight filtering through my blackout curtains.

You don't owe me anything. Glad Cap's doing better. Get some rest yourself, you've earned it.

IZZY

Will do. Sorry for waking you.

No worries! You didn't wake me! I wasn't sleeping anyway.

Why had I said that? Now she'd know I'd been lying there thinking about... what? Her? The situation? The fact that I'd committed the cardinal sin of night shift workers and left my phone on vibrate instead of silent, just in case she needed something?

IZZY

Night shift problems?

Something like that. Sleep well when you get to!

I set the phone down and stared at the ceiling, a smile tugging at the corners of my mouth despite my exhaustion. She'd thought to check on me. Had asked about my schedule, offered to bring me coffee. When was the last time someone had done that?

More importantly, when was the last time I'd cared enough about someone to break the sacred rules of night shift sleep?

I reached over and, for the first time in three years of working nights, deliberately left my phone on vibrate. Just in case.

Then I closed my eyes and tried to convince myself that the warm feeling in my chest was just the satisfaction of a job well done, and not something far more complicated and wonderful and terrifying.

Sleep came eventually, but it was restless and full of dreams I couldn't quite remember when I woke up. Dreams that left me thinking about dark eyes and careful smiles and the way someone's voice could sound like home even when you'd only heard it a handful of times.

When my alarm went off at 4 p.m., the first thing I did was check my phone.

No new messages. But somehow, that was okay. Because in three hours, I'd be back at Metro General, and maybe — just maybe — I'd get to see her again.

chapter
nine

MY DAY off was a study in controlled restlessness. I'd visited Cap that morning — he was stable, settled into a room on the oncology floor, and already complaining about the hospital's attempt at Jell-O. Seeing him gripe was a good sign, but the underlying exhaustion in his eyes, the sallow tint that still clung to his skin, was a constant, dull ache in my chest.

Back at my apartment, I tried to study. The promotion exam to Captain was only a few months away, and my kitchen table was covered in binders thick with departmental policy, incident command structures, and building construction codes. Information I knew, information I could normally recite in my sleep. But today, the words were just black smudges on a white page. My mind kept drifting, replaying the last twenty-four hours: the panic in Margaret's voice, the unforgiving fluorescent light of Cap's bathroom, the steady calm of a nurse's voice cutting through the chaos.

Jimmy.

I had to thank him. Properly. It was a matter of professional courtesy — he'd helped one of our own, and that deserved acknowledgment. The logic felt safe, tactical. It was a box I could check, a mission I could complete.

It has nothing to do with the fact that your hand still feels warm where his touched it, the voice in my head whispered. *Nothing at all.*

I snatched my phone off the counter, my resolve hardening. Direct. Professional.

> Hey, it's Izzy. Hope the post-shift nap was successful.

The line about the nap was calculated — it showed I'd listened, that I understood the rhythms of his world. His reply came quickly:

JIMMY

> It was! Hope you got some rest too. How's Cap doing?

> He's stable. Complaining about the hospital food, which I'm taking as a good sign. Listen, I owe you coffee for everything last night.

I paused, thumb hovering over the keypad. My first instinct was to suggest 9 a.m. tomorrow — but he works nights. He's trying to reset his sleep schedule. For the first time, my tactical mind was assessing a personal situation, anticipating someone else's needs.

> You're on your days off, right? Don't want to mess up your sleep reset. How about this afternoon? Say, 2 p.m.? Or whenever works before you have to flip back to night-owl mode.

JIMMY

> 2 p.m. is perfect. There's a place called The Daily Grind on Main Street. Meet you there?

> See you then.

Mission accomplished. Clean, efficient. So why was my heart hammering against my ribs like it was trying to beat its way out of my chest?

At 1:55, I was sitting in my truck across from The Daily Grind coffee shop, doing nervous surveillance I usually reserved for potential fire scenes. I'd changed clothes twice, settling on dark jeans and a simple blue sweater — put-together without trying too hard.

I saw him before he saw me. Without the baggy scrubs, I could see the lean strength in his arms and shoulders. He looked younger in jeans and a gray henley, his sandy hair catching the afternoon sun. He looked... normal. Somehow, that was more intimidating than facing a whole battalion of chiefs.

When I walked in, he stood immediately, that warm smile spreading across his face.

"Hey," he said, and even that one word carried genuine warmth. "You made it."

"Wouldn't miss it," I said, surprised by how true that felt.

The initial conversation stayed safely clinical — Cap's condition, the stent placement, his improved outlook. But when we settled at a corner table he'd chosen for privacy, something shifted.

"Can I ask you something?" Jimmy said, wrapping his hands around his coffee mug.

I nodded, though my defenses automatically started rising.

"What's it like? Being one of the only women in your department?"

The question surprised me — not because he'd asked, but because of how he'd asked it. Not looking for drama, just genuinely curious.

"Lonely sometimes," I said honestly. "I have to be twice as good to get half the respect. Can't show weakness, can't have bad days, can't make mistakes. The guys I work with are great, but they forget I'm fighting battles they don't even know exist."

Jimmy nodded thoughtfully. "That sounds exhausting."

"It is." I was surprised by my own honesty. "But it's worth it. I love what I do, and I'm good at it. I just wish I didn't have to prove it over and over again."

"For what it's worth," Jimmy said, "watching you advocate for Cap, seeing how you handle yourself — you've already proven it. To the people who matter."

The sincerity in his voice made my chest tight. When was the last time someone had seen past the uniform?

We talked for another hour — about families, about careers, about the weight of choosing jobs that mattered over jobs that impressed people. Jimmy had an easy way of asking questions that made me want to answer them, of listening like my words actually mattered.

"My mother thinks I should have been a teacher," I found myself saying. "Safer, more 'appropriate' for a woman."

"Let me guess — she worries about you."

"Every single day. She lost my dad to the job. And now Cap..." I trailed off, feeling suddenly vulnerable.

"But you can't live your life afraid of what might happen," Jimmy said. "And you can't choose your career based on other people's fears."

I looked up at him, struck by the certainty in his voice. "Sounds like you've given this some thought."

"My parents wanted me to be a doctor. Better money, more prestige. But I like being a nurse. I like the hands-on care, the patient advocacy, the relationships. I don't want to diagnose and move on — I want to be there for the whole journey."

The passion in his voice was unmistakable, and I found myself leaning forward, drawn in by his conviction.

"That's why you were so good with Cap," I said. "You saw him as a person, not just a set of symptoms."

"He deserved that," Jimmy said simply. "You both did."

We sat in comfortable silence for a moment, the shared humor having broken down the initial awkwardness. But I found myself studying Jimmy's face, my mind shifting into evaluation mode. There was something I needed to know about him.

"You've got a day-shift charge nurse named Sophia Mitchell, right?" I said, leaning forward slightly.

Jimmy looked surprised by the shift in topic. "Yeah. She's the best in the hospital. Why?"

"One of my paramedics, Jack McKenzie, seems to agree. Her... public appreciation for him on the radio last month caused a situation at my station." I kept my tone neutral, watching his reaction carefully.

Jimmy's expression didn't change to gossip mode. Instead, he nodded thoughtfully. "I heard some of the chatter. Sophia's very professional. And Jack's a good medic. On our end, that's all that matters."

No fishing for details. No attempts to dish about his colleague. Just quiet respect for both parties involved. Something in my chest loosened

— a test I hadn't realized I was giving, passed without him even knowing he was taking it.

"Good," I said simply. "That's... good to hear."

The moment stretched between us, and I felt that dangerous flutter again. This man understood discretion. Professional boundaries. The kind of person you could trust.

In the comfortable silence that followed, I felt a wave of exhaustion hit me, sudden and profound. The reality of the last day crashed back down.

"It's just... hard," I heard myself say, the words escaping before I could stop them. "I'm used to being the one with the plan. Run into the building, put out the fire, rescue the victim. There are steps. With this... with Cap... there's no plan. There's nothing to fix. I just feel... useless."

The confession hung in the air, raw and exposed. I braced myself for platitudes, for the "I'm sure it'll be okay" that people always said when they didn't know what else to do.

Instead, Jimmy reached across the table and covered my hand with his. His touch was warm and steady — a quiet anchor in the sudden storm of my vulnerability. His hand was large, the back of it dusted with fine hair, a stark contrast to my own calloused, scarred fingers. The simple contact sent a jolt through me, sharp and clean and utterly unexpected.

"You're not useless," he said, his voice soft but firm, his green eyes holding mine. "You're showing up. For him, right now, that's the most useful thing in the world."

I stared at him, unable to speak. The world seemed to narrow to the small space between us, to the feeling of his hand covering mine. He wasn't trying to fix it. He was just... there. Present. Not turning away from the problem or from me.

He pulled his hand back after a moment, and the air rushed back into my lungs.

When we finally left the coffee shop, the afternoon sun felt warmer, the air less heavy. We stood on the sidewalk, and I realized I didn't want this to end.

"I had a really good time," I said. "Thank you. For the coffee, for listening, for... everything."

"Thank you for asking me," he said. "And for trusting me with Cap's care."

"Maybe we could do this again sometime," I said, the words coming out before I could stop them.

Jimmy's smile was answer enough. "I'd like that. A lot."

As I drove home, I caught myself smiling at nothing, replaying conversations and the way he'd looked at me when I'd talked about my work. For the first time in longer than I could remember, I felt seen — not as Lieutenant Delgado or Cap's surrogate daughter or the woman who had to be stronger than everyone else.

Just as Izzy.

chapter
ten

THE TEXT SAT in my drafts folder for forty-seven minutes while I second-guessed every word choice. I'd written it, deleted it, rewritten it, and deleted it again so many times that my phone probably thought I was having some kind of digital seizure.

Would you like to come over for dinner tomorrow? I could cook. Nothing fancy, just...

Delete.

Hey, want to grab dinner at my place tomorrow? I make a mean...

Delete.

I know this is forward, but would you want to come over for a home-cooked meal? I'd love to...

Dear God, that sounded like a dating app message from a serial killer.

I was sitting in the Metro General break room at 11 p.m., nursing my third cup of coffee and trying to convince myself that asking someone to dinner was not, in fact, rocket science. Around me, the night shift moved through its familiar rhythms — Chloe was reviewing medication calculations at the next table, Carly was on the phone with Admitting about bed assignments, and somewhere in the distance, an IV pump was beeping the eternal, mechanical song of its people.

But my mind kept drifting back to yesterday afternoon. To the way Izzy had looked when she'd talked about feeling useless, the vulnerability she'd let slip through her armor. To the moment when I'd covered her hand with mine and watched something shift in her dark eyes.

To the way she'd said my name when she thanked me, like it meant something.

My phone buzzed with an incoming trauma alert, jolting me back to the present. But as I headed toward the trauma bay, I made a decision. Sometimes you just had to take the shot.

During a quiet moment around 2 a.m., I finally sent the message:

> Tomorrow's your last day off this rotation, right? Would you like to come over for dinner? I actually cook — not just reheat things. Fair warning: I tend to go overboard in the kitchen when I'm trying to impress someone.

I hit send before I could lose my nerve, then immediately wanted to crawl under the nearest gurney. *When I'm trying to impress someone?* Could I have been more obvious?

Her response came twenty minutes later:

IZZY

> You want to cook for me? That's... actually really sweet. What time?

> 6 p.m.? I promise not to poison you.

IZZY

> Deal. But just so you know, my standards are pretty low. Last night I had cereal for dinner.

> Challenge accepted.

I spent the rest of my shift planning the menu.

By 4 p.m. the next day, my apartment looked like a Food Network show had exploded in it. I'd been cooking since I got home from my shift, running on three hours of sleep and pure nervous energy. The beef had been braising in red wine and herbs for hours, filling the apartment with rich, savory smells. The polenta was keeping warm on the stove, creamy and perfect, and asparagus spears lay ready for a quick roast in the oven. And on the counter, cooling in individual ramekins, sat six perfect servings of tres leches cake.

I'd stopped at three different grocery stores to find the right ingredients, spent an hour on the phone with my mom getting her polenta technique right (again), and reorganized my living room twice.

At 5:45, I was pacing around my kitchen, checking and rechecking everything for the dozenth time. The beef was perfect, tender enough to shred with a fork. Everything was as ready as it was possible to be.

So why did I feel like I was about to perform surgery without anesthesia?

The knock at my door at exactly 6 p.m. made my heart jump into my throat.

Izzy stood in my doorway holding a bottle of wine, looking slightly uncertain in dark jeans and a soft green sweater that brought out the gold flecks in her brown eyes. Her hair was down, falling in waves around her shoulders instead of her usual severe ponytail.

"Hi," she said, offering the wine. "I wasn't sure what you were making, so I brought some Tempranillo. It goes with most things."

"Perfect," I said, stepping aside to let her in. "And thank you. You didn't have to bring anything."

She stepped into my living room, and I watched her take it all in — the plants lining the windowsills, the cookbook collection that took up an entire wall, the warm light from the salt lamps I'd scattered around the room. Her eyes lingered on the kitchen, where steam was rising from various pots and pans.

"Jimmy," she said slowly, "what exactly did you make?"

"Braised beef," I said, trying for casual and probably missing by miles. "With polenta and asparagus. And, uhm, a surprise for later."

She stared at me for a long moment, then shook her head with something that looked like amazement. "You made all this from scratch?"

"It's not that hard once you get the hang of it," I said, feeling heat creep up my neck. "I, uh, I like to cook. Really cook. It relaxes me."

"Jimmy." Her voice was soft, almost wondering. "No one has ever made me a meal like this before."

The way she said it made my chest tight. Like this simple thing was somehow precious.

"Well," I said, "there's a first time for everything."

We ate at my small dining table by the window, the city lights twinkling beyond the glass. I'd been worried the conversation might be awkward in the intimate setting of my apartment, but it flowed as easily as it had at the coffee shop. Izzy told me stories about firehouse pranks and the ongoing war over condiment theft that apparently rivaled international conflicts in its complexity.

"Wait," I said, laughing so hard I nearly choked on my beer. "Someone actually resold ketchup packets from the McDonald's down the street?"

"Entrepreneurial spirit," Izzy said solemnly, then broke into a grin. "Stopped after a call with the engine and asked them for 'as many ketchup packets as you're legally allowed to give me.' Thompson made seventeen dollars before Cap shut down the operation. The thing is, we could leave five thousand dollars in cash on the table and nobody would touch it. But a bottle of Heinz? Gone like we had ninjas on the loose."

"I cannot even imagine living like that," I said. "Hospital staff'll steal your lunch, but they draw the line at actual condiments."

"Different code of ethics," she agreed. "Though honestly, after eating this, I understand the ketchup wars better. If you could cook like this at the station, people would probably chain you to the stove."

The compliment made me ridiculously happy. Watching her enjoy the food I'd made, seeing her relax into my space, felt better than any performance review or patient commendation I'd ever received.

When we finished the main course, I stood to clear the plates, suddenly nervous about dessert. I'd been second-guessing the tres leches choice all day, but it was too late to change course now.

"There's dessert," I said, carrying the plates to the kitchen. "If you want."

"You made dessert too?" Izzy called from the table. "Jimmy, you're going to spoil me."

I pulled the ramekins from the refrigerator, hands slightly shaking as

I arranged them on a small tray with spoons. "It's tres leches," I said, setting the tray on the table proudly.

Izzy went very still. Her eyes moved from the perfect, cream-soaked cakes to my face, one eyebrow slowly rising.

"Tres leches," she repeated, her voice carefully neutral.

"Yeah!" I exclaimed, excitedly, "I ..."

And then I saw her face.

Oh. Oh shit. Oh shit, oh shit. "I — " I started, then stopped, my face burning. "It's not — I mean, I didn't make it because you're — " The words tangled up in my mouth like fishing line. "I just, I love tres leches, and I thought — "

Izzy stood up from her chair, cutting off my increasingly incoherent rambling. For a terrifying moment, I thought she was going to leave. Instead, she stepped closer, close enough that I could smell her shampoo, something clean and faintly floral.

"Jimmy," she said quietly, her eyes searching mine. "Did you make tres leches because I'm Latina?"

"No!" The word came out too loud, too desperate. "I mean, maybe unconsciously? I don't know, I just — " I ran my hands through my hair, completely flustered. "I make tres leches all the time. It's my go-to dessert when I really want to — " I stopped, realizing what I was about to say.

"When you really want to what?" she asked, stepping even closer.

"When I really want to impress someone," I admitted quietly. "And I really, really wanted to impress you."

For a moment that felt like eternity, she just looked at me. I could see her processing, weighing my words against my obvious panic, my flustered honesty against whatever assumptions she might have had.

Then, without warning, she reached up, cupped my face in her calloused hands, and kissed me.

It was soft at first, tentative, like she was testing the waters. But when I kissed her back, something shifted. Her hands slid into my hair, and I found myself pressing closer, my arms coming up to circle her waist. She tasted like wine and cilantro and something indefinably her, and I thought dimly that this was so much better than any fantasy I'd been trying not to have.

When we finally broke apart, we were both breathing hard. Izzy's cheeks were flushed, her lips slightly swollen, and she was looking at me like she was seeing something new.

"That was — " I started.

"Good," she finished, her voice husky. "That was really good."

We ate the tres leches standing in my kitchen, sharing bites from the same spoon and stealing kisses between tastes. The cake was perfect — rich and sweet and soaked through with cream — but I barely tasted it. I was too distracted by the way Izzy hummed appreciatively with each bite, by the way she kept looking at me like I'd just performed some kind of magic trick.

When it was time for her to leave, we lingered by my door like teenagers reluctant to end a first date. She had her jacket on, her keys in her hand, but neither of us seemed ready to say goodbye.

"This was amazing," she said finally. "The food, the company, all of it. Thank you."

"Thank you for coming," I said. "For trusting me with your last day off."

She smiled, soft and genuine, and I felt my heart do something acrobatic in my chest.

"Uhhh," I said as she turned toward the door, my brain apparently having abandoned all higher functions. "You know, we could, ahh, do that again. Kiss. That was, I mean, wow, it just — "

Before I could finish making a complete fool of myself, Izzy turned back, stepped into my space, and kissed me again. This one was slower, deeper, a promise of more to come.

"Yes," she murmured against my lips when we broke apart. "We definitely could."

And then she was gone, leaving me standing in my doorway watching her taillights fade into the distance.

I closed the door, leaned against it, and let out a breath I didn't know I'd been holding. Then, because there was no one there to witness my complete loss of dignity, I pumped my fist in the air and did a little victory shuffle around my living room that would have made my college football team proud.

"Holy shit," I said to my pothos plant, which seemed to nod approvingly in the lamplight. "She kissed me! Wooo!"

Lieutenant Isabela Delgado, the most competent, intimidating, and beautiful woman I had ever met, had kissed me. In my kitchen.

I was so, *so* gone.

chapter
eleven

Izzy

I MADE it exactly three blocks before I had to pull into the Shell on Maple Street. Not because I needed gas — my tank was three-quarters full — but because my hands were shaking too badly to trust myself on the road.

I pulled up to pump three and just... sat there. The taste of tres leches lingered on my tongue, sweet and rich and somehow perfect. My lips still tingled from that second kiss. The way Jimmy had looked at me when I'd turned back, like I was giving him everything he'd ever wanted just by wanting him back.

God, that kiss.

When was the last time someone had cooked for me? *Really* cooked, not just thrown together a sandwich or picked up takeout? When was the last time someone had been nervous about whether I'd like something they'd made?

When was the last time someone had wanted to *impress* me instead of change me?

A sharp honk from behind made me jump. I looked up to find an irritated-looking guy in a Suburban gesturing at the pump. How long had I been sitting here? The pump wasn't even in my hand — I'd just pulled up and zoned out completely, lost in the memory of Jimmy's hands shaking as he served dessert, the panic in his eyes over the tres leches, the way he'd said "I really, really wanted to impress you."

I waved apologetically at Suburban Guy and fumbled for my phone, my cheeks burning. *Jesus, Delgado, get it together. You're a fire lieutenant who runs into burning buildings, and one kiss from a sweet nurse has you forgetting how gas stations work.*

But my fingers were already typing:

> I sat in my truck for five minutes trying to remember how to drive. Pretty sure that's your fault.

I stared at the message for a second — was it too much? Too forward? — then hit send before I could overthink it. Then, because Suburban Guy was looking increasingly murderous, I actually got out and went through the motions of pumping gas I didn't need.

My phone buzzed:

> JIMMY
>
> Fair is fair. I think my brain is STILL short-circuiting. Thank you for tonight.

Then another:

> JIMMY
>
> And I hope the tres leches didn't give you nightmares about cultural insensitivity.

I found myself grinning at my phone like an idiot as the gas pump clicked off.

> Only nightmares about how good it was. I might have to demand the recipe.

> JIMMY
>
> Trade secret. But I might be convinced to make it again sometime.

> I'd like that.

The three little dots appeared, disappeared, appeared again. I realized I was holding my breath.

Good. Because I'd really like to see you again. Soon.

Me too.

I put my phone away and finally drove home, but my mind kept drifting as I navigated the familiar streets. A text from my mother popped up at a red light:

CARMEN

Hope you're having a good day off, mija. Call me this week?

The message brought back her voice from our last conversation: *You need to find someone nice, Izzy. Someone who can take care of you for once.*

Take care of me. Like I was some fragile thing that needed protecting.

But Jimmy... Jimmy hadn't tried to protect me from anything. He'd just seen me — really seen me — and decided I was worth the effort. Worth impressing.

I started the truck and pulled into traffic, my mind drifting to the last time someone had tried to "take care" of me.

THREE YEARS AGO

"You're never here anymore," Derek had said, his voice tight with accusation as I walked through my apartment door at 7 a.m. after a particularly brutal 48-hour shift. "I feel like I'm dating a ghost."

I'd been too tired to fight, too wrung out from two days of back-to-back calls to do anything but shower and collapse into bed. But Derek had other plans.

"We need to talk about this, Izzy. About us. About your priorities."

"My priorities?" I'd turned from the bathroom doorway, still in my smoky duty uniform. "Derek, I just spent two days pulling people out of burning buildings. I'm exhausted."

"And that's the problem." He'd been sitting on my couch like he owned the place, arms crossed, jaw set in that stubborn line I'd once found attractive. "This job is consuming you. You're becoming someone I don't recognize."

The irony was that the job had made me exactly who I was supposed to be. Confident, capable, strong. But Derek had fallen for the off-duty version of me — the one who wore sundresses to barbecues and laughed at his jokes about women drivers. He'd loved the idea of dating a firefighter until he realized what that actually meant.

"You knew what I did when we started dating," I'd said, leaning against the doorframe because I was too tired to stand without support.

"I thought it was temporary. A phase." Derek had stood up, started pacing around my living room like a caged animal. "But you're talking about taking the Lieutenant's exam, Izzy. You want to make this your whole life."

"It is my whole life."

"And where does that leave me? Leave us?"

I'd stared at him, this man I'd been dating for eight months, and realized he'd never understood me at all. He'd wanted the firefighter fantasy — the calendar girl in turnouts — not the reality of someone who came home smelling like smoke and chemicals, who got called out in the middle of dinner, who had nightmares about the people she couldn't save.

"I don't know," I'd said honestly.

"Well, I do." Derek had grabbed his jacket from the back of my chair, his movements sharp with anger. "You need to choose, Izzy. The job or me. Because I'm not going to sit around waiting for you to decide I'm worth coming home to."

The ultimatum had hung in the air between us like smoke from a structure fire — toxic and impossible to ignore.

"Then I guess you have your answer," I'd said quietly.

He'd looked shocked, like he'd expected me to fold. To choose him over the career I'd built, the crew that depended on me, the calling that had saved me after my father died. Like he'd expected me to choose being comfortable over being myself.

"You'll regret this," he'd said on his way to the door. "You can't marry the job, Izzy. It'll never love you back."

I pulled into my apartment complex, Derek's words still echoing in my head. *You can't marry the job. It'll never love you back.*

Maybe not. But it had never asked me to be smaller, either. It had never demanded I choose between who I was and who someone else wanted me to be.

And before Derek, there had been Marcus — the personal trainer who'd loved my "athletic build" until he realized I was stronger than him. Who'd made increasingly pointed comments about how I should "soften up" my look, grow my hair longer, wear more makeup. Who'd sulked when I could deadlift more weight than him and stopped inviting me to his gym.

Before Marcus, there had been Ryan — the construction foreman who'd been impressed by my "tough chick" persona until I'd gotten promoted to full firefighter and started making more money than him. Suddenly, I was "too ambitious," "too focused on work," "not feminine enough."

All of them had wanted the idea of a strong woman — right up until they had to live with the reality of one.

But tonight... tonight had been different.

I climbed the stairs to my apartment, Jimmy's voice replaying in my head: *I really, really wanted to impress you.*

Not change me. Not fix me. Not make me smaller or softer or more convenient.

Impress me.

He'd spent hours cooking, had worried about every detail, had been nervous about whether I'd like it. He'd been flustered and adorable when I questioned the tres leches, but not defensive. Not angry. Just... honest about his intentions.

And when I'd kissed him, he hadn't tried to take control or turn it into something more aggressive. He'd just kissed me back like he couldn't quite believe it was happening.

I unlocked my apartment and stepped inside, the familiar silence greeting me. But for the first time in years, it didn't feel lonely. It felt... peaceful. Like maybe I wouldn't be filling it with just my own company much longer.

I headed for the shower, still tasting tres leches and possibility. For the first time in three years, I wasn't thinking about Derek's ultimatum or Marcus's insecurities or Ryan's wounded pride.

I was thinking about Jimmy's hands shaking as he served dessert, about the way he'd looked at me like I was something precious, about how he'd cooked for me — really cooked — just because he wanted to make me happy.

Maybe Carmen was wrong. Maybe I didn't need someone to take care of me.

Maybe I just needed someone who wanted to.

And maybe ... I'd found him.

chapter
twelve

THE THING about working nights in the ER is that sometimes the universe decides to have a theme. One night it's all chest pains; the next, it's a parade of kidney stones. Tonight, the theme was norovirus. We were four hours into the shift, and it felt like half the city had decided to simultaneously evacuate their gastrointestinal tracts within the fluorescent-lit walls of Metro General.

"I'm never eating takeout again," Chloe muttered, as we helped our third patient vying to see which direction they could expel more of their internal fluids from.

"Sure you will," I said, handing her a pair of gloves. "You'll just repress this memory. It's a vital nursing skill."

Our fourth patient of the norovirus parade was Mary, a middle-aged woman who looked like she'd been through a blender, clutching a tissue box and eyeing me with the desperate hopefulness of someone who'd been violently ill for the past twelve hours.

"I knew you'd want a sample," she announced proudly from her gurney, clutching her purse to her chest. "So I brought one for you!" She started to unzip a pocket.

My training kicked in with the speed of a defibrillator shock. "NO!" I said, maybe a little too loudly. I softened my voice. "No, no, that's totally fine, Mary. We'll take your word for it. We don't need a sample."

She looked genuinely disappointed. "Oh. Are you sure? It's no trouble. It's double-bagged."

The phrase "double-bagged" made something inside me die a little. "I'm absolutely certain. But I really appreciate you thinking of us."

"But how will you know what's wrong with me if you don't test it?"

This was the part of the job they didn't teach you in nursing school — the delicate art of convincing patients that you believed their symptoms without having to examine whatever they'd thoughtfully preserved at home.

"Mary," I said gently, settling into the chair beside her bed, "generally speaking, people don't go through all the trouble of coming to the ER at two in the morning if they're faking their symptoms. And even if we wanted to run tests, we'd need to obtain fresh samples here in the hospital. But honestly, based on what you're describing and how you're feeling, it sounds like you've got the same bug that's been going around."

"Really?" She looked both relieved and slightly disappointed that her preparation had been unnecessary.

"Really. You're the seventh person tonight with these exact symptoms. There's definitely something making the rounds."

That was the truth. In the past four hours, we'd seen a parade of patients with varying degrees of what was almost certainly norovirus — the cruise ship special, as we called it. Highly contagious, completely miserable, and absolutely nothing you wanted to take home in a plastic bag.

I spent the next few minutes explaining the treatment plan — IV fluids for dehydration, anti-nausea medication, and the universal ER discharge instructions of "rest, clear liquids, and come back if you get worse." By the time I finished getting her situated, Chloe had appeared in the doorway again.

"Room 12 is asking again if we can test their... contribution... for the specific strain," she said, her voice carefully neutral.

I closed my eyes briefly. "Tell them we'll handle all the necessary testing and they can dispose of their sample at home. Where it belongs."

"Copy that."

This was the reality of emergency nursing that nobody talked about — the weird, gross, and occasionally touching ways that people tried to help with their own care. The patient who brought in the tick that bit them, carefully preserved in a jewelry box. The parent who photographed their child's rash from seventeen different angles. The guy who'd written down every single thing he'd eaten in the past week, organized by meal and color-coded by digestive symptoms.

They all wanted to help. They all wanted to make sure we had everything we needed to fix them. And part of my job was accepting that desire to help while gently redirecting it into more useful channels.

"How are you holding up?" I asked Chloe as we restocked the room for the next patient.

"I'm starting to think I should have gone into pediatrics," she said. "Kids might puke on you, but at least they don't bring it in containers."

"Wait until you meet your first frequent flyer who knows more medical terminology than some residents and has seventeen theories about what's wrong with them, all involving rare tropical diseases they definitely don't have."

"Looking forward to it," she said dryly.

The next two hours passed in a blur of IV starts, discharge instructions, and the gentle art of convincing people that they probably didn't need a CT scan for their stomach bug. By one-thirty, the GI rush had finally started to slow, leaving the department in that strange, quiet lull that made you either grateful for the break or suspicious that something worse was about to happen.

I was catching up on charting when the lights flickered.

Just once, a brief flutter that made everyone look up from whatever they were doing. The computers didn't even restart. But in a hospital, any electrical anomaly got immediate attention.

"That's not ominous at all," Carly muttered from the charge desk.

I was about to make a joke about the building being older than some of our patients when Doug came storming out of the supply area, looking genuinely annoyed.

"The ortho room is locked," he announced. "The electronic lock is completely dead. I can't get in there at all."

Carly looked up sharply. "Are you kidding me?"

"Do I look like I'm kidding? We've got no access to cervical collars, splints, backboards — nothing. And before you ask, yes, I tried the manual override. The whole system is fried."

The charge desk went quiet. In an ER, especially one this close to a major interstate, being without orthopedic supplies wasn't just inconvenient — it was potentially dangerous. Any trauma that came through those doors would need immediate spinal immobilization, and all our equipment was locked behind a door that had apparently been defeated by a thirty-second power flicker.

"What's maintenance saying?" Carly asked, already reaching for the phone.

"On call. Could be an hour before they get here."

Carly weighed the options for about ten seconds. "I'm calling 911. This is a facility emergency."

I watched her make the call, explaining the situation to dispatch with the calm professionalism that made her such a good charge nurse. As she hung up, she turned to the rest of us.

"Fire department's responding for forcible entry. Should be here in a few minutes."

Something fluttered in my chest — a mix of anticipation and nervousness that I tried to push down. There were multiple fire stations in the city. It probably wouldn't be Station 2. It definitely wouldn't be Engine 18.

But ten minutes later, when I heard the diesel rumble of a fire engine outside and looked through the windows to see the familiar black and red of Summit County Fire Rescue, I knew exactly which crew had responded.

And when the crew walked through the ER doors — not in full turnout gear but in their dark station pants and department t-shirts, carrying the tools they'd need for a simple forcible entry — I felt my heart do something complicated in my chest.

Lieutenant Isabela Delgado led them in, radiating the same calm, focused authority I'd seen that first night when she'd brought Cap to us. Behind her were three firefighters I didn't recognize, all of them moving with the easy confidence of people who knew exactly what they were doing.

Her eyes found mine across the department, and for just a moment, I saw her professional mask slip. A quick smile, there and gone, but enough to make me feel like an idiot for grinning back.

"Lieutenant Delgado, Engine 18," she said to Carly, all business again. "We're here about your locked door."

"Thank God," Carly said. "Right this way. The electronic lock system fried during a power surge, and we can't access any of our ortho-pedic supplies."

As Carly led them toward the supply area, explaining the situation, Izzy fell into step beside her. But before they disappeared around the corner, she caught my eye again and mouthed, "Hey."

Such a simple thing. One word that wasn't even spoken out loud. But it sent warmth spreading through my chest like I'd just had a shot of something much stronger than hospital coffee.

The actual work took less than five minutes. I could hear the brief discussion about the best approach, then the sharp, decisive sounds of professional competence — metal on metal, the snap of a lock giving way, the satisfied grunt of a job well done.

When they reappeared, Carly was practically beaming. "You guys just saved our night. Maybe our whole week."

"Just doing our job," said one of the other firefighters — an older guy with salt-and-pepper hair who had the weathered look of someone who'd been doing this for decades.

"This is Jimmy," Izzy said, and I realized she was introducing me to her crew. "He's the nurse who took such good care of Cap when we brought him in."

The change in their demeanor was immediate and obvious. The polite professionalism shifted to something warmer, more genuine. The older firefighter — Thompson, according to his name tape — gave me an appraising look that felt like an evaluation.

"Cap speaks highly of you," he said, extending his hand for a firm shake. "Says you actually listened to him instead of just treating him like another old man complaining about pain."

"Cap's good people," I said simply. "Easy to care about."

"Damn right he is," said another firefighter — Martinez, young and eager-looking. "Man taught half the department everything they know about running a scene."

The other firefighter, who'd been quietly coiling up their entry tools, looked up. "Thanks for taking care of our guy."

It was such a simple exchange, but I could feel the weight of it. This wasn't just polite conversation. These were Cap's people, and they were taking my measure. The fact that I'd treated their mentor with respect and competence had apparently earned me something valuable — their approval.

"We should get going," Izzy said, though I noticed she didn't move toward the door immediately. "Let you guys get back to work."

Her crew started heading for the exit, but she lingered for just a moment, letting them get a few steps ahead.

"Cap's doing better, by the way," she said quietly. "Margaret said he's been sleeping through the night, and his appetite's coming back."

"That's great to hear," I said, and meant it. "I was wondering how he was doing."

"Thanks again for everything you did for him that night. For both of us."

"Just doing my job."

"No," she said, and there was something in her voice that made me look at her more carefully. "It was more than that."

We stood there for a moment, the noise of the ER fading into the background. There was something in her eyes, something that made me think about tres leches cake and the taste of possibility, about the way she'd kissed me in my kitchen and left me standing there like a lovesick teenager.

"Lieutenant?" Martinez's voice carried from the doorway. "We're good to roll."

The spell broke. Izzy's professional mask snapped back into place, but not before I caught a glimpse of something that looked like regret.

"Be safe out there," I said.

"Always am," she replied, but she was smiling when she said it.

I watched them leave, the diesel rumble of Engine 18 fading as they pulled away from the hospital. The ER settled back into its normal rhythm, but I found myself standing there for a moment longer, replaying the brief conversation, the way her crew had looked at me, the moment when her guard had dropped just enough to let me see the woman behind the lieutenant's uniform.

"Earth to Jimmy," Carly called from the charge desk. "You planning to stand there all night, or are you going to help me figure out why Room 3 is asking for a priest and a lawyer?"

I shook my head, clearing away the lingering warmth of Izzy's smile. "On my way."

But as I headed toward Room 3 and whatever fresh crisis awaited, I couldn't stop thinking about the way she'd said "more than that," like maybe what I'd thought was just professional courtesy had meant something deeper to her.

Like maybe I wasn't the only one who'd been replaying that kiss in my kitchen, wondering when we'd get another chance to be alone together.

The thought should have been distracting. In a few hours, it would prove to be exactly that. But for now, it just made the rest of my shift feel a little brighter, like maybe the universe was finally starting to line up in my favor.

I had no idea how wrong I was about to be.

chapter
thirteen

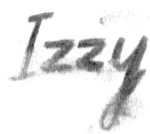

THE TONES DROPPED at 2:47 a.m., cutting through the quiet murmur of late-night conversation in the station day room.

"Engine 18, respond to Metro General Hospital, Emergency Department, for a public assist, facility emergency."

I was up and moving before the dispatcher finished speaking, muscle memory taking over. Around me, my crew stirred into action with the practiced efficiency of people who'd done this dance a thousand times.

"Metro General?" Thompson said, grabbing his radio from the charger. "What are the odds it's something actually interesting?"

"Slim to none," Martinez replied, but he was already pulling on his boots. "Probably a stuck elevator or a door that won't open."

"Facilities emergency means they need us now," I said, checking my radio and clipping it to my belt. "Let's roll."

It wasn't until we were pulling out of the bay that my brain fully processed where we were headed. Metro General. Jimmy's hospital. Jimmy, who worked nights, who would be there right now, who I'd been thinking about more than was probably healthy since our dinner three days ago.

The thought sent a jolt of nervous energy through me that I immediately shoved down. This was a call. A job. Nothing more. The fact that I might see him was irrelevant.

Keep telling yourself that, Delgado.

"What's the over-under on this being an actual emergency versus someone who doesn't want to wait for maintenance?" Rodriguez asked from the back seat.

"Even money," Thompson said. "But hey, it's a nice night for a drive."

The drive to Metro General took eight minutes through the quiet city streets. Eight minutes for me to lecture myself about professionalism, about maintaining boundaries, about not letting personal feelings interfere with the job. Eight minutes that felt like an eternity.

We pulled up to the emergency department entrance, and I forced myself into lieutenant mode. Professional. Focused. In command.

"Alright, let's see what they've got for us," I said, grabbing the halligan bar from its mount. "Rodriguez, bring the flathead. Keep it simple until we know what we're dealing with."

The automatic doors slid open, and we walked into the familiar chaos of the ER. Bright lights, the smell of antiseptic, the constant background hum of medical equipment. I'd been here dozens of times bringing in patients, but tonight felt different. Tonight, I was looking for —

And there he was. At the nurses' station, updating a chart, looking tired but solid in his navy scrubs. Our eyes met across the department, and for just a moment, his professional mask slipped. Recognition. Warmth. That same nervous energy I was trying so hard to suppress.

I gave him the barest nod and mouthed "Hey" before forcing myself to focus on the charge nurse's explanation.

The lock was simple, the kind that failed spectacularly when the power hiccupped wrong. Rodriguez and I had it open in thirty seconds — one quick pop with the halligan, metal on metal, the satisfying snap of a job well done. My crew moved with automatic efficiency, but I was hyperaware of Jimmy watching from across the department, of the way my hands were steadier than they should have been for such a simple task.

When the charge nurse thanked us — genuine relief in her voice about accessing supplies that could mean the difference between life and death — I found myself introducing Jimmy to my crew. Not because protocol demanded it, but because it felt important. Because I wanted these men I trusted with my life to know the man who'd taken such good care of Cap.

I watched Thompson's expression shift when he heard Jimmy's name. The way the usual firefighter-to-nurse politeness transformed into something warmer, more genuine. Martinez perked up with interest. Rodriguez gave Jimmy an appraising look that seemed to find him acceptable.

This was the gauntlet every civilian had to run — firefighter scrutiny, the unspoken question of whether you understood what the job demanded. Whether you'd resent the missed dinners, the interrupted sleep, the thousand small ways the work claimed us.

But Jimmy didn't look intimidated. He looked honored. Like meeting my crew mattered.

It settled something I hadn't realized was a question.

"We should get going," I said, though part of me wanted to linger. "Let you guys get back to work."

My crew started heading for the exit, and I let them get a few steps ahead before I spoke again.

"Cap's doing better, by the way," I said quietly, stepping slightly closer to Jimmy. "Margaret said he's been sleeping through the night, and his appetite's coming back."

"That's great to hear," Jimmy replied, and I could see that he genuinely meant it. "I was wondering how he was doing."

"Thanks again for everything you did for him that night. For both of us."

"Just doing my job."

"No," I said, and suddenly it felt important that he understand this. "It was more than that."

We stood there for a moment, and I felt that same pull I'd experienced in his kitchen three nights ago. The urge to step closer, to reach out, to close the distance between us. But we were in his workplace, surrounded by his colleagues, and I was still in uniform with my crew waiting.

"Lieutenant?" Rodriguez's voice carried from the doorway, slightly amused. "We're good to roll."

The spell broke, and I stepped back, my professional mask sliding back into place. But not before I caught something in Jimmy's eyes that looked like regret — the same regret I was feeling.

"Be safe out there," he said.

"Always am," I replied, allowing myself a small smile.

As we walked back to the engine, I could feel my crew's eyes on me. Thompson was grinning in a way that meant I was going to hear about this later. Rodriguez looked thoughtful, like he was filing away information for future use. Martinez just looked pleased, like he'd witnessed something entertaining.

"Nice guy," Thompson said as we climbed back into the engine, his tone carefully neutral.

"Yeah," I agreed, probably too quickly. "He is."

"Seems competent," Rodriguez added. "Cap's got good judgment about people."

"That he does."

Martinez, bless him, seemed oblivious to the undercurrents. "Cool that we got to meet him. Not often we get to put faces to the people who help our guys."

The drive back to Station 2 was quiet, each of us lost in our own thoughts. But I could feel the weight of unspoken observations, the way my crew had noticed the way Jimmy and I looked at each other, the way I'd lingered to talk to him.

Back at the station, as we reset our equipment and returned to whatever we'd been doing before the call, Thompson appeared at my elbow.

"So," he said, his voice low enough that the others couldn't hear. "How long?"

"How long what?" I asked, though I knew exactly what he meant.

"How long have you been seeing the nurse?"

I could have denied it. Should have denied it. But Thompson had twenty-three years on the job and eyes that missed nothing.

"It's new," I said finally. "Really new."

He nodded thoughtfully. "He seems like a good guy. Cap obviously likes him, and Cap's not easy to impress."

"No, he's not."

"Just..." Thompson paused, choosing his words carefully. "Be careful, L.T. This job's hard enough without having to worry about someone who doesn't understand it."

"He understands it," I said, surprised by the certainty in my voice. "He gets it."

Thompson studied my face for a long moment, then nodded. "Alright then. Just wanted to make sure you knew we've got your back, whatever happens."

"I know you do."

He clapped me on the shoulder and headed back to the day room, leaving me alone with my thoughts and the lingering warmth of Jimmy's smile.

I settled into my office to finish the incident report — simple public assist, no injuries, no complications. But as I filled out the forms, my mind kept drifting back to that moment in the ER, to the way Jimmy had looked at me like I was the best part of his night.

For the first time in years, I found myself looking forward to getting off shift for reasons that had nothing to do with sleep or solitude. I found myself thinking about calling him, maybe suggesting another dinner, maybe taking the risk of letting him see a little more of who I was behind the uniform.

Maybe, just maybe, it was time to stop being so careful all the time. Waiting for chance encounters at the hospital wasn't a plan. It was leaving things to fate, and I didn't believe in fate. I believed in assessing a situation and acting. This situation required action.

My thumb hovered over his contact. My heart hammered against my ribs. This was a different kind of risk, a vulnerability that felt more dangerous than walking into a burning building. But the memory of his smile, of the quiet strength in his hands, pushed me forward.

> Thanks for letting my crew feel useful. They get restless when they're not breaking things.

It was a safe opening. Acknowledging the professional context. I watched the three little dots appear and disappear, my breath held tight in my chest.

JIMMY

Anytime. Glad we could call in the
professionals. Hope we didn't interrupt your
night too much.

Our night was a biohazard-in-a-bag festival.
Breaking down a door was a welcome
change of pace.

JIMMY

Ha. I know that feeling. Noro Night is a
special kind of hell.

The easy back-and-forth felt comfortable, familiar. I took a deep
breath and typed the real reason I was texting.

When's your next day off?

The question hung there, direct and unambiguous. It was a clear
statement of intent. My intent.

The dots appeared again, slower this time. I could almost picture
him on the other end, surprised, maybe trying to figure out if he was
reading it right.

JIMMY

Tomorrow night- tonight?- whatever 12-16
hours from now is, is my Friday. I'm off for
the next two.

Good. I'm taking you to dinner tonight. My
treat. You can tell me more stories about
what people bring to the ER in Ziploc bags.

I hit send, a feeling of pure, terrifying resolve settling over me. I had
taken control. I had made a plan. And whatever happened next, it
would be on my terms.

JIMMY

I'd like that. A lot.

A slow smile spread across my face. Maybe this was how it was supposed to feel. Not like being taken care of, but like meeting someone halfway, an equal partnership built on mutual respect and a shared understanding of the beautiful, messy, chaotic world we lived in. Maybe, just maybe, this was what hope felt like.

chapter
fourteen

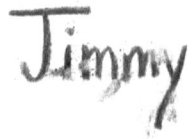

THE HIGH FROM seeing Izzy was still coursing through me as I updated patient charts at the nurses' station. Her crew's approval, that moment when she'd said "it was more than that," the way she'd looked at me like I was the best part of her night — it all felt like a promise of something good coming.

My phone buzzed with another text from her:

> IZZY
>
> Looking forward to tomorrow. Any restaurant preferences?

I was typing back when the ambulance bay doors hissed open. Two paramedics wheeled in a woman who looked like she'd been through hell, her left eye swollen shut, her arm cradled against her chest. Walking beside the gurney was a man in his forties, doing all the talking.

"She fell down the stairs," he was saying to anyone who'd listen. "Clumsy as hell, my Lisa. Always tripping over something."

I looked up from my phone, and my stomach dropped. The woman — Lisa — wasn't making eye contact with anyone. She was staring at the ceiling, her visible eye glazed with the particular kind of numbness I'd seen before.

"Chloe," I called quietly. "Room 6."

She appeared at my elbow, took one look at the incoming patient, and I saw her face change. Only three months on the job — still a "toddler" in ER terms — and she was already starting to develop the instincts.

"Fell down the stairs?" she whispered.

"So they say."

We got Lisa settled in Room 6, the man hovering at her bedside like a guard dog. He answered every question I directed at her, his hand never leaving her shoulder in what might have looked like comfort but felt like control.

"Lisa, I need to ask you directly about your pain level," I said, ignoring him. "On a scale of one to ten — "

"She's about a six," the man interrupted. "Aren't you, baby? Not too bad."

Lisa nodded mutely, but I caught the way she flinched when he squeezed her shoulder.

"We need to get some X-rays," I said, my voice professionally neutral. "Sir, I'll need you to step out to the waiting room while we position her."

"I'm not leaving her alone," he said, his voice taking on an edge. "She gets confused when she's hurt. Needs me here."

"Hospital policy," I said firmly. "Radiation safety. I'll come get you as soon as we're done."

He started to argue, but I was already moving, opening the door and gesturing toward the hallway. "Just for a few minutes. There's coffee in the waiting room."

The moment he was gone, I turned to Chloe. "Get Carly. Now."

"Jimmy, what — "

"Trust me. Get Carly, and make sure that guy stays in the waiting area."

Carly appeared within minutes, took one look at Lisa, and I saw the same recognition in her eyes. We'd both been here before.

"Lisa," Carly said gently, pulling up a chair beside the bed. "How are you really doing?"

Lisa's composure cracked just slightly. "I'm fine. Just clumsy."

"The stairs must have been really steep," I said carefully. "Those injuries on your ribs look like they came from multiple impacts."

Lisa's good eye flicked to the door, then back to me. Fear. Pure, undiluted fear.

"He's not here," Carly said softly. "It's just us. You're safe."

For a moment, I thought she might open up. Her lips parted, and I could see her fighting with herself. Then she shook her head.

"I fell down the stairs," she repeated, but her voice was hollow.

Carly and I exchanged glances. We both knew what we were looking at, but without Lisa's cooperation, our hands were tied.

"Lisa," I said, leaning forward, "if you're not safe at home, we can help you. There are places you can go, people who can keep you safe. You don't have to — "

"I can't... there's nowhere..." Her voice broke. "The money, he... I don't even..." She gestured helplessly at her purse. "No cards. Nothing."

There it was. The trap that kept so many women locked in hell.

"We can help with that too," Carly said. "There are resources, programs — "

"You don't..." Lisa shook her head frantically. "He said he'd find me. Always finds me. And anyone who..." Her eyes darted to the door. "He means it. You don't know him."

Lisa's phone, sitting on the bedside table, lit up with a text. She glanced at it and went even paler.

"Can I see that?" I asked gently.

With trembling hands, she turned the phone toward me. The message was brutal:

> Get your ass out here now or I'm coming in
> there and dragging you out.

Another text came through as I watched:

> And if any of those heroes try to stop me I'll
> put bullets in every one of them.

"Lisa," I said urgently, "this is him threatening you. And threatening us. We can — "

"Please," she whispered. "Please just let him back in. If you don't... he'll take it out on me later. You know he will."

Carly was already on the phone with security, but I could see the impossible calculation in Lisa's eyes. Stay here and face his escalated rage later, or leave now and face it immediately.

"We can protect you," I said desperately. "We can — "

"No, you can't." Her voice was flat, certain. "You can't be there when your shift ends. You can't be there tomorrow, or next week. But he will be."

The man's voice echoed from the hallway — loud, demanding, getting closer despite security's presence. "Where is she? Where's my wife?"

"Lisa, please," I said, standing up. "Let us help you."

She was already reaching for her IV line. "Take this out."

"Lisa — "

"Take it out, or I'll pull it out myself."

I met her eyes, saw the resignation there, the terrible clarity of someone who'd calculated her odds and found them wanting. With shaking hands, I removed the IV.

The man appeared in the doorway, brushing past security like they weren't there. "There you are, baby. Come on, we're leaving. These people don't know what they're talking about."

He reached for Lisa's arm, and something in me snapped.

I stepped between them, close enough that I could smell his cologne, close enough to see the veins in his bloodshot eyes.

"Back off," I said quietly.

He looked at me like I was an insect. "Move, nurse boy."

"Make me."

The words came out flat, emotionless. I could feel Chloe's shock from across the room, could see Carly reaching for her phone, but I didn't care. I stared into this man's eyes and willed him to give me a reason.

"Do it," I said, my voice barely above a whisper. "Put your hands on me. I *dare* you. Do it."

For a moment, I thought he would. I could see the calculation in his eyes, the same predator's instinct that had trapped Lisa. But he was too smart, too controlled.

He stepped back, hands raised in mock surrender. "Whatever, man. This place is a joke anyway." He turned to Lisa. "Come on. Your stuff's going in the trash if you're not in the car in two minutes."

Lisa slid off the bed like a ghost, not looking at any of us. At the door, she paused for just a moment.

"Thank you for trying," she whispered.

And then they were gone.

I stood there for a long moment, my hands shaking with unused adrenaline. Chloe was staring at me with wide eyes.

"What just happened?" she asked.

I forced my voice back to professional calm. "Domestic violence case. Sometimes they leave anyway."

"But you... you were ready to fight him."

"Sometimes that's what it takes." I looked at her, saw the questions in her eyes. "Chloe, you're going to see this again. Patients who are being hurt by people who claim to love them. And sometimes, no matter what we do, no matter how hard we try, they go back to their abusers. It doesn't mean we stop trying."

She nodded slowly. "What do we do now?"

"We document everything. We call the police and file a report. We hope that next time, she'll be ready to accept help." I started toward the computer to begin the incident report. "And we don't let it stop us from fighting for the next one."

But as I sat down to type, my hands were still shaking. Because I knew, with terrible certainty, that Lisa was driving home to face the consequences of our intervention. And there wasn't a damn thing I could do about it.

After they left, I called the police from the nurses' station. The officer who answered was sympathetic but firm.

"Look, we get it," he said. "We see these cases all the time. But without the victim asking for help, without her pressing charges or asking for protection, there's not much we can do. We can do a welfare check, but if she answers the door and says she's fine..."

"Even with the threats to hospital staff?"

"You can file a report about that, and we'll document it. But the domestic situation? Our hands are tied until she's ready to ask for help."

I hung up feeling hollower than before. Somewhere across the city, Lisa was facing the consequences of our intervention, and the system that was supposed to protect her was as helpless as I was.

The text from Izzy about dinner felt like it came from another life-time. I stared at it for a long moment, then put my phone away without responding.

Some battles, you just couldn't win.

chapter
fifteen

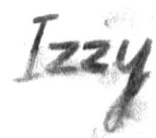

I **WALKED** out of the fire station at 7 a.m. with a smile on my face, which was unusual enough that it took me a moment to remember why. Then it all came flooding back — Jimmy's text about his days off, my bold move asking him to dinner, his response that he'd like it "a lot."

For the first time in years, I had butterflies about a date. Actual, honest-to-God butterflies, like I was sixteen again instead of a twenty-eight-year-old fire lieutenant who could dismantle a car engine or coordinate a multi-agency rescue without breaking a sweat.

I walked into my apartment and headed to the kitchen to make coffee, my phone in hand, expecting to see his response to my question about restaurant preferences. Nothing. Well, he was probably just getting off right now too — night shift schedules were brutal that way.

By nine a.m., I was standing in front of my closet, actually considering my options. When was the last time I'd cared what I wore on a date? Derek had always wanted me in dresses, the more feminine the better. Marcus had preferred tight workout clothes that showed off what he called my "athletic assets." But with Jimmy... I just wanted to look like myself. Maybe the green sweater he'd complimented, or the dark jeans that actually fit well.

I checked my phone again. Still nothing.

By noon, the butterflies had died and been replaced by something colder. I'd sent the restaurant question twelve hours ago. Jimmy had been quick to respond to every other text, sometimes within seconds. The silence was starting to feel deliberate.

I sat on my couch, staring at my phone like it might spontaneously generate a message. Had I misread everything? The dinner at his place, the way he'd looked at me at the hospital, the easy conversation, that moment when our eyes had met across the ER — had I imagined the connection?

Maybe you came on too strong, the voice in my head whispered. *Maybe "I'm taking you to dinner" was too aggressive. Maybe he likes the chase and you took that away from him.*

The optimistic buzz from our date began to curdle into a familiar, sour dread, as the ghosts of past failures began whispering in my ear.

"You're never here anymore," Derek's voice echoed in my head.

"You need to soften up," Marcus had complained.

"You're too ambitious," Ryan had accused.

Maybe he's just another flirty nurse, the voice continued. *Maybe you were just another conquest, and now that he's gotten you interested, the game's over.*

Had Jimmy gotten a taste of the real me — the demanding job, the walls I couldn't seem to fully dismantle — and decided it was too much? The confident lieutenant who had taken charge and asked him to dinner was replaced by a woman staring at a blank phone screen, feeling the sting of a dozen old rejections. I'd let my guard down, and this was the price. I felt like a fool.

By 2 p.m., I was pacing my apartment like a caged animal. This was ridiculous. I was a fire department lieutenant. I commanded emergency scenes, made life-and-death decisions under pressure, earned the respect of men who'd initially written me off as a diversity hire. I didn't pace around waiting for some guy to text me back.

But the silence was eating at me. Not just because my feelings were hurt — though they were — but because it was wrong. This level of radio silence from Jimmy, who'd been so open and communicative, wasn't normal. It didn't fit the pattern.

I stopped pacing. My commander's instincts were kicking in, the same ones that told me when something was off at a scene, when the smoke pattern didn't match the reported fire location, when a victim's story didn't align with their injuries.

This wasn't ghosting. This was a distress signal.

Jimmy had been on shift when I'd texted him. Something had happened. Something bad enough to make a man who'd been excited about our date go completely silent.

I grabbed my keys.

Jimmy's apartment building looked the same as it had four nights ago, but everything felt different now. I stood outside his door, still in my uniform from the night shift, my heart hammering against my ribs for entirely different reasons than it had the last time I was here.

I knocked softly. No answer.

I knocked again, louder. "Jimmy? It's Izzy."

I heard movement inside, then footsteps. The door opened, and my breath caught.

Jimmy looked like he'd been hit by a truck. His eyes were hollow, ringed with dark circles. His hair was disheveled, and he was wearing the same clothes he'd had on yesterday, wrinkled now like he'd slept in them. But it was his expression that broke my heart — empty, defeated, like something essential had been carved out of him and left a void behind.

"Izzy," he said, his voice rough. "I... I'm sorry, I meant to text you back, I just — "

"Is your family okay?" I asked quietly.

He blinked, confused by the question. "What? Yeah, they're... they're fine."

I nodded. I'd needed to rule out personal tragedy first. Which meant this was work. Which meant I understood.

"Bad case?" I asked, even though I already knew the answer.

His face crumpled slightly, and I saw him fighting to hold it together. "I... yeah. Really bad."

I stepped past him into his apartment, closing the door behind me. "Okay."

"Izzy, I'm not... I'm not good company right now. Maybe we should — "

"Jimmy." I turned to face him, my voice gentle but firm. "I'm not leaving. I don't know what happened, and you don't have to tell me. But I know that look. I've seen it on my crew after a bad call. I've seen it in the mirror. You're not okay, and you don't have to be. But you're not going to be alone with it."

He stared at me for a long moment, and I could see the exact moment his carefully maintained composure finally cracked. His shoulders sagged, and he looked so lost, so unlike the confident, caring man I'd been getting to know.

"Come here," I said softly, opening my arms.

He didn't move at first, like he wasn't sure he deserved comfort. So I went to him, wrapping my arms around him and pulling him against me. He was taller than me, but he seemed to fold into himself, his head dropping to my shoulder.

"I tried to help someone," he whispered against my neck. "I had a plan. I did everything right. And she... she left anyway. Because I couldn't protect her."

"I know," I said quietly, my hand stroking his hair. "I know."

And then he told me everything.

We stood there in his living room for a long time, his weight against me, my arms around him. I could feel the exhaustion in his body, the way he was finally letting himself lean on someone after hours of carrying this alone.

"Come on," I said finally, guiding him toward his bedroom. "When's the last time you slept?"

"I don't know. I keep seeing her face, hearing what he said to her..." He rubbed his eyes with the heels of his hands. "I wanted him to hit me, Izzy. I wanted him to give me a reason to escalate it, to call security, to do something. I looked him in the eye and told him to do it. And the bastard was too smart."

My heart broke a little more. This gentle, caring man had been willing to take a beating to protect someone, and it still hadn't been enough.

"That's not your fault," I said.

"Isn't it? I'm supposed to help people. I'm supposed to keep them safe. And I couldn't..." His voice broke. "There was nothing I could do. Nothing at all."

I guided him to sit on the edge of his bed, then settled beside him.

Without hesitation, I pulled him down with me, positioning him so his head was resting on my chest, my arm around his shoulders. It wasn't sexual — it was pure comfort, the kind of anchor I'd wished for after my own worst calls.

"Sometimes there's nothing you can do," I said quietly, my fingers running through his hair. "Sometimes the system fails, or people make choices we can't understand, or the bad guy is just too smart. It doesn't mean you failed. It means the world is broken in ways that one person can't fix."

He was quiet for a long time, his breathing gradually evening out as the exhaustion finally started to win over the adrenaline and guilt.

"I keep thinking about what's happening to her right now," he murmured. "What he's doing to punish her for talking to us."

"I know," I said. "But you planted a seed. You showed her that someone cared, that someone saw what was happening to her. Maybe next time, she'll remember that. Maybe next time, she'll be ready."

"Maybe," he said, but he didn't sound convinced.

I held him closer, feeling his body gradually relax against mine. "You did everything you could, Jimmy. You were willing to take a beating for someone you barely knew. That matters, even if it didn't work out the way you wanted."

He didn't respond, and after a few minutes, I realized his breathing had deepened into sleep. The man who spent his nights taking care of everyone else had finally let someone take care of him.

I lay there holding him, watching the afternoon light filter through his bedroom curtains, and realized something had fundamentally shifted between us. This wasn't about attraction anymore, or the thrill of a new relationship. This was about trust. About seeing each other at our most vulnerable and choosing to stay anyway.

I thought about all the men who'd wanted me to be softer, smaller, more manageable. None of them would have understood this moment — me in my rumpled clothes, holding a man who'd just had his heart broken by his own compassion. They'd have seen weakness where I saw strength, neediness where I saw courage.

But Jimmy had let me see him shattered, and somehow that made me want to protect him even more fiercely than I protected my crew.

He'd trusted me with his pain, and I'd do whatever it took to help him carry it.

Outside, the city moved on with its day, oblivious to the quiet revolution happening in a nurse's bedroom, where two people who spent their lives taking care of others had begun to learn to take care of each other.

I pressed a soft kiss to the top of his head and settled in to keep watch while he slept. Whatever came next, we'd face it together.

chapter
sixteen

I WOKE UP SLOWLY, the way you do when your body has finally been allowed to rest after carrying too much for too long. For a moment, I was disoriented — the light was wrong, the shadows unfamiliar. Then I became aware of the warmth beneath me, the steady rise and fall of breath that wasn't my own, of gentle fingers still moving through my hair.

Izzy.

I was lying on her chest, my head tucked into the curve of her shoulder, one arm wrapped around her waist. She was still in her uniform shirt, though it had come untucked from her pants. My own clothes were wrinkled and uncomfortable, but I didn't want to move. I didn't want to break whatever spell had brought us to this moment.

"Hey," she said quietly, and I realized she'd been awake, probably for a while.

"Hey." My voice came out rough with sleep. "How long was I out?"

"A few hours. It's almost seven."

7 p.m. I'd slept through the afternoon, something I never did. But then again, I'd never had someone hold me while I fell apart, either.

I started to pull away, suddenly self-conscious. "I should — "

"Should what?" Her arm tightened around me, keeping me close. "You needed sleep. I needed to make sure you were okay."

I looked up at her, really looked at her. Her dark hair was mussed from lying against my pillow, and there were new lines of exhaustion around her eyes. She'd stayed awake watching over me while I slept off my crisis.

"You didn't have to do that," I said.

"Yes, I did." Her voice was matter-of-fact, but her hand was still stroking my hair with infinite gentleness. "That's what you do for people you care about."

People you care about. The words settled something in my chest that I hadn't realized was still raw.

I shifted, propping myself up on my elbow so I could see her better. "Izzy — "

"You don't have to talk about it," she said quickly. "I meant what I said earlier. You don't owe me explanations."

"I know. But I want to." I traced a pattern on her shirt with my finger, gathering my thoughts. "I became a nurse because I wanted to help people. To protect them. And when I can't..." I shook my head. "It makes me question everything."

"That's because you care," she said simply. "That's why you're good at what you do."

"Sometimes caring isn't enough."

"No," she agreed. "Sometimes it's not. But it's still worth doing."

We lay there in the gathering dusk, her hand in my hair, my weight against her solid warmth. The apartment was quiet except for the distant hum of traffic, the world outside moving on while we existed in this small pocket of peace.

I became aware, gradually, of other things. The way her breath hitched slightly when my thumb brushed against the exposed skin at her waist. The way she was looking at me, her dark eyes holding something I hadn't seen before. The way the space between us seemed to be shrinking without either of us moving.

"Jimmy," she said, my name barely a whisper.

"Yeah?"

"I'm not going anywhere."

Something shifted in the air between us. The comfort and protection she'd offered was transforming into something else, something that made my pulse quicken and my skin feel too tight.

I leaned down and kissed her, soft and tentative at first, giving her every chance to pull away. Instead, she kissed me back, her hand sliding from my hair to cup the back of my neck, pulling me closer.

This kiss was different from the ones in my kitchen. Those had been sweet, exploratory, full of possibility. This one was deeper, more certain. It tasted like trust and want and the kind of intimacy that came from seeing someone at their most vulnerable and choosing to stay.

When we broke apart, we were both breathing harder. I searched her face, looking for any sign of hesitation, any indication that this was too much, too fast.

"Are you sure?" I asked.

"I've never been more sure of anything," she said, and pulled me back down to her.

What followed was unlike anything I'd ever experienced. There was no urgency, no rush toward a finish line. We moved slowly, carefully, learning each other with a patience that felt almost sacred. Her hands were gentle but sure as she helped me out of my wrinkled shirt, her fingers tracing the lines of my shoulders like she was memorizing them.

When I returned the favor, carefully unbuttoning her uniform shirt, she watched my face with an intensity that made my chest tight. There was trust in her eyes, and something that looked like wonder, as if she couldn't quite believe this was happening.

"You're beautiful," I whispered against her collarbone, and felt her shiver beneath me.

She reached for me again, guiding me in slowly, her breath catching as our bodies connected. There was nothing frantic in it — no surge of lust demanding urgency. Just heat, deep and steady, rising with every long, unhurried thrust.

Her legs wrapped around my hips as I moved within her, the friction exquisite, building with each stroke like the slow burn of a fire catching. Her fingers dug into my shoulders, grounding herself, and when I dipped my head to kiss her again — soft, lingering — she made a sound low in her throat that almost undid me, a breathy, half-laugh.

"What?" I asked, brushing my lips along her collarbone.

"I just ..." She tilted her head back, eyes fluttering shut. "This is already the longest sex I've ever had."

I paused, blinking, unsure I'd heard her right.

"What do you mean?"

"I mean," she said dryly, "that most men treat foreplay like a formality, and actual sex like a sprint. This? This feels like you're trying to learn my body, not just get off."

I sat back slightly, one hand still resting on her hip. "I am."

Her breath caught.

"Izzy, I want to *wreck* you," I said, voice low and reverent. "But only in ways you want. I'm not in a rush. I've got all night. You're not a race."

She pulled me back down to her with a ferocity that made my blood roar. "Then shut up and keep going."

I obeyed, slowly dragging my mouth down the column of her throat, lingering at the sensitive spot just below her ear. Her breath hitched.

I kissed my way across her chest, teasing, savoring. When my hand slid between her thighs, she gasped and arched into me like she couldn't help it.

"God," she murmured, her hands threading into my hair. "Why does that feel so good?"

"Because I'm not in a hurry," I said, lips brushing against her hip. "Because you deserve this. Every second of it."

She didn't respond with words — just a low, hungry sound that made me want to worship her for hours. And I did.

I teased her until she was shaking. I mapped every inch of her skin with my hands and mouth, catalogued every sound she made, every way she responded to my touch. She was strong and soft and fierce and vulnerable all at once, and when she finally came apart in my arms, her back arching off the bed and my name falling from her lips like a prayer, I thought I might die from the sheer privilege of witnessing it.

Her breath was still stuttering when I curled around her, pressing a kiss to the sweat-damp skin at the back of her neck. She reached for my hand and laced our fingers together without a word.

We lay like that for a while, skin to skin, heartbeats finding the same rhythm. I couldn't remember the last time sex had felt like this — like a promise instead of a transaction.

"That was..." she started, then trailed off.

"Yeah," I agreed, pressing a series of feather-lite kisses to the top of her head. "It was."

We dozed for a while, but by ten p.m., my stomach was making demands that couldn't be ignored. I started to disentangle myself from her warm limbs.

"Where are you going?" she asked, catching my wrist.

"To make you dinner," I said. "Or breakfast. Whatever meal this counts as when you work nights."

She smiled, lazy and satisfied. "You don't have to — "

"I want to." I leaned down to kiss her forehead. "Stay right there."

I pulled on my boxer shorts and padded to the kitchen, flipping on the light and taking stock of what I had available. My sourdough starter sat in its usual place on the counter, ready for its nightly feeding. Perfect.

I was in the process of stirring flour and water into the jar when Izzy appeared in the kitchen doorway, wearing one of my t-shirts and nothing else. The sight of her — hair mussed, lips still swollen from kissing, my shirt hanging loose on her frame — made me forget what I was doing entirely.

"Is that sourdough?" she asked, hopping up to sit on the counter beside me.

"Mmhmm." I tried to focus on the starter, but she was sitting close enough that I could smell her shampoo, could see the faint marks my mouth had left on her neck. "Daily feeding ritual. You have to keep the culture alive, or it dies."

She watched me seal the jar and return it to its spot. "How long have you had it?"

"Two years. Started it from scratch when I moved into this place." I pulled a covered bowl from the refrigerator. "But the fun part is what I made yesterday."

Inside was a round of dough that had been cold-fermenting overnight, properly risen and ready for the final steps. I turned it out onto my floured work surface and grabbed my lame — a small blade designed specifically for scoring bread.

"What's that for?" Izzy asked, genuine curiosity in her voice.

"Watch." I made quick, confident cuts across the top of the loaf in a pattern I'd perfected over hundreds of loaves. "The scoring lets the bread expand in the oven without tearing randomly. Plus it looks cool."

She laughed, the sound rich and unguarded. "You're such a nerd about this."

"Guilty." I slid the scored loaf into my preheated Dutch oven. "Thirty-five minutes, then we can eat it warm with butter and honey."

I set the timer and washed the flour from my hands. When I turned around, Izzy was still sitting on the counter, watching me with an expression I couldn't quite read.

"This is nice," she said eventually, swinging her legs back and forth.

"What is?"

"This. The quiet. Usually after..." She gestured vaguely. "Usually I'm ready for them to leave. Or I leave."

I looked up at her, understanding exactly what she meant. "And now?"

"Now I'm thinking about what it would be like to wake up next to you."

The words hit me square in the chest. I stepped between her legs, my hands settling on her thighs.

"I'd like that," I said. "A lot."

She leaned forward and kissed me, soft and sweet.

"Come home with me," she said against my lips. "When this is done. I want to show you my place."

I thought about her neat, precise apartment, about seeing her in her own space, about waking up in her bed instead of mine.

"Yeah," I said. "I'd like that, too."

The bread would take another thirty-five minutes to bake, then needed time to cool. Plenty of time to fall into each other again, to explore this new territory we'd discovered. And then I'd follow her home, to her carefully controlled world, and maybe find new ways to make her fall apart in my arms.

For the first time in twenty-four hours, the future felt bright with possibility.

chapter
seventeen

I'D BEEN SITTING on Jimmy's kitchen counter for twenty minutes, and I was pretty sure I'd broken him.

It had started innocently enough — well, mostly innocently. I'd wandered into the kitchen wearing nothing but his t-shirt and my panties, genuinely curious about the sourdough process. But the moment I'd hopped up onto the counter and seen his eyes go wide, something wicked had awakened in me.

For the first time in my adult life, I had a man's complete, undivided attention, and I was enjoying every second of it.

I'd watched him feed his starter with methodical precision, explaining the process like he was teaching a class. Then he'd pulled out this gorgeous round of dough from the fridge and scored it with quick, confident strokes that made me think about his hands doing other things. And when he'd slid it into the Dutch oven and set the timer?

That's when I decided to make his waiting time *very* difficult.

I crossed my legs, letting the hem of his shirt ride up slightly, and watched his eyes track the movement. He was cleaning flour from his hands at the sink, trying to act normal, but I could see the exact moment he lost focus.

"So how long did you say this takes?" I asked innocently, uncrossing my legs and letting them swing slightly apart.

"Uhhh..." Jimmy's voice came out rougher than intended. He

cleared his throat, his hands stilling under the running water. "About thirty-five minutes to bake, then it needs to cool for a bit."

I leaned forward, ostensibly interested in the oven, but really giving him a better view down the loose neckline of his shirt. "That's a long time to wait."

His hands gripped the edge of the sink. "Izzy."

"Mmm?" I stretched my arms above my head, arching my back slightly, watching his eyes follow the movement of my body beneath the thin cotton.

"You're doing this on purpose."

"Doing what?" I asked, all innocence, as I recrossed my legs in the opposite direction.

Jimmy dried his hands and stepped closer, his hands settling on my thighs. "Driving me crazy."

"Is it working?" I asked, sliding my hands up his chest.

"You know it is."

I did know. And God, I loved it. This wasn't Derek demanding I dress a certain way, or Marcus critiquing my appearance, or Ryan wanting me to be more "feminine." This was Jimmy, completely undone by the sight of me in his kitchen, wanting me exactly as I was.

"Good," I said, pulling him down for a kiss that tasted like honey and promises.

By the time the bread was done — golden and crackling as Jimmy pulled it from the oven — I was pretty sure we'd both worked up an appetite for more than just food. But Jimmy outdid himself with the meal: fresh sourdough bread still warm enough that the butter melted into it, perfectly scrambled eggs with herbs from his windowsill garden, and coffee that was somehow better than anything I'd ever had.

"How do you make everything taste so good?" I asked, stealing another bite of his eggs.

"Practice," he said, but he was smiling, pleased by my obvious enjoyment. "And good ingredients. Those eggs are from a farmer's market vendor who actually named all her chickens."

I laughed. "Of course they are. You probably know her life story, too."

"Mary's a retired teacher who started raising chickens because her grandkids were afraid of them. She figured if she could teach seventh graders, she could handle a few hens."

"See? I knew it." I shook my head in amazement. "You collect people's stories."

"Don't you?"

I considered this. "I collect tactical information. Exit strategies. Structural weaknesses." I paused. "But you collect the human parts."

"Maybe that's why we work," he said quietly.

The words hung between us, heavy with possibility. We work. Not worked, past tense, but work — present, ongoing, future.

"Maybe we do," I said, and meant it.

An hour later, we were driving through the city in my truck, Jimmy taking in the neighborhoods I'd grown up in, the places that had shaped me into who I was.

"That's where I went to high school," I said, pulling over to really look at the building. "I used to sit on those steps during lunch, watching the popular kids and wondering what it would be like to fit in anywhere." I paused, surprised by the admission. "I never told anyone that before."

Jimmy was quiet for a moment, then: "Did you want to fit in?"

"I thought I did. But really, I just wanted someone to see me as more than just 'the strong girl' or 'the weird girl who could outrun the boys.' I wanted someone to see me as... me."

Jimmy looked at the building, then at me. "Their loss."

"Easy to say now," I said, turning onto a tree-lined street. "Harder to believe when you're seventeen and the guy you have a crush on tells you that you're 'too much' for him to handle."

"What was his name?"

"Kyle Reynolds. Why?"

"Just want to know who to punch if I ever meet him."

100

I laughed, surprised by the fierce protectiveness in his voice. "I think I can handle Kyle Reynolds."

"I know you can. Doesn't mean I wouldn't enjoy it."

Something warm unfurled in my chest. Not because I needed him to fight my battles, but because he wanted to. Because in his mind, an insult to me was an insult to him.

"This is where my dad used to take me to practice driving," I said, pulling into an empty parking lot behind a defunct shopping center. "He'd sit in the passenger seat and let me figure out how to parallel park between traffic cones."

"What was he like?"

I put the truck in park and really considered the question. "Patient. Funny. The kind of guy who would give you his last dollar if you needed it, but would lecture you for an hour about being more careful with money." I smiled at the memory. "He used to say that being a firefighter wasn't about being brave — it was about being too stubborn to quit when things got scary."

"Sounds like where you get it from."

"The stubbornness? Definitely." I pulled back onto the road, heading toward downtown. "What about you? What were your parents like?"

"Good people. My mom's a second-grade teacher who still sends care packages to her former students when they go to college. My dad teaches high school history and coaches JV baseball. They're the kind of people who have never missed a school play or a parent-teacher conference."

"Sounds nice."

"It was. Is." Jimmy paused. "They worry about me, though. Think I'm wasting my potential by 'just' being a nurse."

"That's ridiculous."

"I know. But they come from a generation where success was measured by how far up the ladder you climbed, not by how much good you did on the way."

I turned onto the main drag, where the bars and restaurants were just starting to come alive for the evening. "There's this place I like," I said, nodding toward a dive bar with a neon sign that flickered intermittently. "Best beer selection in the city, and they don't water down their whiskey."

Jimmy looked at the bar, then at me, and I saw something shift in his expression. "Izzy."

"Yeah?"

"I don't really want a drink right now."

The way he said it, low and rough, made heat pool in my stomach. "No?"

"No." His hand found my thigh, fingers tracing small circles through my jeans. "I want to see your place. I want to see where you live, where you sleep, where you feel safe."

I was already making a U-turn, heading back toward my apartment. "Good," I said, pressing down on the accelerator. "Because I want to show you."

My apartment had never felt smaller than it did with Jimmy in it, but not in a bad way. In a way that made me hyperaware of every space, every surface, every possibility.

"It's very you," he said, taking in the clean lines, the functional furniture, the complete absence of clutter.

"Is that a good thing or a bad thing?"

"It's perfect." He turned to face me, and I saw something in his eyes that made my pulse quicken. "It's honest. No pretense, no trying to be something you're not."

I stepped closer, backing him toward my bedroom. "Speaking of honest..."

"Yeah?"

"I've been thinking about getting you out of those clothes since we left your place."

His laugh was low and rough. "Have you now?"

"Mmhmm." I pushed him gently onto my bed, climbing up to straddle his hips. "I've been thinking about a lot of things."

"Such as?"

Instead of answering, I pulled my shirt over my head, watching his eyes go dark as he took in the sight of me above him. This was different from the slow, tender exploration at his place. This was hunger, pure and simple.

"Such as this," I said, and leaned down to him deeply, savoring the taste and feel of him beneath me. His hands roamed over my bare skin, igniting sparks wherever they touched. The slow, tantalizing friction between our bodies had me aching for more.

He sat up slightly, lips dragging down my neck, murmuring something incoherent against my skin. I shifted to straddle him more firmly, guiding him with a practiced hand as I lowered myself onto him, inch by delicious inch. He gasped, hands gripping my hips as he filled me completely.

We paused there for a moment, both of us adjusting to the sensation. Then I began to move, slowly at first — rocking my hips in a rhythm that was more teasing than anything else. He met my movements with increasing urgency, his fingers digging into my skin as he whispered my name like a prayer.

The room around us faded into the background. There was only the heat of our bodies, the ragged cadence of our breathing, the wet, needy sound of our connection. Every movement drew a new sound from him, every grind of my hips pushing him closer to the edge.

He broke the kiss, breathless. "God, Izzy — "

"You want me to say it, don't you?" I teased softly, nipping gently at his jawline.

He drew in a shaky breath. "Say ... what?"

I rocked my hips against his, watching his eyes flutter closed briefly. "You know exactly what. You want me to say it."

His hands tightened on my hips, almost painfully. "I really don't — "

"Just admit it."

His eyes opened, blazing with intensity. His voice was barely a whisper. "Yes."

I leaned close, my lips brushing his ear, voice dripping honey and heat. "*Ayyy, papi.*"

His reaction was immediate and overwhelming. He gasped sharply, body tensing beneath me, hips bucking involuntarily as he lost control entirely.

"Oh *fuck*, Izzy!" His voice broke, raw and undone as he shuddered beneath me, grabbing my shoulders with both hands and bringing me down into his chest, squeezing me tightly as he made a noise that was somewhere between a moan and a whimper.

I couldn't hold back my delighted laugh, thrilled by my power over him. "You really like that, don't you?"

He groaned, half-laughing, half-mortified. "You're d-d-dangerous."

I grinned, rolling onto my back, pulling him with me. I was still catching my breath, satisfied in a way I hadn't expected. Honestly, that might've been enough. Most guys I'd been with? That's where things ended. No expectation, no follow-through. And I'd gotten used to it. It's just how things worked, right?

Jimmy had other ideas.

He shifted downward, trailing kisses down my body, until he paused, looking up with wicked intent from between my thighs.

I hesitated. "Jimmy, there's ... a lot of you still there."

He grinned devilishly, eyes dark. "I don't care what's still in you. I've got a job to do here."

I opened my mouth to protest, but then his mouth was on me, skillful and determined, silencing me instantly. My head fell back, pleasure overtaking all coherent thought as he worked me relentlessly, pulling me to the edge with devastating precision.

Then his hands slid beneath me, gripping my ass with firm, possessive strength, using the leverage to pull me harder against his mouth.

"Jimmy — oh God — " I gasped, overwhelmed by the new pressure, the unrelenting rhythm.

He paused, just for a moment, and looked me directly in the eyes.

"Louder, baby. Let's make the neighbors jealous."

It didn't take long — he was thorough and relentless, bringing me crashing over the edge with an intensity that stole my breath, leaving me trembling and completely undone beneath him.

When he finally moved back up beside me, we were both breathing hard, tangled together, sated and sweaty and utterly content.

"Still think I'm dangerous?" I teased breathlessly.

"Jesus," Jimmy said eventually.

"Good Jesus or bad Jesus?"

"Very, *very* good Jesus." He pulled me closer, pressing a kiss to my shoulder. "I think you might have actually killed me."

"Don't be dramatic," I said, but I was smiling. "You're very much alive."

"Barely."

I propped myself up on my elbow to look at him. His hair was completely disheveled, his lips swollen from kissing, and there were marks on his neck that I'd definitely left there. He looked thoroughly debauched, and I felt a surge of possessive satisfaction.

"You look like you've been thoroughly ravaged," I said.

"I have been." He traced a finger down my spine, making me shiver. "And I loved every second of it."

"Good," I said, settling back against his chest. "Because I'm not done with you yet."

"Promise?"

"Promise."

Outside, the city hummed with its usual nighttime energy, but inside my bedroom, we existed in our own bubble of contentment. For the first time in years, I felt completely satisfied — not just physically, but emotionally. Like I'd found something I didn't even know I was looking for.

Jimmy's breathing was starting to even out, and I could feel him relaxing into sleep. I should have been tired too, but instead I felt energized, alive in a way I hadn't in months.

Maybe this was what happiness felt like. Maybe this was what it was like to be with someone who didn't want to change you, who didn't see your strength as a threat, who could match your intensity without being intimidated by it.

Maybe this was what love felt like.

The thought should have scared me. Instead, it felt like coming home.

chapter
eighteen

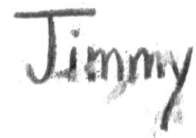

I **WALKED** into Metro General at 6:45 p.m. with what I was pretty sure was a permanent grin plastered on my face. The automatic doors seemed to open faster, the fluorescent lights seemed less harsh, and even the familiar smell of antiseptic and industrial cleaner felt welcoming instead of sterile.

I was in love. Or falling in love. Or had fallen so hard I was still bouncing. The specifics didn't matter — what mattered was that Izzy Delgado existed in the world, and for some miraculous reason, she wanted to exist in it with me.

"Well, well," Brenda said as I walked into the break room for report. "Someone's looking chipper tonight."

"It's a beautiful evening," I said, still grinning as I hung my stethoscope around my neck.

"It's a busy night in the ER," Chloe pointed out, but she was smiling, too. "What's got you so happy?"

Before I could answer, my phone buzzed with a text. Izzy.

> IZZY
>
> Just got to the station. Thompson's already asking about "that nurse" again.

I couldn't help the laugh that escaped me as I typed back:

> Tell him I said hi. And that I still remember where he lives.

"Oh my God," Brenda said, reading over my shoulder without shame. "You're texting someone. During report."

"I am not — "

"You absolutely are." She grinned. "And you're blushing. This is amazing."

Before I could defend myself, Kellen appeared at my elbow. Our night shift charge nurse looked like he'd been run over by the same truck that had apparently delivered me to paradise. Late forties, with disheveled silver-blonde hair and wrinkled scrubs, he had the thousand-yard stare of someone who'd been working nights for a couple decades too long.

"Alright, folks, welcome to another night in paradise," he said drolly, addressing the room. "Looks like it'll be a busy one. Inpatient beds are hard to come by, and we've been holding patients since this morning. Just have to keep everyone alive until seven-oh-five. Any questions?"

"Boy," I said aloud, cheerfully, "this job sure would be a lot easier if it weren't for all the sick people."

Kellen's voice could have flash-frozen coffee. "Mr. Dalton, are you having some kind of neurological event? Should I call Dr. Peterson?"

"Nope, I'm okay! Just in a good mood."

"Well, contain it," Kellen said, walking away. "It's disturbing."

Brenda was trying not to laugh. "Did you just make a joke to the man who considers smiling a sign of weakness?"

"It seemed funny at the time."

"It was funny. He's just dead inside." She patted my shoulder. "Don't let him kill your buzz. Whatever's making you this happy, hold onto it."

The first few hours of my shift passed in a haze of cheerful efficiency. Every patient seemed like an opportunity to spread a little joy, every interaction a chance to make someone's night a little better.

My first patient was Harold, a frequent flyer who came in monthly with various complaints that usually turned out to be anxiety manifesting as physical symptoms. Tonight he was convinced he was having a heart attack because he'd felt his pulse skip while watching television.

"Jimmy!" Harold called out as I entered his room. "Thank God it's you. These other nurses don't understand my condition."

"What condition is that, Harold?" I asked, pulling up a chair. Harold was lonely more than sick, and sometimes what people needed most was someone to listen.

"I've got a very sensitive cardiovascular system. It responds to stress."

"Ah, the stress. What were you watching that got your heart racing? Let me guess — Netflix true crime?"

Harold looked sheepish. "*The Bachelor.*"

I managed to keep a straight face. "Reality TV. That'll do it. Very high-stress situation. All that drama, people making bad decisions, rose ceremonies. It's basically psychological warfare."

"Exactly!" Harold said, looking vindicated. "You get it."

Twenty minutes later, after a normal EKG and some gentle reassurance, Harold was ready to go home with instructions to maybe stick to cooking shows for a while.

My next patient was Marjorie Dicesare, an elderly woman who'd come in with her husband for what appeared to be a minor cut on her hand from a kitchen knife.

"I'm so sorry to bother you," she said as I examined the small bandage. "It's really nothing, but Frank insisted we come in."

"Mrs. Dicesare, you never need to apologize for seeking medical care," I said, carefully unwrapping the bandage. "And Frank's a smart man. Kitchen accidents can be tricky." I looked over at Frank, gave him a knowing wink, and said, "Sir, I have to say, your daughter here is charming."

Mrs. Dicesare giggled like a teenager. "Oh, you flatterer!" Frank smiled, despite being in on the joke.

"You're just looking for a tip, aren't you?" he asked, chuckling.

The cut was indeed minor — clean, shallow, already mostly stopped bleeding. As I cleaned it and prepared a proper dressing, I asked Mrs. Dicesare "How long have you two been married?"

"Forty-three years next month," Frank said proudly.

"Forty-three years? That's incredible! You'll have to tell me your secrets."

"Never go to bed angry," Mrs. Dicesare said immediately.

Frank nodded. "And always say 'I love you' before you leave the house. You never know what might happen."

"Also," Mrs. Dicesare added with a mischievous smile, "learn to cook. Nothing says 'I love you' like a good meal."

Mrs. Dicesare was beaming, and when I finished her bandage, she patted my hand. "You're a good boy. Your mother raised you right."

As they left, I heard Mrs. Dicesare telling her husband, "Such a nice young man. Very handsome, too. I wonder if he's single?"

I was grinning as I updated her chart, my phone buzzing with another text from Izzy.

IZZY

Martinez just asked if you're single. I told him you were taken. He seems disappointed.

I typed back:

Tell him I'm very flattered, but my heart belongs to his lieutenant.

IZZY

Smooth talker. How's your shift?

Perfect. Everything's perfect.

My third patient was walking so slowly down the hallway that I thought she might be having a stroke. Agnes Murphy was eighty-seven and apologizing with every step.

"Are you sure you don't want a wheelchair, ma'am?" I asked her, as we made our way to the exam room at the speed of continental drift. Mrs. Murphy waved me off.

"Absolutely not. I'm not going to be around walking much longer, and I'm going to do it until I can't anymore. But," she said, sheepishly, "I am sorry. I know you're busy, and here I am holding everyone up."

"Mrs. Murphy," I said cheerfully, "don't you worry about it. They pay me by the hour. You walk whatever speed you want."

She stopped walking entirely and looked at me, then burst into delighted laughter. "Oh, you're terrible! By the hour! George used to say things like that."

"George sounds like a smart man."

"He was. Fifty-five years married, and he never stopped making me laugh." She paused, looking a little sad. "I miss that."

"Well," I said, offering her my arm, "maybe I can fill in just for tonight. Did I tell you about the patient who came in last week convinced they were allergic to vitamin D?"

By the time we reached her room, Agnes was laughing again, and I was feeling that familiar warmth that came from making someone's day a little brighter.

The night continued in the same vein. A college student convinced WebMD that his runny nose was actually a rare autoimmune disorder turned out to have garden-variety allergies. A construction worker with a splinter the size of a toothpick spun a twenty-minute tale about workplace hazards and OSHA violations that ended with me removing said splinter in about thirty seconds.

Every patient got my full attention, every interaction felt effortless, and I found myself humming while I charted — something that didn't go unnoticed.

"Okay, what's going on?" Chloe asked during a rare quiet moment around 2 a.m.. "You've been walking around here like you won the lottery."

"Just having a good night," I said, not looking up from my computer.

"Jimmy." She lowered her voice. "You're humming. You just told a patient his hangnail was 'practically a medical emergency' and made him laugh."

I looked up at her. "Did I really say that?"

"Word for word."

"Wow. I sound like a joy to work with!"

"You are, usually. But this version of you is... different." She studied my face. "Good different. You look happy."

Before I could respond, Kellen appeared again, this time carrying a cup of coffee that looked like it could dissolve paint.

"Dalton," he said, settling into a chair with the exhausted grace of a man who'd given up on life somewhere around 2003. "You brought cookies."

It wasn't a question. I had, in fact, brought cookies — chocolate chip with sea salt, a recipe I'd been perfecting for months.

"I did."

"They're good."

"Thank you."

"Too good." Kellen took another sip of his coffee. "What's in them?"

"Chocolate chips. Brown butter. Love."

Kellen stared at me. "Love."

"It's a secret ingredient."

"Right." He stood up slowly, like his joints hurt. "Dalton, I've been doing this job since you were in elementary school. In that time, I've seen nurses come and go, burn out, flame out, and occasionally spontaneously combust in the break room. But you... you're different tonight."

"Good different or bad different?"

"Aggressively cheerful different. Disturbingly optimistic different." He paused. "Are you on drugs? Too much Zyn and Celcius?"

"I'm high on life, Kellen."

"That's worse." He started to walk away, then turned back. "Whatever it is, bottle it. The rest of us could use some."

As he disappeared into the medication room, Chloe shook her head. "I think that's the most I've ever heard Kellen say at once."

"He's a man of few words."

"He's a man of *no* words. Usually he just grunts and points." She leaned closer. "Seriously, Jimmy. What's going on? And don't say 'nothing' because you've been grinning like an idiot for six hours."

I looked at her, this young nurse who I'd been mentoring for months, and realized I wanted to tell someone. I wanted to shout it from the rooftops.

"I met someone," I said quietly.

"Ahhhh, I knew it!" Chloe practically bounced in her chair. "Tell me everything. What's her name? What does she do? How did you meet?"

"Her name is Izzy. She's a firefighter. And it's... it's good, Chloe. *Really* good."

"A firefighter?" Chloe's eyes went wide. "That's so cool. Is she tough?"

I thought about Izzy holding me while I fell apart, about her showing up at my apartment because she'd known something was wrong, about the way she'd taken charge in my kitchen and my bedroom with equal confidence.

"Yeah," I said, unable to keep the dopey smile off my face. "She's tough."

"And she makes you happy."

"Ridiculously happy."

"Good." Chloe patted my arm. "You deserve it. You take care of everyone else all the time. It's nice to see someone taking care of you."

My phone buzzed again.

IZZY

Shift's quiet. Thinking about you.

Same here. Can't wait to see you tomorrow.

IZZY

Me too. Sweet dreams when you get home.

I was still staring at my phone when Kellen reappeared, refilled coffee cup in hand.

"Dalton."

"Yeah?"

"That's the face."

"What face?"

"The face that explains the humming and the love cookies and the aggressive cheerfulness." He took a long sip of coffee. "You're in love."

It wasn't a question.

"Maybe," I said.

"Definitely." Kellen sat back down, studying me like I was a particularly interesting specimen. "How long?"

"How long what?"

"How long have you been in love with her?"

"I didn't say it was a her."

Kellen gave me a look that could have curdled milk. "Dalton."

"Okay, fine. It's a her. And I don't know how long. It's new."

"New love." Kellen nodded sagely. "That explains it. You're in the honeymoon phase. Everything's perfect, the sun shines brighter, the birds sing sweeter, and you make cookies with love as an ingredient."

"You sound like you speak from experience."

"I do." He took a sip of his coffee. "Been married to her for seventeen years. Couldn't be happier."

I stared at him, trying to reconcile this information with the man who spoke in monotone, moved like he was underwater, and treated every shift like a personal affront to his existence was... happily married?

"Really?"

"Really." His expression didn't change one bit. "Best thing that ever happened to me. She thinks I'm funny."

"You're... funny?"

"Hilarious." Still completely deadpan. "She laughs at everything I say. She's obviously got great taste."

I was trying to process this when he stood up, still moving with the enthusiasm of a sloth on sedatives.

"Point is, Dalton, enjoy it. The honeymoon phase doesn't last forever, but if you're lucky, what comes after is even better."

He walked away before I could respond, leaving me sitting there with a strange mix of happiness and something that might have been worry.

But then my phone buzzed again — Izzy sending me a picture of her truck's dashboard with the radio playing our song (we didn't have a song, but apparently we did now) — and the worry disappeared. Everything was perfect. Everything was going to stay perfect.

I was sure of it.

chapter
nineteen

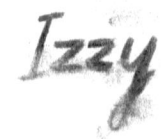

THE FIRST SIGN something was off came when Martinez emerged from the shower bay, hair still dripping, looking genuinely baffled.

"L.T.," he called out, "did we get a delivery I missed?"

"What kind of delivery?" I asked, looking up from the apparatus checks.

"Shampoo. The dispenser's bone dry."

Thompson appeared from the kitchen, already scowling. "Let me guess. A-shift."

"Has to be," Martinez said. "Thing was full last time I checked it."

Benny wandered over, wiping his hands on a shop rag. "How much shampoo could they possibly need? Half of A-shift is bald. What the fuck were they shampooing?"

The question hung in the air, absurd and infuriating in equal measure. It was such a small thing, but that was the point. It was the kind of petty, inexplicable theft that served no purpose except to annoy us.

"Maybe Santoro's back hair finally achieved sentience," Thompson suggested darkly. "Demanded its own personal care routine."

"Or they're washing the engine," Martinez added. "God knows they don't clean anything else properly."

I shook my head, trying to push down the irritation. This was exactly the kind of petty bullshit that made the job harder than it needed to be. "Just add it to the supply list. We'll bill it to their shift."

"Should we booby-trap the next bottle?" Thompson asked hopefully. "Little food coloring? Make them look like Smurfs for a week?"

"Absolutely not," I said, but I was fighting a smile. "We're professionals."

"*Boring* professionals," Thompson muttered.

The first twelve hours of my shift passed in a state of quiet, humming contentment despite the shampoo situation. For the first time in years, the fire station didn't feel like my only sanctuary; it felt like one of two. My mind kept drifting back to Jimmy's apartment, to the easy warmth of his kitchen and the dizzying intimacy of his bed. A text from him would buzz on my phone, and I'd have to fight to keep a goofy, unprofessional smile off my face.

JIMMY

Thinking about you. Hope the shift is quiet.

Quiet so far. Thinking about your sourdough.
Might be ruined for all other bread now.

JIMMY

I can live with that.

Even the routine calls — a fender bender on the interstate, a lift assist at a nursing home — felt lighter, easier. The constant, low-grade tension that usually hummed beneath my skin had been replaced by a steady, hopeful warmth.

The illusion of peace shattered at 9 p.m.

The tones dropped with a violent urgency that promised something real. "Engine 18, Truck 12, Battalion 3, respond for a residential structure fire. 417 Elm Street. Reports of heavy smoke and possible entrapment of an elderly resident."

"Time to earn that paycheck, boys," I called out, already moving. As we pulled out of the bay, the dispatcher's voice crackled over the radio again: "Engine 18, Truck 12, multiple callers reporting person trapped."

The address was in The Grid, an old part of the city with narrow streets, cars parked bumper-to-bumper, and postage-stamp-sized front yards cluttered with fences and overgrown hedges. It was a tactical nightmare, a place where every second counted.

"Engine 18 responding," I radioed, my eyes already scanning the map on the dashboard computer. "Benny, it's a tight street. Position us just past the building — we'll stretch back. Need to leave room for Truck 12 to get their stick up."

"Copy that, L.T."

We were the first on scene. Smoke, thick and black, was pouring from the second-story windows of a small, two-story brick house. This was a working fire.

"Engine 18 on scene," I reported, my voice calm and clipped. "We have a two-story residential with heavy smoke showing from the second floor, Alpha side. Engine 18 requesting the working fire assignment."

"Copy Engine 18, transmitting working fire assignment."

"Martinez, Thompson, grab the crosslay," I ordered, swinging out of the officer's seat as Benny positioned us past the building. "We're stretching back to the front door. Let's move!"

This was our bread and butter. The Minuteman load my crew practiced relentlessly was designed for exactly this scenario — a fast, one-person deployment around the inevitable obstacles of a cramped residential scene.

Martinez pulled the loops from the hose bed and started toward the front door. The hose began paying out clean, then suddenly — nothing. The line went taut, stopped cold.

"What the hell?" Martinez yanked harder, and the entire bundle tumbled out of the bed onto the ground. Disconnected. The fucking pigtail wasn't connected to the discharge.

"Shit!" Thompson was already moving, diving for the connection. But we all knew what this meant. Someone had pulled this line and hadn't reconnected it properly.

Rage, cold and pure, surged through me. On a call with a reported entrapment, this wasn't just an oversight. Lives hung in the balance while Thompson scrambled to thread the coupling.

"Forget it!" I yelled, my mind racing through contingencies. "Benny, charge the bumper line! Thompson, forcible entry. Martinez, with me!"

We lost forty-five seconds — an eternity on a fireground. Forty-five seconds of smoke banking down, of heat building, of whoever was trapped inside running out of time.

We made up for it with brutal efficiency. Thompson popped the front door with a single, perfectly placed strike of the Halligan.

Martinez and I advanced the backup line into the house, the heat rolling over us in a physical wave.

We found the fire in an upstairs bedroom and knocked it down quickly. The truck crew arrived and performed a search, finding the elderly homeowner passed out from smoke inhalation in a back hallway. They brought her out, alive.

It was a good stop. A successful rescue. But as we stood outside in the aftermath, covered in soot and sweat, all I could feel was a cold rage.

Back at the station, the mood was tense. The crew knew what had happened, and how close we had come to a catastrophe.

"L.T.," Benny said quietly as we cleaned our equipment, "A-shift got held over this morning for that mutual aid call to Pine County."

The realization hit me like a physical blow.

"Some of their guys were still here when we came on shift. They took our engine to that warehouse fire while we were on the medical run to Riverside."

Thompson looked up from coiling hose, his face darkening with understanding. "They used our crosslay."

"And didn't reconnect it," Martinez added, his voice tight with anger.

The full scope of what had happened settled over me like ice water. When you use another crew's equipment, you put it back the way you found it. When you disconnect something, you reconnect it. It was fire-fighting 101, drilled into every rookie from day one.

A-shift had used our primary attack line and left it disconnected. They'd left us a ticking time bomb, assuming we'd have a quiet night. Assuming there wouldn't be a life on the line.

"It was deliberate, L.T.," Thompson continued, his voice low and dangerous. "No way that was an accident. You don't just forget to reconnect a crosslay."

"I know," I said, my own anger a cold, hard knot in my stomach.

I stripped off my gear and walked straight to Battalion Chief Evans's office. Even with the late hour, he was at his desk, reviewing the incident report.

"Good stop tonight, Delgado," he said without looking up. "Textbook search and rescue."

"We got lucky, sir," I said, my voice tight. "A-shift used our engine on that mutual aid call today and left our crosslay disconnected. Cost us almost a minute getting water on the fire."

Evans finally looked up, a frown creasing his forehead. He took a slow sip of his coffee. "Are you sure it wasn't just missed in the rush? Those overtime holdovers, everyone's tired..."

"Forgetting to reconnect a primary attack line isn't being tired, sir. It's gross negligence. At *best*."

He leaned back in his chair, his expression unreadable. "That's a serious accusation, Lieutenant. I'm sure it was just an oversight. These things happen when crews are held over."

"With all due respect, sir, this goes beyond simple oversight. This is a safety issue. This is the kind of mistake that gets people killed."

"Look," he said, his tone shifting to one of paternalistic weariness. "I'll mention it at the officer's meeting. Remind everyone about equipment checks. But you need to be careful here, Delgado. You're up for promotion. Making accusations against other shifts isn't a good look. Maybe you should have checked the connections when you got your apparatus back."

I stared at him, my anger solidifying into a cold, hard certainty. He wasn't going to do anything. He was telling me it was our fault for not catching their "mistake." He was telling me that my crew's safety was less important than keeping the peace between shifts.

"Yes, sir," I said, my voice flat and devoid of emotion. "I understand perfectly."

I turned and walked out of his office, the full weight of the situation settling on me. This wasn't just about a disconnected hose or shift rivalry. This was the system protecting its own. To get this promotion, to protect my crew, I wasn't just fighting Santoro. I was fighting the quiet, insidious culture that would rather risk a firefighter's life than deal with an uncomfortable conversation.

And I knew, with a certainty that chilled me to the bone, that if I wanted to protect my crew, I was going to have to do it alone.

chapter
twenty

I WOKE up to the smell of coffee brewing and the sound of Izzy's voice drifting from the kitchen, sharp with exasperation and tinged with the kind of fondness that only came from dealing with people you'd trust with your life but wouldn't trust to plan a grocery list.

"No, Thompson, we are *not* having 'leftover chili dogs' again tomorrow night," she was saying into her phone, already dressed in her uniform pants and department t-shirt. "That's a health code violation, not a meal... Yes, I know you like it. You also like wrestling, that doesn't make it a good idea."

I smiled, staying quiet in the doorway to watch her. Three weeks into whatever this was between us, and I was still getting used to the small intimacies — the way she looked completely at home in my kitchen, how she'd claimed the left side of my bed without discussion, the spare hoodie draped over my reading chair like it belonged there. She was getting ready for her forty-eight-hour shift, making coffee for both of us with the automatic efficiency of someone who'd done this routine many times before.

"Martinez, you're supposed to be the responsible one," she continued, and I could hear the eye-roll in her voice. "Don't encourage him... Because we're not nineteen anymore, that's why."

The station clearly had strong opinions about dinner plans. I'd heard enough stories over the past few weeks to know that Station 2's B-shift took their meals seriously — it was one of the ways they bonded, took care of each other, maintained the family atmosphere that made them so tight-knit. But apparently, left to their own devices, they defaulted to the culinary sophistication of college freshmen.

"Look, just... don't buy anything yet, okay? I'll figure something out." She hung up and turned around, startling slightly when she saw me. "How long have you been standing there?"

"Long enough to hear about the chili dog situation," I said, stepping closer and slipping my arms around her waist. "Do you *have* to go to work today?" I pulled her against me, letting my hands slide down to squeeze her ass. "I have some things I want to do with you."

She laughed, rising up on her toes to kiss me softly. "Soon enough, loverboy. I've got forty-eight hours to get through first."

"That's too long," I murmured against her lips.

"It'll go fast. And then I'll have four days off." She handed me the coffee she'd poured, perfect temperature, just enough cream. "Thompson thinks leftover chili dogs count as a planned meal for tomorrow night. Martinez is encouraging him because he thinks it's funny. Benny's staying out of it because he's smart, and the truck guys are probably going to order pizza and laugh at us." She shook her head, but her expression was fond. "They're like children. Incredibly competent, life-saving children who can dismantle a car engine but can't plan a balanced meal."

An idea began forming in my mind — the kind of idea that felt both generous and slightly terrifying. I watched Izzy's face, noting the way she worried about her crew, how their well-being was always on her mind even during her time off.

"You know," I said carefully, "I could cook for you guys tomorrow night. For the whole shift."

She paused with her coffee mug halfway to her lips, then laughed — a short, surprised sound. "Ha! That's funny. Wait..." She looked at me more closely, her expression shifting from amusement to something like amazement. "Oh my God, you're serious."

I could practically see the wheels turning in her head, the tactical part of her brain clicking into gear. This wasn't just her boyfriend offering to cook dinner. This was strategic. She knew what my food could do to people — she'd experienced it herself. And I'd already proven myself with Cap, shown that I understood how to treat the people who mattered to her.

"Dead serious," I said. "I want to meet them properly anyway. And I can guarantee it'll be better than leftover chili dogs. Plus, I've got all day to prep while you're working."

Her smile was brilliant, the kind that made my chest tight with something I was still getting used to feeling. "Jimmy, that's... that's actually brilliant. They're going to love you. Like, immediately and completely love you."

"That's the plan."

She set down her coffee and stepped closer, reaching up to cup my face in her hands. "You know that the way to a firefighter's heart is through their stomach, right? And that these guys would literally adopt you if you feed them well?"

"I was hoping for that reaction."

She kissed me then, soft and grateful and just a little bit amazed, like she couldn't quite believe I was real. When she pulled back, her eyes were bright with something that looked like pride.

"Tomorrow night then," she said. "I'll let them know." She grabbed her keys and gear bag, pausing at the door. "I'll let the crew know they can invite a plus one, if that's okay?"

"Absolutely," I confirmed, "the more, the merrier."

The next evening, I was standing in the parking lot of Station 2, my arms full of grocery bags and prep containers, wondering if I'd lost my mind. I'd spent the entire day shopping and prepping. The building was imposing in the early evening light — all red brick and bay doors, with massive fire trucks visible through the open apparatus bays. The scale of everything was bigger than I'd expected, more industrial, designed for serious business.

This wasn't just meeting the girlfriend's friends. This was auditioning for her family.

Izzy appeared from a side door, already in her uniform — dark navy pants and a department t-shirt that somehow made her look both professional and completely gorgeous. She grinned when she saw me struggling with my load.

"Need help?"

"I think I've got it," I said, then reconsidered as one of the bags started to slip. "Actually, yes."

She took half my burden, and together we walked through a side entrance into what was clearly the heart of the station. The day room was exactly what I'd imagined — large and comfortable, with a kitchen that opened onto a dining area, worn but well-maintained furniture, and a massive TV currently showing some kind of tactical training video with the sound off.

"Guys," Izzy called out, "Jimmy's here."

The response was immediate. Men emerged from various corners of the station — some in uniform, others in workout clothes or casual wear. I recognized them from Izzy's stories, but seeing them in person was different. I'd seen them all briefly in the ER when they responded to the door jam, but now, out of their turnout pants ... they were all bigger than I'd expected. I suppose that made sense, with the kind of physical presence that came from years of hauling equipment and pulling people out of burning buildings.

"Thompson," Izzy said, gesturing to a stocky guy with graying hair and sharp eyes, "meet Jimmy. Jimmy, this is Thompson, my bar man and the station's unofficial comedian."

Thompson looked me up and down with the kind of assessment I imagined he usually reserved for burning buildings. "Thanks again for taking such good care of Cap."

"Like I said, he's good people," I said simply. "No need to thank me for telling the truth."

Something in Thompson's expression shifted, approval replacing assessment. "Yeah. Damn right."

The introductions continued. Martinez, young and eager, with the kind of enthusiasm that reminded me of new nursing grads. Benny Carter, the driver, older and steady, with callused hands and the quiet confidence of someone who'd seen everything. From the truck crew: Miller, the captain with the easy smile and competitive gleam in his eye; O'Malley, whose Irish accent was barely detectable until he got excited; Rodriguez, who looked like he could bench press a small car.

They were polite but reserved, the way people are when they're sizing up someone new to their circle. I understood it — they were protective of Izzy, protective of their crew dynamic. I was an outsider until proven otherwise.

"What did you bring us?" Martinez asked, eyeing the containers with barely concealed hope.

"Chicken Parmesan," I said, setting down my bags. "Bacon panko mac and cheese. Caesar salad. And New York-style cheesecake for dessert."

The silence that followed was profound. Thompson blinked slowly, like he was processing a particularly complex technical manual.

"From scratch?" Benny asked carefully.

"Is there another way?"

Miller clapped his hands together. "I like him already."

"Save some room for judgment until after you taste it," I said, but I was smiling. The ice was starting to crack.

The bay doors rumbled open, and Sophia appeared, hand-in-hand with Jack, the Kiwi paramedic I knew she'd been dating. Seeing Sophia out of her charge nurse element was strange — she looked younger, happier, completely at ease.

"*Kia ora*, everyone!" Jack called out as they entered. "Hope we're not too late for the tucker."

I'd met Jack briefly at the hospital, but this was different — casual clothes, relaxed posture, Sophia's hand in his. They looked happy together, settled in a way that spoke of a relationship that had found its footing.

"Jimmy," Jack said warmly, "good to see you again, mate."

Sophia stepped forward, and I understood immediately why she commanded so much respect at Metro General. Even in jeans and a sweater, she had an aura of competence and quiet authority. We'd crossed paths plenty of times at shift change — me coming in at seven p.m. as she was wrapping up her day, brief conversations about patients we'd shared.

"Hey, Jimmy," she said with a warm smile. "Good to see you outside the hospital for once."

"Likewise. How'd that guy in room 12 make out yesterday? The one with the pneumonia?"

"Discharged this morning, actually. Responded beautifully to the antibiotics." She looked around at the prep containers. "Jack told me you were cooking for everyone. That's really sweet of you."

Jack held up a bottle of wine — something with an elegant label that looked expensive. "McKenzie Estate," he said, handing it to me. "For you and Izzy to take home later. Can't show up empty-handed when someone's doing all the cooking."

The gesture was small but significant. They weren't just being polite — they were marking me as part of the group, someone worth investing in. The wine was clearly good stuff, the kind of thing you shared with people who mattered.

"Thank you," I said, meaning it. "That's really thoughtful."

"Right then," Jack said, clapping his hands together. "What can we do to help?"

The next hour was controlled chaos in the best possible way. The Station 2 kitchen was clearly designed for feeding a crew — commercial-grade appliances, plenty of counter space, multiple ovens. It was a pleasure to work in, especially with so many willing hands.

Martinez appointed himself my sous chef, following instructions with the kind of precision he probably brought to checking equipment. Thompson manned the salad station with surprising skill, admitting that he'd learned to cook during his first marriage. "Back when I thought romance meant more than just not leaving dirty dishes in the sink," he said with a self-deprecating grin.

Benny and Miller fell into an easy rhythm setting the long dining table, while O'Malley and Rodriguez argued good-naturedly about proper Caesar dressing technique. Jack and Sophia worked together with the kind of seamless coordination that spoke of a established relationship, and Izzy moved between groups, supervising and encouraging like the natural leader she was.

"Smells incredible in here," Miller called out as the chicken came out of the oven, golden and bubbling.

"Wait until you taste it," Izzy said, and there was pride in her voice that made my chest warm.

The mac and cheese was the real showstopper — bacon and panko breadcrumbs on top, three different cheeses, and a hint of mustard powder that made it complex without being fancy. When I pulled the pan from the oven, the silence was reverent.

"My God," Thompson breathed. "That's not mac and cheese. That's art."

"It's comfort food," I corrected. "Just done right."

We loaded the table with serving dishes, and for a moment, everyone just stood there looking at the spread. It wasn't just the quantity — though there was plenty — it was the care that was obvious in every dish. This wasn't institutional cooking or fast food. This was the kind of meal you made when you wanted to show people they mattered.

"Alright," Izzy said, "let's eat before it gets cold."

The first bite was met with the kind of silence that every cook hopes for — the complete, focused attention of people discovering something unexpectedly wonderful. Then the compliments started, overlapping and enthusiastic.

"This is incredible."

"How did you get the chicken so tender?"

"The mac and cheese is better than my grandmother's, and I'm Italian."

"Can you move in here?"

I found myself relaxing into the rhythm of their conversation, the easy way they included me without making a big deal of it. They asked about my work, but in the way people do when they're genuinely interested, not just being polite. I told them about the ER, about what it was like working nights.

"So you see all the weird stuff," Rodriguez said. "Give us your best 'there's no way that's real' story from this week."

I thought for a moment, then grinned. "Patient came in last week convinced he was allergic to vitamin D. Not lactose intolerant — allergic to the actual vitamin. He'd been avoiding sunlight for six months because he read on some conspiracy website that vitamin D was a government plot to control people's minds."

Thompson nearly choked on his beer. "You're kidding."

"Scout's honor. Took three different doctors and a nutritionist to convince him that vitamin D deficiency was going to cause more problems than mind control."

"What is it with people and conspiracy theories?" Martinez asked. "We had a guy last month who was convinced his house fire was started by government satellites."

"Turned out he'd been hoarding fireworks in his basement," Miller added. "But sure, satellites."

The conversation flowed easily from there — work stories, station gossip, good-natured arguments about sports teams. They included me naturally, asking follow-up questions, building on my comments. The engine versus truck rivalry emerged in the form of playful insults about intellectual capacity and job importance, and I found myself following the rhythm of it, understanding that the constant ribbing was actually a form of affection.

"The thing about truckies," Thompson explained to me with mock seriousness, "is that they think breaking windows makes them elite. We're over here doing the actual work — you know, putting water on fire — and they're playing with ladders and feeling superior."

"Says the guy whose idea of technical skill is pointing a hose," Miller shot back. "We're creating ventilation opportunities and performing complex search patterns while you're standing around getting wet."

"Complex search patterns," Thompson repeated. "Is that what we're calling 'wandering around lost in the smoke' now?"

I laughed, raising my hands in mock surrender. "As an outsider, I'm staying neutral in this particular war."

"Smart man," Sophia said. "I've been watching this argument for years. Neither side has won yet."

The food kept disappearing — not just polite portions, but genuine appreciation, with guys going back for seconds and thirds. Thompson declared the mac and cheese "life-changing." Martinez asked for the recipe, claiming his mother would want to add it to her repertoire. Even Miller, who struck me as the type who didn't give compliments easily, admitted it was "restaurant quality."

"I don't know why we don't do this more often," Rodriguez said, loading his plate with a third helping of chicken. "This is incredible. Really, *why* don't we cook like this more often?"

The timing couldn't have been more perfect. Just as the words left his mouth, the station alarm erupted in a cacophony of tones and static, cutting through the comfortable conversation like a blade.

"Engine 18, Truck 12, Battalion 3, respond to a working structure fire at 1247 Cedar Street. Reports of heavy smoke showing, possible entrapment."

"Oh, right. *That's* why."

The transformation was instantaneous and stunning. One moment we were sitting around a dinner table, laughing and arguing about seasoning techniques. The next, every firefighter in the room was moving with purpose and speed that defied belief.

Chairs scraped back. Plates were abandoned mid-bite. The comfortable, familial atmosphere evaporated, replaced by focused urgency.

"Working fire," Izzy said, already standing. Her voice had changed completely — gone was my warm, laughing girlfriend, replaced by Lieutenant Delgado, calm and authoritative. "Let's go, guys."

Thompson paused in his rush toward the apparatus bay, doubled back to the table, grabbed a handful of cheesecake with his bare hand, shoved it in his mouth, and mumbled "Oh my *God*" through the mouthful as he ran for the engine.

Even in the middle of the controlled chaos, I had to smile. That was the highest compliment my dessert could have received.

"Izzy," I called out as she headed for the bay.

She turned back, and for just a moment, I saw both versions of her — the lieutenant and the woman I was falling for.

"Be safe," I said.

Her smile was quick but genuine. "Always am."

And then they were gone, bay doors rumbling closed behind them, sirens fading into the distance. The station fell silent except for the hum of fluorescent lights and the distant murmur of dispatch radio traffic.

I stood in the sudden quiet, surrounded by the remnants of dinner and the echo of laughter, feeling like I'd just witnessed something profound. The speed of the transition, the way they'd moved as one unit despite having been completely relaxed moments before — it was beautiful and terrifying in equal measure.

"Quite something, isn't it?" Sophia said beside me.

I turned to find her starting to clear plates, moving with the automatic efficiency of someone who'd done this many times before.

"I've never seen anything like that," I admitted. "The way they just... switched."

"It never gets old," she said. "Jack's the same way. One minute he's telling terrible jokes, the next he's loading someone into the back of an ambulance and saving their life."

I joined her in clearing the table, grateful for something to do with my hands. "How do you handle it? The not knowing if they're coming back okay?"

Sophia paused, a stack of plates in her hands. "You learn to trust their training. And you learn to focus on what you can control." She gestured around the kitchen. "Like making sure there's food waiting when they get back."

We worked in comfortable silence for a few minutes, loading the dishwasher and packing up leftovers. There was something oddly intimate about it — two people who cared about the same group of first responders, taking care of them in the only way available at the moment.

"You know," Sophia said eventually, "you should think about transferring to days. We could use someone with your skills, and the schedule's more predictable. Join the 'real world'. Better work-life balance."

I looked up from wrapping the remaining mac and cheese. "Are you trying to poach me?"

"Maybe." She grinned. "Is it working?"

I smiled. "I'm flattered, Sophia, but I'm a creature of the night. The vibes are better. *You're* the one who should come over to the dark side. We have better snacks."

"Better snacks aren't going to save you when you're three deep in the waiting room and holding six ICU patients."

"That's why we need you!" I countered. "Kellen's nice, but ... let's be honest, he can't be long for the ER. The man is totally burned out."

Sophia shook her head. "Nah. I did nights for two years. It's not for me." Then her expression shifted, becoming more thoughtful. "You know, Kellen was my preceptor when I started at Metro General."

That surprised me. "Really? I would never have guessed."

"Yeah, he's been around longer than any other nurse in our ER. He was a different man back then," she said, her voice soft with something like sadness. "Getting him to smile was almost as easy as getting him to volunteer for overtime."

I frowned, leaning against the counter. This was entirely unlike the Kellen I knew. "He seems... I don't know. Burned out, I guess. Like he's just going through the motions."

"Kellen's still one of the best nurses I've ever worked with," Sophia said firmly. "His patients trust him completely, he never misses anything critical, his clinical judgment is flawless. But that many years in the ER ..." She trailed off, looking for the right words.

"What changed?"

"He used to organize all the holiday parties. He remembered everyone's birthdays, brought cake, coordinated gift collections when someone was having a rough time. He was the heart of the unit." Sophia's smile was sad. "Now he does his job perfectly, but somewhere along the way, he stopped doing those small gestures."

The parallel hit me like a physical force. I thought about my own approach to work — the cookies I baked, the extra time I spent with difficult patients, the way I tried to make everyone's day a little brighter. Was that sustainable? Could I still be doing that in ten years? Fifteen?

"What do you think happened?" I asked.

Sophia considered this for a long moment. "I think he cared too much for too long without enough support. Emergency medicine asks you to absorb everyone else's worst day, over and over again. Some people build walls to protect themselves. Kellen built them so high he can't remember how to let people in."

The weight of her words settled over me like a heavy blanket. I thought about the domestic violence patient I'd tried to help last month, the way her situation had haunted me for days. I thought about every patient I'd lost, every family I'd had to comfort, every code blue that didn't end the way we hoped.

"But he stayed," I said finally.

"He stayed because it still matters to him," Sophia agreed. "The people who really don't care? They leave. They find easier jobs, ones that don't ask them to carry other people's pain. Kellen stayed because he can't not care, even when caring hurts."

We finished cleaning in silence, but her words echoed in my head. Was this my future? Would I become like Kellen — competent but hollow, going through the motions of caring without feeling it?

"The trick," Sophia said, as if reading my thoughts, "is finding ways to keep your heart open without letting it break completely. People like Jack, like Izzy — they help. Having someone who understands the work but reminds you who you are outside of it."

I thought about Izzy, about the way she'd looked at me during dinner — proud and grateful and just a little amazed. About how she'd worried about her crew's nutrition while planning their shifts. About the careful balance she maintained between professional competence and personal warmth.

"Is that what Jack does for you?"

Sophia's smile was soft and genuine. "Among other things. He reminds me that saving people is important, but so is living your own life. Hard lesson to learn in this business."

The sound of vehicles approaching interrupted our conversation. They were coming back.

"That was quick," I said.

"Good thing. Means it wasn't as bad as it could have been."

The bay doors opened with their familiar rumble, and the apparatus backed in with practiced precision. I could hear voices, tired but not traumatized, the kind of post-call energy that came from a job well done.

Izzy appeared in the kitchen doorway, her face streaked with soot, her hair escaping from its ponytail. She looked exhausted but satisfied.

"How'd it go?" I asked.

"Good stop. Kitchen fire, contained to one room. Nobody hurt." She looked around at the cleaned kitchen, the neatly packed leftovers. "You didn't have to clean up."

"Sophia helped. Teamwork."

"He's good people," Sophia said, joining us. "You should keep him around."

"Planning on it," Izzy replied, and something warm unfurled in my chest.

The rest of the crew filtered in, shedding gear and gravitating toward the leftovers with the single-minded focus of people who'd just spent an hour doing physical labor in extreme heat. Thompson made a beeline for the remaining cheesecake, while Martinez heated up another plate of mac and cheese.

"Verdict?" I asked Thompson as he loaded a fork with dessert.

He paused mid-chew, his expression serious. "You can cook for us anytime, man. You're alright."

Coming from Thompson, that sounded like it was practically a declaration of love. I caught Izzy's eye across the room and saw her trying not to smile too broadly. Mission accomplished.

The evening wound down gradually. Sophia left first, with promises to do this again soon and reminders to call if we needed anything. The crew gradually dispersed to their individual routines — some to the gym, others to watch TV or catch up on paperwork.

I found myself saying goodbye to each of them individually, surprised by how genuinely fond I'd become of this group of people in just a few hours. They weren't just Izzy's coworkers anymore — they were starting to feel like family.

"Thanks for dinner," Martinez said, shaking my hand. "Really. Best meal we've had in months."

"Thanks for letting me cook for you," I replied. "It was fun."

Benny clapped me on the shoulder as he headed out. "You're good for her," he said quietly. "Don't mess it up."

The simple directness of it — no threats, no warnings, just a statement of fact — was somehow more meaningful than any elaborate speech could have been.

Finally, it was just Izzy and me in the quiet station. She walked me out to my car, the bottle of wine in her hand, her other arm linked through mine.

"So," she said as we reached my car, "what's the verdict? Think you can handle dating a firefighter?"

I thought about the evening — the easy acceptance, the sudden shift to emergency mode, the way her crew had looked at her with such obvious respect and affection. I thought about Sophia's words about Kellen, about the cost of caring too much for too long.

"I think," I said carefully, "that I'm starting to understand what your world looks like. And I want to be part of it."

She smiled, stepping closer. "Good. Because after tonight, you're definitely part of the family. Thompson doesn't give out approval lightly."

"What about you?" I asked, reaching up to tuck a strand of hair behind her ear. "Do I have your approval?"

Instead of answering, she kissed me — soft and grateful and tasting faintly of the stress and smoke of the call. When she pulled back, her eyes were bright with something that looked like pride.

"You more than have my approval," she said. "You have my gratitude. And my heart, if you want it."

The words hung between us, more significant than either of us had probably intended. We'd been dancing around the deeper feelings for weeks, but this felt like the first time either of us had acknowledged them directly.

"I want it," I said simply. "All of it. The good days and the bad calls and everything in between."

She smiled, the kind of smile that made my chest tight with the magnitude of what I was feeling. "Good. Because you've got it."

I looked at her standing there in the parking lot, still smelling faintly of smoke, her crew's approval still warm in the air around us, and the words rose up from somewhere deep in my chest.

"I love you."

Her smile became something radiant. "I love you, too."

I drove home with the windows down, the wine safe in my passenger seat, and Sophia's words echoing in my head. The evening had been everything I'd hoped for — acceptance, integration, the beginning of something that felt like belonging. But underneath the satisfaction was a new awareness, a question I hadn't considered before.

How do you love someone who runs toward danger for a living? How do you build a life with someone whose job asks them to absorb other people's worst moments? And how do you do it without losing yourself in the process?

I didn't have answers yet. But I knew, with the certainty that had been growing over the past weeks, that I wanted to find out. Whatever challenges lay ahead — for Izzy, for us, for the future we were building together — I wanted to face them as part of her family, her crew, her life.

The rest would figure itself out as we went along.

chapter
twenty-one

THE ALARM TONES at Station 2 had been mercifully quiet for the past hour, giving my crew time to recover from the three-call marathon that had kicked off our shift. Thompson was sprawled on the day room couch, remote in hand, flipping between a cooking show and what appeared to be a documentary about people who collected vintage lunch boxes. Martinez was at the kitchen table, meticulously filling out equipment inspection logs with the kind of attention to detail that made me proud. Benny had claimed the recliner and was dozing with a copy of *Fire Chief* magazine draped over his face.

It was the kind of peaceful moment that usually made me grateful for this job, this crew, this second family I'd built. But tonight, an undercurrent of unease ran beneath my skin like a low-grade fever. I couldn't shake the image of Cap from the dinner I had with Margaret and him three days ago — the way he'd pushed food around his plate more than he'd eaten it, the new lines of exhaustion etched around his eyes, the careful way he'd moved when he thought no one was watching.

My phone buzzed on the table beside me.

JIMMY

How is Cap?

I stared at the message, my stomach dropping. It was an odd question — direct and immediate in a way that felt urgent. Jimmy knew Cap had been struggling, but this felt different. More pointed.

He's been better. Why?

The three dots appeared and disappeared several times, like he was typing and deleting responses. That made my unease spike into something closer to alarm.

JIMMY

Just checking.

Something was wrong. I could feel it in the careful neutrality of his words, the way he was dancing around something. I was about to type back when my phone rang. Margaret's name on the screen.

"Margaret?" I answered, already standing.

"Izzy, honey." Her voice was thin, strained. "I'm at Metro General. Michael... he collapsed at home about an hour ago. They're running tests, but..." She trailed off, and I could hear the controlled panic she was trying to keep at bay.

"I'm on my way," I said, already grabbing my keys from the table. "Which room?"

"Emergency department. They haven't moved him upstairs yet."

I hung up and looked around at my crew, all of them now alert and watching me with the kind of focused attention that meant they knew something serious was happening.

"Cap's at Metro General," I said simply. "I need to go."

"Go," Thompson said immediately, already reaching for his radio. "I'll call Battalion, get you released for the rest of the shift."

"Thompson —"

"L.T." His voice was firm but gentle. "Cap's family. Go take care of family."

Twenty minutes later, I was pushing through the familiar doors of Metro General's emergency department, my heart hammering against my ribs. The charge nurse — a competent-looking woman I'd seen during previous visits — looked up as I approached.

"I'm here for Michael O'Sullivan," I said. "His... I'm Izzy. Margaret, his wife, called me."

Recognition flickered in her eyes. "Room 4. Margaret's with him."

I walked down the familiar hallway on unsteady legs, past the controlled chaos of the night shift, past the rooms where I'd brought countless patients over the years. But this felt different. This felt personal in a way that made my professional armor feel thin and useless.

Bay 4's curtain was pulled partially closed. I could hear voices inside — Margaret's soft murmur, a deeper voice I didn't recognize, and underneath it all, Cap's familiar rumble, weaker than usual but definitely present.

I knocked softly on the doorframe. "Can I come in?"

"Izzy!" Margaret's voice carried relief and something that might have been gratitude. "Of course, sweetheart."

I pushed through the curtain and stopped short. Cap was propped up in the hospital bed, looking smaller than I'd ever seen him. His skin had that waxy, yellow tinge that spoke of liver problems, and there were dark circles under his eyes that hadn't been there three days ago. But his eyes were alert, annoyed, and very much alive.

"There she is," he said, his voice rough but warm. "Knew you'd show up. Stubborn as your old man. Come to bust me out of this place?"

"Depends," I said, moving to his bedside and taking the chair Margaret had vacated for me. "Are you planning to behave yourself?"

"Not if I can help it."

A doctor I didn't recognize — young, serious-looking, with the kind of careful bedside manner that meant he was delivering news no one wanted to hear — cleared his throat.

"Mrs. O'Sullivan? Ms. Delgado? I'm Dr. Lee. I've been treating Mr. O'Sullivan tonight."

I nodded, my hands instinctively reaching for Cap's. His fingers were cold, but his grip was still strong.

"What we're dealing with," Dr. Lee continued, "is ascites — fluid buildup in the abdominal cavity — along with some severe pain that's not responding to his current medication regimen. The cancer has progressed, and we need to drain the fluid and adjust his pain management. We're looking at a few days for treatment and to get him stabilized."

The words washed over me like static. Ascites. Fluid buildup. Pain management. All clinical terms that boiled down to one simple truth: Cap was getting sicker, faster than any of us had expected.

"How long?" I asked quietly.

Dr. Lee exchanged a glance with Cap, who nodded slightly.

"We're looking at a few days for the procedure and recovery, assuming everything goes smoothly."

That wasn't what I'd been asking, and we all knew it. But it was the only answer I was going to get tonight.

"Well," Cap said after Dr. Lee left, "this is a hell of a thing."

Margaret reached for his other hand, her eyes bright with unshed tears. "The important thing is that you're here, and you're getting help."

"The important thing," Cap said, looking directly at me, "is that I'm not going anywhere yet. I've got too much left to do."

I felt something crack open in my chest — a hairline fracture in the armor I'd been wearing for so long I'd forgotten it was there. This was Cap. Cap, who'd taught me how to read smoke, how to command a scene, how to earn respect without compromising who I was. Cap, who'd been at my father's funeral and promised to look after me. Cap, who was more of a father to me than anyone else had ever been.

And he was dying. Maybe not tonight, maybe not next week, but soon. Sooner than any of us were ready for.

"Hey," he said quietly, squeezing my hand. "I'm okay, kiddo. I'm still here."

I nodded, not trusting my voice. Behind me, I heard the soft rustle of scrubs, and I turned to see Jimmy in the doorway. He looked tired, concerned, but not surprised — which confirmed my suspicion that he'd known Cap was here before I did.

"Sorry to interrupt," he said, his voice professionally neutral. "I just wanted to check on how everyone was doing."

"Jimmy," Cap said, his face brightening. "Good to see you, son."

"Good to see you too, Cap. Though I wish it was under better circumstances."

I caught Jimmy's eye, and in that brief moment, I saw the careful concern there, the way he was trying to balance his professional obligations with his personal feelings. He'd known Cap was here, had probably been the one taking care of him, and had found a way to let me know without crossing any lines.

"Thank you," I said quietly, and he understood I wasn't just talking about tonight.

"Just doing my job," he replied, but his smile was warm and real.

As he left to check on other patients, I settled back into the chair beside Cap's bed. Margaret had found another chair on the other side, and the three of us sat in the kind of comfortable silence that came from people who'd been through hard things together.

"You know," Cap said eventually, his voice thoughtful, "I've been thinking about your father a lot lately."

My chest tightened. Cap didn't often talk about my dad, understanding that the subject was still raw for me even after all these years.

"He would have been so proud of you, Izzy. The woman you've become, the officer you are. He always said you had the heart for this job, even when you were just a kid following him around the volunteer house."

"I miss him," I said quietly.

"I know you do. I miss him, too." Cap's grip on my hand tightened slightly. "But he's not really gone, you know. He's in every decision you make on the fireground, every time you put your crew's safety first, every time you refuse to let someone tell you that you don't belong."

Margaret reached across the bed to squeeze my other hand. "Your father would be amazed by the woman you've become."

I sat there in the fluorescent-lit hospital room, holding hands with the two people who knew me best in the world, and felt something I hadn't allowed myself to feel in a long time: vulnerable. Not weak, but open. Not broken, but human.

Outside, Metro General continued its nightly rhythm of healing and heartbreak. Somewhere in the hospital, Jimmy was taking care of other patients, bringing his quiet competence and gentle humor to people having the worst nights of their lives. My crew at Station 2 was probably handling calls without me, Thompson stepping into the leadership role with the gruff efficiency that made him such a good firefighter.

But here, in this small bay surrounded by medical equipment and the soft beeping of monitors, I was just Izzy. Not Lieutenant Delgado, not the woman who had to be stronger than everyone else, just a daughter afraid of losing another father.

"I'm scared," I admitted, the words coming out barely above a whisper.

"I know you are," Cap said. "But fear don't make you weak, kiddo. Fear makes you human. And being human is what makes you a good leader."

Tears were streaming down my face now, hot and silent.

"That nurse ..." Cap continued, his eyes finding mine again. "Jimmy. He's a good man. I see the way he looks at you." He took a shallow, rattling breath. "It's good to see you happy, kiddo. Really good."

He squeezed my hand, his grip surprisingly weak. "Promise me you'll let yourself be happy. You deserve that."

"I promise, Cap," I said, my voice breaking.

He just smiled, a sad, knowing smile, his eyes already starting to drift shut from the effort. "Good girl."

He was asleep in seconds, his breathing evening out into the shallow rhythm of the monitors.

I sat there for a long time, holding his hand, his words echoing in my head. He hadn't given me a roadmap or a solution. Just an observation and a simple permission slip — permission to be happy. The last link to my father, the man who had been my compass, my anchor, my family, was slipping away. And for the first time in my life, I felt the terrifying, untethered certainty of being completely and utterly alone.

I tried to say goodbye to Jimmy, but he was caught with an emergent patient, a patient in an unstable cardiac rhythm. I saw his eyes flick up and he nodded briefly as I waved, though I saw the look that crossed his face momentarily that made it clear he'd have come running out to me if he could.

The drive back to my apartment was a blur of city lights and the kind of bone-deep exhaustion that had nothing to do with physical tiredness. By the time I pulled into my parking space, my hands were shaking slightly, the adrenaline of the crisis finally wearing off.

My phone buzzed as I climbed the stairs to my apartment.

JIMMY

How are you holding up?

I stared at the message for a long moment, then typed back:

Can I see you tonight? After your shift?

JIMMY

Of course. My place or yours?

> Yours. I need... I need to not be alone right now.

JIMMY

> Go over whenever you want. Let yourself in.
> There's tres leches in the fridge. Help
> yourself, beautiful.

I smiled, despite myself. I let myself into my apartment, changed out of my uniform, took a shower, and tried to find something to do with my hands until Jimmy's shift ended. But everything felt hollow, temporary, like I was just marking time until the next crisis, the next loss, the next reminder that nothing good lasted forever.

At 7 a.m., I walked through Jimmy's apartment door, my overnight bag in hand and my carefully constructed walls finally starting to crumble.

When he opened the door, still in his scrubs but with tired, compassionate eyes, I didn't say anything. I just stepped into his arms and let him hold me while I finally allowed myself to fall apart.

He didn't ask questions. He didn't try to fix anything. He just held me against his chest while I shook, one hand stroking my hair, the other wrapped securely around my waist. I could smell the faint scent of antiseptic clinging to his scrubs, mixed with something that was purely him — clean and warm and safe.

"I've got you," he whispered against the top of my head. "I've got you."

We stood there in his doorway for what felt like hours, my face pressed against his shoulder, his arms creating a barrier between me and the rest of the world. When the trembling finally stopped, when I could breathe without feeling like my chest was going to cave in, I pulled back to look at him.

His green eyes were soft with concern, searching my face. "Cap?"

"He's..." I swallowed hard. "He's fighting. But he's getting weaker. The cancer's spreading." The words came out in fragments, pieces of a reality I wasn't ready to face. "He told me about my father. About being proud of me. About giving myself permission to be happy."

Jimmy's hand came up to cup my cheek, his thumb brushing away tears I didn't realize I was still crying. "And what do you want, Izzy? What would make you happy?"

The question hung between us, simple and profound. What did I want? I'd spent so many years focused on what I had to do, what was expected of me, what would prove I belonged. But what did I actually want?

"This," I said quietly, my hand coming up to cover his. "You. Right now, I just want to forget about everything else and be here with you."

Something shifted in his expression — not just desire, though I could see that too, but understanding. He leaned down and kissed me, soft and careful, like I was something precious that might break.

"Then that's what we'll do," he said against my lips.

He led me through his apartment, past the kitchen where we'd laughed and cooked together, past the living room where we'd talked about everything and nothing. In his bedroom, he turned to face me, his hands settling gently on my waist.

"Are you sure?" he asked. "We don't have to — "

I silenced him with a kiss, pouring everything I couldn't say into the press of my lips against his. The fear, the exhaustion, the desperate need to feel something other than grief. He responded immediately, his arms tightening around me, pulling me closer.

We undressed each other slowly, carefully, like we had all the time in the world. His fingers traced the lines of my shoulders, the curve of my waist, mapping me with a reverence that made my breath catch. When his scrub top hit the floor, I pressed my palms against his chest, feeling the steady rhythm of his heartbeat beneath my hands.

"You're beautiful," he whispered, his voice rough with emotion. "So beautiful."

I'd never felt beautiful during sex before. Desired, yes. Wanted, certainly. But beautiful? That was new. That was Jimmy seeing something in me that I'd never seen in myself.

He guided me to his bed, his movements gentle but sure. When he settled over me, his weight warm and solid, I felt something I hadn't expected — safety. Not just physical safety, but emotional shelter. The weight of his body wasn't a burden; it was an anchor, grounding me when everything else felt like it was spinning out of control.

"I've got you," he said again, his forehead resting against mine. "Let me take care of you."

For once in my life, I didn't fight those words. I didn't insist that I could take care of myself, didn't push back against the offer of protection. I just nodded and let myself sink into the feeling of being held, being cherished, being safe.

He undressed me slowly, like he needed to touch every part of me before I disappeared. His hands skimmed over my skin with maddening patience — his fingertips tracing down my arms, over my hips, the swell of my thighs.

It wasn't greedy. It was *tender*, reverent — like he was grounding himself in the shape of me. His palms molded to me, firm and unhurried, pulling me closer so I could feel every inch of him against me.

"Izzy," he murmured against my throat, planting featherlight kisses along my collarbone.

I arched into him, needing more, needing everything. But he kept the pace slow, drawing it out like he wanted me to burn for it.

He kissed his way down the slope of one breast, then the other, his tongue teasing, his hands cradling the weight of them with aching gentleness. When he sucked a nipple into his mouth, my back bowed off the bed. I couldn't stop the whimper that escaped.

"That's it," he whispered, his breath hot against my skin. "Let me feel you."

His hands roamed everywhere — trailing down my ribs, stroking the dip of my waist, spreading heat with every pass of his fingers. When he reached between my thighs, I gasped at the brush of his touch — slow, purposeful, coaxing rather than demanding. He kissed the inside of my knee before pushing gently, guiding my legs open.

"Izzy. You're *perfect*."

When he finally came over me, I felt the full weight of him settle, and something in me *broke open*.

I didn't want to lead. Didn't want to guide. I just wanted to *feel*.

He kissed me then — mouth on mine, soft and consuming — while he pushed inside me with a slow, delicious stretch that made my whole body clench around him. This wasn't about passion or hunger — though both were there, simmering beneath the surface. This was about connection, about finding each other in the dark, about being present for this moment when everything else felt uncertain.

His hands framed my face as he moved above me, his eyes never leaving mine. "Stay with me," he whispered, and I knew he meant more than just physically.

"I'm here," I whispered back. "I'm right here. I'm not going anywhere."

The rhythm we found was slow, deliberate, like we were trying to memorize each other. His weight pressed me into the mattress, surrounding me, creating a world that existed only for us. Every kiss, every touch, every soft sound he made was a promise that I wasn't alone, that someone saw me and wanted me exactly as I was.

He rocked into me with a rhythm that made the rest of the world vanish. No noise. No grief. Just skin and breath and the steady beat of his heart against my chest.

His hands framed my face, and then — God — he ran the back of his fingers down my cheek, slow and reverent, like he was memorizing every detail.

"Look at me," he whispered, kissing the corner of my mouth, then my jaw, then the tip of my nose. "You're the most beautiful thing I've ever seen."

My eyes burned. My body was wound so tight I couldn't tell if I was crying or coming or both. He bent to kiss the tears from my cheeks, never breaking his rhythm.

When the pleasure built, it was like a warm tide rising, gentle but inevitable. I felt myself letting go in ways I'd never allowed before — not just physically, but emotionally. The walls I'd spent years building crumbled completely under the weight of his care, his attention, his absolute focus on me and what I needed.

"Let go," he breathed against my ear. "I've got you. Let go."

And I did. I let myself fall apart in his arms, let myself be vulnerable and open and human. The release was more than physical; it was a shattering of everything I thought I had to be, replaced by the simple truth of who I was when someone loved me well.

He followed me with a ragged breath, his whole body shuddering above me. And then he stayed — his weight resting on me, warm and heavy and safe.

I curled my arms around his shoulders, let him bury his face in my neck, and for the first time in days, I didn't feel like I was falling.

"You're safe," he whispered again. "I've got you. Every part of you."

Afterward, we lay tangled together, his arm around me, my head on his chest. I could feel his heartbeat gradually slowing, could hear the quiet rhythm of his breathing. The morning light filtered through his curtains, painting everything in soft gold.

"Thank you," I whispered against his skin.

His arm tightened around me. "For what?"

"For holding me. For seeing me. For..." I struggled to find the words. "For making me feel like I don't have to carry everything alone."

He pressed a kiss to the top of my head. "You don't. Not anymore."

We dozed in the warm bubble of his bed, wrapped around each other like we could keep the rest of the world at bay through sheer force of will. For those few hours, it felt possible. It felt like maybe Cap was right — maybe I did deserve to be happy.

Maybe this was what that looked like.

chapter
twenty-two

I WOKE up to the feeling that the world had fundamentally shifted on its axis overnight.

The early afternoon light was filtering through my blackout curtains in thin golden lines, painting everything in my bedroom with a soft, warm glow. But it wasn't the light that felt different — it was everything else. The air itself seemed charged with possibility, heavy with the weight of what had happened between us just hours before.

Izzy was still asleep beside me, her back to me, her breathing deep and even. Her dark hair was fanned across my pillow, catching the light, and I could see the gentle rise and fall of her shoulders beneath the sheet. She looked peaceful in a way I'd never seen before — not the controlled calm of Lieutenant Delgado, but the soft vulnerability of someone who had finally allowed herself to rest.

I lay there for a long time, just watching her, trying to process the magnitude of what had shifted between us. This wasn't just a relation-ship milestone, wasn't just another step in the progression of dating someone new. This was something else entirely.

Last night, I had witnessed the strongest, most self-contained person I'd ever known completely fall apart and trust me to be her safe harbor. And she wasn't weak for it — she was incredibly, impossibly brave. She had let me see her at her most vulnerable, had allowed me to hold her pain and help carry it, even if just for a few hours.

I thought about the way she'd felt in my arms, the way she'd looked at me when I'd asked what would make her happy. The way she'd surrendered control — not because she was weak, but because she trusted me enough to be strong for both of us when she couldn't be strong for herself.

The weight of that trust was both humbling and terrifying. I was no longer just her boyfriend, no longer just some guy she was dating. I had become something more essential — her primary emotional support during one of the worst crises of her life. The responsibility of that felt enormous, but I wouldn't trade it for anything. She had chosen me. Of all the people in her carefully controlled world, she had chosen to let me in.

I slipped out of bed as quietly as I could, not wanting to wake her. She needed the sleep, needed the peace of not having to think about Cap's decline or the weight of command or any of the hundred other burdens she carried. For these few hours, I could let her just be Izzy, not Lieutenant Delgado.

In the kitchen, I started the coffee and pulled out my sourdough starter, already planning something special. This morning called for more than toast and scrambled eggs. This morning deserved thick-cut French toast made from bread I'd baked myself, crispy bacon, fresh berries. A meal that said *I'm taking care of you* without having to speak the words aloud.

As I mixed the custard for the French toast — eggs, cream, vanilla, a touch of cinnamon — I found myself smiling for no reason other than pure contentment. My apartment felt different with her in it, warmer somehow, more like home than it had ever felt when it was just mine.

I had the bacon sizzling in the pan and the first pieces of French toast browning in the skillet when I heard her footsteps on the hardwood floor. I turned to see her padding into the kitchen wearing one of my t-shirts and nothing else, her hair tousled from sleep, looking soft and beautiful and completely at ease in my space.

"Good morning," she said, her voice still rough with sleep.

"Good morning," I replied, reaching for the coffee pot. "How did you sleep?"

"Better than I have in a while." She accepted the mug I handed her, inhaling the steam with a satisfied sigh. "You know exactly how I like my coffee."

"Lucky guess," I said, though it wasn't luck at all. I'd been paying attention from the first time I'd made her coffee in this kitchen, cataloging the details of what made her happy.

She hopped up onto the counter beside the stove, the same spot where she'd sat that first night when she'd driven me crazy just by existing in my space. But this morning felt different. This morning, she belonged here.

"French toast?" she asked, watching me flip the golden slices.

"Sourdough French toast," I corrected. "With fresh berries and real maple syrup. You deserve better than frozen waffles and coffee for breakfast."

"You're going to spoil me," she said, but she was smiling, and there was something in her voice that sounded like wonder, like she couldn't quite believe someone wanted to take care of her this way.

"That's the plan."

We ate at my small dining table, and the conversation flowed easily — small talk about her crew's reaction to my cooking, gentle teasing about my tendency to overcomplicate breakfast, comfortable silence punctuated by shared glances that carried the weight of everything that had changed between us.

It felt domestic in the best possible way. Natural. Like we'd been doing this for years instead of hours.

"I have to go in soon," she said eventually, checking the time on her phone. "I need to catch up on paperwork after leaving early yesterday, and Thompson texted that C-shift is having vehicle issues. I should probably help them out if they need it."

The reminder that the outside world existed, that our bubble of morning intimacy couldn't last forever, sent a small pang of disappointment through my chest. But I understood. Her sense of duty was part of what made her who she was, part of what I loved about her.

"Of course," I said. "Do what you need to do."

She stood and carried her plate to the sink, then turned back to me, something shifting in her expression. The easy domesticity of the morning gave way to something more intense, more charged with the memory of last night.

"Thank you," she said quietly. "For everything. For last night, for this morning, for just... being here."

I stood and moved closer, my hands settling on her waist. "You don't have to thank me for wanting to take care of you."

"Yes, I do," she said, her hands coming up to rest on my chest. "Because no one ever has before. Not like this."

The words hit me square in the chest, a reminder of how carefully she'd had to guard herself, how rarely she'd been able to let someone else be strong for her. I leaned down and kissed her, soft and lingering, trying to pour everything I felt into the connection between us.

"I love you," I said against her lips.

"I love you too," she replied, and the words felt different now than they had before. Deeper. More certain. Like they carried the weight of everything we'd shared and everything we were building together.

An hour later, I stood in my doorway watching her walk to her truck, already missing her even though she'd only been gone for thirty seconds. The apartment felt too quiet without her laughter, too empty without her presence filling the spaces between my furniture.

I was loading the last of the dishes into the dishwasher when my phone rang. Unknown number, but with a local area code, the first digits of which were ones I recognized for numbers that usually came from our hospital.

"Hello?" I answered.

"Mr. Dalton? This is Sarah Martin from Metro General Legal Affairs. I'm sorry to bother you on your day off, but we've received a subpoena regarding your patient care, and we need you to come in to discuss it. Can you come in tomorrow at 2 p.m.?"

I paused, dish towel in hand. "Tomorrow? That seems kind of urgent."

"I know it's short notice, and I apologize. But we need to review the details with you before we respond to the court."

I ran through my mental calendar. "Yeah, I can make 2 p.m. work. Is this about a DUI blood draw? Those are usually pretty straightforward."

"We'll discuss all the details when you come in," Sarah said, her voice professionally neutral. "Just bring your employee ID and we'll take care of everything else."

"Okay," I said, though something nagged at the back of my mind. Usually these subpoenas came through email, with a simple "acknowledge receipt" response required. A face-to-face meeting seemed like overkill for routine blood work testimony.

But then my phone buzzed with a text ...

> **IZZY**
>
> My crew won't stop asking what you're cooking next. You've ruined them for normal food.

... and the warm glow of contentment pushed away any lingering concerns about work.

I typed back:

> Tell them I'm thinking carnitas next time. If they're good.

> **IZZY**
>
> They'll be angels. I'll make sure of it.
> Promise. Love you.

I set my phone down and finished cleaning the kitchen, humming under my breath. Tomorrow's legal meeting was probably nothing more than another routine court appearance, the kind of administrative hassle that came with working in emergency medicine. DUI blood draws, accident reports, the occasional assault case — it was all part of the job.

Right now, all I wanted to think about was the woman who'd trusted me with her heart, who'd let me take care of her when she needed it most, who'd made my apartment feel like home just by being in it.

Everything else could wait.

chapter twenty-three

I PULLED into the Station 2 parking lot at three in the afternoon feeling more centered than I had in weeks. The morning with Jimmy had done something to me — not just the physical intimacy, though that had been revelatory, but the simple act of letting someone else carry the weight for a few hours. Cap's words echoed in my head: permission to be happy. Maybe I was finally learning how to accept that gift.

The bay doors were open, and I could see C-shift's apparatus positioned with the kind of casual indifference that immediately set my teeth on edge. Engine 18 was parked crooked, not lined up with the bay markings. The front bumper had what looked like dried mud caked on it, and someone had left a coffee cup sitting on the running board.

Small things. But in the fire service, small things mattered.

I walked through the apparatus bay, doing my own informal inspection as I headed for the office. The crosslay hose bed looked like it had been packed by someone in a hurry — uneven folds, loose coupling connections, the kind of sloppy work that could cost precious seconds on a fireground. The SCBA brackets were empty, masks hanging loose instead of properly secured.

"L.T.!"

I turned to see Firefighter Danny Kozak from C-shift emerging from the equipment room, looking surprised to see me. Danny was a decent enough guy, but he'd absorbed the shift's culture of doing just enough to get by.

"Hey, Danny. How's the rig running?"

"Oh, fine, fine. No issues." He glanced back at Engine 18, and I could see him noticing the same things I was noticing. "We, uh, we had a pretty quiet shift. Just a couple lift assists and a fender bender on Highway 9."

"Good to hear." I kept my voice neutral, professional. "I'm just here to catch up on some paperwork. Don't mind me."

"Sure thing, L.T. Phillips is in the office if you need anything."

Lieutenant Ryan Phillips. C-shift's officer, and everything I never wanted to become. I found him in the station office, feet up on the desk, scrolling through his phone while some mindless reality show played on the small TV in the corner.

"Delgado," he said without looking up. "Heard you had a family emergency yesterday. Everything okay?"

"Thanks for asking. Just some personal stuff." I settled at the other desk, pulling up the incident reports I needed to review. "How was the shift?"

"Quiet. Easy money." Phillips finally looked up from his phone, his expression smug. "Sometimes I think you B-shift guys make the job harder than it needs to be. All that training, all those drills. Half the time we just sit here anyway."

I bit back my initial response, focusing on my computer screen. This was exactly the attitude that was poisoning the department. The idea that because you weren't currently fighting a fire, the job didn't matter. That preparation and professionalism were optional.

"Better to be ready and not need it," I said carefully.

"Sure, sure. But you've got to admit, some of you guys take it pretty seriously. Like it's life or death every day."

Because it is, I thought, but kept typing. Phillips represented everything wrong with the modern fire service — the guys who saw it as a job instead of a calling, who forgot that citizens trusted us to be ready when their worst day happened.

I was deep into reviewing training records when I heard the rumble of another engine pulling into the bay. Not one of ours — the pitch was different, the timing wrong. I glanced out the window and felt my stomach tighten.

Engine 5. And climbing down from the officer's seat was Lieutenant Mark Santoro.

"Looks like you've got company," Phillips said, following my gaze. "Santoro. That guy's going places. Knows how to play the game."

I didn't respond, but my jaw clenched involuntarily. Phillips was right about one thing — Santoro did know how to play the game. The question was what game he was playing here.

I watched him walk into the station with the confident swagger of someone who owned every room he entered. He was handsome in a conventional way — square jaw, perfect posture, the kind of groomed appearance that looked good in department publicity photos. Everything about him screamed "future chief."

"Phillips," he called out as he entered the office. "How's C-shift treating you?"

"Can't complain. Easy living." Phillips straightened up slightly, the kind of automatic deference people showed Santoro. "What brings you to our little corner of paradise?"

"Just wanted to check on some equipment transfer paperwork from last week. Heard you guys borrowed our thermal camera for that warehouse call."

It was a lie. Equipment transfers went through dispatch and battalion, not individual lieutenants making house calls. But Phillips just nodded along, apparently not catching the inconsistency.

"Yeah, yeah, that's all sorted. Paperwork's in the system."

Santoro's eyes found mine across the room. "Delgado. Didn't expect to see you here on your day off."

"Catching up on paperwork," I said evenly. "You know how it is."

"I do indeed." He smiled, but it didn't reach his eyes. "Mind if I have a word? Professional matter."

Phillips took the hint, gathering his things with more energy than he'd shown all afternoon. "I'll just go check on the guys. Make sure they're not burning the place down."

When we were alone, Santoro's facade dropped slightly. The political smile remained, but something harder showed in his eyes.

"So," he said, settling into Phillips's abandoned chair. "How's Captain O'Sullivan doing? Heard he's been having some health issues."

The casual way he mentioned Cap's illness made my skin crawl. "He's fighting. Thanks for asking."

"Good, good. Terrible thing, cancer. Makes you think about the future, doesn't it? About who's going to step up when the old guard moves on."

I kept my expression neutral, but every instinct was telling me this conversation was going somewhere I wouldn't like.

"The department needs strong leadership," I said carefully.

"Absolutely. Leadership that understands the big picture. The politics, the relationships, the way things really work." He leaned back in the chair, perfectly relaxed. "Not everyone gets that. Some people think it's all about tactics and training records."

"Those things matter."

"Of course they do. But they're not everything." His smile widened. "Take that mutual aid call last month. Your crew did excellent work. Really excellent. But afterwards, there were some... concerns raised."

My blood pressure spiked. "What kind of concerns?"

"Oh, just some questions about equipment protocols. The crosslay connections. How information gets passed between shifts." He examined his fingernails with casual interest. "Nothing major. The kind of thing that gets noted in files, though. The kind of thing that comes up when promotion boards review candidates."

I stared at him, the full scope of what he was saying sinking in. He was talking about the incident where A-shift had used our engine and left our attack line disconnected, nearly costing us crucial time on a structure fire. The incident that had been their fault, their negligence.

"That was A-shift's error. Your crew used our engine on a mutual aid call," I began, my voice low and controlled. I wasn't going to yell. Yelling was a loss of control, and I was in complete command of this situation. "When it came back, our crosslay was disconnected from the discharge. My crew almost paid the price for that on the Elm Street fire."

He had the gall to look surprised, then concerned. It was a masterful performance. "Whoa, Delgado, I had no idea. The guys were probably just exhausted after that warehouse fire. These things happen when you're running on fumes. No harm, no foul, right? You got the job done."

"We got the job done *in spite* of your crew's negligence," I corrected him. "Leaving a primary attack line disconnected isn't a mistake. It's a reckless disregard for basic safety that could have gotten a civilian killed. It could have gotten my crew killed."

He dropped the concerned act, his expression hardening. "Look, nobody got hurt. What's the big deal? You're making this into something it's not."

"The big deal," I said, stepping closer, "is that you seem to think professionalism is optional. That the rules don't apply to you. That my crew's safety is less important than your shift's convenience."

His smooth facade finally cracked. A flash of genuine anger lit his eyes. He took a step toward me, his voice dropping to a low, condescending sneer.

"Funny thing about errors," Santoro said, his voice quieter and more dangerous, "They're often a matter of perspective. Who reports them, how they get interpreted, what context they're given." He stood up, straightening his uniform shirt. "The brass tends to trust officers who've demonstrated good judgment. Political judgment."

"Is that a threat?"

"A threat?" He looked genuinely shocked. "Delgado, I'm trying to help you. I'm trying to explain how things work in the real world. You're a good tactical officer — nobody disputes that. But there's more to leadership than running calls."

He moved closer, his voice dropping to a confidential tone. "Look, I like you. I respect your work. But you've got to understand, the promotion process isn't just about test scores and fireground performance. It's about relationships. It's about fitting in with the command structure. It's about understanding that sometimes you need to work within the system instead of against it."

"And what if the system is wrong?"

He shook his head. "You know, Delgado, your problem is you think this job is just about kicking down doors and putting out fires. It's not. It's about people. It's about relationships. And some of us are better at that than others."

I just stared at him, my silence a more potent weapon than any shouted retort.

"You can be the best tactical officer in this whole department," he continued, a cruel smile touching his lips. "But it doesn't mean a damn thing if the guys upstairs don't *like* you. And they like me. They play golf with me. Their wives have lunch with my wife. And when that Captain's list comes out, who do you really think they're going to choose? The girl who's always making waves and filing complaints, or the guy who knows how to play the game?"

It was all out in the open now. The ugly, unspoken truth of the department. It wasn't about merit. It was about politics.

"This isn't about making waves, Santoro," I said, my voice dangerously quiet. "This is about my firefighters going home to their families at the end of their shift. Something you clearly don't give a damn about."

He laughed, a short, ugly sound. "Don't be so dramatic. You're not the first woman to try and climb the ladder in this department, and you won't be the last. But you all make the same mistake. You think being better at the job is enough." He leaned in, his voice dropping to a whisper. "It's not. It never has been."

He straightened up, his professional mask sliding back into place. "Good luck on the exam, Lieutenant," he said, the title dripping with condescension. "You're gonna need it."

The door closed behind him with a soft click, leaving me alone in the office with the taste of bile in my mouth and the absolute certainty that Mark Santoro had just declared war.

I sat there for a long moment, staring at the computer screen without seeing it. The equipment transfer paperwork had been a lie, just like I'd suspected. He'd come here to deliver a message, to make sure I understood exactly where I stood in his political calculation.

The message was clear: play by his rules, or watch my career get destroyed by "concerns" and "questions" that would somehow always trace back to my "poor judgment" and "emotional instability."

My phone buzzed with a text:

JIMMY

Hope your paperwork isn't too boring.
Missing you already.

I stared at the message for a long moment, Santoro's words echoing in my head. *The company you keep... the relationships you form. Everything reflects on your professional judgment.*

Even Jimmy wasn't safe from this bastard's political games.

I typed back:

> Just finishing up. Can't wait to see you tonight.

But as I packed up my things and headed for my truck, I couldn't shake the feeling that Santoro's visit was just the opening move in a much larger game. A game where the rules were rigged, the referees were bought, and people like me were expected to just accept it.

The hell with that.

If Mark Santoro wanted a war, he'd get one. But he'd learn that underestimating Isabel Delgado was the first and last mistake he'd make.

chapter
twenty-four

THE METRO GENERAL LEGAL AFFAIRS office was located in the administrative wing of the hospital, a part of the building I'd only visited once before during my initial hiring process. The hallways were sterile and corporate, all beige walls and motivational posters about "excellence in patient care" and "teamwork makes the dream work." It felt like a different world from the controlled chaos of the emergency department.

I found room 314 easily enough and knocked on the door at exactly 2 p.m.

"Come in," called a voice from inside.

Sarah Martin turned out to be a woman in her forties with short, graying hair and the kind of professionally neutral expression that gave nothing away. Her office was small and functional, dominated by a conference table surrounded by chairs that had seen better days.

"Mr. Dalton, thank you for coming in on such short notice," she said, gesturing for me to take a seat. "I know this interrupts your sleep schedule."

"No problem," I said, settling into the offered chair. "Though I have to admit, I'm curious about what's so urgent it couldn't wait for the usual email notification."

Sarah's expression didn't change, but something flickered in her eyes — a momentary hesitation that made my stomach tighten with the first whisper of unease.

"Mr. Dalton, this isn't about a routine subpoena," she said carefully. "This is about a patient you treated approximately three weeks ago. Lisa Harris, thirty-eight years old, brought in by EMS on the night with injuries consistent with domestic violence."

The name almost dropped me to my knees. Lisa. The woman with the swollen eye and the cradled arm, the one whose boyfriend had hovered like a predator, answering every question for her. The one I'd tried so hard to help, who'd left against medical advice because she was more afraid of what would happen later than what was happening then.

"I remember her," I said quietly.

"Ms. Harris was found deceased in her apartment two days ago," Sarah continued, her voice gentle but relentless. "The cause of death was blunt force trauma to the head, consistent with repeated blows. Her boyfriend, a Ronald Lawfer, has been arrested and charged with second-degree murder."

The room seemed to tilt sideways. I gripped the edge of the table, trying to process what she was saying. Lisa was dead. The woman I'd tried to save, the one who'd looked at me with such desperate hope when I'd offered her resources and safety planning, was dead.

"The district attorney's office is building their case," Sarah went on. "They want to establish a pattern of escalating violence, and your inter-actions with Ms. Harris on the night she was here are part of that time-line. You'll likely be called to testify about her injuries, her demeanor, and any statements she made about her home situation."

I nodded numbly, though I wasn't really hearing her anymore. All I could see was Lisa's face, the way she'd flinched when her boyfriend touched her shoulder, the quiet desperation in her voice when she'd whispered, "I don't have anywhere else to go."

"Mr. Dalton? Are you alright?"

I looked up to find Sarah watching me with concern. "I'm sorry, what?"

"I asked if you have any questions about the legal process. The subpoena is fairly straightforward — you'll be asked to testify about what you observed and documented during her visit."

"I tried to help her," I said, the words coming out hoarse. "I gave her resources, safety planning information. I tried to convince her to stay, to let us call someone for her."

"I'm sure you did everything you could," Sarah said softly. "This isn't about your care, Mr. Dalton. By all accounts, you followed protocol perfectly. The documentation in her chart shows you provided appropriate resources and education. Sometimes... sometimes the system fails, despite everyone doing their job correctly."

But I wasn't listening to her reassurances. I was back in that room with Lisa, seeing the hope in her eyes when I'd promised to help her find somewhere safe to go. I'd convinced her to trust me, to believe that there were people who could protect her, that she didn't have to face this alone.

And then she'd walked out of the hospital and back to the man who killed her.

"Did she... did she ever use any of the resources I gave her?" I asked.

Sarah consulted her notes. "The victim's advocate tried to contact her the next day, but the phone number was disconnected. There's no record of her reaching out to any of the domestic violence services in the area."

The phone number was disconnected. Of course it was. He'd probably taken her phone away the moment they got home, another layer of control and isolation. I'd sent her back into that nightmare with nothing but a business card and my empty promises of safety.

"Mr. Dalton, I want to be very clear about something," Sarah said, leaning forward slightly. "Nothing about Ms. Harris' death reflects poorly on your care or judgment. You did everything protocol requires, and more. Her decision to leave against medical advice was her choice to make, not yours to prevent."

"But I could have — "

"Could have what?" Sarah's voice was firm. "Held her against her will? That would have been illegal. Called the police? They can't arrest someone for being a victim. The sad reality is that leaving an abusive relationship is the most dangerous time for a victim. Statistics show that seventy-five percent of domestic violence homicides occur when the victim is attempting to leave or has recently left their abuser."

The statistics felt like stones in my stomach. I'd known them, of course — they were part of every domestic violence training I'd ever attended. But knowing them intellectually was different from living them, from looking into the eyes of someone who would become part of that statistic.

"The DA will likely ask you about your observations of the relationship dynamic," Sarah continued. "Mr. Laufer's behavior in the emergency department, any controlling behaviors you witnessed, Ms. Harris' demeanor and responses. Your testimony will help establish the pattern of abuse that led to her death."

I thought about Ron Laufer — the way he'd answered every question directed at Lisa, the proprietary hand on her shoulder, the cold calculation in his eyes when he'd sized me up as a potential threat. I'd wanted him to hit me, wanted him to give me a reason to escalate the situation, to force some kind of intervention.

But he'd been too smart for that. Too controlled. He'd known exactly how to play the system, how to walk the line between suspicious and actionable.

"When will I need to testify?" I asked.

"The trial isn't expected to begin for several months. You'll receive formal notice with plenty of advance warning." Sarah gathered her papers, signaling that the meeting was winding down. "Mr. Dalton, I know this is difficult news. If you need to speak with someone — the hospital has employee assistance programs, counseling resources..."

I shook my head, standing up on legs that felt unsteady. "I'm fine. Thank you for letting me know."

But I wasn't fine. I was the opposite of fine. I was a man who spent his nights trying to heal people, to protect them, to be their advocate when they were at their most vulnerable. And I had failed completely and utterly.

The walk back to my car was a blur. I sat in the driver's seat for a long time, staring at the steering wheel, trying to make sense of what had just happened. Three weeks ago, I'd held Lisa's hand and promised her that there were people who could help, that she didn't have to be afraid anymore.

Three weeks ago, I'd been naive enough to believe that caring was enough. That good intentions and proper protocol could save someone from a system designed to fail them.

My phone buzzed with a text from Izzy:

How did the legal meeting go? Routine
subpoena stuff?

I stared at the message, my thumb hovering over the keyboard. How could I explain that everything I thought I knew about my ability to protect people had just been shattered? How could I tell her that the man she'd trusted with her vulnerability, the one she'd let take care of her when she was falling apart, was actually useless when it came to saving anyone who really needed it?

I typed back:

Just routine stuff. Nothing to worry about.

It was a lie, but it was the only response I could manage. Izzy had enough to deal with — Cap's declining health, her own professional challenges. She didn't need to know that the man she was falling in love with was a fraud, someone who could make French toast and offer empty comfort but couldn't actually protect anyone when it mattered.

I drove home in a daze, Lisa's face haunting every mile. At my apartment, I sat on my couch and stared at the wall, trying to reconcile the man I thought I was with the reality of what I'd just learned. The nurturing, protective instincts that defined my sense of self felt like cruel jokes now. What good was the desire to heal if you couldn't actually save anyone?

When my phone rang an hour later with Izzy's ringtone, I almost let it go to voicemail. But she'd already texted, and not answering her call would worry her. She had enough to deal with.

"Hey," I said, forcing normalcy into my voice.

"Hi." She sounded tired but warm. "How are you feeling? You sounded kind of off in your text."

"Just tired," I lied smoothly. "You know how these legal meetings drag on. How was your paperwork marathon?"

"Frustrating. C-shift left the station looking like a disaster zone." There was something else in her voice, an edge I couldn't quite identify. "And Santoro showed up."

Every instinct told me to ask what happened, to dig deeper, to be the supportive partner she needed. But I felt hollowed out, like there was nothing left of me to give.

"Sounds like that was a lot of fun," I said instead, the response automatic and insufficient.

A pause. "Yeah. It was."

I should have pressed. Should have heard the weight in her voice and responded to it. But all I could think about was Lisa's face, the hope in her eyes when I'd promised her safety I couldn't deliver.

"Alright, beautiful, I should probably try to get some sleep before my shift tonight," I said, the excuse tasting bitter in my mouth.

"Of course. I love you."

"Love you too," I replied, the words feeling like a betrayal. How could I love her when I couldn't even protect a stranger who'd trusted me?

After I hung up, I sat in the growing darkness of my apartment, wondering how many other people I'd failed without even knowing it, and whether I'd ever be able to look at myself in the mirror again.

chapter
twenty-five

THE SHIFT WAS A "GOOD" one, as far as they went. The calls were routine; a fender bender with no injuries, a lift assist at a nursing home, a dumpster fire behind a restaurant that we knocked down before it could even think about extending to the main building. Between calls, the station was filled with an easy, comfortable energy. The tension with A-shift over the hose load incident had simmered down, and my crew was back to their usual rhythm of training, checks, and relentless, good-natured insults.

My own internal landscape was quieter, too. The constant, low-grade hum of anxiety had been replaced by a steady warmth that had its epicenter in my phone.

> JIMMY
>
> Thinking about you. Hope it's a quiet one.

> So far, so good. Just watching Martinez try to parallel park the engine. It's a terrifying and beautiful thing to behold.

> JIMMY
>
> Be nice. He's learning.

I was smiling at my phone, feeling a lightness that was still unfamiliar, when the tones dropped. The sound was different this time — sharper, more urgent.

"Engine 18, Truck 12, Medic 402, respond to Highway 45 eastbound at Maple Street for motor vehicle accident with possible entrapment. Be advised, caller reports at least two vehicles involved, unknown injuries."

I was moving before the dispatcher finished speaking, Thompson and Martinez already heading for their gear. The afternoon had been quiet — routine equipment checks, some training drills, the kind of shift that let you catch up on sleep and paperwork. But highway accidents had a way of changing everything in an instant.

"Let's go," I called out, swinging into the officer's seat as Benny fired up the engine. "Thompson, pull a full extrication setup. If we've got entrapment, we'll need the works."

The drive to Highway 45 took four minutes through moderate traffic. Four minutes to run through the tactical considerations — positioning for safety, traffic control, coordination with the truck company for any heavy lifting. Four minutes to prepare for whatever we'd find at the scene.

We were first on location. What we found made my stomach drop.

A family sedan — a grey Honda CRV — had been T-boned by a semi truck at the intersection. The impact had crumpled the driver's side like a tin can, pushing the car nearly thirty feet from the point of collision. The truck sat jackknifed across both eastbound lanes, its driver standing beside the cab with his hands on his head, looking dazed but uninjured.

"Engine 18 on scene," I radioed, my voice automatically shifting into command mode. "We have a two-vehicle MVA, one passenger car with severe damage, one semi. Establishing command. Engine 18 will handle patient care and extrication. Truck 12, secure the scene and set up for heavy rescue if needed."

I began my 360-degree survey of the vehicle, my boots crunching on shattered glass. The two adults in the front seats ... were gone. The injuries were catastrophic, incompatible with life. My mind registered it with a cold, professional detachment. A problem that could not be solved. My focus immediately shifted. "Check the back seat!" I yelled to Martinez, who was right behind me.

A child's voice, thin and frightened: "Mommy? Daddy? Wake up. *Please.*"

Through the spider-webbed rear window, I could see a little girl, maybe six or seven years old, still strapped into her booster seat. She appeared physically unharmed — no visible blood, moving normally — but she was reaching forward, trying to touch the motionless forms in the front seats.

"Mommy, we need to go home now. Daddy, wake up."

"Martinez, C-spine precautions, but I'm going in with you," I said, my voice tight. "Thompson, get the Halligan, but hold off on the hydraulics until I say so. I don't want to scare her more than we have to."

I moved to the rear passenger door, my hands already assessing the damage. The frame was twisted but not severely — this would be a relatively straightforward extrication. The real challenge would be everything else.

"Hi there, sweetheart," I said, kneeling down to the child's eye level through the broken window. "My name is Izzy. I'm a firefighter, and I'm here to help you."

She looked at me with wide brown eyes, tears streaking down her cheeks. She had dark hair in pigtails, a pink t-shirt with a cartoon character I didn't recognize, and the kind of trusting expression that made my chest tight.

"My mommy and daddy won't wake up," she said, her voice steady despite the tears. "I keep calling them, but they're not answering."

Behind me, I could hear Thompson and Martinez setting up the extrication equipment, the controlled efficiency of a crew that had done this hundreds of times. Miller's truck company was establishing traffic control, setting up cones and flares to protect our work area. The organized chaos of a rescue operation in full swing.

But all of that faded into background noise as I focused on the small face in front of me.

"What's your name, honey?" I asked, my voice gentle.

"Amelia," she said. "Amelia Rose Patterson. I'm seven."

"That's a beautiful name, Amelia. And seven is a very important age." I was working on the door mechanism as I talked, testing the latches and hinges. "Amelia, I need to ask you something very important. Does anything hurt? Your head, your arms, your tummy?"

She shook her head solemnly. "No, nothing hurts. But I can't get out of my seat, and Mommy always helps me with the buckles."

The door was stuck but not crushed. Thompson appeared at my shoulder with the Halligan bar.

"L.T., we can pop this in about thirty seconds," he said quietly. "How do you want to play it?"

I glanced toward the front seat, then back to Amelia. She couldn't see her parents from her position — the seats blocked her view of the worst of the damage — but that wouldn't last long once we got her out.

"Nice and easy," I said. "Let me talk her through it first."

I turned back to Amelia, forcing my voice to stay calm and reassuring. "Amelia, we're going to help you get out of your car seat, okay? My friend Thompson is going to open the door, and then I'm going to help you with those buckles."

"But what about Mommy and Daddy?" she asked, craning her neck to try to see into the front seat. "They need to get out, too."

The question threatened to overwhelm me. How do you explain death to a seven-year-old? How do you tell a child that the two most important people in her world are never waking up?

"My other friends are taking care of Mommy and Daddy right now," I said carefully. "They're very good at their jobs, just like I'm good at mine. But they need to go to the hospital so the doctors can help them. Right now, my job is to take care of you."

Thompson worked the door with practiced efficiency, the metal groaning as it gave way. Amelia watched with fascination rather than fear — to her, we were just more adults taking charge of a confusing situation.

"There we go," I said as the door swung open. "Now let's get you out of there."

I reached across her to work the car seat buckles, my hands steady despite the emotions churning in my chest. This close, I could smell her shampoo — something fruity and sweet — and see the small details that made her real. A friendship bracelet on her wrist, a tiny scar on her chin, a stuffed animal clutched in her lap.

"Who's this?" I asked, nodding toward the toy as I freed the last buckle.

"Mr. Bear," she said seriously. "He was scared in the car, so I've been holding him."

"That's very brave of you, taking care of Mr. Bear when he was scared."

I lifted her out of the car seat, surprised by how naturally she came to me, her small arms wrapping around my neck as I carried her away from the wreckage. She was so light, so trusting, and something deep in my chest cracked open at the feeling of her weight against me.

Jack from Medic 402 had arrived and was setting up his equipment. I caught his eye and mouthed "parents are code," and he nodded grimly, understanding immediately. Thompson and Martinez waited until she was safely out, in my arms, and well away from the car before anyone touched the front seats. That was the unspoken rule — we protected them from as much as we could, even when we couldn't protect them from everything.

"Amelia," I said, settling down on the ambulance's rear bumper with her still in my arms. "The doctors at the hospital are going to want to make sure you're okay, even though you feel fine. Is that alright with you?"

She nodded, then looked back toward the car where Thompson and Martinez were now working to extract her parents' bodies. "When will Mommy and Daddy come home from the hospital?"

The question caught in my throat. Around us, the scene continued its organized efficiency — traffic being diverted, equipment being packed up, reports being written. Normal things happening while a little girl's world had just ended.

"I don't know, sweetheart," I said honestly. "The doctors will know more after they see them. But right now, someone is going to call your family to come get you. Do you have grandparents? Aunts and uncles?"

"Grandma Susan lives in the blue house with the big garden," Amelia said. "She makes cookies that look like flowers."

"That sounds wonderful. I bet Grandma Susan is going to want to see you very much."

Jack appeared beside us, his medical bag in hand. "Amelia, I'm Jack," he said, his Kiwi-accented voice gentle and smooth. "I'm a paramedic, which means I help people feel better. Can I check to make sure you're okay?"

As Jack did his assessment — checking her pupils, her reflexes, asking her simple questions — I found myself studying Amelia's face, memorizing the details. The way she answered Jack's questions with serious concentration. The way she kept Mr. Bear close but allowed the examination. The way she trusted us completely, even as her world fell apart around her.

"She looks good," Jack said quietly. "No signs of head injury, no physical trauma. But they'll want to do a full workup at University Hospital's pediatric center, just to be sure."

I made a command decision. "Benny," I called out. "You're acting Lieutenant. Finish the scene cleanup." I turned to Jack. "I'm riding with you to University Hospital."

Jack raised an eyebrow. That wasn't standard protocol — once the patient was in their care, the fire department's job was typically done. But he saw something in my face that made him nod.

"Sure, L.T. We'll make room."

As we loaded into the ambulance, Amelia still clutching Mr. Bear, she looked up at me with those trusting brown eyes.

"Izzy, are you going to stay with me?"

"For as long as I can, sweetheart," I said, settling onto the bench beside her stretcher. "For as long as I can."

The ride to University Hospital was one of gentle conversation and careful monitoring. Amelia told me about her school, about her best friend Kayla, about how she was learning to read chapter books. Normal seven-year-old chatter that became heartbreaking when you knew the context.

When we couldn't think of anything else to talk about, I found myself telling her stories — modified fairy tales where the princesses were firefighters and the dragons were just misunderstood. She listened with rapt attention, occasionally asking questions or adding her own details to the narrative.

"Do you think the princess could teach real dragons to be nice?" she asked as we pulled into the hospital.

"I think if anyone could do it, it would be her," I said. "Princesses are very good at understanding what dragons need."

At the hospital, things moved quickly. A whole team of medical professionals descended on Amelia with the kind of gentle efficiency that made University Hospital's pediatric unit famous. Through it all, Amelia stayed calm, answering questions and following instructions with the resilience that children somehow managed even in impossible circumstances.

I stayed until a social worker arrived with news that Amelia's grandmother was on her way from three hours upstate. Until child protective services had established temporary custody. Until Amelia was settled in a room with a nurse who specialized in helping children process trauma.

"Will I see you again, Izzy?" Amelia asked as I prepared to leave.

"I hope so, sweetheart," I said, giving her one last hug. "You take care of Mr. Bear for me, okay?"

"I will. And Izzy? Thank you for telling me stories about the dragon and the princess."

The ride back to Station 2 with Jack was quiet. We'd both seen enough tragedy to know that some calls stayed with you, that some faces you never forgot.

"You did good with her," Jack said as we pulled into the station.

"She did all the hard work," I replied. "I just tried to keep up."

But as I climbed out of the ambulance and headed back into the station, I couldn't shake the feeling that something fundamental had shifted inside me. Holding Amelia, comforting her, being the steady presence she needed — it had felt natural in a way that surprised me. More than natural. It had felt right.

For the first time in my adult life, I found myself thinking about children not as abstract concepts for "someday," but as real possibilities. As futures I might actually want. Amelia's trust, her need for comfort and protection, had awakened something in me that I hadn't even known was sleeping.

I thought about Jimmy, about the conversation we'd never had about what we wanted our future to look like. I thought about the quiet domesticity of our morning together, the way he'd taken care of me when I was falling apart. I thought about what it might be like to build something lasting with him, something that included the possibility of small voices calling our names and bedtime stories about dragon princesses.

The realization hit me like a physical force: I wanted that. I wanted all of it.

I wanted mornings that began with little feet on the floor. I wanted bedtime stories. I wanted someone to call me Mama. I wanted the messy, complicated, beautiful reality of being responsible for someone else's happiness and safety.

I wanted it with Jimmy.

But then I stopped. I remembered our last phone call, the one after my confrontation with Santoro. I'd been so wrapped up in my own anger and frustration that I hadn't even asked him how he was. He'd sounded distant, tired. And I had been so preoccupied with my own battles that I hadn't been there for him. My mind, now raw and vulnerable, twisted the memory. *He needed me, and I was closed off. I failed him.*

The thought was a fresh wave of guilt, compounding the grief from the call. I couldn't just pack this away. I couldn't just show up and expect him to fix me when I hadn't been willing to do the same for him. If this thing between us was going to be real, if it was going to survive the unique horrors of our jobs, I had to be the one to prove it. I had to show him that he could trust me with his pain, by trusting him with mine.

I pulled out my phone, thinking about calling him, about sharing what had just happened and what it had shown me about what I wanted. But my shift wasn't over, and he was probably trying to sleep before his own shift started. The moment passed, and the phone went back into my pocket.

Later, I told myself. We'd talk about all of it later.

But as I filled out the incident report for Amelia's accident, writing down the clinical details of what had been anything but clinical, I couldn't shake the feeling that "later" was becoming a dangerous word in our relationship. That the space between what we felt and what we said was growing wider, even as we tried so hard to take care of each other that we forgot to let ourselves be taken care of.

Amelia Rose Patterson. Seven years old. No injuries. Parents deceased. Transported to University Hospital for evaluation.

The facts looked so simple on paper. They didn't capture the weight of her in my arms, or the way she'd trusted me to keep her safe, or the way the whole experience had cracked something open in me that I hadn't even known existed.

They didn't capture the way it felt to realize you wanted something you'd never let yourself imagine, just as the person you wanted it with was starting to feel unreachable.

My hands were shaking as I typed the text. It was a cry for help. But it was also a promise.

> Bad call. Really bad. Can I see you later?

I hit send, terrified but resolute. I had let someone see the cracks in my armor. Now I had to let him see what was inside.

chapter
twenty-six

THE PRE-DAWN quiet of my apartment felt different this morning. Not empty, but expectant, like the space itself was holding its breath. I'd gotten home from my shift an hour ago, and instead of the usual post-work exhaustion, I found myself restless, unable to settle.

I was sitting on my couch with a cup of coffee, looking at a text Izzy had sent me earlier in her shift:

> **IZZY**
>
> The crew wants to know when the next dinner night is, and they're fighting over each other on what to ask you to make.

The message had made me smile when I'd first read it, a warm reminder of how easily I'd been accepted into her work family. But now, in the quiet of my apartment, it felt like evidence of something precious I was in danger of losing.

The Lisa Harris meeting had left me feeling hollow, disconnected from everything that usually brought me joy. I'd been going through the motions for days now — responding to Izzy's texts, asking about her shift, saying the right things. But I hadn't really been present. Not the way she deserved.

I thought about our phone call yesterday, how distant I'd sounded when she'd mentioned Santoro. She'd needed my support, my attention, and I'd given her polite deflection instead. The guilt sat heavy in my chest, a constant reminder that I was failing the person who mattered most to me.

I need to be better for her, I thought, staring at my phone. *I can't let one case, one failure, poison this. She deserves someone who shows up completely.*

My phone buzzed in my hands, and I looked down expecting another playful text from her shift. Instead, the message made my stomach drop:

IZZY

Bad call. Really bad. Can I see you later?

The coffee mug hit the table harder than I'd intended. This wasn't casual conversation or flirting between calls. This was a distress signal. "Bad call" was code in our world — it meant trauma, the kind of call that stayed with you long after the sirens stopped.

My guilt amplified instantly. She'd been dealing with something terrible, and where had I been? Wrapped up in my own head, nursing my own wounds, being exactly the kind of partner she didn't need.

Not anymore, I told myself, already moving toward my phone. *Whatever this is, whatever she needs, I'm going to be there. Really there.*

My response was immediate:

Of course. Anything you need. My place or yours? When does your shift end?

IZZY

Yours. I get off at 7.

I looked at the clock. Four hours. Four hours to transform my apartment into whatever she needed it to be. A safe harbor, a quiet refuge; a place where she could fall apart if necessary.

I moved through my apartment with purpose, each action deliberate and caring. Fresh coffee went into the pot — not the bitter stuff I drank when I was alone, but the good beans I saved for special occasions. I pulled out the softest throw blanket I owned, the one that felt like a hug, and draped it over the couch. The tres leches from yesterday went to the front of the fridge where she'd see it immediately, a quiet offering of sweetness when everything else felt bitter.

I changed the lighting, switching off the harsh overhead fixtures in favor of the warm lamps that made everything feel calmer. I put on music — instrumental jazz, nothing with words that might jar against whatever she was carrying. Every decision was made with one question: What would help her feel safe?

By the time I finished, my apartment felt different. Not like a bachelor pad or even a romantic setting, but like a sanctuary. A place designed for healing.

I showered and changed into my softest clothes — worn jeans and a cotton t-shirt that had been through a hundred washes. Nothing that would scratch against her skin if she needed to be held. Nothing that would remind her of hospitals or uniforms or any of the professional armor we both wore.

Then I sat on my couch and waited.

The knock on my door at 7:23 a.m. was soft, tentative. I opened it to find Izzy standing in the hallway, still in her uniform, looking like she'd been hit by something she couldn't quite name. Her eyes were red-rimmed but dry, her posture carefully controlled in the way that meant she was holding herself together through sheer force of will.

"Hey," she said quietly.

"Hey yourself," I replied, stepping aside to let her in. "Come here, beautiful."

She didn't hesitate. She walked straight into my arms, and I folded her against my chest, feeling some of the tension leave her body as I held her. She smelled like smoke and antiseptic and something indefinably sad.

"You don't have to talk about it if you don't want to," I said against her hair. "But I'm here. Whatever you need."

She pulled back to look at me, and I saw surprise in her eyes — pleasant surprise, like she'd been expecting something else.

"Thank you," she said. "I just... I need to sit down."

I guided her to the couch, and she sank into it gratefully, pulling the throw blanket around herself like armor. I settled beside her, close enough to touch but giving her space to breathe.

"Do you want coffee? Food? Anything you want."

"Coffee sounds good," she said. "And maybe... maybe you could just sit with me for a minute?"

I got up to pour the coffee, adding cream the way she liked it, and when I returned, she was staring at her hands, gathering herself for whatever she needed to say.

"There was an accident," she began, her voice carefully controlled. "Highway 45. A family."

I set the coffee within her reach and settled back beside her, one hand resting on her leg in quiet support.

"The parents didn't make it," she continued. "But there was a little girl in the back seat. Seven years old. Amelia."

The story came out in pieces — the extrication, the child's questions about her parents, the ride to the hospital, the long wait until family could take custody. I listened without interrupting, asking gentle questions when she paused, letting her set the pace.

"She was so trusting," Izzy said, her voice finally starting to crack. "She believed me when I told her everything would be okay. She held my hand and told me stories about her grandmother's cookies and asked if the dragon princess could teach real dragons to be nice."

"You kept her safe," I said quietly. "In the worst moment of her life, you made sure she wasn't alone."

"But Jimmy..." She turned to look at me, and there were tears in her eyes now. "Holding her, taking care of her, being what she needed... it felt so natural. So right. And I realized something I've never let myself think about before."

I waited, sensing she was building toward something important.

"I want that," she said, her voice barely above a whisper. "I want kids. I want a family. I want to have little voices calling my name and bedtime stories about dragons and princesses and all of it." She paused, looking directly at me. "I want it with you."

The words hit me upside the head. Kids. Family. The future she was describing, the one she wanted with me, required something I wasn't sure I could give: the ability to protect the people who mattered most.

All I could see was Lisa Harris' face. The hope in her eyes when I'd promised her safety. The way she'd trusted me to keep her alive, and how spectacularly I'd failed.

How could I promise to protect a child, a family, when I couldn't even save one woman who'd put her faith in me?

"Jimmy?" Izzy's voice seemed to come from very far away. "You okay?"

I realized I'd gone completely still, completely silent. She was watching me with growing concern, and I could see the exact moment when my lack of response registered as rejection.

"I mean, not right now, obviously," she said quickly, her voice taking on a forced lightness. "Someday. Maybe. It's just something I realized today, holding Amelia. I've never really thought about it before, but — "

"Izzy," I managed, but my voice came out hoarse, strange.

She stopped talking, studying my face. I wanted to explain, wanted to tell her about Lisa, about how the thought of being responsible for protecting the people I loved most terrified me beyond rational thought. But the words wouldn't come.

"I'm sorry," she said quietly. "I shouldn't have brought it up. It's too much, too soon. I just... today was intense, and I wasn't thinking clearly."

"No, it's not — " I started, but she was already pulling away, both physically and emotionally.

"You know what? Let me tell you about something else that happened," she said, clearly trying to change the subject. "Something with work that you might actually be able to help me think through."

I nodded, grateful for the reprieve even as I hated myself for needing it.

"Santoro came by the station yesterday," she said, her voice taking on a different quality — harder, more controlled. "He basically threatened my promotion chances. Made it clear that the good ol' boy network doesn't want me moving up, and that he's got the political connections to make sure I don't."

The shift from personal to professional was jarring, but I found myself able to focus on this in a way I couldn't with the family conversation. This was a problem I could understand, maybe even help with.

"What exactly did he say?" I asked, my protective instincts finally kicking in.

She told me about the conversation — Santoro's veiled threats, his manipulation of the hose incident, his casual mention of how "everything reflects on your professional judgment," including the company she kept.

"He basically said that being better at the job isn't enough," she finished. "That it's all about relationships and politics, and I don't play that game."

Anger flared in my chest, clean and simple compared to the complicated terror of the family conversation. This was something concrete, something I could potentially do something about.

"That's total bullshit," I said firmly. "You're the best officer in that department. Anyone with eyes can see that."

"That's not how it works, though," she said with a bitter laugh. "Merit only matters if the people making decisions want it to matter."

I listened, feeling my protective instincts surge. This was concrete, something I understood. Not the terrifying abstraction of family and children and protection, but a clear injustice that could maybe be addressed.

An idea began forming in the back of my mind. Maybe ... but I pushed the thought aside for now. This wasn't the time for solutions. This was the time to listen.

"I'm sorry," she said suddenly, looking down at her hands. "I should have told you about this sooner. About Santoro, about the pressure at work. I was trying to protect you from it, but that just made me... closed off. Distant. And then today happened, and I realized I can't keep doing that. If we're going to make this work, I need to trust you with the hard stuff."

She settled back against me, and for the first time since she'd arrived, some of the tension seemed to leave her body.

"Thank you," she said quietly. "For listening, for understanding, for wanting to help. I know today was a lot, and I probably dumped too much on you."

"You didn't dump anything on me," I said. "I want to be here for all of it. The good days and the bad calls and everything in between."

She nodded against my chest, but I could feel something had shifted between us. The easy intimacy we'd had this morning felt strained now, complicated by words said and unsaid.

We sat in silence for a while, both of us processing the conversation in our own ways. I held her close and told myself that love was about more than just matching dreams for the future. That supporting her career was just as important as sharing her vision of children and family.

But deep down, I knew that something fundamental had changed between us. She'd shown me her heart's desire, and I'd failed to meet her there. The idea forming in my mind felt like an apology, a way to prove I could be the partner she needed, even if I couldn't be the father she wanted.

I just hoped it would be enough.

chapter
twenty-
seven

THE ALARM TONES at 0041 should have been a relief — something concrete to focus on, a problem with a clear solution. Instead, as I swung into the officer's seat of Engine 18 and listened to dispatch rattle off the details of a kitchen fire on Rio Road, all I could think about was the careful space Jimmy had put between us on his couch three nights ago.

"Structure fire, 412 Rio Road. Single family residence, kitchen fire, occupants evacuated."

"Engine 18 responding," I radioed, forcing my voice into its usual crisp professionalism. But my mind wasn't on the call. It was stuck on the moment when I'd told Jimmy I wanted children, wanted a family, wanted it with him — and watched him go completely still, like I'd just told him I wanted to burn his apartment down.

"L.T.?" Martinez's voice cut through my spiraling thoughts. "You good?"

I realized I'd been staring out the passenger window for the entire three-minute response, not doing my usual pre-arrival assessment. Thompson was giving me a look from the back seat that suggested he'd noticed, too.

"Fine," I said quickly, grabbing my radio. "Just thinking through positioning."

But I wasn't fine. I was the opposite of fine. I was a woman who'd finally found the courage to be vulnerable with someone, only to discover that vulnerability came with a price I wasn't sure I could afford to pay.

The kitchen fire turned out to be a grease fire that had already burned itself out by the time we arrived. Fifteen minutes of ventilation, a quick inspection for extension, and we were clearing the scene. Routine. Simple. The kind of call that usually left me feeling satisfied with our efficiency.

Instead, I felt hollow.

"Nice work, everyone," I said as we backed into the bay at Station 2. "Thompson, make sure the exhaust fan on the engine gets cleaned. Martinez, I want the attack line repacked and pressure-tested."

Standard post-call routine, but my crew exchanged glances. I was being more formal than usual, more distant. They knew something was off, but they were too professional to call me on it in front of the others.

Back in the station, I tried to lose myself in paperwork. Incident reports, training schedules, equipment logs — all the administrative busy work that came with the lieutenant's bars. But every few minutes, my phone would buzz with a text from Jimmy.

> JIMMY
>
> Hope the shift is going well. Miss you.
>
> Thinking about you. Can't wait to see you tomorrow.
>
> Love you, beautiful.

Sweet messages. Normal messages. The kind of things he'd been sending me for weeks. But now they felt different. Careful. Like he was trying to paper over the crack that had opened between us with forced normalcy.

I stared at the latest message, my thumb hovering over the keyboard. What was I supposed to say? *Love you too, but I'm terrified that wanting children makes me incompatible with the man I'm falling for? Thanks for the sweet text, but can we talk about why you looked like I'd suggested we join a cult when I mentioned kids?*

Instead, I typed:

> Love you too. See you soon.

Safe. Noncommittal. Exactly the kind of careful response that was becoming our new normal.

"L.T." Thompson appeared in the doorway of the office, holding two cups of coffee. "You look like you could use this."

I accepted the mug gratefully. Thompson had been my bar man for two years, and he could read my moods better than most people could read a book.

"Anything bothering you?" he asked, settling into the chair across from my desk.

"No, just tired." The lie came easily, but Thompson's raised eyebrow suggested he wasn't buying it.

"Uh-huh. And I'm the Queen of England." He took a sip of his coffee, studying me with the kind of direct assessment he usually reserved for potentially dangerous situations. "You've been off all shift. Want to talk about it?"

Part of me did want to talk about it. Thompson was married, he had kids, two daughters he adored. He might understand the weight of realizing you wanted something fundamental that your partner might not be able to give you.

But Thompson was also my subordinate, and this was a firehouse. Personal problems stayed personal, especially for female officers who couldn't afford to be seen as "too emotional."

"Just some stuff with Cap," I said, which wasn't entirely a lie. Cap's declining health was a constant worry, even if it wasn't what was keeping me up at night right now.

Thompson nodded, accepting the deflection. "How's he doing?"

"Better, actually. Saw him yesterday, and he seemed almost like his old self. Complaining about the hospital food, giving me grief about my paperwork. Margaret said his appetite's been good."

That, at least, was true. Cap had seemed stable during our visit yesterday, more alert and energetic than he'd been in weeks. It was the one bright spot in an otherwise confusing and emotionally exhausting few days.

"That's good news," Thompson said. "Man's too stubborn to go down easy."

"Yeah, he is."

We sat in comfortable silence for a few minutes, drinking our coffee and listening to the familiar sounds of the station — Rodriguez and O'Malley arguing about something on Truck 12, the distant hum of equipment being cleaned and checked.

"You know," Thompson said eventually, "whatever's eating at you, it'll work itself out. You're too smart and too stubborn to let anything keep you down for long."

I smiled, the first genuine smile I'd managed all day. "Thanks, Thompson. I appreciate that."

"Just speaking the truth, L.T. Now, you want to tell me why you've been checking your phone every thirty seconds like you're expecting either really good news or really bad news?"

I glanced down at my phone, which I'd unconsciously placed face-up on my desk so I could see any incoming messages. Another text from Jimmy had come in while we were talking.

JIMMY

Off work in an hour. Want me to pick up
dinner on the way over?

The message was perfectly normal, perfectly sweet. So why did it make my chest feel tight with something that might have been dread?

"Just coordinating with someone," I said, which was technically true.

Thompson gave me another one of his assessing looks but didn't push. "Well, whoever it is, they're lucky to have you worrying about them."

If only it were that simple.

Two hours later, I was standing in my apartment bathroom, the morning sun shining through the window, staring at my reflection and trying to figure out how to act normal when Jimmy arrived. We hadn't seen each other since the morning after Amelia's accident, when I'd told him I wanted children and watched something fundamental shift in his expression.

Since then, we'd texted constantly, talked on the phone twice, and made plans for tonight like nothing had changed. But everything had changed, hadn't it? The easy intimacy we'd built over the past few weeks now felt fragile, complicated by unspoken questions about futures that might not align.

My phone buzzed with his signature knock at the door. I took a deep breath, checked my reflection one more time, and went to let him in.

"Hey, beautiful," he said, leaning in to kiss me softly. He smelled like the hospital — that familiar mix of antiseptic and laundry detergent — and carried a bag from our favorite Thai place.

"Hey yourself," I replied, accepting the kiss and trying to ignore the way it felt different. Not bad, just... careful. Like we were both being more cautious with each other.

"How was your shift?" he asked, following me into the kitchen and starting to unpack the food with the easy familiarity of someone who'd done this dozens of times.

"Quiet. One kitchen fire, couple of EMS calls. Nothing dramatic." I grabbed plates from the cabinet, grateful for something to do with my hands. "How about you? Busy night?"

"Moderately. Had a guy come in convinced his ingrown toenail was a flesh-eating bacteria. Took three different medical professionals and a PowerPoint presentation to convince him otherwise."

I laughed, and for a moment it felt normal. This was us — sharing stories from our respective wars, finding humor in the chaos of emergency services. This was the easy rhythm we'd fallen into, the comfortable domesticity that had made me think we could build something lasting together.

But then Jimmy started telling me about his patient, and I found myself studying his face, looking for some sign of how he really felt about our conversation. Did he want children? Had he ever thought about it? Was my admission a dealbreaker he was still figuring out how to address?

"Izzy?" His voice cut through my spiraling thoughts. "You okay? You seem distracted."

"Sorry," I said quickly. "Just tired. It's been a long few days."

He nodded, accepting the explanation, but I caught the way his eyes lingered on my face. He was reading me the same way I was reading him, both of us looking for clues about what the other was really thinking.

We ate dinner (breakfast, whatever you wanted to call this post-shift meal), making small talk about work, the weather, a documentary he'd watched about sourdough starters. Normal couple conversation, but underneath it all was this new awareness, this careful distance that neither of us was acknowledging.

Afterwards, we settled on my couch to watch a movie, and I became acutely aware of how we positioned ourselves. Usually, Jimmy would pull me against his side, and I'd curl up with my head on his shoulder. Tonight, we sat close but not touching, each of us claiming our own space on the couch.

The movie was some action thriller that required no emotional investment, but I found myself barely following the plot. Instead, I was thinking about Amelia Patterson, about the way it had felt to hold her small, trusting weight in my arms. About the realization that had cemented itself in my soul: *I wanted that.* I wanted bedtime stories and scraped knees and first days of school. I wanted the messy, complicated, beautiful reality of being responsible for someone else's happiness.

But I wanted it with Jimmy. And Jimmy... Jimmy had looked at me like I'd suggested we jump off a bridge together when I'd told him.

"This is a terrible movie," Jimmy said during a particularly ridiculous action sequence.

"Yeah, it really is," I agreed, though I couldn't have summarized the plot if my life depended on it.

"Want to watch something else?"

"Sure."

But instead of reaching for the remote, he turned to face me on the couch. "Izzy, are we okay?"

The question hung between us, loaded with everything we weren't saying. I could deflect, make a joke, pretend I didn't know what he meant. Or I could be brave and address the elephant that had taken up residence in my living room.

"I don't know," I said honestly. "Are we?"

Jimmy's expression grew thoughtful, like he was choosing his words carefully. "I feel like there's something we're not talking about."

The children conversation, I thought. *The way you went completely silent when I told you what I wanted. The way you've been treating me like I'm made of glass ever since.*

But I couldn't say that. Couldn't push him on something he clearly wasn't ready to discuss. The relationship was still too new, too fragile. And maybe... maybe I wasn't ready to hear his answer anyway.

"We're fine," I said instead. "Just adjusting to being in a relationship with someone who understands the job. It's different."

It was a safe answer, focusing on our professional compatibility rather than our personal incompatibilities. Jimmy nodded, seeming to accept it, but I caught the relief in his expression. He didn't want to have the difficult conversation any more than I did.

"You're right," he said. "It is different. Good different."

"Yeah. Good different."

We turned back to the terrible movie, and Jimmy's arm came around me in our usual position. I settled against his side, breathing in his familiar scent, trying to convince myself that this was enough. That love was about more than matching visions for the future. That maybe wanting children was just a passing phase brought on by trauma from a difficult call.

But even as I told myself these things, I knew I was lying. The realization I'd had while holding Amelia wasn't going away. If anything, it was growing stronger, more certain with each passing day.

I wanted children. I wanted a family. And I wanted it with Jimmy.

The question was whether Jimmy wanted it too, or if this was where our story ended — not with a dramatic fight or betrayal, but with the quiet incompatibility of two people who loved each other but wanted different futures.

As the credits rolled on the movie neither of us had watched, Jimmy's phone buzzed with a work notification. He glanced at it and sighed.

"I should probably head home," he said. "Early shift tonight, and I want to get some actual sleep."

"Of course," I said, even though he'd slept here plenty of times before early shifts. Another small distance, another careful boundary that hadn't existed a week ago.

He kissed me goodbye at the door, soft and sweet and just a little too brief. "I love you," he said, and I could hear the sincerity in his voice.

"I love you too," I replied, and meant it completely.

He stepped back, reaching for his keys, and something desperate clawed at my chest. The careful distance, the unspoken tension, the way we'd been dancing around each other for days — I couldn't let him leave like this. Not when it felt like we were slipping away from each other one polite goodbye at a time.

"Jimmy, wait." The words came out more breathless than I'd intended.

He turned back, concern flickering in his green eyes. "What's wrong?"

"Nothing's wrong, I just..." I swallowed hard, my pride warring with my desperation. "You could stay. It's been a while since we had a morning together."

The words hung between us, and I saw the exact moment he understood what I was really asking. Not for sex, exactly, but for connection. For proof that we were still us, that whatever had shifted between us could be fixed with closeness, with skin against skin and the familiar rhythm of bodies that knew each other.

Something broke in his expression — not rejection, but something that looked almost like pain.

"Okay," he said quietly, stepping back inside and closing the door behind him. "Okay, I'll stay."

Relief flooded through me, followed immediately by shame. When had I become the kind of woman who had to ask? When had Jimmy become someone who looked like staying the night was an act of charity rather than something he wanted?

We moved through my apartment with careful quiet, the easy domesticity we'd once shared now feeling fragile and forced. In my bedroom, we undressed without words, without the playful teasing that usually accompanied this ritual. Jimmy's hands were gentle as he helped me out of my shirt, but there was a reverence to his touch that felt more like goodbye than hello.

We slipped under the covers, and Jimmy pulled me against his chest, my back to his front, his arm solid and warm around my waist. It was intimate without being sexual, close without being passionate. Just two people holding onto each other in the dark.

"Thank you," I whispered, though I wasn't entirely sure what I was thanking him for.

"Shh," he murmured against my hair. "Just sleep, beautiful. Just sleep."

But sleep didn't come easily. I lay there listening to Jimmy's breathing, feeling the rise and fall of his chest against my back, and wondered when holding the person I loved had started to feel like holding onto something that was already slipping away.

Behind me, Jimmy's breathing never settled into the deep rhythm of sleep. We lay there, skin against skin, closer than we'd been in days but somehow further apart than ever.

chapter twenty- eight

I LAY in Izzy's bed, my arm around her sleeping form, and felt like the biggest fraud who'd ever drawn breath.

Her back was pressed against my chest, her breathing finally deep and even after what felt like hours of restless shifting. The digital clock on her nightstand glowed 4:23 a.m. in harsh red numbers, mocking me. I'd been awake for every single minute since we'd climbed into bed, my mind a relentless cycle of self-recrimination and terror.

She'd asked me to stay. Not demanded, not manipulated — just asked, with a vulnerability in her voice that had nearly brought me to my knees. And I'd said yes because I was too much of a coward to face what saying no would mean. Too selfish to give her the space she deserved to find someone who could actually give her what she wanted.

You could stay. It's been a while since we had a morning together.

The careful way she'd phrased it, the hope hidden beneath the casual words — Christ, it had broken something inside me. She was trying so hard to bridge the gap that had opened between us, and all I could do was lie here like a corpse, pretending to sleep while my chest felt like it was caving in.

She would have said yes to anything tonight. If I'd pushed, if I'd taken what she was offering instead of just holding her, she would have given me her body even while her heart was breaking. The thought made me sick. The strongest, most self-possessed woman I'd ever known had been willing to use sex as a bridge across the chasm I'd created, and I was such a failure that she'd felt like she had to.

I thought about what Izzy had told me about the Amelia Patterson call, the way her voice had broken when she'd described how the little girl had looked at her. *"She trusted me completely, Jimmy. This seven-year-old who'd just lost everything, and she looked at me like I could fix the whole world."* The wonder and pain in Izzy's voice when she'd said it, the way she'd realized in that moment what she wanted for her future.

She was going to be the most incredible mother someday. Any child would be lucky beyond measure to have her love, her protection, her fierce loyalty.

And I was the bastard who was going to rob her of that future because I was too broken to be what she needed.

How can I promise to protect a child when I couldn't even keep Lisa safe?

The thought gutted me, the same way it had every night since Sarah Martin had told me about the murder. Lisa Harris, thirty-eight years old, beaten to death by the man who'd stood in my ER and threatened my colleagues while I'd tried so desperately to save her. I'd given her resources, safety planning, promises that there were people who could help. And she'd walked out anyway, back to the man who killed her three weeks later.

I'd failed her completely. Failed at the one thing that defined who I was supposed to be — a protector, a healer, someone who made things better instead of worse.

How could I promise Izzy I'd protect our children when I couldn't save one woman who'd trusted me to keep her alive?

My arm tightened involuntarily around Izzy's waist, and she stirred slightly, making a soft sound that drove another spike of self-loathing through my chest. Even in sleep, she was reaching for connection, seeking comfort from the man who was slowly destroying everything good between them.

I remembered the first time I'd seen her in command — that night when she'd brought Cap to the ER, all professional competence and barely controlled fear. The way she'd advocated for him, demanded the best care, never backed down even when she was terrified. And later, watching her crew respond to her orders with absolute trust, seeing the respect in their eyes when they talked about her.

She was a leader. A protector. Someone who ran toward danger because that's what the job demanded, and she was brave enough to do it perfectly.

And I was lying in her bed like a parasite, taking her comfort while giving nothing back except my own damage.

The digital clock continued counting the minutes. Izzy's breathing remained steady, finally deep in real sleep after the emotional exhaustion of the past few days. Carefully, moving with the same precision I used when starting an IV on a difficult patient, I began to extract myself from her arms.

But first, barely breathing, I let my hand trace the curve of her hip, the dip of her waist, the constellation of freckles across her shoulder that I'd memorized during lazy Sunday mornings. Every scar from her years of running toward danger, every soft curve, every strong line of muscle earned through years of hauling equipment and pulling people from wreckage. I was trying to memorize her, knowing this might be the last time I'd have the right to touch her like this.

She murmured something unintelligible as I slipped away, her hand searching for me across the sheets. I had to bite my lip to keep from making a sound as I pulled on my clothes in the dark, every movement feeling like a betrayal.

At her bedroom doorway, I looked back. She was curled on her side now, dark hair spilled across the pillow, one hand still reaching toward the empty space where I'd been lying. Beautiful. Strong. Deserving of so much more than what I could give her.

I let myself out of her apartment as quietly as I'd ever done anything, the soft click of the lock engaging behind me sounding like a door closing on everything I'd ever wanted but was too damaged to keep.

The drive home through the empty streets felt like a funeral procession. Dawn was breaking over the city, painting everything in that flat, gray light that made everything look tired and used up. My phone sat in the cup holder, silent. No messages from work, no emergencies requiring my attention. Just me and the growing certainty that I was going to lose the best thing that had ever happened to me because I wasn't brave enough to be what she deserved.

Back in my apartment, I made coffee with shaking hands and sat at my kitchen table, staring at my laptop screen. The cursor blinked in the empty document, waiting. I'd been thinking about this for days, ever since I'd realized how badly I'd handled the children conversation. I couldn't give Izzy the future she wanted, but maybe — maybe I could give her the career she'd earned.

I began to type:

To Whom It May Concern:

I am writing to provide a character reference for Lieutenant Isabela Delgado of Summit County Fire Rescue, whom I have had the privilege to observe in both professional and personal contexts over the past several months.

The words came easier than I'd expected, flowing from a place of absolute certainty. This, at least, I could do right. I could tell the truth about her competence, her leadership, her unwavering commitment to the people under her command. I could fight for her promotion even if I couldn't fight for our relationship.

Lieutenant Delgado's tactical decision-making under pressure is exceptional. I have witnessed her coordinate complex emergency scenes with a level of professionalism and calm that would be impressive in an officer with twice her experience...

I paused, thinking about the conversation Izzy had shared with me about Santoro's threats. She'd been so frustrated, so angry at the political games being played with her career. Jimmy's fingers hovered over the keyboard. Evans was a good man, a professional who would surely want to know if one of his officers was being undermined by political maneuvering. This was exactly the kind of information a fair-minded leader would need to make the right decision.

I feel compelled to share an incident that speaks to Lieutenant Delgado's character, though I know she would never bring this to your attention herself due to her professionalism. During a recent interaction, Lieutenant Mark Santoro approached her with what appeared to be veiled threats regarding her promotion prospects, suggesting that her "emotional" responses and "the company she keeps" might reflect poorly on her professional judgment. Rather than escalating the situation or filing a formal complaint, Lieutenant Delgado handled the matter with remarkable restraint and dignity.

I believe this incident demonstrates exactly why Lieutenant Delgado deserves advancement - she faces challenges that male officers rarely encounter, yet maintains her professionalism even when subjected to inappropriate political pressure. Her ability to focus on the mission rather than personal grievances shows the kind of leadership this department needs.

The letter continued with specific examples of her competence, her crew's loyalty, her technical expertise. By the time I finished, it felt like a bulletproof case for her promotion. Evans would have to be willfully blind not to see that Izzy was the best candidate for the job.

I wrote about the night she'd brought Cap to us, the way she'd advocated for him without ever crossing professional lines. I wrote about watching her crew respond to her commands with absolute trust, the respect in their voices when they talked about their lieutenant. I wrote about her technical competence, her emotional intelligence, her ability to balance compassion with the kind of firm leadership that kept people alive.

What I didn't write about was the way she looked when she laughed at something stupid I'd said, or how she'd held me when I'd fallen apart after Lisa's death, or the careful way she'd told me about wanting children while watching my face for signs of rejection.

I didn't write about how she was the strongest person I'd ever known, and how that strength made my own weakness feel like a chasm I'd never be able to cross.

I sat back, satisfied that I'd given Evans the full picture. Surely a battalion chief would see Santoro's behavior for what it was — unprofessional intimidation that had no place in personnel decisions. Evans would appreciate Izzy's restraint and recognize that she was being held to an impossible standard.

When I finished, the letter was three pages long and probably the most honest thing I'd ever written. I attached it to an email addressed to Battalion Chief Evans, added a brief note explaining my professional relationship with Lieutenant Delgado through her mentor's medical care, and hit send before I could lose my nerve.

Then I sat back in my chair and waited for my heart to stop feeling like it was trying to beat its way out of my chest.

I'd done what I could. Maybe it would help her get the promotion she deserved. Maybe it would make some small difference in a system that seemed determined to overlook her qualifications.

And maybe, when she found someone who could give her everything she wanted — the marriage, the children, the future I was too broken to provide — she'd remember that I'd tried to fight for her in the only way I knew how.

Outside my kitchen window, the city was waking up. People were starting their days, heading to jobs where they'd make decisions and solve problems and build things that mattered. Normal people with normal lives, who didn't carry the weight of everyone they'd failed to save.

I closed the laptop and headed for my bedroom, exhaustion finally winning over the adrenaline that had kept me awake all night. In a few hours, I'd have to go back to work, put on my scrubs and my professional smile, and pretend I was still the competent, caring nurse everyone thought I was.

But for now, I could sleep. And maybe, if I was lucky, I wouldn't dream about Lisa Harris or little Amelia Patterson or the look in Izzy's eyes when she'd asked me to stay and I'd known I was the wrong answer to every question she'd ever have about the future.

chapter
twenty-
nine

I WOKE to the cold shock of an empty bed and the immediate, crushing awareness that something fundamental had shifted in the night. The space where Jimmy had been lying was cool to the touch, the indentation in the pillow the only evidence he'd been there at all. I rolled over, squinting at the clock. He'd left sometime early, slipping away while I slept.

The memory of last night hit me in fragments — my desperate plea for him to stay, the careful way we'd held each other without really connecting, the hollow feeling that we were going through the motions of intimacy without any of its substance. I stared at the ceiling, trying to decide if I was relieved or devastated that he'd left.

My phone buzzed with a text message:

> JIMMY
>
> Had to leave for shift prep. Didn't want to wake you. I love you.

I stared at the message for a long moment, my thumb hovering over the keyboard. What was I supposed to say? That I loved him too, but I wasn't sure love was enough anymore? That his careful distance felt like another kind of abandonment?

> Ok. Have a good shift.

Safe. Neutral. The kind of response that said nothing while saying everything.

I was still holding my phone when it rang, Margaret's name on the screen sending ice through my veins.

"Izzy?" Her voice was thin, stretched tight with panic. "You need to come. Now. The doctor said... oh God, Izzy, it's time."

I went numb. For a moment, I couldn't even move. Pancreatic cancer was notorious for this — long periods of relative stability followed by a rapid, irreversible decline. I'd known this call would come eventually, but knowing and being ready were two entirely different things.

"I'm on my way," I said, already throwing off the covers. "Twenty minutes. Is he...?"

"He's still here. But Izzy, hurry."

I was dressed and out the door in under five minutes, my mind shifting into the tactical mode that had carried me through every crisis of my adult life. Traffic patterns. Fastest route. Parking at Metro General. The practical details that kept me from thinking about what waited at the end of the drive.

The ICU at Metro General was quiet in the way that intensive care units were quiet — not peaceful, but hushed with the weight of lives hanging in the balance. I found Margaret outside Cap's room, looking smaller and more fragile than I'd ever seen her. She fell into my arms the moment she saw me, and I held her while she cried, my own grief a tight knot in my chest that I couldn't afford to untangle. Not yet.

"He's been waiting for you," she whispered against my shoulder. "I think... I think he's been holding on."

Cap's room was dim, lit only by the soft glow of monitors and the early morning light filtering through the window. He looked impossibly small in the hospital bed, his skin the waxy yellow that spoke of liver failure, his breathing shallow and labored. But his eyes were open when I approached, those sharp, intelligent eyes that had seen me through every crisis of the past twelve years.

"Hey, Cap," I whispered, taking his hand. His grip was weak but present, his fingers curling around mine with the ghost of his former strength.

He couldn't speak — the effort of breathing was taking everything he had — but his eyes held mine with the same intensity that had always made him such a good commander. I saw recognition there, and love, and something that might have been pride.

"I'm here," I said, settling into the chair beside his bed. "I'm right here."

Margaret took his other hand, and the three of us existed in a bubble of quiet intensity, listening to the steady rhythm of the monitors, the soft sounds of the hospital carrying on around us. I found myself talking to him in low whispers, telling him about the crew, about station politics, about the mundane details of daily life that suddenly felt precious because I was sharing them with him for the last time.

"Please," I heard myself whisper, my voice breaking for the first time. "Please don't go. I'm not ready. I don't know how to do this without you."

His hand tightened slightly around mine, and with tremendous effort, he lifted his other hand to my face, his thumb brushing away a tear I hadn't realized I'd shed. His touch was gentle, final, a last blessing from the man who'd been more of a father to me than my own.

I leaned forward, resting my head on his chest, feeling the uneven rhythm of his heart beneath my cheek. His hand came up to stroke my hair with the same gentle touch he'd used when I was a rookie, when I'd come to him broken and scared after a bad call.

"I love you," I whispered against his chest. "Thank you for everything. Thank you for taking care of me."

I felt his lips press against the top of my head, so soft I might have imagined it.

At 7:23 a.m., Michael O'Sullivan took his last breath. The silence that followed was profound and terrible ... the absence of sound after a lifetime of presence. Margaret's quiet sobs, the flatline tone of the heart monitor that seemed to go on forever before someone mercifully turned it off, and underneath it all, the hollow echo of another piece of my world crumbling away.

I stayed where I was for a long moment, my head on his still chest, feeling the warmth slowly leave his body. This was the end, the closing of a chapter that had defined my entire adult life. When I finally sat up, I felt something fundamental shift inside me — not breaking, but hardening. Crystallizing into something colder and more impenetrable than anything I'd built before.

The hours that followed blurred together in a haze of necessary tasks. Paperwork. Phone calls. Margaret's endless, heartbroken tears that I absorbed while staying dry-eyed myself. I called Thompson first, knowing he'd handle telling the rest of the crew with the right mixture of respect and practicality.

"Aw, fuck," Thompson said when I told him, his voice rough with emotion. "How's Margaret? How are you?"

"We're managing," I said, the lie coming easily. "I need you to coordinate with the Honor Guard. Full department funeral. He earned it."

"Copy that, L.T. Anything you need, anything at all — "

"Just take care of the crew. They're going to take this hard."

My phone buzzed constantly — texts from colleagues, from other departments, from firefighters across the region who'd known Cap. I answered them mechanically, professionally, my responses growing shorter and more formal with each one.

> MARTINEZ
>
> L.T., just heard about Cap. I'm so sorry. He was the best of us.

>> Thank you. Funeral arrangements TBD.

> BENNY
>
> Kiddo, you know we're here for you. Cap would want us taking care of you.

>> I'm fine. Focus on the arrangements.

> RODRIGUEZ (TRUCK 12)
>
> Heard about Cap. Whole department's gonna miss him. You hanging in there?

>> Managing. Thank you.

My mother called around noon, her voice thick with sympathy. "Mija, I just heard. I'm so sorry. Michael was a good man."

"Yes, he was."

"Do you want me to come up? I could drive up today, help with whatever you need — "

"I'm fine, Mom. Thank you."

"Izzy, you don't have to be strong all the time. It's okay to — "

"I have arrangements to make," I cut her off. "I'll call you with the funeral details."

I hung up before she could respond, before her kindness could crack the wall I was building brick by careful brick.

Jimmy texted throughout the day, his messages growing more worried as my responses grew more distant.

> JIMMY
>
> Thompson called. I'm so sorry about Cap. I know how much he meant to you.

> Thank you.

> JIMMY
>
> Do you want me to come over? I could bring food, or just sit with you. Whatever you need.

> I'm busy with arrangements.

> JIMMY
>
> Izzy, please let me help. You don't have to go through this alone.

> I'm fine.

> JIMMY
>
> You're not fine. No one would be fine. It's okay to not be fine.

I stared at that message for a long time, feeling something twist in my chest. But I couldn't afford to not be fine. Fine was all I had left.

> Funeral is Saturday 10 a.m., Ridge Street Station.

> JIMMY
>
> I'll be there. I love you.

I didn't respond to that one.

The next few days passed in a controlled blur of preparation. The Honor Guard took charge of the ceremonial details while I focused on the logistics — coordinating with surrounding departments for mutual aid coverage, arranging for the honor guard from stations across three counties, working with the bagpiper from the Emerald Society. Every detail had to be perfect. Cap deserved perfect.

Thompson found me in the station office Thursday night, meticulously reviewing the funeral program for the dozenth time.

"L.T.," he said, settling into the chair across from my desk. "You've been here for twelve hours. When's the last time you went home?"

"I'm fine."

"That's not what I asked." His voice carried the gentle firmness of someone who'd known me for years. "You haven't eaten today. Martinez brought you a sandwich at lunch and it's still sitting there, untouched."

I looked down at the forgotten sandwich, surprised to see it there. "I'll eat later."

"Izzy." The use of my first name made me look up. Thompson's eyes were kind but worried. "Cap wouldn't want you running yourself into the ground over his funeral. You know that."

"Cap would want everything done right."

"Cap would want you to take care of yourself." Thompson leaned forward. "Talk to me, kid. What's going on in that head of yours?"

I met his eyes, saw the genuine concern there, and felt something crack in my chest. For just a moment, I wanted to tell him everything — about Jimmy's distance, about my fears for the promotion, about the crushing weight of being strong when all I wanted to do was fall apart.

Instead, I felt the wall slam back into place, stronger than before.

"I'm fine, Thompson. Just want everything to be right for him."

Thompson studied my face for a long moment, then nodded slowly. "Alright. But I'm driving you home tonight. And you're eating that sandwich first."

Saturday morning dawned gray and cold, appropriate weather for a line-of-duty funeral. I stood in front of my bedroom mirror, adjusting my dress uniform with mechanical precision. Black mourning band across my badge. White gloves spotless. Every brass button polished to a mirror shine. Cap had always said you could tell everything you needed to know about a firefighter by how they maintained their dress uniform.

The Ridge Street Station was transformed into a staging area for what would be one of the largest firefighter funerals the region had seen in years. Departments from across three states had sent representatives. The apparatus bay had been cleared and filled with chairs, the massive overhead doors open to accommodate the overflow crowd that spilled onto the street.

I found myself checking and rechecking details that had already been checked — the positioning of the honor guard, the timing of the bagpiper, the route for the procession. Control. I could control these things when I couldn't control anything else.

"Lieutenant Delgado?" A young firefighter from a neighboring department approached me nervously. "I'm supposed to tell you the color guard is in position, and the honor guard is ready for your signal."

"Thank you. Five minutes."

I stepped outside, needing air, needing space. The street was lined with fire apparatus from dozens of departments, their lights flashing in synchronized silence. Firefighters in dress uniforms stood in perfect formation, their faces solemn. At the far end of the street, I could see news crews setting up their cameras. Cap would have hated the media attention, but he'd have understood it. This was how the fire service honored its own.

"Izzy."

I turned to find Jimmy approaching from the parking area. He was in a dark suit, looking handsome but out of place among all the uniforms. His eyes were red-rimmed and worried, focused entirely on me.

"How are you holding up?" he asked softly.

"Fine," I said automatically.

"No, you're not." He stepped closer, his voice gentle. "You don't have to be fine for me. Not today."

Something in his tone, the careful way he was looking at me, made me want to scream. Or cry. Or both. Instead, I felt the wall grow thicker.

"I need to get back inside. The service is starting soon."

"Izzy, wait." He caught my arm gently. "I just wanted to say... Cap was a good man. I'm so sorry."

I looked at his hand on my arm, then back at his face, and nodded. "Yeah."

I pulled away from his touch and walked back into the station, leaving him standing on the sidewalk. Inside, the crowd had settled into respectful silence. Every seat was filled, with firefighters and paramedics standing along the walls and spilling out into the apparatus bay. I recognized faces from stations across the region, men and women who'd traveled hours to pay their respects to a firefighter they'd probably never met but understood completely.

The service was everything Cap would have wanted — respectful, solemn, focused on his service rather than his death. The department chaplain spoke about sacrifice and brotherhood. The fire chief read a letter from the governor. Margaret spoke briefly about Cap's dedication to his department family.

And then it was my turn.

I stepped to the podium, looking out at a sea of dress uniforms and badges draped in black mourning bands. The silence was complete, respectful, waiting.

"How do I explain who Captain O'Sullivan was?" I began, my voice carrying clearly through the packed station. "He'd want you to know he was a fireman. A truckie. He wouldn't brag about his thirty-two years of service, or tell you that he was considered the senior man not just on his truck, but for the entire department."

I found Jimmy in the crowd, standing at the back near the apparatus bay doors. Our eyes met briefly, and I saw the pain there, the love, the desperate wish to comfort me. But I felt nothing. The grief was there, locked away, but I couldn't access it. Wouldn't access it.

"He was a member of the Honor Guard," I continued, "and he would travel anywhere, on his own time and his own dime, to be there for the family of someone he'd never met. He believed that when a firefighter fell, we all fell a little. And when we gathered to honor them, we all stood a little taller."

My voice caught slightly, the only crack in my composure. I paused, gathering myself, aware of the hundreds of eyes watching me.

"But mostly, he was kind. I remember one day when I was having a particularly hard time. I was sitting in the station lounge, feeling sorry for myself, probably not hiding it very well. Cap found me there, and he didn't ask what was wrong or try to fix anything. He just pulled me out of that chair and gave me a hug. That was Cap. He left kindness in his wake."

I stepped back from the podium as the honor guard prepared for the ceremonial elements. The presentation of the flag to Margaret, folded with military precision. The three-volley salute that made me flinch — not from the sound, but from the finality of it. And then, carried on the cold morning air, the haunting notes of "Amazing Grace" played on bagpipes.

The music cut through me like a blade, piercing through the wall I'd built to reach something raw and broken inside. But I didn't let it show. I stood at attention, dry-eyed and controlled, as the most important person in my life was honored and mourned and finally laid to rest.

And then, the last call came over our radios ... dispatch honoring Cap with the traditional final call for a fallen firefighter.

"*Summit County Dispatch to Captain Michael O'Sullivan, Badge Number 2847.*"

Silence.

"*Captain O'Sullivan, Badge Number 2847.*"

The static stretched on, heavy with meaning.

"*Captain Michael O'Sullivan, your service to Summit County Fire Rescue and the citizens you protected has ended. Your watch is complete. Rest in peace. Ridge Street Station is out of service for Captain Michael O'Sullivan.*"

The radio fell silent, and with it, an era ended.

The reception was a subdued affair, firefighters sharing stories and memories over coffee and sandwiches that no one seemed to have much appetite for. I moved through the crowd like a ghost, accepting condolences with practiced grace while feeling nothing. My crew hovered nearby, protective and worried, but I kept them at arm's length, too. This new wall I'd built didn't discriminate. It kept *everyone* out.

I needed air. Space. Something other than the weight of sympathetic eyes and careful voices offering comfort I couldn't accept. The crowd was suffocating in its kindness, every well-meaning touch and whispered condolence pressing against the wall I'd built until I thought it might crack.

Cap's office door was open, the light off. I slipped inside and closed the door behind me, grateful for the sudden quiet. His coffee mug still sat on the desk — a chipped ceramic piece that read "World's Okayest Captain," a gag gift from last year's Christmas party. His reading glasses were folded beside a stack of reports he'd never finish. The little wooden sign that had hung behind his desk for as long as I'd known him — "Can't outrank dirty dishes" — seemed to mock the pristine order of a space that would never be lived in again.

I picked up his pen, the cheap Bic he'd used for everything from incident reports to birthday cards. My fingers closed around it, and for a moment I felt something crack in my chest, something that threatened to spill out and drown me.

A soft knock on the door made me straighten, schooling my features back into careful neutrality.

"L.T.?" Thompson's voice was gentle, concerned. "You okay in there?"

I set the pen down carefully, precisely where I'd found it. "I'm fine."

"Mind if I come in?"

I opened the door to find Thompson standing there with Benny, both of them wearing the kind of careful expressions people used around unexploded ordnance.

"Just needed a quiet moment," I said.

"When's the last time you ate?" Benny asked, his voice carrying the gentle authority of someone who'd been looking after rookies for two decades.

"I'm not hungry."

"That's not what I asked." Thompson stepped closer, his eyes scanning my face with the kind of assessment that came from years of reading people under stress. "You've been taking care of everyone else all day. Cap wouldn't want you running yourself into the ground."

"Cap would want me to do my job."

"Your job isn't to carry this alone," Thompson said quietly. "We're your crew. Let us help."

I looked at these two men — good firefighters, loyal friends, the closest thing to family I had left — and felt the wall I'd built grow another layer of concrete. They meant well. They always meant well. But well-meaning had already destroyed everything else in my life.

"I'm fine," I repeated. "Just need to freshen up before I head home."

Thompson and Benny exchanged a look, some wordless communication passing between them. Finally, Thompson nodded.

"Alright, L.T. But if you need anything ..."

"I know where to find you."

I walked past them toward the women's restroom, feeling their worried eyes on my back. The bathroom was mercifully empty, just me and the harsh fluorescent lights that made my dress uniform look washed out in the mirror. I turned on the cold water and splashed it on my face, letting the shock of it center me.

My reflection stared back — composed, controlled, every brass button in perfect alignment. Cap had always said you could tell everything you needed to know about a firefighter by how they maintained their dress uniform. Mine was flawless. Empty, but flawless.

I straightened my tie, checked that my mourning band was properly positioned, and rebuilt the professional mask that had carried me through the worst day of my life. Whatever came next, I would meet it with the same cold competence that had gotten me this far.

I walked out of the bathroom — which is when Santoro found me. He materialized at my elbow with the calculated timing of a predator, offering the kind of carefully practiced sympathy that made my skin crawl.

"Tough loss," he said, his voice pitched just loud enough for nearby firefighters to hear. "Cap was a good man. Old guard. But things are changing around here."

"Are they?" I replied, my voice perfectly neutral.

His smile was sharp, predatory. "Oh yes. BC Evans just posted the new Captain's list this morning. You know, I really should thank you."

Something cold settled in my stomach. "Should you?"

"The promotion. Station 12. I got it." His smile widened as he watched my face for a reaction. "Thanks for making it so easy."

Cold fury exploded into my chest, but I kept my expression perfectly controlled. Around us, conversations continued, oblivious to the destruction happening in their midst.

"Congratulations," I said evenly.

"You know what the funny thing is?" Santoro continued, clearly savoring the moment. "BC Evans told me the deciding factor was your 'lack of professional judgment.' Something about letting your personal relationships interfere with your duties. Amazing how quickly these things can turn around, isn't it?"

My blood turned to ice. "What are you talking about?"

"Oh, you don't know?" His expression was all false concern, his voice dropping to a confidential whisper. "Your boyfriend wrote a letter to Evans. Three pages about what a wonderful firefighter you are. Really touching stuff."

The world tilted sideways. Jimmy. Jimmy had written a letter. About me. To my battalion chief.

"Problem is," Santoro continued, his voice like poison, "it just proved what we've been saying all along. You can't handle your own battles. You need a man to fight for you. Evans knows what the brass wants, and they don't want officers who let their boyfriends interfere in department business."

I felt something die inside me — not break, but calcify into something harder and colder than anything I'd ever felt before.

"I don't believe you," I said quietly.

"Ask Evans yourself. He's got the whole thing printed out in his office." Santoro's smile was vicious now, triumphant. "Three pages of your boyfriend explaining how the mean old department is being unfair to his poor girlfriend. Really sealed the deal."

He walked away, leaving me standing there with the wreckage of my career scattered at my feet. Around me, the reception continued — firefighters sharing memories of Cap, talking about his legacy, his impact on the department. But all I could hear was the sound of the last pillar holding up my world crashing down around me.

I found Evans in his office, looking uncomfortable and deliberately avoiding my eyes. The coward's guilt was written all over his face — the carefully averted gaze, the way his hands fidgeted with paperwork he wasn't actually reading.

"I want to see the letter," I said without preamble.

He sighed deeply, the sound of a man who'd been dreading this conversation. "Izzy, I can explain — "

"Show me the letter."

Evans wouldn't meet my eyes. He simply pulled a manila folder from his desk drawer with the reluctance of someone handling evidence of his own corruption. The letter was three pages long, printed on Metro General letterhead, and signed by James Dalton, RN.

I read every word, feeling something inside me crystallize into perfect, cold clarity. Jimmy's love for me was evident in every line — his admiration for my competence, his respect for my leadership, his passionate defense of my character. And there, in the second paragraph, the poison that had destroyed everything: his naive account of Santoro's threats, his well-intentioned belief that exposing the political maneuvering would somehow help my case.

It was the most beautiful, loving thing anyone had ever written about me.

And it was the weapon they had used to destroy me.

"With Cap gone," I said, my voice deadly quiet, "you finally let this happen, didn't you?"

Evans couldn't meet my eyes. "Izzy, that's not fair. My hands were tied — "

"No," I said, my voice dangerously quiet. "Your hands were free. You just chose not to use them. With Cap gone, you figured you could finally let this happen without looking him in the eye, didn't you? With him gone, there was no one left to defend me, no one whose opinion you actually respected."

"The promotion board made the decision based on multiple factors, but, yes ... they reviewed it," Evans mumbled. "They felt ... they felt it showed a lack of professional boundaries. That your personal relationships could compromise your command decisions."

"You're a coward," I said, my voice cutting through his excuses like a blade. "You know I'm the better candidate. You know Santoro's promotion is about politics, not merit. But you chose the easy path because that's what cowards do. You took the ammunition my boyfriend handed you and used it to justify what you were always going to do anyway."

"Izzy — "

"Don't." I stood, looking down at him with something that might have been pity. "Cap believed in you. He thought you were better than this. But he's not here to see what you really are, is he? How convenient for you."

I left him sitting there, unable to defend himself because we both knew I was right. The second pillar of my life — my career, my future, everything I'd worked for — lay in ruins behind me. But I wasn't broken. I was something else entirely now, something harder and more focused than I'd ever been before.

There was still one more pillar to demolish.

I found Jimmy waiting by his car in the station parking lot, looking lost and uncertain. The reception was winding down, firefighters heading home or back to their stations, the normal rhythm of the fire service resuming despite the loss of one of its own. He straightened when he saw me approaching, hope flickering in his green eyes like a candle in the wind.

"Izzy," he said softly. "How are you holding up? I know today was — "

"Did you write a letter to my battalion chief?" I asked, my voice perfectly controlled.

The hope died in his eyes, replaced by something that looked like terror. His face went pale, and I saw him swallow hard before answering.

"I... yes. I thought it would help — "

"You thought wrong." I stepped closer, and he actually took a step back, responding to something in my voice that was colder than anything I'd ever directed at him before. "Did you really think that would help? Did you, an outsider, think you could write a letter and fix a system that's been destroying women for fifty years?"

"I was trying to help you — "

"You weren't helping me, Jimmy." My voice remained perfectly level, each word precisely chosen for maximum impact. "You were proving their point. You handed them exactly what they needed — evidence that I'm too emotional, too weak to handle my own battles without my boyfriend intervening."

Jimmy was crying now, tears streaming down his face. His hands were shaking, and I could see him struggling to find words, to explain, to somehow undo what had been done.

"I just wanted to fight for you," he said, his voice breaking. "I thought if they just knew how good you are, how much you deserve — "

"What you thought doesn't matter," I cut him off. "What matters is what you did. You gave them my career on a silver platter because you don't understand the first thing about the world I live in."

"Izzy, please, I never meant — "

"You took away my chance to fight my own battle," I continued relentlessly. "You made me look weak when I needed to look strong. You destroyed everything I worked for because you were too naive to understand that good intentions aren't enough."

Tears were streaming down his face now, and I could see him struggling to hold himself together, his breath coming in ragged gasps. Part of me — a small, buried part — wanted to comfort him, to tell him I knew he'd meant well. But that part was locked away behind the wall I'd built, unreachable and irrelevant.

"I'm sorry," he whispered. "God, Izzy, I'm so sorry. I thought... I love you so much, and I just wanted to help — "

"Love isn't enough," I said quietly. "Not when it comes with this kind of destruction."

I turned to walk away, but his voice stopped me.

"What does this mean?" he asked, his voice broken. "For us?"

I looked back at him — this man who'd held me when I cried, who'd cooked for me, who'd made me believe for a brief, shining moment that I could have both strength and softness, competence and vulnerability.

"Stay away from me," I said. "Don't call. Don't text. Don't show up at my apartment or my station. We're done."

I walked away, leaving him standing there in the parking lot, destroyed by the weight of his own good intentions. The third and final pillar of my life — love, hope, the possibility of a future with someone who understood me — crumbled to dust behind me.

But I didn't look back. I couldn't afford to. I had nothing left now except my competence, my tactical mind, and the cold, hard shell I'd built to protect what remained of myself.

It would have to be enough. It was all I had left.

chapter
thirty

I MADE it home on autopilot, the drive from Station 2 passing in a blur of stoplights and empty streets. My hands were steady on the wheel, my breathing controlled, my mind carefully blank. It wasn't until I walked through my apartment door and closed it behind me that the silence hit me like a tangible thing.

The apartment felt different. Wrong. Every surface, every corner held memories of her — Izzy laughing at my terrible movie choices, Izzy cooking breakfast in my kitchen, Izzy curled against me on the couch while I read her stories from nursing school. The ghost of her presence filled every room, making the emptiness feel vast and suffocating.

I walked into the kitchen, and that's where it all came crashing down.

The counter where she'd sat that first night, driving me crazy just by existing in my space. The stove where we'd cooked together, where I'd made her tres leches and watched her face light up with surprise and pleasure. The table where we'd shared breakfast after the best night of my life, where she'd told me she wanted children and I'd failed her so completely.

The sob that escaped me was raw, animalistic, a sound I didn't recognize as coming from my own throat. My legs gave out, and I found myself on the kitchen floor, my back against the cabinets, wracked with the kind of crying that had no sound — just pure, physical agony that felt like my chest was being torn apart.

I destroyed everything.

The thought circled through my mind like a mantra, each repetition driving the knife deeper. I hadn't just lost Izzy — I'd destroyed her. I'd taken her trust, her vulnerability, her dreams for the future, and I'd crushed them with my own stupidity. She'd told me exactly how her world worked, warned me about the politics and the way women like her were treated, and I'd ignored it all because I thought I knew better.

Lisa trusted me, too.

The memory hit me like another blow. Lisa Harris, sitting in that hospital bed, looking at me with desperate hope when I'd promised her safety. And weeks later, she was dead because I couldn't save her. Because I'd been naive enough to think that good intentions and proper protocol could protect someone from a system designed to fail them.

I was poison. Everything I touched turned to ash. Every person who trusted me ended up worse for it.

The tears came harder now, silent and devastating. I pulled my knees to my chest and let them come, let the grief and guilt and self-loathing wash over me in waves. There was no fighting it, no controlling it. This was what I deserved — to be alone on my kitchen floor, choking on the wreckage of everything I'd tried to protect.

My phone rang, cutting through the silence. My mother's ringtone — "Sweet Caroline," because she'd insisted on it after a particularly wine-soaked family barbecue. For a moment, I considered letting it go to voicemail. But something desperate in me reached for the phone, needing to hear a voice that still loved me, even if I didn't deserve it.

"Hi, Mom," I managed, my voice hoarse and broken.

"Jimmy? Honey, what's wrong?" Her maternal radar had always been flawless. One word from me and she could diagnose everything from a bad day to a broken heart.

"I messed up, Mom," I said, fresh tears starting. "Really bad."

"What happened? Are you hurt? Do you need me to come up there?"

The concern in her voice almost broke me all over again. Here was unconditional love, offered without question or judgment, and I couldn't even explain why I didn't deserve it.

"No, I just... I hurt someone. Someone really important to me. And I can't fix it."

"Oh, sweetheart." Her voice was soft, full of the kind of motherly comfort that had gotten me through skinned knees and broken friendships and every other crisis of my life. "What did you do?"

I tried to find the words to explain, but how could I tell her about the letter without admitting how completely I'd failed to understand the woman I claimed to love? How could I explain that I'd destroyed Izzy's career with good intentions?

"I tried to help her," I said finally. "I thought I was helping, but I just made everything worse. She was right to leave me. I'm not... I'm not good enough for her."

"James Daniel Dalton," my mother said, her voice taking on the firm tone she'd used when I was a child and needed correction. "That is not the son I raised talking. The son I raised doesn't give up on people he loves."

"But what if I'm the problem, Mom? What if I'm the one who hurts everyone I try to help?"

There was a long pause on the other end of the line. When she spoke again, her voice was gentler. "Honey, loving someone means risking hurt. It means making mistakes and learning from them. If this girl is worth fighting for — "

"She is," I said without hesitation. "She's the strongest, most incredible person I've ever met."

"Then you fight for her. You figure out how to be the man she deserves. But giving up? That's not love, baby. That's fear."

We talked for a few more minutes, her voice a lifeline in the darkness of my apartment. But when I hung up, the silence rushed back in, heavier than before. She was wrong. This wasn't about fear — it was about facing the truth. I wasn't the man Izzy deserved. I'd proven that spectacularly.

The best thing I could do for her was stay away. Let her find someone who wouldn't destroy her career with misguided love letters. Someone who could protect her instead of failing her at every turn.

I went back to work the next day and threw myself into the job with the kind of desperate focus that felt like drowning in reverse. If I couldn't be the man Izzy needed, if I couldn't save the patients who trusted me, then I'd be perfect at everything else. I'd be the most competent, most careful, most thorough nurse Metro General had ever seen.

I picked up extra shifts. Covered for colleagues who needed time off. Stayed late to double-check charts and triple-check medication calculations. The easy smile I'd worn for years disappeared, replaced by a professional mask that never slipped. The cookies stopped appearing in the break room. The birthday celebrations I'd organized became someone else's responsibility.

I became a ghost of myself — technically flawless but completely hollow.

My first patient of the night was Harold, my frequent flyer who usually came in convinced his anxiety symptoms were heart attacks. In the past, I'd spend time with him, talking him through his fears with gentle humor and patience. Tonight, I ran through his assessment with mechanical efficiency.

"Mr. Brennan, your EKG is normal, your troponins are negative, and your vital signs are stable," I said, not meeting his eyes as I updated his chart. "Dr. Ward will be in shortly to discuss discharge."

"Jimmy?" Harold looked confused, maybe a little hurt. "Don't you want to know what I was watching when it started? You always ask about that."

"The important thing is that your cardiac workup is normal," I replied, already moving toward the door. "Is there anything else you need right now?"

Harold shook his head, but I could see the disappointment in his eyes. In the past, our conversations had been the highlight of his visits — someone who listened without judgment, who treated his anxiety as real without feeding into it. Now I was just another nurse going through the motions.

"Mr. Patton, I need to check your pain level one more time," I said to the patient in Room 7, a construction worker who'd fallen from a scaffold. I'd already assessed him twice in the past hour, but the gnawing fear that I'd missed something wouldn't let me rest.

"I told you, it's a six," he said, looking at me with mild concern. "You feeling alright? You've asked me that three times."

"Just being thorough," I replied, updating his chart with mechanical precision. "I'll be back to check on you in thirty minutes."

In Room 3, an elderly woman named Mrs. Kim had been waiting for test results for her abdominal pain. She'd been asking about her grandson, trying to make conversation the way patients did when they were scared and alone. In the past, I'd have pulled up a chair, asked about her family, maybe even shown her pictures on her phone to pass the time.

"Mrs. Kim, your CT results should be back within the hour," I said, checking her IV line. "Are you experiencing any nausea or increased pain?"

"No, dear, but I was wondering — "

"I'll update you as soon as we have results," I cut her off, not unkindly but with a finality that ended the conversation. I had other patients to check, other assessments to complete. There wasn't time for stories about grandchildren.

In the hallway, I ran into Dr. Delaney Ward, one of the ER attendings. Ward was known for her razor-sharp intellect and ice-cold competence — the kind of doctor who could diagnose rare conditions with Sherlock Holmes-like deductive reasoning but had the bedside manner of a particularly efficient computer.

"Dalton, what's going on with Mr. Patton?" she asked, her voice crisp and direct. "His chart shows pain assessments every twenty minutes for the past four hours."

"I want to make sure we're not missing anything," I said. "Pain can be an indicator of complications."

Ward frowned, pulling up his chart on her tablet. "His vitals are stable, his imaging is unremarkable, and his pain is appropriately controlled for his injury. You're documenting at a frequency that suggests either deterioration or paranoia. Which is it?"

I met her cool gaze, recognizing something in her clinical detachment that felt familiar. "Just being thorough."

"Thoroughness has a clinical definition, Mr. Dalton. This is something else." She studied me for a moment with the same analytical intensity she brought to difficult diagnoses. "When's the last time you took time off?"

"I'm fine," I said, the phrase becoming as automatic as checking blood pressure.

Ward's expression didn't change, but something flickered in her eyes that might have been concern. "See that you are. Hypervigilance can be as dangerous as negligence."

Two weeks later, I was assigned to precept Chloe again. She bounded into the department with her usual enthusiasm, her face lighting up when she saw me at the nurses' station.

"Jimmy!" she said, practically bouncing on her toes. "I'm so excited to work with you again. I've been practicing my IV starts, and I think I'm finally getting the hang of the butterfly technique you taught me."

"That's good," I replied, not looking up from the patient assignment sheet. "We've got a full board tonight. Room assignments are posted."

Chloe's smile faltered slightly. "Okay... so what's our game plan? Should we start with the chest pain in Room 4, or do you want to tackle the psych patient first?"

"We'll start with the most acute and work our way down. Standard triage priorities." I handed her the assignment sheet and started walking toward Room 4. "Patient is a fifty-six-year-old male with chest pain onset two hours ago. I'll take the history while you prepare for the EKG."

"Right, but..." Chloe hurried to keep up with me. "Don't you want to hear about Mrs. Murphy? She asked about you last week. Said you were the only nurse who made her laugh during her gallbladder surgery admission."

"Patient rapport is important, but we have twelve patients to assess," I said, pushing open the door to Room 4. "We need to prioritize efficiency."

I watched Chloe's face fall, confusion replacing her earlier excitement. In the past, I'd have asked about Mrs. Murphy, probably would have made a note to stop by and say hello if she was still in the hospital. Now it just felt like a distraction from the work that needed to be done.

The chest pain assessment went perfectly — textbook history taking, flawless EKG placement, appropriate medication administration. But when Chloe tried to engage the patient in light conversation while we waited for lab results, I cut her off.

"Mr. Williams, we'll have your results within the hour," I said. "Chloe, Room 6 needs vitals."

In the hallway, Chloe caught my arm. "Jimmy, are you okay? You seem... different."

"Different how?"

"I don't know. Distant? You used to tell jokes during procedures, ask patients about their families. You made everyone feel comfortable. Now you're all business."

I looked at her earnest face, this young nurse who still believed that caring was enough, that good intentions could save people. I'd been like her once — optimistic, invested, convinced that the right combination of compassion and competence could fix anything.

"This job isn't about making friends, Chloe," I said quietly. "It's about providing safe, effective care. Everything else is secondary."

"But you taught me that connecting with patients was part of good care — "

"I was wrong." The words came out harsher than I'd intended. "Focus on the clinical skills. That's what matters."

I walked away, leaving Chloe standing in the hallway looking like I'd just told her that Santa Claus wasn't real. Which, in a way, I had. I'd shattered her illusion that caring and competence could coexist, that you could protect your patients without protecting yourself from them.

The rest of the shift passed in mechanical precision. Perfect medication calculations, flawless assessments, comprehensive documentation. But every interaction felt hollow, devoid of the warmth that had once made this job feel like more than just work.

During our break, Chloe tried one more time. "Jimmy, I don't know what's going on with you, but you're scaring me a little. This isn't the nurse who taught me to see patients as people, not just diagnoses."

"Maybe that nurse was naive," I said, not looking up from my charting. "Maybe he hadn't learned yet that caring too much just leads to disappointment."

"Is this about a patient? Did something happen?" A pause, and then, "Did I do something wrong?"

Everything happened, I thought. *I failed a woman who trusted me to keep her safe. I destroyed the career of the woman I love. I proved that I'm not worthy of the trust people place in me.*

"No. You're just fine. Nothing happened," I said instead. "I just learned to prioritize appropriately."

But Chloe wasn't buying it. She studied my face with the kind of intensity I'd taught her to bring to patient assessment. "The Jimmy who taught me would never talk like this. He'd say that caring is what makes us good nurses, not just technicians."

The truth of her words rocked me a little, but I pushed it down. That Jimmy had been a fool. This Jimmy understood the world better.

"Get some rest," I said, ending the conversation. "Long night ahead."

Three weeks into my new routine, I was finishing a particularly brutal stretch — six twelve-hour shifts in as many days — when Sophia appeared at my elbow as I gathered my things from the nurses' station to leave for the morning.

"Jimmy," she said, her voice gentle but concerned. "What's going on? You look like you haven't slept in a week."

I kept my eyes on my bag, mechanically checking that I had everything I needed. My apartment had become a place I barely recognized — dishes in the sink, laundry piling up, the refrigerator containing nothing but energy drinks and takeout containers. I'd stopped cooking, stopped cleaning, stopped doing anything that wasn't directly related to work.

"I'm fine. Just tired."

"No, you're not." She stepped closer, lowering her voice. "You used to light up this whole department. People looked forward to working with you. Now you move around here like a ghost. Talk to me."

For a moment, I was tempted to tell her everything. Sophia had always been easy to talk to, a natural listener who seemed to understand people's pain without judgment. But the words wouldn't come. How could I explain that I'd destroyed the best thing in my life because I was too broken to be what she needed?

"Just going through some stuff," I said, slinging my bag over my shoulder. "I'll be fine."

"Jimmy — "

"I need to get home," I cut her off, not unkindly but with a finality that ended the conversation. "Long shift tomorrow."

I walked away, leaving Sophia standing at the nurses' station with worry written all over her face. I could feel her eyes on me as I headed for the exit, but I didn't look back. There was nothing she could do to help me. Nothing anyone could do.

This was who I was now — a nurse who could start IVs on impossible patients and calculate drip rates in his sleep, but who couldn't save the people who mattered most. A man who'd learned to keep his distance from anything that might require him to be more than technically competent.

It was safer this way. For everyone.

As I drove home through the empty pre-dawn streets, I thought about Kellen — the way he moved through the department like a machine, competent but untouchable. I'd always felt sorry for him, wondered what had happened to make him so closed off.

Now I understood. This was what happened when you cared too much and failed too often. You didn't break.

You just stopped feeling anything at all.

Maybe it was better this way. Maybe this was who I was supposed to be.

But as I pulled into my apartment complex and saw the empty parking space where Izzy's truck used to sit when she stayed over, the hollowness in my chest felt so vast I could barely breathe.

Perfect competence, it turned out, was a cold comfort when you had no one left to be competent for.

chapter
thirty-one

THE NEWSPAPER ARTICLE was waiting on my desk when I arrived for shift, folded open to the Metro section like someone had wanted to make sure I wouldn't miss it. The headline read "Rising Star: Lt. Mark Santoro Named Captain of Station 12," and below it was a professionally staged photo of Santoro in his dress uniform, all polished brass and political smile.

I read the article with the same clinical detachment I brought to incident reports, cataloging each carefully crafted quote like evidence in a case file.

"Captain Santoro brings a fresh perspective to Station 12," said Battalion Chief Evans. "His ability to build relationships and work collaboratively with all levels of the department makes him an ideal leader for the next generation of firefighters."

"I'm honored to serve in this capacity," Santoro was quoted as saying. "The fire service is about teamwork and trust. I look forward to building those bonds with my new crew and continuing Summit County's tradition of excellence."

The words were professionally meaningless, the kind of corporate speak that said nothing while sounding impressive. But beneath the sanitized language, I could read the real message. *Teamwork. Building relationships. Working collaboratively.* All coded language for "plays politics better than his female competition."

There was even a sidebar about his "community involvement" —

charity golf tournaments, youth sports coaching, the kind of visible civic engagement that looked good in personnel files and promotion boards. The article mentioned his "strong family values" and included a quote from his wife about how proud she was of his advancement.

I folded the paper closed and dropped it in the trash. The first cut was always the deepest, and this one had been designed to wound. Someone — probably Santoro himself — had made sure this would be the first thing I saw when I came to work. A reminder of what I'd lost, what he'd won, and how easily the system had discarded me.

But the blade that was meant to break me only made me harder.

Station 2 felt different now. The easy camaraderie that had defined B-shift for years had been replaced by something more careful, more professional. My crew still respected me — that had never been in question — but the warmth was gone, locked away behind the wall I'd built to protect what remained of myself.

"Morning, L.T.," Thompson said as I walked through the apparatus bay. His greeting was perfectly respectful, but I caught the way his eyes searched my face, looking for some sign of the person I used to be.

"Thompson," I replied with a curt nod. "Equipment checks complete?"

"Yeah, we're all set. Martinez is finishing up the hose bed, and Benny's got the pump panel squared away." He paused, clearly wanting to say something more. "Hey, did you see that bullshit in the paper about — "

"I saw it." My voice was flat, final. "Is there anything requiring my attention?"

Thompson's face fell slightly, the easy joke he'd been building toward dying on his lips. "No, ma'am. We're good to go."

I moved past him toward the engine, checking systems that had already been checked, inspecting equipment that was already perfect. It was busy work, but it kept my hands occupied and my mind focused on concrete, controllable tasks.

Martinez emerged from the back of the engine, looking proud of his work on the hose bed. "L.T., I went with the Minuteman load like you showed me. Took me three tries, but I think I got it right."

I climbed up to inspect his work, noting the precise folds and proper coupling placement. It was flawless — exactly the kind of attention to detail that kept people alive on the fireground.

"Acceptable," I said, jumping down from the truck bed.

Martinez's face fell. In the past, good work had earned him praise, maybe even one of my rare smiles. Now it earned him a single word that felt more like a dismissal than recognition.

"Is there... anything I could do better?" he asked tentatively.

"No. It meets standard."

I walked away, leaving him standing there looking confused and hurt. Behind me, I heard Thompson mutter something to Benny, their voices too low to make out the words but their concern clear in the tone.

The first call of the shift came in just after ten — a vehicle accident with possible entrapment on Highway 45. As we rolled out of the bay, I felt the familiar shift into tactical mode, my mind calculating response times, positioning options, and resource needs.

"Engine 18 on scene," I radioed as we pulled up to find a sedan on its side against a guardrail. "We have one vehicle, driver conscious and alert, possible entrapment. Engine 18 establishing command."

The scene was straightforward — a minor roll-over with the driver trapped by a jammed door. In the past, I would have worked the problem with my crew, teaching Martinez about extrication techniques while Thompson positioned equipment. Today, I issued orders with military precision.

"Martinez, stabilize the vehicle. Thompson, get the spreaders. We're taking the door on the A-side."

"Copy, L.T." Martinez moved to position the cribbing blocks, but he was moving too slowly, checking and double-checking his placement.

"Martinez, move faster," I snapped over the radio. "We don't have all day."

The correction was technically appropriate — speed mattered in extrication — but my delivery was harsh, public, designed to cut rather than teach. Martinez flinched at the tone, his confidence visibly shaking as he hurried to complete the task.

Thompson shot me a look from across the vehicle, something between surprise and concern. In the past, I would have handled Martinez's hesitation with a quiet word, maybe moved him to a different position where he could build confidence. Now I just wanted the job done efficiently, without the messy complications of feelings or mentorship.

We had the driver out in six minutes — a clean, professional operation. But as we packed up equipment, I could feel the tension radiating from my crew. They'd done good work, but none of them looked satisfied. They looked rattled.

"Nice work, everyone," I said as we prepared to clear the scene. But the words felt hollow, a box I was checking rather than genuine appreciation.

Back at the station, the quiet was oppressive. Thompson and Martinez spoke in low voices as they cleaned equipment, shooting occasional glances in my direction. Benny focused on his paperwork with unusual intensity, avoiding eye contact entirely.

I retreated to my office and closed the door.

The call that broke everything came three hours later — an apartment fire with multiple units involved. As we rolled up to the scene, I could see heavy smoke pushing from the second floor of a three-story building. Real fire. Real danger.

"Engine 18 on scene," I radioed. "We have a working structure fire, two-story apartment building, heavy smoke showing from the Charlie side. Engine 18 establishing command."

I positioned our apparatus and began sizing up the scene, my tactical mind processing the variables. Exposures, water supply, ventilation needs, search priorities. Everything was clicking into place with mechanical precision.

"Thompson, Martinez, pull the attack line. Primary search of the second floor. Benny, get me a water supply from the hydrant on the corner."

My crew moved with professional efficiency, but I could see the hesitation in Martinez's movements, the way Thompson kept glancing back at me for confirmation. The harsh correction from our last call had shaken their confidence, and now, when confidence mattered most, they were second-guessing themselves.

"Martinez, what's your status?" I barked into my radio as they advanced the line into the building.

"Interior, advancing on the seat of the fire," came his reply, but I could hear the uncertainty in his voice.

"Move faster. You're not on a sightseeing tour."

It was the kind of comment I would have made before, but then it would have been delivered with wry humor, a way to keep spirits up during dangerous work. Now it was just cruel, another public cut that served no purpose except to vent my own frustration.

The fire was contained quickly — good stop, no injuries, property damage minimal. But as we stood outside packing up equipment, I could see the damage I'd done to something more important than the building we'd just saved.

Thompson approached me as I updated the incident report. "L.T., can I have a word?"

I looked up from my paperwork, noting the careful distance he was maintaining, the formal way he'd phrased the request.

"What is it, Thompson?"

"It's about Martinez. Kid's shook up. Thinks he did something wrong back there."

"Did he?"

Thompson's jaw tightened. "No, ma'am. He did good work. Followed orders, kept his head down, got the job done. But you've been riding him hard lately, and he's starting to lose confidence."

I set down my pen and looked at Thompson directly. "Is there a problem with my command decisions, Firefighter Thompson?"

The use of his last name hit like a slap. For two years, he'd been "Thompson" or even "Thomps" when I was feeling playful. Now he was "Firefighter Thompson," relegated to the formal distance of rank and regulation.

"No, ma'am," he said quietly. "No problem."

"Good. Then we're done here."

Thompson stood there for a moment, clearly wanting to say more. But the wall I'd built was impenetrable, and he finally just nodded and walked away.

Jack McKenzie found me twenty minutes later as we were preparing to clear the scene. The paramedic approached with his usual easy confidence, but I could see the concern in his eyes.

"Good work in there, Lieutenant," he said, checking his notes from the patient transport. "Clean operation. How's your crew holding up?"

It was a perfectly normal question — paramedics and firefighters worked closely enough that checking on personnel welfare was common courtesy. But something in his tone, the careful way he was watching my face, told me this wasn't just professional interest.

"My crew is fine, Medic McKenzie," I replied, my voice clipped. "Is there a medical issue that requires your input?"

Jack blinked, clearly taken aback by the formal tone. We'd worked dozens of calls together over the years, had shared easy conversation and mutual respect. Now I was treating him like a stranger, and it showed.

"No medical issues," he said carefully. "Just checking. Some of the other crews have mentioned that Station 2 seems... different lately. Thought I'd see if you needed anything."

"We don't." I turned back to my paperwork, making it clear the conversation was over. "Thank you for your concern."

Jack stood there for a moment, clearly debating whether to push further. "Izzy — "

"*Lieutenant* Delgado," I corrected without looking up.

"Right. Lieutenant. Look, I know you've been through a lot lately, with Cap and everything. If you ever need to talk — "

"I don't." My voice was ice. "Is there anything else, Medic McKenzie?"

Jack's expression shifted from concern to something that looked like pity. "No. Nothing else."

He walked away, and I felt a small stab of satisfaction. Another boundary established, another relationship moved to safe, professional distance. It was better this way. Cleaner.

I didn't need Jack's concern or Thompson's worry or Martinez's confused hurt. I needed them to do their jobs with the same mechanical precision I brought to mine. Feelings were a luxury I could no longer afford.

Back at the station, the atmosphere was toxic in a way I'd never experienced before. My crew went about their post-call duties with grim efficiency, but the easy banter that usually followed a good stop was absent. They cleaned equipment in silence, checked inventory without their usual complaints about missing supplies, and avoided making eye contact with me whenever possible.

Benny found me in my office an hour later, his weathered face creased with worry.

"Kiddo," he started, then caught himself. "L.T., can we talk?"

I looked up from the incident report I was reviewing for the third time. "What is it, Firefighter Carter?"

The formal address stung him, I could tell. Benny had known me since I was a rookie, had worked with my father, had earned the right to call me "kiddo" through years of loyalty and quiet wisdom. Reducing him to his rank and last name was cruel, and we both knew it.

"Is there an issue with an order?" I continued when he didn't immediately respond.

"No, ma'am," he said quietly. "No issues."

But he didn't leave. He stood there in my doorway, looking at me with the kind of patient concern he'd shown when I was a scared rookie making mistakes.

"Benny, was there something else?"

"Just... you sure you're okay? You seem different since..."

"Since what?"

"Since the funeral. Since Cap." His voice was gentle, careful. "We're worried about you."

The kindness in his voice almost cracked something inside me, but I pushed it down, locked it away behind the wall that kept me safe.

"I'm fine," I said. "Better than fine. I'm focused."

"Maybe too focused," Benny said quietly.

"Is there a problem with my performance, Firefighter Carter?"

He flinched at the formal address again, but didn't back down. "No. Your performance is perfect. That's the problem."

"I don't understand."

"L.T., the boys are spooked. They'll follow you into hell, you know that. But they're losing confidence. Not in your orders, but in themselves. You used to be one of us. Now you're just our boss." His voice carried twenty years of experience, two decades of watching officers come and go. "There's a difference."

I stared at him, feeling nothing but cold certainty. "The difference is professionalism. The difference is focus. The difference is not letting personal feelings interfere with operational effectiveness."

"The difference," Benny said sadly, "is that we used to *want* to follow you. Now we just *have* to."

He left me sitting there with those words hanging in the air like smoke from a structure fire — invisible but toxic, seeping into everything and making it hard to breathe.

That night, I sat alone in my office after the shift had ended, staring at the framed photo of Cap that sat on my desk. It had been taken at last year's department picnic, back when he was still healthy, still laughing, still the anchor that kept me grounded.

In the photo, he was telling some story to a group of younger firefighters, his hands animated, his face bright with the joy of sharing hard-won wisdom. That was who he'd been — a teacher, a mentor, a man who built people up instead of tearing them down.

I felt the grief rise in my chest, sharp and sudden, threatening to crack the wall I'd built. For just a moment, I wanted to let it out, to cry for the man I'd lost and the woman I used to be. But I pushed it down, locked it away with everything else I couldn't afford to feel.

Emotions were weakness. Caring too much was what had cost me everything — my promotion, my relationship, my future. The only way to survive was to be perfect, untouchable, professionally flawless.

But as I sat there in the empty station, surrounded by the equipment and traditions that had once felt like home, I couldn't shake Benny's words.

We used to want to follow you. Now we just have to.

I told myself it didn't matter. Leadership wasn't about being liked — it was about being effective. My crew would follow my orders because they were good orders, tactically sound and professionally appropriate. Their feelings about it were irrelevant.

But even as I told myself these things, even as I reinforced the wall that kept me safe and isolated, I couldn't quite silence the voice in the back of my mind that sounded suspiciously like Cap.

Be brave enough to keep your heart open. Even when it hurts. Especially when it hurts.

I pushed the voice away and focused on my paperwork. Hearts were fragile things, easily broken. Walls were stronger. Walls lasted.

Even if they kept everyone else out.

chapter
thirty-two

THE AUTOMATIC DOORS of Metro General slid open with their familiar whisper, and I stepped into the controlled chaos of shift change. The fluorescent lights felt harsher than usual, cutting through the exhaustion that had become my constant companion. I'd picked up this call shift because the alternative — sitting alone in my apartment, staring at walls that still held echoes of Izzy's laughter — was unbearable.

The elevator ride to the ER felt endless. Almost two months now since Cap's funeral. Since I'd watched the strongest woman I'd ever known look at me like I was a stranger who'd destroyed her life. Three weeks of perfect, hollow competence that left me feeling like a ghost haunting my own existence.

The elevator dinged, and I stepped out into the familiar chaos of the emergency department. But something was off. Sophia was standing at the nurses' station with Carly, both charge nurses looking up as I approached with expressions I couldn't quite read.

"Oh, gosh, Jimmy," Sophia said, her voice carrying a note of apologetic surprise that didn't quite ring true. "My mistake. We double-scheduled tonight. We don't actually need you."

I stopped walking, my exhausted brain struggling to process what she was saying. "What?"

"I know, I know. Total screwup on our part." She exchanged a glance with Carly that lasted a fraction of a second too long. "We'll pay out your call-time anyway since it's our fault. Sorry you drove all the way in for nothing."

The disappointment almost shattered me, desperation rising in my chest. The prospect of twelve hours of methodical, mind-numbing work had been the only thing getting me through the day. Now I'd have to go home, back to the silence and the memories and the constant replay of every mistake I'd made.

"Are you sure?" I asked, hearing the desperation in my own voice. "I could work anyway, help out with — "

"We're fully staffed for tonight," Carly said firmly. "Go home. Get some rest."

I nodded numbly, turned around, and headed back toward the elevator. Behind me, I caught a fragment of whispered conversation between Sophia and Carly, something about "had to try", but the words felt distant and unimportant.

The parking garage was dimly lit and mostly empty, my footsteps echoing off concrete walls as I made my way toward my car. All I wanted was to get home, maybe drink myself into unconsciousness, anything to stop the endless cycle of self-recrimination that had become my default state.

"Dalton."

The voice cut through the silence like a blade. I turned to see Kellen standing beside a beat-up Chevy Silverado, his expression as unreadable as ever. He was wearing a zipped hoodie and navy blue EMS-style cargo pants.

"You're coming with me," he said. Not a request. Not a suggestion. A statement of fact delivered in that flat, emotionless tone that was his bread and butter.

I stared at him, too tired to be surprised, too hollow to argue. "What? Where?"

"Just get in the truck, Dalton."

Something in his voice — a note of authority that brooked no disagreement — made my legs move without conscious thought. I climbed into the passenger seat of his pickup, noting the meticulous cleanliness, the lack of personal items, the way even his vehicle seemed to reflect his emotional distance.

Kellen started the engine without another word, and we pulled out of the garage into the night.

The drive took us through parts of the city I barely recognized. Industrial areas filled with warehouses and chain-link fences, neighborhoods where the streetlights were sparse and the buildings looked like they'd given up on better days. Kellen navigated the empty streets with obvious purpose, never explaining where we were going or why.

We pulled up in front of a squat, windowless cinderblock building with a single flickering neon sign that simply read "BAR." No name, no decoration, just a statement as blunt and uncompromising as the man who'd brought me here.

"Come on," Kellen said, climbing out of the truck.

The interior was exactly what the exterior had promised — dark, smelling of stale beer and industrial-strength bleach, populated by a handful of people who looked like they'd been carved from the same unforgiving stone as the building itself. The bartender, a woman who appeared to have been working here since the Earth was young, looked up as we entered with the kind of practiced indifference that suggested she'd seen everything and been impressed by none of it.

Kellen steered me toward a booth in the back, the kind of scarred wooden table that had probably absorbed decades of bad decisions and worse conversations. I slid into the worn vinyl seat, still too confused and exhausted to question what was happening.

"Two glasses, please," Kellen told the bartender when she materialized beside our table.

I watched, my confusion deepening, as he unvelcroed a leg pocket on his cargo pants and withdrew a bottle that made my eyebrows rise. Blanton's. Single barrel bourbon that cost more than most people spent on groceries in a month.

"Hey, buddy, you want to drink here, you buy it here. State Beverage Commission'll fine the shit out of us," the bartender said, unimpressed by the expensive liquor.

Kellen pulled out his wallet, extracted a one-hundred dollar bill from it, and placed it on the table. "Two glasses, one with ice. We don't need anything else. Thanks."

His voice carried that same flat authority that made attending physicians instantly defer to his judgment. The glasses appeared with only the briefest delay.

When we were alone, Kellen poured two generous measures of bourbon, the amber liquid catching the dim light from the flickering fixture overhead. He pushed the glass with ice toward me and raised his own.

"Drink," he said.

I took a sip and immediately started coughing. The bourbon was smooth but powerful, burning its way down my throat with the kind of authority that demanded respect. Kellen drained half his glass without so much as a wince, then set it down evenly.

"Jesus," I wheezed, my eyes watering.

"Good stuff, isn't it," Kellen said, a statement rather than a question. He topped off my glass without asking. "Drink up, Dalton. We've got things to discuss."

I took another drink, feeling the warmth spread through my chest. "What things?"

"You've been different lately," he said, his flat voice making it sound like a medical diagnosis. "Going through the motions. I've been watching you."

The bourbon was starting to soften the edges of my exhaustion, but his words made me defensive. "I'm fine. Just tired."

"Bullshit." Kellen's expression didn't change, but there was something sharp in his voice. "I've seen tired. This isn't tired. This is something else."

I took another drink, larger this time, feeling the alcohol burn away some of my resistance. "I don't know what you're talking about."

"The hell you don't." He leaned back in the booth, studying me with the same clinical assessment he brought to difficult diagnoses. "You used to light up the whole department. People looked forward to working with you. Now you move around there like a ghost."

The bourbon was making me feel loose, unmoored. "Maybe that's just who I really am."

"No." Kellen's voice was firm, certain. "I know who you really are,

Dalton. I've watched you with patients, with the new grads, with families having the worst day of their lives. You're not this hollow thing pretending to be a nurse."

I finished my glass and reached for the bottle. Kellen didn't stop me. "You don't know anything about me."

"I know you're in love with that firefighter," he said, and the words landed like a sledgehammer. "I know you're walking around here like a man who's lost everything that mattered to him. And I know you're doing exactly what I did years ago."

"What's that?"

"Trying to protect yourself from caring by pretending you don't." He poured himself another drink, his movements deliberate and controlled. "How's that working out for you?"

The bourbon was making my tongue loose, my defenses crumbling. "I'm fine."

"You're a liar." But there was no anger in his voice, just a tired certainty. "And you're an idiot if you think shutting down is going to save you from the pain."

I felt something crack open in my chest, a fissure in the wall I'd built around my grief. "You don't understand."

"Oh I don't, do I?" Kellen's eyes met mine across the table, and for the first time since I'd known him, I saw something human there, a flicker of amusement. "Tell me, then, Jimmy. What don't I understand?"

The way he said my first name — gentle, almost paternal — broke something in me. The bourbon and the exhaustion and the weight of carrying it all alone for weeks finally overwhelmed my resistance.

"I failed someone," I whispered. "Someone who trusted me to keep them safe, and I failed them."

"Tell me about it."

So I did. The words poured out of me like blood from a wound. Lisa Harris, the domestic violence case, the promises I'd made that I couldn't keep. The way she'd looked at me with desperate hope when I'd given her those useless resources. The phone call from legal affairs telling me she was dead.

"I tried to save her," I said, my voice breaking. "I gave her everything we're supposed to give them ... safety planning, resources, phone numbers. And three weeks later she was dead because I wasn't enough."

But I wasn't done, and in short order, it all came tumbling out.

"And then there's Izzy," I continued, the words coming faster now. "The firefighter. I was in love with her, and I thought... God, I thought I could help her, too. She was being passed over for promotion because of politics, because she's a woman in a good 'ole boys' club, and I wrote this letter to her battalion chief. Three pages about how amazing she was, how unfair they were being."

I laughed bitterly, the sound harsh in the dim bar. "I thought I was being supportive. I thought I was fighting for her. Instead, I handed them proof that she was 'too emotional' to handle command, that she needed her boyfriend to fight her battles."

Kellen listened without interruption, his expression never changing.

"She lost the promotion," I whispered. "They gave it to some political asshole who plays golf with the brass. And when she found out about the letter... she looked at me like I'd betrayed her. Like I'd destroyed everything she'd worked for." My voice cracked completely. "Because I had."

Kellen kept listening, pouring me another drink when my glass emptied, his expression implacable. When I finally finished, he was quiet for a long moment.

"You think you're the first nurse to lose a patient to something you couldn't control?" he asked finally. "Or the first man to destroy something he loved by trying to protect it?"

"It feels like it."

"It always does." He took a small sip from his glass. "The patient, that's the job. Sometimes we lose them no matter what we do. But the woman..." He paused, studying me with those flat eyes. "That's harder. That's the kind of mistake that comes from caring too much and understanding too little."

I felt fresh tears start, but he wasn't done.

"You want to hear about failure, Jimmy? Real failure?"

I nodded, not trusting my voice.

"You remember when those basketball players got shot?" he said. "You'd have been in, oh ... high school, maybe middle school. It was national news."

I nodded vaguely, my memory conjuring fragments of news reports, images of a campus in lockdown.

"I was the charge nurse that night," Kellen continued, his voice maintaining that same flat monotone that somehow made the words more chilling. "When they came in. Kids, all of them just barely old enough to vote. The EMS captain, it was her first night after her promotion, and *that's* what she got thrown into."

He took another small sip of bourbon, his eyes focused on something beyond the stained walls of the bar.

"It was bad. I'm sure I don't have to go into the details with you. But one of them... one of the kids was effectively black-tag when he came in. We tried anyway, of course. We always try. But sometimes..." He shrugged, the gesture carrying the weight of a thousand failed attempts at salvation.

I found myself leaning forward, drawn into the story despite my growing intoxication.

"I'm at the charge desk," Kellen went on, "and the secretary goes white. Tells me there's a call I have to take. It's one of the kids' fathers. Says he's been trying to call his son, text his son. Says his son always answers his calls, always answers his texts, and now he's not. Says he heard something about a shooting at a pick-up court near campus."

Kellen's hand, I noticed, was trembling slightly as he lifted his glass. It was the first crack I'd ever seen in his emotional armor.

"Now, I have no reason to disbelieve this guy is who he says he is. And, of course, I found out later he *is* the kid's dad. But I can't take that for granted. I have no way to verify it, and the kid doesn't have any next of kin listed in our system because he's never been a patient before. Gunshot trauma, first time through our doors."

He paused, and for a moment I thought I saw something that might have been moisture in his eyes.

"So I've got a father who I know has had his world destroyed. No parent should outlive their children. And I'm listening to him on the phone, not even begging, just... 'My son always answers. Please.'"

The words hung in the air between us, heavy with implications I was only beginning to understand.

"I have to be circumspect, of course," Kellen continued. "I have to give a non-answer. HIPAA, protocols, all the legal bullshit that keeps the hospital from getting sued. But the father... he takes my non-answer as an indication that his son *isn't* in our ER, that he might just be okay. In a more rational state, he would have understood what I was really saying. He probably logically knew what was true. But when you're desperate, you'll grab onto any reason not to believe the worst."

Kellen's voice dropped even lower, and I had to strain to hear him over the ambient noise of the bar.

"I gave him hope when I should have found a way to prepare him. I made it worse by trying to follow the rules. And that kid died on the table twenty minutes later while his father was probably thinking his son was going to be okay."

I felt something crack open in my chest. The bourbon burned, but not as much as the image Kellen had painted — a father racing through the night, clinging to false hope because a nurse had been too careful in order to be kind.

"That's just one," Kellen said, refilling both our glasses. "One incident out of dozens, hundreds like it. I had a two-year-old once. Mom's boyfriend got angry at him for crying. Turned off the safety on their water heater, threw the kid in the bathtub, gave him third-degree burns. Had to watch that kid suffer for weeks."

His voice never changed, never wavered from that same flat delivery, but I could see the cost of each memory in the lines around his eyes.

"There's a local politician. Had to report him to Adult Protective Services for how he was treating his elderly mother. Abuse, neglect, the works. But I still get to watch his campaign commercials every election season, see him talking about family values and community service, and I can't say a goddamn thing."

The bourbon was hitting me hard now, making everything feel loose and unmoored. I was crying without realizing when it had started, tears streaming down my face as the weight of his words sank in.

"The job will eat you alive if you let it," Kellen said, his voice carrying a weariness that seemed to come from his bones. "It ate me. Look at me, Dalton. This is what it looks like when you let the job win."

I looked at him — really looked at him — and saw not just the emotionally distant charge nurse I'd worked with for years, but a man who'd been hollowed out by too many impossible choices, too many moments when doing the right thing felt indistinguishable from inflicting cruelty.

"But you don't have to do what I did," he said, his eyes meeting mine for the first time since we'd sat down. "You need someone. Like that fire-fighter. I saw how you looked at her."

The mention of Izzy hit me like a physical blow. I felt my face crumple, the careful control I'd maintained for weeks finally beginning to crack completely.

"I destroyed that," I sobbed. "I tried to help her and I destroyed everything."

"Maybe," Kellen said. "Or maybe you made a mistake that can be fixed. Believe it or not, I feel the same way about my wife, even after seventeen years, even if it doesn't show. She's the only thing that keeps me from *truly* becoming... this."

He gestured at himself, a bitter smile flickering across his face.

"Don't lose yourself," he said quietly. "And don't you dare lose that." His voice dropped even lower. "It's okay, son."

The words undid me entirely. This broken, distant man — who I'd never seen show a single emotion, who moved through the hospital like a competent ghost — had just claimed me as family. I started crying harder, raw, ugly sobs that seemed to come from somewhere deeper than my chest.

"Atta boy," Kellen said magnanimously, patting me on the shoulder. "Let it all out."

"Hey." A voice cut through my grief — not Kellen's, but someone else's. "What's wrong with your friend? Can't handle his liquor?"

I looked up through my tears to see a man standing beside our table, probably in his fifties, wearing a stained Carhartt work shirt and the kind of sneer that suggested he'd been looking for trouble all evening. He reeked of cheap beer and bad decisions.

"Nothing wrong with him," Kellen said, his voice carrying that same flat authority it always did.

"Looks like he's having a breakdown to me," the man continued, his voice getting louder. "Maybe you should take him home before he starts crying all over everyone."

I felt Kellen go very still, even across the table. When I looked at him, his expression hadn't changed, but something dangerous had entered his eyes.

"I think you should walk away, pal," Kellen said quietly.

"What if I don't want to?" The drunk took a step closer, apparently mistaking Kellen's calm for weakness. "What if I think you and your crying boyfriend should find somewhere else to — "

It happened so fast I almost missed it. One moment, the drunk was standing there running his mouth; the next Kellen had him by the scruff of his shirt as he lifted the man slightly off his feet.

"I'm sorry. You were saying?" Kellen's voice was perfectly calm. Conversational, even ... which somehow made it more terrifying.

The drunk's reply came in a whisper. "N-n-nothing, I didn't mean nothing by it."

Kellen held him there for another moment, then released him. The man stumbled backward, surprise still evident on his face.

"That's what I thought," Kellen said, settling back into the booth as if nothing had happened.

The drunk looked like he was considering saying something else, then thought better of it and retreated quickly to the far end of the bar. Around us, the other patrons had gone very quiet, all of them suddenly finding their drinks fascinating.

I stared at Kellen in shock. "Jesus Christ."

"Finish your drink, it's expensive as hell," he said calmly, almost with a yawn. "About time we go, anyway."

The bourbon was hitting me hard now, making the room spin slightly. I drained my glass and tried to stand, only to discover that my legs weren't quite working the way they should.

"Whoa," I said, grabbing the table for support.

Kellen was beside me immediately, his arm steady under mine. "Come on, lightweight. Let's get you home."

The walk to his truck was a struggle. The alcohol seemed to hit me all at once, and my legs felt like they belonged to someone else. Kellen half-carried me across the parking lot, his strength surprising given his build.

"Waaait," I mumbled as Kellen helped me toward his truck, my words slurring together. "Soph ... Sop... she didn't really double-schedule me, did she?"

Kellen didn't answer. He just kept steering me forward.

"She set this up," I continued, the pieces clicking together in my drunk brain. "She fucking ... fucking ... she knew you were gonna..."

"Get in, Dalton."

"She was worried about me?" The realization hit me like another shot of bourbon. "Jesus, Kellen, how bad have I been?"

"Bad enough," he said quietly, helping me into the passenger seat. "Bad enough that people who care about you started making plans."

The drive back to my apartment passed in a dizzying blur of streetlights and gentle motion. I must have dozed, because the next thing I knew, Kellen was helping me out of his pickup and toward my building.

"Keys," he said.

I fumbled in my pockets, eventually producing them with the kind of concentration that simple tasks required when you were this drunk. Kellen took them and unlocked the door, then helped me up the stairs to my apartment.

"Jesus, Dalton," he muttered as I stumbled on the landing. "I'm getting too old for this bullshit."

Inside my apartment, he guided me to my bedroom and helped me sit on the edge of the bed.

"Think you can manage from here?" he asked.

I nodded, though I wasn't entirely sure. "Thanks, Kellen. For everything."

"Don't thank me yet," he said. "Thank me when you fix what's broken."

He started to leave, then paused at the bedroom door. "I'm going to sleep on your couch tonight. Make sure you don't choke on your own vomit or something equally stupid."

"You don't have to — "

"Yeah, I do." He was already walking toward the living room. "Get some sleep, Jimmy. Tomorrow you start figuring out how to get your life back."

I lay back on the bed, still fully clothed, and closed my eyes. The room was spinning, but for the first time in weeks, the chaos felt manageable. Kellen had given me something I didn't even know I needed: permission to be human. Permission to fail without being destroyed by it.

And most importantly, permission to fight for the things that mattered, even when I wasn't sure I deserved them.

I woke up feeling like I'd been hit by a truck, then backed over for good measure. Sunlight was streaming through my bedroom window with the kind of aggressive cheerfulness that seemed designed to mock the hungover. My mouth tasted like something had died in it, and my head was pounding with the rhythm of my heartbeat.

But underneath the physical misery, I felt something I hadn't experienced in weeks: clarity.

From the kitchen, I could hear Kellen's voice, low and warm in a way I'd never heard before. He was on the phone.

"...yeah, he's still sleeping it off," he was saying. "Kid's been through hell... No, no, nothing like that. Just heartbreak and a case that went bad. You know how it is."

There was a pause, and I could hear the faint sound of a woman's voice responding.

"She's a firefighter," Kellen continued. "Strong, competent. Sounds like his kind of person, if he doesn't screw it up completely... Honestly, hon, she'd be damn lucky to have someone like him. If she doesn't see that, her loss."

Another pause, longer this time.

"Mmm. Yeah. Hey, did you remember to take your medication this morning?" His voice shifted, becoming gentler, more concerned. "Good. And yes, I'll pick up some milk on the way home. Do we need anything else? What? Nah, we're not out. I bought some yesterday. Check the cabinet above the stove."

I heard what sounded like warm laughter from the other end.

"I love you, too, beautiful," Kellen said quietly, the endearment sounding natural, well-worn. "See you soon."

I lay there for a few more minutes, processing what I'd heard. Not just the phone call, but the warmth in his voice, the easy domesticity, the way he'd defended me to his wife. After seventeen years of marriage, after everything that had hollowed him out, he still had that. He was still capable of love, still capable of being loved.

And he thought I was worth fighting for.

I stumbled to the kitchen, drawn by the smell of coffee, and found Kellen sitting at my small dining table with a mug and the morning paper. He looked exactly the same as always; composed, unreadable, like he hadn't spent the previous evening getting me drunk and sharing his deepest traumas.

"Coffee's fresh," he said without looking up from the sports section.

I poured myself a mug with shaking hands, grateful for the caffeine and the excuse to avoid conversation until my brain started working again.

"How do you feel?" Kellen asked.

"Like I got hit by a truck."

"Good. That means you're alive." He folded the paper and looked at me directly. "You remember what we talked about?"

"Most of it." I took a sip of coffee, feeling it burn its way down my throat. "Thank you. For last night. For staying."

"Don't mention it." He stood and rinsed his mug in the sink with his usual methodical precision. "We need to get you back to your car. You ready to drive?"

I checked my internal systems — headache, nausea, but functional. "Yeah, I think so."

The drive back to the hospital was quiet, both of us lost in our own thoughts.

Kellen pulled up next to my car. I climbed out of his Chevy, the morning air hitting me like a slap, and fumbled for my keys.

"Thanks," I said, turning back toward him. "For everything. I — "

"Don't mention it," he said, his voice returning to its usual flat tone. "Not a problem. Have a great morning, Jimmy."

I started to close his truck door, but before I could, Kellen caught it with his hand, looking at me with something I couldn't quite read.

"Hey. By the way."

"Yeah?" I asked.

"That firefighter of yours," he said, after a moment's pause. "She's worth fighting for. Don't let pride or fear keep you from at least trying."

I nodded, not trusting my voice.

"And Jimmy?" He used my first name again, and hearing it from him still felt like a gift. "You're a good nurse. Don't let this job make you forget that."

He nodded at me, released the door, and I closed it. Kellen drove off without another word, leaving me standing there in the parking lot with something I hadn't felt in weeks: hope.

I sat there for a moment, watching him disappear into traffic, then pulled out my phone. I scrolled through my contacts until I found the number I'd been avoiding for weeks.

Izzy.

My thumb hovered over her name, and for a moment, all my old fears came rushing back. What if she wouldn't see me? What if I'd destroyed things too completely to repair? What if I wasn't worthy of the love I'd thrown away?

But then I heard Kellen's voice in my head: *You're a good nurse. Don't let this job make you forget that.*

And underneath that, something else: *She's worth fighting for.*

I pressed the call button before I could change my mind.

It rang once. Twice. Three times.

Then, just as I was about to hang up, she answered.

"Jimmy?"

Her voice was cautious, surprised, but she'd answered. That had to count for something.

"Izzy," I said, my voice rough with emotion and too much bourbon. "I know I don't deserve it, but... can we talk?"

There was a long pause, and I held my breath, waiting.

"Where?" she said finally.

chapter
thirty-three

THE CALL CAME on a Thursday morning, a month deep into what had become my new normal — mechanical coffee, mechanical shower, mechanical existence in an apartment that felt more like a holding cell than a home. I was sitting at my kitchen table, staring at incident reports that didn't need reviewing, when my phone rang.

"Izzy?" Margaret's voice was small, fragile in a way that made my chest tighten. "I'm sorry to bother you, honey, but I... I'm trying to go through some of Michael's things. His clothes and... I can't do it alone. Would you... could you come sit with me?"

The request threatened to overwhelm me, but I pushed down the emotion immediately. This was duty. This was what you did for family.

"Of course," I said, already reaching for my keys. "I'll be right there."

"Thank you," she whispered. "I just... I can't face it by myself."

Twenty minutes later, I was standing in Cap and Margaret's bedroom, surrounded by the detritus of a life well-lived. The room still smelled like him — Old Spice aftershave and the faint scent of smoke that never quite washed out of a firefighter's skin. Margaret was sitting on the edge of the bed, holding one of his uniform shirts like it might disappear if she let go.

When she spoke, her voice seemed to echo strangely in the half-empty space, bouncing off surfaces that had absorbed thirty-two years of shared conversations and now had only one voice left to fill them.

"I don't know where to start," she said, her voice barely above a whisper.

"We'll take it slow," I said, settling beside her. "One box at a time."

We worked in companionable silence for a while, sorting through the accumulated possessions of thirty-two years of marriage. Tax forms from the early 90s. Old warranty papers for appliances that had been replaced years ago. A shoebox full of takeout menus from restaurants that no longer existed. The mundane paperwork of a shared life that somehow felt more intimate than love letters.

Margaret kept getting distracted by memories, and each one felt like a small explosion in my chest.

"Oh, this old thing," she said, pulling out a faded Station 4 t-shirt with holes in the shoulders. "I can't believe I even remember this, but..." She paused, a small smile crossing her face. "Aaron used to — God, he was maybe three? — and Michael would come home just *destroyed* from a shift. Awake for twenty-four hours, sometimes forty-eight if they had mutual aid calls. And this little voice would go 'WRESTLE ME, DADDY!' and I'd think, 'Please, no, Aaron, Daddy needs to sit down,' but Michael..."

She trailed off, her fingers tracing the worn fabric.

"He'd just drop right to the floor," she continued, her voice thick with memory. "Right there in the hallway, still in his work boots, and they'd have these elaborate wrestling matches. Michael would make these ridiculous sound effects, let Aaron pin him for the count. 'OH NO, I'M DEFEATED BY THE MIGHTY AARON!' he'd yell. The neighbors probably thought we were insane."

Someone who would have made time, I thought, the realization hitting me like a sucker punch. *Someone who would have gotten on the floor, no matter how tired.*

"He never said he was too tired," Margaret said softly. "Not once. Even when I could see how exhausted he was."

I nodded, not trusting my voice, and reached for another box. Inside were photo albums mixed with old Christmas cards, insurance papers, and a collection of coffee mugs from vacation spots they'd visited over the years.

Margaret's face lit up as she opened the first photo album.

"Our Mediterranean cruise," she said, pointing to a picture of her and Cap on what looked like a ship's deck. "Twentieth anniversary. I'd always wanted to do something like that, and Michael planned the whole thing. Saved for two years." She laughed, but it came out watery. "I shouldn't be laughing about this, but he insisted on trying 'authentic Turkish street food' when we stopped in Kusadasi. Swore he had an iron stomach from all those years of firehouse cooking."

She turned the page, revealing a photo of Cap looking green around the gills, giving a weak thumbs up from what was clearly a ship's cabin.

"Twenty-four hours," Margaret said, shaking her head. "Poor man was a prisoner in our bathroom for an entire day. But you know what he was most upset about? That he'd 'ruined' my dream vacation. He kept apologizing, like getting food poisoning was somehow a personal failing. I had to convince him that taking care of him was exactly where I wanted to be."

That's what I threw away, the thought hit me like a physical blow. *Someone who would stay. Someone who would worry about disappointing me more than his own suffering.*

We moved on to another box — old kitchen gadgets, a broken watch he'd never gotten fixed, reading glasses from three different prescriptions. Margaret pulled out a small appointment book, and her eyes filled with tears.

"He never forgot," she said suddenly. "Our anniversary, the kids' birthdays, even stupid little things like the day we adopted our first dog. I didn't realize how special that was until I talked to other wives. Some of my friends' husbands couldn't remember their own anniversary without Facebook reminding them."

She flipped through the pages, showing me entries in Cap's careful handwriting. *Margaret flowers,* one read. *Aaron science fair. Izzy promotion exam.*

My name in his handwriting made something crack inside my chest. He'd been keeping track of my life the same way he'd kept track of his family's milestones.

I don't even know his birthday, I realized with a sick feeling. *What kind of person does that make me?*

"I keep thinking about all the ordinary moments," Margaret said, closing the appointment book and setting it aside with a stack of old utility bills. "The times he'd come home grumpy about some administrative bullshit, and I'd make him sit at the kitchen table while I cooked dinner, and he'd just... decompress. Tell me about his day. The silly fights we had about whose turn it was to take out the trash, or how he insisted on watching the Weather Channel every morning even though I told him his phone had a weather app."

She was crying now, quiet tears that she didn't bother to wipe away.

"I miss him telling me I was loading the dishwasher wrong. Isn't that stupid? I miss being annoyed at him for leaving his coffee mug on the bathroom counter every single morning for twenty-six years."

I miss him more than I miss the promotion, the thought hit me with stunning clarity. *I miss the man I pushed away more than anything.*

We worked for another hour, sorting through bank statements and old birthday cards, Christmas ornaments and expired coupons. The accumulated treasures and detritus of a marriage that had lasted through shift work and dangerous calls and the thousand small challenges that came with loving someone in a job that could take them away. With each story Margaret shared, I felt another piece of my carefully constructed armor crack.

This was what I'd wanted, deep down. Not the fairy tale version of love from movies, but the real thing — someone who showed up, who remembered what mattered, who chose you every single day, even when they were tired. Even when it was hard.

I'd had that. For a brief, shining moment, I'd had someone who cooked for me, who held me when I fell apart, who was willing to fight for me even when he didn't understand the rules of the war.

And I'd thrown it away because I was too afraid to be vulnerable.

"Oh, what's this?" Margaret said, pulling something from between the pages of an old fire manual. "It's addressed to you, honey."

She handed me a sealed envelope, my name written in Cap's careful script across the front. My hands started shaking before I even opened it.

"He must have written this for you and forgotten to give it to you," Margaret said. "You should take it home."

I stared at the envelope, feeling like I was holding a live grenade. "Are you sure?"

"Of course. He'd want you to have it."

The drive home passed in a blur. The envelope sat on my passenger seat like it was radioactive, and I found myself glancing at it every few seconds, as if it might disappear.

At a red light, I watched an elderly couple walking hand-in-hand on the sidewalk, the man adjusting his pace to match his wife's slower steps. In the grocery store parking lot, a young father was loading bags while his toddler "helped" by handing him items one at a time, both of them laughing at some private joke. Ordinary moments. The kind Cap and Margaret had shared for thirty-two years. The kind I'd convinced myself I didn't need.

Back in my apartment, I set it on my kitchen table and stared at it for a long time. The handwriting was shaky — he must have written it when he was already getting sick. My name looked different in his failing penmanship, more fragile somehow.

With trembling fingers, I tore open the envelope.

Izzy,

If you're reading this, then I'm gone, and Margaret found this where I hid it. I'm writing this on one of my good days, when the pain meds aren't making me too fuzzy to think straight. There are things I need to tell you while I still can.

My vision blurred immediately. I had to set the letter down and wipe my eyes before I could continue.

First, your father would be so proud of the woman you've become. Miguel always said you had more heart than anyone had a right to, and he was right. You fight for people who can't fight for themselves. You run toward danger when everyone else is running away. That's not just courage, kiddo — that's love in action.

"Kiddo," I whispered aloud, my voice breaking on the word. He'd called me that since I was a rookie, even when I'd grown into my lieutenant's bars.

But more than that, I'm proud of you for something your father never got to see. I see you with that nurse — Jimmy — and it makes my heart glad. For the first time since your father died, I see you letting someone in. I see you choosing love over fear. That takes more courage than running into any burning building, kiddo.

I had to stop reading. My hands were shaking so badly I couldn't hold the paper steady, and tears were falling fast enough to threaten the ink. This was so much worse than if he'd been disappointed in me. He'd been *proud* of me for letting Jimmy in, proud of me for being vulnerable, proud of me for choosing love.

And I'd destroyed it all.

I know you're scared. Lord knows this job will break your heart if you let it. But you can't love people from behind a wall, Izzy. You can't live a full life if you're too afraid to let people in. I've watched you with Jimmy, and I've never seen you happier. Don't let fear cost you that.

I was sobbing now, ugly, gut-wrenching sobs that seemed to come from somewhere deeper than my chest. The letter was getting wet from my tears, the ink starting to smudge, but I couldn't stop.

Your crew doesn't need a commander, Izzy. They need a leader. There's a difference. And that young man loves you — I can see it in the way he looks at you, the way he takes extra care when he's treating me because he knows what I mean to you. Don't throw that away because you're afraid of being vulnerable. Love isn't a weakness, kiddo. It's the only thing that makes any of this worthwhile.

Your father once told me that the strongest steel is forged in the hottest fire, but even the strongest steel has to cool down to be useful. You've been through the fire, Izzy. You've been tested and proven. Now let yourself cool down. Let yourself be human.

I know you think you have to be perfect, but perfection is just another word for fear. The people who love you don't need you to be perfect. They need you to be real.

Take care of yourself, kiddo. Take care of your crew. And for God's sake, hold onto that love you found. Life's too short to do anything else.

All my love, Cap

P.S. — Your father always said you were stubborn as a mule. He meant it as a compliment. But even mules know when to stop kicking.

The letter fell from my hands as I doubled over, the grief making me claw at the air, like it was a physical thing. I slid off my chair onto the kitchen floor, curling into myself, my knees pulled up to my chest. The sound that came out of me wasn't crying — it was something primal and raw, the kind of wailing that came from the deepest part of the soul.

I wasn't just crying for Cap anymore. I was crying for everything — for my father, for the promotion I'd lost, for the woman I used to be before I'd built these walls around my heart. But mostly, I was crying for Jimmy. For the way I'd looked at him that day in the parking lot, like he was a stranger who'd betrayed me instead of the man who'd loved me enough to fight for me. For the way his face had crumpled when I'd told him to stay away from me. For the way I'd thrown away the best thing that had ever happened to me because I was too afraid to let him in.

I lay there on my kitchen floor for what felt like hours, Cap's letter clutched against my chest, letting myself fall apart completely. The walls I'd built so carefully, the armor I'd wrapped around my heart — it all crumbled at once, leaving me raw and exposed and more vulnerable than I'd ever been.

But for the first time in weeks, I could breathe.

For the first time since Cap died, I felt like myself again.

And I knew what I had to do.

Two days later, I was sitting on my couch, Cap's letter spread out on my coffee table, reading it for the dozenth time. I'd called in sick to work — the first time I'd ever used a sick day for something that wasn't physical. But I needed time to think, to process everything that had broken loose inside me.

I'd picked up my phone to call Jimmy at least fifty times, but I couldn't make myself dial the number. What was I supposed to say? *Sorry I said you destroyed my career prospects and told you to stay away from me when all you did was love me?*

My phone had been buzzing all morning with texts from my crew, checking on me. Even they were worried about the ice queen taking a sick day.

> THOMPSON
>
> L.T., you okay? Need anything?
>
> MARTINEZ
>
> Feel better soon. Station's not the same without you.
>
> BENNY
>
> Rest up, kiddo. We'll hold down the fort.

Kiddo. Even Benny was using Cap's word for me now.

I was staring at Jimmy's contact information, trying to work up the courage to call, when my phone rang. For a wild moment, I thought it might be him, that maybe he'd felt the same pull I'd been feeling for days.

But it was my mother's name on the screen.

"Mija," Carmen said, her voice soft with sympathy. I could hear the maternal concern that had been missing from our relationship for years. "I'm so sorry, baby. I know how much he meant to you."

The kindness in her voice almost undid me all over again. "Thanks, Mom."

"How are you holding up?"

It was such a simple question, but it broke something loose inside me. "I'm not," I said, my voice cracking. "I'm really not okay."

"Oh, sweetheart. Do you want me to come up there? I could drive up today — "

"I don't know." I was crying again, which seemed to be my default state lately. "Everything's falling apart, Mom. My career, my personal life... I don't know what I'm doing anymore."

There was a pause, and when Carmen spoke again, her voice carried a gentle but unmistakable note of satisfaction. "Maybe this is a sign, mija."

The words hit me like cold water. "What?"

"I mean, maybe this is the universe telling you it's time to come home. Like we talked about, you could go back to school, get your nursing degree. David's connections at Metro General are still there — "

"Mom." My voice was flat.

"I'm just saying, you've proven yourself. You've shown everyone how strong you are. But maybe it's time to choose something safer. Something that won't put you through this kind of pain."

The disappointment was crushing. Even my own mother couldn't see me as anything but a woman who needed to be rescued from her own choices.

"You think I should quit," I said.

"I think you should consider your options. You're still young, mija. You could have a family, a normal life — "

"With someone like David, you mean. Someone safe."

"There's nothing wrong with safe, Izzy. Look what this job has cost you already. Your father, Captain O'Sullivan, and now this whole mess with that nurse... How much more can you take?"

I closed my eyes, feeling more alone than I ever had in my life. "I have to go, Mom."

"Izzy, wait — "

I hung up and threw my phone across the room, watching it skitter across the hardwood floor. Even my own mother thought I should give up, should choose security over passion, should settle for a smaller life because the big one was too scary.

I picked up Cap's letter again, my vision blurring with fresh tears.

Love isn't a weakness, kiddo. It's the only thing that makes any of this worthwhile.

I was still sitting there, holding the letter and feeling more isolated than I'd ever felt in my life, when my phone rang again. I'd retrieved it from where it had slid under my coffee table, expecting another call from my mother.

But it wasn't Carmen's name on the screen.

It was Jimmy's.

My heart stopped. For a moment, I just stared at the phone, afraid that if I moved, the call would disappear like a mirage.

Then, with shaking hands, I answered.

"Jimmy?"

"Izzy." His voice was rough, uncertain. "I know I don't deserve it, but... can we talk?"

I looked down at Cap's letter, at his final words about not letting pride cost me the best thing that had ever happened to me.

"Where?" I said.

chapter
thirty-four

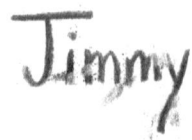

THE DAILY GRIND looked exactly the same as it had all those weeks ago when we'd sat at this corner table. Same chipped mugs, same indie music playing too loud, same barista with the elaborate sleeve tattoos who remembered everyone's order except mine.

But everything else was different. I was different. Broken down and rebuilt by bourbon and brutal honesty in a dive bar that smelled like decades of bad decisions. Hollow from weeks of mechanical competence that fooled everyone except the people who actually mattered.

I checked my phone for the dozenth time. 2:47 p.m. She was seventeen minutes late, and I was starting to wonder if she'd changed her mind. If the woman I'd heard on the phone — careful, guarded, but still willing to meet — had reconsidered in the harsh light of day.

The bell above the door chimed, and I looked up to see her.

Izzy stood in the doorway for a moment, scanning the café until her eyes found mine. She looked... tired. Beautiful, always beautiful, but worn down in a way that made my chest ache. Her dark hair was pulled back in its usual severe ponytail, and she was wearing jeans and a simple gray sweater that somehow made her look smaller than I remembered.

But it was her eyes that broke my heart. Those fierce, intelligent eyes that had first caught my attention were carefully neutral, guarded in a way they'd never been even when we were strangers.

She walked over to my table with the measured stride of someone approaching a crime scene, and I stood up too quickly, nearly knocking over my coffee mug.

"Izzy." Her name came out rougher than I'd intended.

"Jimmy." She nodded formally, like we were colleagues meeting to discuss a patient. "Thank you for... for meeting me."

For meeting you? I thought. *You're thanking me for the privilege of letting me grovel?*

"Of course," I said instead. "Can I... do you want coffee? I can — "

"I'll get it." She was already moving toward the counter, and I watched her order — medium dark roast, no cream, no sugar. The same order she'd gotten that first time, when I'd teased her about drinking coffee that could strip paint.

When she came back, we sat across from each other like awkward strangers. The silence stretched between us, heavy with everything we weren't saying.

"How's work?" I asked finally, because it seemed safer than any of the things I actually wanted to say.

"Fine." Her voice was clipped, professional. "Busy. You?"

"Same. Yeah, it's been..." I trailed off, realizing how absurd this was. We were sitting here making small talk like we hadn't torn each other's lives apart, like we were distant acquaintances catching up instead of two people who'd once been so in love it hurt to breathe.

"Izzy," I said, abandoning the pretense. "I need to — "

"Jimmy, I — "

We spoke at the same time, then both stopped. For just a moment, I saw a flicker of the old Izzy — the one who would have laughed at the awkwardness, who would have said something sarcastic about our timing.

"You first," she said quietly.

I took a deep breath, hearing Kellen's voice in my head: *Fix what's broken.*

"I need to apologize," I said. "For everything. But mostly for the letter."

Her face went very still.

"I'm sorry my letter destroyed your promotion. I'm sorry they used it as evidence that you were 'too emotional' to handle command." The words tasted like ash in my mouth. "I was arrogant and naive. I thought

I was helping, but I was just an outsider who didn't understand your world. I am so, so sorry I took your fight away from you."

Izzy's carefully controlled expression cracked slightly. "You wrote three pages about how amazing I was."

"And handed them exactly what they needed to destroy you." I leaned forward, desperate for her to understand. "I should have asked you. I should have listened when you explained how things worked in your department. Instead, I charged in like some white knight and proved everything they'd been saying about you needing a man to fight your battles."

She was quiet for a long moment, staring into her coffee cup. When she finally looked up, her eyes were bright with unshed tears.

"Do you know what the worst part was?" she asked, her voice barely above a whisper. "It wasn't losing the promotion. It wasn't watching Santoro get everything I'd worked for. It was knowing that you — the person who was supposed to understand me better than anyone — had fundamentally misunderstood who I was."

Her words loomed over me ominously, panic clawing at my chest. "Izzy — "

"You saw me as someone who needed protecting instead of someone who was already protecting herself. You saw a victim instead of a fighter." She wiped her eyes with the back of her hand, the gesture angry and vulnerable at the same time. "And maybe... maybe I let you. Maybe I was so tired of fighting alone that I forgot how to let someone stand beside me instead of in front of me."

I felt something crack open in my chest. "I'm sorry for pulling away, too. After the letter, after everything went wrong... I didn't know how to face you. I was drowning in my own failure, and I was a coward."

"What failure?" she asked, confusion flickering across her face.

This was it. The thing I'd never told her, the wound that had been festering for months.

"The patient I told you about," I said slowly. "The domestic violence case. The one that came in beaten up, and I... I gave her all the resources, set up safety planning, convinced her that people could help her."

Izzy's expression softened slightly, but I pressed on.

"She was murdered. Beaten to death by the same man who'd stood in my ER and threatened to put bullets in anyone who tried to help her." My voice cracked. "She trusted me, Izzy. She looked at me with this desperate hope when I promised her safety, and I failed her completely."

"Jimmy," she said softly.

"When you told me you wanted kids, all I could see was her face. All I could think was, 'How can I promise to protect a child when I couldn't even keep one woman safe?' How could I give you a child, Izzy, when I still wake up wondering if I even deserve to be someone's father?"

The silence that followed was profound. I watched emotions flicker across her face — surprise, understanding, something that might have been pain.

"You pulled away because you were trying to protect me," she said finally. "From your own fears."

"And you pulled away because you were trying to protect yourself from mine." I managed a bitter laugh. "God, we're idiots."

"Speak for yourself," she said, but there was the faintest hint of a smile in her voice. "I'm a professionally trained idiot."

Despite everything, I felt my lips twitch. "Is that better or worse than a regular idiot?"

"Worse. We have credentials."

The moment of levity felt like sunlight breaking through storm clouds. But then her expression grew serious again.

"Jimmy, you can't save everyone. No one can. Not me, not you, not anyone in our line of work." She reached across the table, her fingers barely brushing mine. "But that doesn't mean we stop trying. It doesn't mean we're not worthy of love or family or happiness."

"I know that now," I said. "Intellectually, anyway. I'm working on believing it."

"And I know that I can't keep pushing people away every time I'm scared of getting hurt." Her fingers pressed against mine, the contact warm and familiar. "I became someone I didn't recognize, Jimmy. I turned into this cold, untouchable thing because I thought it would keep me safe. But it just made me alone."

"You're not alone," I said fiercely. "You're never alone. Not if I have anything to say about it."

She was crying now, silent tears streaming down her face. "I missed you so much. Every day. Every call, every quiet moment, every time something funny happened and I wanted to text you about it. I missed *us*."

"I missed us, too." I turned my hand palm up, letting her fingers interlace with mine. "I missed your terrible movie choices and the way you steal the covers and how you make everything taste better just by being there while I cook."

"Jimmy," she said, her voice thick with tears and something else. Something that sounded like hope. "I don't want to do this here. I don't want to fall apart in public."

I understood immediately. This conversation needed privacy, needed space for the kind of vulnerability that couldn't happen over coffee in a crowded café.

"Your place or mine?" I asked.

"Mine," she said without hesitation. "I want... I need you to choose to come home with me. Not because it's convenient, but because you want to."

I stood up, leaving tip money on the table for both our coffees. "Lead the way."

chapter
thirty-five

THE DRIVE to my apartment felt like the longest eight minutes of my life. In my rearview mirror, I could see Jimmy following in his Honda, and something about that simple act — him choosing to follow me home — made my chest tight with emotions I'd been suppressing for weeks.

My hands were trembling slightly on the steering wheel. Cap's letter sat heavy in my jacket pocket, a tangible weight against my ribs. The conversation at the coffee shop had cracked something open inside me, something I'd spent weeks trying to keep locked away. Jimmy's raw honesty about Lisa Harris, about his fears of not being worthy of fatherhood — it had shattered the last of my carefully constructed walls.

He was trying to protect me by leaving, I thought, the realization still stunning in its clarity. *And I was trying to protect myself by pushing him away.*

We'd both been so busy trying to save each other from our own perceived failures that we'd nearly destroyed the one thing worth saving.

I pulled into my parking space and sat there for a moment, watching Jimmy park beside me. Through his windshield, I could see his profile, the familiar line of his jaw, the way he ran his hand through his hair when he was nervous. God, I'd missed him. I'd missed the simple pleasure of knowing someone was there, of having someone to come home to, someone who understood the weight of carrying other people's lives in your hands.

He was waiting by my truck when I climbed out, his green eyes searching my face with the same careful attention he brought to his patients.

"You okay?" he asked softly.

I nodded, not trusting my voice. We walked to my building in silence, the familiar ritual of unlocking doors and climbing stairs feeling surreal with him beside me again. How many times had we done this before? How many evenings had ended with his gentle presence filling my carefully controlled space?

Inside my apartment, I felt the full weight of what I was about to do. This wasn't just letting him back into my bed — it was letting him back into my life, my heart, my carefully guarded vulnerabilities. I was choosing to tear down every wall I'd built since Cap died, every barrier I'd erected to protect myself from the pain of loving someone and losing them.

"There's something I need to show you," I said, my voice steadier than I felt. I walked to my kitchen table where Cap's letter had been sitting for days, waiting for this moment.

I handed Jimmy the envelope, watching his confusion turn to understanding as he read Cap's shaky handwriting. The letter had broken me open when I'd first read it, but seeing Jimmy's face as he absorbed Cap's words — that was almost worse. I watched his throat work as he swallowed hard, saw the way his eyes brightened with unshed tears.

When he finished, he looked up at me with something that looked like wonder.

"He believed in us," he said, his voice thick with emotion.

"He did. Even when I didn't." I took the letter back, folding it with the reverence it deserved. "He said you loved me, that he could see it in the way you looked at me. He was right, wasn't he?"

"Yes," Jimmy said without hesitation, the word carrying the weight of weeks of separation, of mistakes and misunderstandings and the desperate hope that we could find our way back to each other. "God, yes. I love you, Izzy. I never stopped, not for a single day."

The words hit me like a physical force, and suddenly I was crying again — not the controlled tears I'd allowed myself over the past weeks, but the raw, honest grief of someone who'd convinced herself she'd lost everything that mattered.

"I love you too," I whispered, the admission feeling like stepping off a cliff. "I tried to stop, tried to make myself not care, but I couldn't. You're in my bones, Jimmy. You're part of me."

We stood there in my living room, looking at each other across the space that had once felt like home and now felt like a battleground we'd somehow survived. The weight of everything we'd said, everything we'd been through, hung between us like smoke from a structure fire — invisible but toxic, needing to be cleared before we could breathe again.

"So what now?" Jimmy asked, and I could hear the vulnerability in his voice, the fear that we might have talked ourselves into forgiveness but not back into love.

I smiled then — the first genuine smile I'd managed in weeks. Something was shifting inside me, the ice queen I'd become finally melting away to reveal the woman underneath. The woman who'd fallen in love with a gentle nurse who made tres leches cake and held people when they were breaking apart.

"Now you come here and hold me while I figure out how to be brave enough to let you stay," I said.

He crossed my living room in three quick strides, and then his arms were around me, solid and warm and achingly familiar. I buried my face in his neck, breathing in the scent of him — soap and laundry detergent and something indefinably Jimmy that I'd been craving for weeks without admitting it.

"I'm not going anywhere," he murmured against my hair, his voice rough with emotion. "Not unless you tell me to."

"Don't you dare," I said fiercely, my arms tightening around his waist. "Don't you dare leave me again."

"Never," he promised, and I felt the truth of it in the way he held me, like I was something precious he'd thought he'd lost forever. "Not ever again."

We stood there for a long time, just holding each other, just breathing the same air. I felt something inside me unclenching, the constant tension I'd been carrying since Cap died finally beginning to ease. This was what I'd missed — not just the physical comfort, but the simple peace of being held by someone who understood the weight I carried, who didn't need me to be perfect or strong or anything other than myself.

When I finally pulled back to look at him, I saw my own relief reflected in his green eyes. But underneath it was something else — desire, yes, but also a kind of desperate hunger that had nothing to do with sex and everything to do with connection. We'd been starving for each other, and now that we were here, now that we'd said the words that needed saying, the need was overwhelming.

"Take me to bed, Jimmy," I said, my voice steady despite the way my heart was racing. "I want to remember what it feels like to be yours."

His breath caught, and I saw the exact moment when the careful distance we'd been maintaining finally collapsed. His hands came up to frame my face, his thumbs brushing away the tears I hadn't realized were still falling.

"Are you sure?" he asked, his voice soft but intense. "Because once we cross this line, I don't think I can go back to pretending I don't need you."

"I don't want you to pretend," I said, leaning into his touch. "I'm tired of pretending. I'm tired of being careful and controlled and afraid of feeling too much. I want to feel everything, Jimmy. I want to feel alive again."

He studied my face for a moment longer, searching for any sign of hesitation. What he saw there must have satisfied him, because he leaned down and kissed me — soft at first, tentative, like he was afraid I might disappear if he moved too fast.

But I was done with careful. I was done with tentative. I kissed him back with six weeks of suppressed longing, my hands fisting in his shirt to pull him closer. He made a sound low in his throat, part surprise and part relief, and then his arms were around me, lifting me slightly as he deepened the kiss.

"Bedroom," I breathed against his lips, and he nodded, his forehead resting against mine.

"Are you sure — "

"Jimmy," I interrupted, looking directly into his eyes. "I've never been more sure of anything in my life."

He swept me up then, literally lifting me off my feet, and I wrapped my legs around his waist as he carried me toward my bedroom. I felt powerful and cherished at the same time, strong enough to choose this vulnerability, brave enough to trust him with the parts of me I'd kept hidden for so long.

In my bedroom, he set me down gently beside the bed, his hands settling on my waist with a reverence that made my breath catch. The afternoon light filtered through my curtains, painting everything in gold, making this moment feel suspended outside of time.

"I've missed you," he said, his voice rough with emotion. "God, Izzy, I've missed you so much."

"Show me," I whispered, reaching for the hem of his shirt. "Show me how much."

What followed was unlike anything we'd shared before. In the past, our lovemaking had been passionate but careful, two people learning each other's bodies and boundaries. This was different. This was reunion and reconciliation and the desperate need to prove to ourselves that we were real, that this was real, that we hadn't lost everything that mattered.

Jimmy's hands shook slightly as he helped me out of my sweater, his fingers tracing the lines of my shoulders like he was memorizing them all over again. When I reached for his shirt, pulling it over his head and running my hands over the familiar planes of his chest, he closed his eyes and made a sound that was part groan, part prayer.

We undressed each other slowly, carefully, like we were unwrapping something precious. When Jimmy's hands found the clasp of my bra, his eyes met mine, asking permission even though we'd been here before. I nodded, and when the fabric fell away, he looked at me like I was a miracle he couldn't quite believe in.

"Beautiful," he breathed, his hands coming up to cup my breasts, his thumbs brushing over my nipples with a touch so gentle it made me arch into him. "So beautiful."

I reached for his belt, my fingers working the leather with more urgency than finesse. When he was finally naked, when we were both standing there in the golden afternoon light with nothing between us but air and possibility, I felt something shift inside me. This wasn't just about sex, though desire was pooling low in my belly like liquid heat. This was about choosing to be vulnerable, choosing to trust, choosing love over fear.

"Come here," I said, pulling him down onto the bed with me.

Jimmy settled over me, his weight warm and solid and achingly familiar. For a moment, we just looked at each other, drinking in the reality of being here, together, whole.

"I love you," he said, his voice thick with emotion. "I love your strength, your courage, the way you protect everyone around you. I love that you're brave enough to save people for a living, and I love that you're brave enough to let me love you."

The words broke something open inside me, something that had been locked away since the day I'd told him to stay away from me. I pulled his face down to mine, kissing him with everything I had — all the love I'd tried to suppress, all the need I'd tried to deny, all the hope I'd been afraid to feel.

"I love you too," I whispered against his lips. "I love how gentle you are, how you see people when they're broken and help put them back together. I love that you're brave enough to care about strangers, and I love that you're brave enough to fight for us."

What followed wasn't lovemaking.

It was reclamation.

"I thought I'd lost this," he murmured, his palms spanning my hips like he needed to anchor himself. "I thought I'd lost you."

"You didn't," I said, pressing my mouth to the hollow of his throat. "But I almost lost myself not having you."

The way he kissed me then — open, hungry, barely controlled — set every nerve ending on fire. His mouth moved with purpose, rediscovering me with aching need, and I responded in kind. We undressed with reverence and urgency all at once, tugging and pausing, kissing each new stretch of revealed skin like it mattered. Because it did.

I arched into his touch when he cupped my breasts, the pads of his thumbs teasing across sensitive peaks until I whimpered. My hands roamed over the planes of his back, pulling him closer, needing to feel the weight and heat and reality of him. By the time he slipped my panties down and kissed the inside of my thigh, my whole body felt like a live wire.

"Lie back," he whispered, voice ragged, "please, baby — I need to look at you."

I obeyed, limbs shaking as I settled onto the bed, and watched him stand at the edge of it like he wasn't sure whether to worship or devour me.

"Come here," I said again, soft but commanding.

He climbed over me slowly, fitting our bodies together with a precision that felt like coming home. And when he pushed inside me — deep, careful, reverent — everything else disappeared. I let out a broken sound, clutching at his shoulders, and he stilled.

"Okay?" he whispered, forehead pressed to mine.

"Perfect," I breathed. "You're perfect."

We moved together in slow, hypnotic rhythm, our hands roaming, our mouths finding each other over and over again. There was no rush. Just rediscovery. Just awe. Just Jimmy murmuring praise against my skin like a litany: *So beautiful. So strong. So fucking brave.*

Rain had started pattering against the windows, creating a gentle rhythm that matched our breathing. "I missed this," I gasped as he found that spot inside me that made stars explode behind my eyelids. "I missed you touching me like this."

"Like what?" he asked, his breath hot against my ear.

"Like I matter," I said, the words coming out more honest than I'd intended. "Like I'm worth fighting for."

Jimmy stilled for a moment, pulling back to look at me with something that might have been anguish.

"Izzy," he said, his voice rough. "You are worth fighting for. You're worth everything. Don't ever doubt that."

When his hand slipped between us to circle my clit with steady pressure, my voice cracked on his name. "Jimmy — God — I'm — "

"Let go," he said, voice thick with emotion. "I've got you, Izzy. I've always had you."

And I did. I let go of the control I'd been clinging to for weeks, let go of the fear that loving him would cost me everything I'd worked for, let go of the idea that I had to be perfect to be worthy of love. The orgasm that crashed over me was more than physical — it was emotional, spiritual, a complete surrender to the man above me and the love between us.

Jimmy followed me over the edge with a broken cry of my name, his body shuddering against mine as he buried his face in my neck. We clung to each other as the aftershocks faded, both of us breathing hard, both of us trying to process what had just happened.

We lay tangled in silence for a long time, just breathing, just holding each other. But something restless thrummed beneath our skin.

We weren't done. Not nearly.

As our breathing slowed, as the golden light outside began to fade toward evening, Jimmy began pressing soft kisses to my collarbone, my throat, the sensitive spot behind my ear that made me shiver. He kissed the curve of my shoulder, then the underside of my breast, then lower, letting his mouth trace a path that sent shivers racing through me.

"Baby?" he murmured.

"Mmm?" I murmured in return.

"Baby?" he asked again, his voice suddenly taking on a playful note I hadn't heard in weeks.

He sang softly, and began humming a familiar tune, swaying his hips against mine in a way that made me laugh despite myself.

"Are you seriously serenading me with Marvin Gaye right now?" I asked, but I was grinning, feeling lighter than I had in months.

"Maybe," he said. "Is it working?"

"Jimmy Dalton," I said, mock-seriously, "you are absolutely ridiculous."

"Ridiculously in love with you," he countered, punctuating his words with a roll of his hips that made me gasp.

This time, there was nothing careful or tentative about what happened between us. This was celebration, pure and simple — a joyous reclaiming of our bodies, our connection, our future. Jimmy moved above me with a rhythm that was part dance, part worship, making me laugh and moan in equal measure.

What followed was athletic, urgent, a little bit ridiculous, and absolutely perfect. We moved together with the kind of abandon that comes from knowing you're safe, knowing you're loved, knowing that the person above you would do anything to make you feel cherished.

It wasn't careful this time. It wasn't tender.

It was *hungry*.

Afterward, we lay tangled together in my rumpled sheets, both of us breathing hard, both of us grinning like idiots.

"So," I said, tracing lazy patterns on his chest, "that happened."

"That definitely happened," he agreed, pressing a kiss to the top of my head. "Twice."

"I was keeping track. And now, I need water," I murmured against Jimmy's shoulder. "And you probably do, too."

"I'll get it," he said, but I was already sliding out of bed, suddenly aware of my own body in a way I hadn't been in weeks. I felt powerful, feminine, alive.

In the kitchen, I filled two glasses from the tap, the ordinary act feeling surreal after everything that had happened. When I turned around, Jimmy was there, wearing nothing at all, watching me with an expression of quiet wonder.

"What?" I asked, suddenly self-conscious.

"You," he said simply. "Here. Real." He stepped closer, taking one of the glasses. "I keep thinking I'm going to wake up and this will all have been a dream."

"It's real," I said, touching his face. "We're real."

We drank our water standing there in my kitchen, and somehow that simple act — hydrating together in comfortable nakedness — felt as intimate as anything we'd done in the bedroom.

We went back to bed and dozed for a while, wrapped around each other like we were afraid the other might disappear. When I woke up, the golden afternoon light had faded to deep purple twilight, and the rain had stopped. Jimmy was still there, still solid and warm beside me, his arm a comfortable weight across my waist. The digital clock on my nightstand indicated we'd been lost in each other for hours.

I reached over to my nightstand and carefully placed Cap's letter in the drawer. Not hiding it, not throwing it away, but keeping it close while moving forward. He would always be part of me, but I was ready to write the next chapter of my story.

The next chapter that included Jimmy.

"Hey," Jimmy said softly, his voice rough with sleep. "You okay?"

I turned in his arms, studying his face in the dim light. He looked peaceful, content, younger somehow than he had in weeks. This was what happiness looked like, I realized. Not the absence of problems, but the presence of someone who chose to face them with you.

"We're going to be okay, aren't we?" I asked, the question coming out more vulnerable than I'd intended.

Jimmy's arms tightened around me, and I felt him press a soft kiss to my forehead.

"Yeah," he said, his voice carrying absolute certainty. "We are."

I settled deeper into his embrace, feeling safer than I had in months. But there was something restless in the way his fingers traced patterns on my shoulder, like he was working up to saying something.

"What?" I asked, recognizing the signs.

He was quiet for a moment, then: "I keep thinking about what you said. About wanting kids."

My heart did a little flutter. "Yeah?"

"I want that with you," he said simply. "I want all of it. The chaos, the sleepless nights, the tiny firefighter costumes for Halloween."

I laughed, turning in his arms to see his face. "Tiny firefighter costumes?"

"Oh, absolutely. And I want to teach them to make bread and read them bedtime stories about brave princesses who save dragons instead of the other way around." His voice grew softer, more serious. "I want to hear them call you Mama."

The words hit me right in the chest, warm and perfect and everything I'd been afraid to hope for.

"How many kids are we talking about here?" I asked, trying to keep my voice light even though my heart was doing somersaults.

"However many you want," he said immediately. "One, five, somewhere in between. I'll be there for all of it." His hand found mine in the dim light. "I'll be the guy cheering you on when you're Chief someday, staying home with the kids if that's what it takes. Hell, I'll pack their lunches and make TikToks about what a smoke show their mom is in a turnout coat."

I burst out laughing, partly from the absurdity of the image and partly from pure joy. "You did not just say you'd make TikToks about me."

"Oh, I absolutely did."

"You know what I want?" I said, my fingers tracing patterns on his chest. "I want Sunday mornings where we don't have to get up for calls or shifts. I want to watch you teach our kids to make pancakes while I'm still in my pajamas, complaining about how loud you all are. I want family dinners where they tell us about their days and we pretend to be shocked by their adventures." I paused, my voice growing softer. "I want to be the kind of parents who are still disgustingly in love after twenty years, the kind our kids roll their eyes at but secretly hope to find for themselves."

"Sounds good, as long as I get to be the embarrassing dad who brags about his wife to anyone who'll listen. 'That's my wife running into that burning building. Yeah, she's a badass. Yeah, I'm lucky.'"

"You're ridiculous," I said, but I was grinning so hard my cheeks hurt.

"Ridiculously in love with you," he said, echoing our earlier conversation. "And speaking of practicing for our future..." His hand drifted lower, fingers tracing lazy circles on my hip. "I heard birth control is 99% effective, but those sound like odds I'm willing to challenge."

"Jimmy Dalton," I said, trying to sound scandalized but failing completely. "Are you suggesting we try to beat the statistics?"

"I'm suggesting we keep practicing," he said innocently. "For science. You know, when we're ready."

"Soon, loverboy," I said, leaning down to kiss him softly. "But we've got some things to figure out first. Like whether you can actually handle being married to a firefighter."

"Try me," he said, his voice taking on that confident tone that made my toes curl. "I've got excellent stamina for long-term projects."

"Is that your professional medical opinion?"

"That's my personal guarantee." He rolled us over so he was looking down at me, his green eyes warm in the streetlight filtering through my curtains. "I want everything with you, Izzy. The good calls and the bad ones, the boring Tuesday nights and the emergency room visits. All of it."

"Even when I come home grumpy because C-shift left the station a disaster and my crew's complaining about the hose loads again?"

"Especially then. I'll make you dinner and let you vent about incompetent colleagues while I plot ways to anonymously send them proper training materials."

I reached up to cup his face, feeling the slight roughness of stubble under my palms. "I love you so much it scares me sometimes."

"Good," he said, pressing a kiss to my palm. "Love should be a little scary. It means it matters."

"It matters," I agreed. "You matter. This matters."

"Then we'll take care of it," he said simply. "We'll take care of each other."

"Promise?"

"Promise." He settled back down beside me, pulling me close again. "Now get some sleep, future Fire Chief. You've got a department to revolutionize and a boyfriend to wear out."

"Is that a challenge?"

"That's a promise," he said, and I could hear the smile in his voice. "We've got all the time in the world to practice."

EPILOGUE: IZZY

six months later

THE LATE AFTERNOON sun cast long shadows across the apparatus bay at Station 2, the light catching on the polished chrome of Engine 18. It was a perfect autumn day, the kind that felt full of promise. I leaned against the front of the truck, a comfortable warmth settled deep in my chest, and watched my crew.

Thompson and Martinez were locked in a merciless game of cornhole on the apron, their insults escalating with each errant toss. Benny was in his usual spot in the recliner, pretending to read *Fire Chief* magazine but actually dozing. It was a scene of perfect, mundane normalcy, and six months ago, I would have given anything for it.

The past few months had been a study in rebuilding. After the disastrous promotion cycle and the raw grief of losing Cap, I had thrown myself into being the kind of leader he had always believed I could be. The cold, impenetrable armor was gone, replaced by a strength that was quieter, more confident. I still pushed my crew to be their best, but the teaching moments had returned. The easy banter was back. I was still their lieutenant, but I was one of them again.

It turned out that being the kind of leader people chose to follow was infinitely more satisfying than any rank the department could have given me.

I'd heard through the grapevine that Station 12's response times had been slipping. Nothing catastrophic ... just consistently slower than they should be. Martinez had mentioned that his buddy on C-shift said Santoro was "still figuring out the administrative side." Last week, Thompson had casually dropped that Evans had to smooth something over with the mayor's office. "Protocol issue at 12," he'd said with a shrug.

I didn't ask for details. Didn't need them.

Santoro was exactly what I'd always known he was: a politician who'd gotten promoted beyond his competence. The system would protect him, cover for him, make excuses. That was how it worked. Some days, that still made me angry. Most days, I just didn't care anymore.

I had my crew. I had my future. I had something real to build instead of a rank to chase.

My phone buzzed with a text.

JIMMY

On my way. Don't let Thompson eat all the burgers before I get there.

I smiled, typing back.

No promises. He's in a mood. Just lost ten bucks to Martinez.

JIMMY

Savage. See you in five. I love you.

I love you, too.

The words felt as natural as breathing now. After our reconciliation, after we had painstakingly pieced our relationship back together, we had found a new rhythm. Jimmy had made a huge change, switching to the chaotic 3 p.m. to 11 p.m. midshift in the ER. It was a brutal schedule — five days a week, right in the thick of the hospital's busiest hours. But the ER scheduler, grateful for his willingness to take on the difficult shift, had given him a set schedule where his days off now perfectly aligned with my "off" days. It was a quiet, profound sacrifice on his part, a daily testament to his commitment. It meant we had real time together, time to build a life.

The side door to the bay opened, and Jack and Sophia walked in, Jack carrying a cooler.

"Reinforcements have arrived," Jack announced, his Kiwi accent echoing in the cavernous space.

"Just in time," I said. "Thompson was about to start grilling the hot dogs from last week."

Sophia laughed, giving me a hug. "Never change, B-shift. Never change."

Our little family had grown, the lines between the station and the hospital blurring into a comfortable, easy community. I saw Jack and Sophia almost as much as I saw my own crew.

Then the door opened again. And my smile faltered in pure, unadulterated shock.

Kellen, the stoic, burnt-out charge nurse from Jimmy's night shift, was standing there, looking deeply uncomfortable but undeniably present. He was holding what looked like a store-bought potato salad.

My brain stalled. Kellen? Here? At a firehouse BBQ? It didn't compute.

"Kellen," Sophia said, her voice warm and welcoming as she went to greet him. "I'm so glad you could make it."

He just gave a curt nod, his eyes scanning the bay like a man assessing a disaster scene. What in the world was he doing here?

My eyes darted around the station. My whole crew was here. Jack and Sophia. Now Kellen. Something was happening. This wasn't just a BBQ.

But before I could fully process why, something small and white and fluffy came bounding across the apparatus bay floor, trailing what looked like a red ribbon.

A puppy. A small white and tan cocker spaniel puppy with enormous brown eyes and ears that were too big for its head. It was wearing a tiny red collar with something attached to it, and it was headed straight for me with the kind of unbridled enthusiasm that only puppies could manage.

"Oh my God!" I breathed, automatically dropping to my knees as the little furball launched itself into my arms. "Whose dog is this? What is — "

And that's when I saw Jimmy.

He was emerging from behind Truck 12, looking nervous and excited and absolutely terrified all at the same time. He was wearing his good jeans and the blue button-down I'd bought him for his birthday, and he was carrying a small velvet box in his hands.

Time slowed down like it does in those movies where the hero suddenly realizes the guy walking toward them is an assassin, except instead of mortal danger, my brain was processing something infinitely more earth-shattering.

The puppy. The entire crew from both stations. Sophia and Kellen from his work. Jimmy in his good clothes with a ... ring box.

"Oh my God," I said again, this time with a completely different inflection. "OH MY GOD."

Jimmy was walking toward me now, and I could see the exact moment when his nervousness transformed into that quiet confidence I'd fallen in love with. The puppy in my arms was wiggling with excitement, and I could feel something attached to its collar — a small tag that I was too stunned to read.

"Hi, beautiful," Jimmy said, stopping a few feet away from where I was still kneeling on the apparatus bay floor with a puppy in my lap. "How was your shift?"

"Jimmy," I managed, my voice coming out as barely a whisper. "What is... who is... what's happening?"

"Well," he said, his mouth quirking up in that smile that still made my knees weak, "it seems we have a dog now." He gestured to the puppy, who had apparently decided that my turnout coat was the most fascinating thing in the world and was trying to chew on one of the reflective stripes. "His name is Sunny."

I looked down at the tag attached to his collar. In neat script, it read:

Sunny Delgado-Dalton

"*Jimmy,*" I said again, my heart hammering against my ribs.

"And I figure," he continued, his voice steady despite the fact that his hands were trembling slightly, "if we have a dog together, we should probably make it official."

That's when he dropped to one knee.

The apparatus bay went completely silent except for the sound of Sunny's tiny paws scrambling for purchase on my turnout coat and my own ragged breathing. In my peripheral vision, I could see our entire combined family — firefighters and paramedics and nurses, the people who understood the weight of what we did every day — watching with barely contained excitement.

"Isabela Delgado," Jimmy said, opening the velvet box to reveal a ring that caught the light streaming through the bay doors. It was perfect — simple, elegant, exactly what I would have chosen if I'd been brave enough to dream this big. "You are the strongest, bravest, most incredible woman I've ever known. You run into burning buildings to save people you've never met. You lead with your heart and your head in equal measure. You make me want to be better than I am, and somehow you love me even when I fall short."

Tears were streaming down my face now, and I couldn't have spoken if my life depended on it.

"I want to spend the rest of my life supporting your dreams, celebrating your victories, and holding you through the hard calls."

I let out a shaky breath, tears streaming down my face now.

"I want to pack our kids' lunches and embarrass them at school events by bragging about their mom, the fire chief. I want to grow old with you and argue about proper hose loads and whose turn it is to walk Sunny."

A laugh escaped me through the tears — only Jimmy would include hose load arguments in a proposal.

He paused, taking a shaky breath, and I saw his eyes flick briefly to the crowd of people watching us. Thompson was grinning like an idiot, Martinez looked like he might cry, and Sophia had her hands pressed to her mouth like she was trying to contain her excitement.

"Will you marry me?" Jimmy asked, his voice soft but carrying clearly through the apparatus bay.

I looked down at Sunny, who had apparently decided that this was the perfect moment for a nap and had curled up in my lap like he'd always belonged there. I looked at Jimmy, kneeling on the concrete floor of Station 2 in his good clothes, holding a ring that represented everything I'd been afraid to want. I looked at our combined families — blood and chosen, fire and medical, all the people who had supported us through the worst of times and were here to celebrate the best.

"Yes," I whispered, and then louder, "Yes, you ridiculous man. Yes."

The apparatus bay erupted. Thompson let out a whoop that probably violated several noise ordinances. Martinez started clapping so enthusiastically that he nearly fell over. Jack was grinning and taking pictures, and Sophia was definitely crying now.

Jimmy slipped the ring onto my finger with hands that were steady despite the chaos around us, and then he was kissing me while I held a sleeping puppy and our entire found family cheered in the background.

"I love you," he said against my lips.

"I love you, too," I replied. "But we're going to have to have a serious conversation about your planning skills. A puppy and a proposal on the same day? That's a lot of life changes at once."

"Says the woman who wants five kids," he pointed out, standing up and pulling me with him, careful not to disturb Sunny.

"Fair point." I looked down at our dog — *our dog*, I was still getting used to that — and felt something settle into place in my chest. "Sunny Delgado-Dalton?"

"I figured we should practice hyphenating," he said with a grin. "For when you're Fire Chief Delgado-Dalton."

"And you'll be Mr. Delgado-Dalton?"

"I'll be whatever you want me to be, as long as I get to be yours."

Thompson appeared at my elbow, his eyes suspiciously bright. "So, L.T.," he said in his usual gravelly voice, "I guess this means we're getting a new station cook?"

"Don't get ahead of yourself, Thompson," I said, but I was smiling. "He hasn't passed the firehouse pancake test yet."

"Challenge accepted," Jimmy said immediately. "But first, I think Sunny needs to be introduced to his new family properly."

As if he'd been waiting for her cue, Sunny opened his eyes and looked around at the crowd of firefighters and medical professionals surrounding us. His tail started wagging, and he let out a tiny bark that somehow conveyed pure joy.

"He's perfect," I said, scratching behind his ears.

"Just like his mom," Jimmy replied, and kissed me again while our family cheered and Sunny decided that this was definitely the best day ever.

Three hours later, after the impromptu engagement party had finally wound down and everyone had gone home, Jimmy and I were sitting on my couch with Sunny asleep between us, planning our future over leftover station house coffee and the kind of comfortable silence that came from knowing you'd found your person.

"So," I said, playing with my new ring and marveling at how right it felt on my finger. "Five kids and a dog. Think we can handle it?"

"With you?" Jimmy said, reaching over to squeeze my hand. "I think we can handle anything."

Outside, Station 2 sat quiet in the afternoon sun, ready for whatever calls might come. But inside my apartment, surrounded by wedding magazines Sophia had somehow already procured and puppy toys Jack had insisted on buying, I felt the kind of peace that came from knowing that no matter what chaos tomorrow brought, I'd have Jimmy and Sunny by my side.

We were going to be more than okay.

We were going to be *extraordinary*.

A NOTE FROM THE AUTHOR

Captain Michael O'Sullivan — "Cap" — is an homage to Dennis Lynn Brent, one of the finest firefighters I ever had the privilege to know.

Dennis was exactly the kind of man who would have corrected me for calling him "one of the finest firefighters I've ever known." He would have told you he was just a fireman. A truckie. He wouldn't have mentioned his thirty-eight years of service, or that he'd been chief of his local Volunteer Fire Department, or that he was considered the senior man not just for his shift, but for the entire Charlottesville Fire Department. He would never have bragged about being a National Honor Guard Academy graduate who traveled the country without notice to honor fallen firefighters he'd never met.

Dennis was the kind of man who spoke of his family with such love that it inspired everyone around him to be better fathers, better husbands, better people. He was a natural teacher who placed the needs of others before himself with grace, humility, and love. He left kindness in his wake, ripples that are still spreading outward, even today.

I learned what it meant to be a leader by watching him. I learned that true strength comes not from being the loudest voice in the room, but from knowing when someone needs to be pulled out of a chair for a hug they didn't know they needed.

On December 1, 2018, occupational cancer took Dennis from us. The Virginia General Assembly honored him with a joint resolution recognizing his decades of selfless service, but the politicians' words on paper could never capture who he really was: the man who hugged a heartbroken firefighter on their last day together, who showed up for strangers' funerals because he understood that when one of us falls, we all fall a little.

Dennis's story is tragically common. Across this country, firefighters run into burning buildings, breathe toxic smoke, and absorb chemicals that accumulate in their bodies over decades of service. They develop cancers at rates *far* higher than the general population. And then they have to fight (often for *years*) to have their illnesses recognized as line-of-duty injuries.

The same politicians who call firefighters "heroes" every election cycle have dragged their feet on passing presumptive cancer legislation. It took until 2019 — *eighteen years* after 9/11 — for Congress to finally reauthorize the September 11th Victim Compensation Fund, and only after Jon Stewart shamed them into action. States across the country have been glacially slow to pass their own presumptive cancer laws, forcing dying firefighters to prove in court that their cancer came from the job that everyone knows causes cancer.

We send these men and women into toxic environments, then make them lawyers in their final years instead of letting them focus on fighting for their lives and spending time with their families.

I never once saw Dennis be bitter about this. I never saw him be anything but gracious and grateful for the time he had left and the family who surrounded him. But *I* can be bitter for him. *I* can be angry for all the firefighters who die from occupational cancers, for their families who have to fight for benefits while they're grieving, for a system that honors heroes in speeches but abandons them when they need help most.

If you've read this far, if this story moved you, then please remember the real firefighters like Dennis Brent who inspired it. Support presumptive cancer legislation in your state. Donate to organizations that help firefighters and their families navigate cancer treatment. Remember that every time you see a fire truck, there are people inside who have chosen to risk their health and their lives for strangers.

And if you know a firefighter — active or retired — who seems to be having a hard time, maybe pull them out of their chair and give them a hug. Sometimes that's all it takes to remind someone they're not alone.

Dennis would have been embarrassed by this dedication, but he would have understood why it matters. Because when we remember the good ones, when we tell their stories, when we refuse to let their sacrifices be forgotten? That's how we honor not just their memory, but everyone who still answers the call.

If you'd like to honor Dennis's legacy, consider supporting the Firefighter Cancer Support Network, the National Fallen Firefighters Foundation, or your local volunteer fire department.

Rest easy, Dennis.

— Cari

POST-CREDITS SCENE

sophia

I was waiting up for Jack when he finally dragged himself through our front door at nearly midnight, his paramedic uniform wrinkled and his face carrying that particular exhaustion that came from twelve hours of dealing with humanity at its worst.

"Long shift?" I asked, though I already knew the answer from the way his shoulders sagged.

"The longest." He dropped his gear bag by the door and collapsed onto the couch beside me, his head falling back against the cushions. "Had a call with Engine 18 today. Tried to talk to Izzy about... well, everything. She shut me down completely. Called me 'Medic McKenzie' like we hadn't been friends for two years."

I felt my chest tighten. I'd been watching Jimmy deteriorate for weeks now, moving through the hospital like a ghost of himself. The easy warmth that had made him everyone's favorite nurse had been replaced by mechanical competence that fooled no one who actually cared about him.

"She's hurting," I said, though the words felt inadequate.

"They both are." Jack scrubbed his hands over his face. "It's like watching two people drown in the same pool while refusing to reach for each other."

I knew exactly what he meant. Jimmy had been picking up extra shifts, working himself into the ground with the kind of desperate focus that came from trying to outrun your own thoughts. And from what

Jack had told me about his interactions with Izzy's crew, she was doing the same thing — burying herself in work and pushing everyone away.

"They're both too stubborn and too broken to reach out," I said, more to myself than to Jack.

"Someone needs to do something," he said quietly. "They're going to lose each other if this keeps up."

I sat there in our quiet living room, thinking about the two people who'd become so important to both of us. They belonged together. Anyone with eyes could see it. But sometimes the people involved were the last ones to figure it out.

An idea started forming in my mind — the kind of plan that would either bring them back together or backfire spectacularly. But looking at Jack's exhausted face, thinking about Jimmy's hollow smile and Izzy's careful distance, I decided the risk was worth it.

"I need to make a phone call," I said, reaching for my phone.

Jack raised an eyebrow. "At this hour?"

"Trust me," I said, already scrolling through my contacts for a number I hadn't called in months. "Sometimes you have to deploy the secret weapon."

I found Kellen's contact and hit the dial button before I could lose my nerve. The phone rang twice before his familiar gravelly voice answered.

"What."

No greeting, no pleasantries. Just Kellen being Kellen.

"Kellen, it's Sophia." I let my voice warm, shifting into the tone I'd use with an old friend instead of a colleague. "Remember that night back in 2011, when we just had the one big ER bay with only curtains, back when we were still doing paper charting? We had that chest pain in 'Room' 7? The guy the doc ordered sublingual nitro for?"

There was a pause, and I could practically hear the wheels turning in his head. "Mmmhmm."

Perfect. He was listening. Now I just had to remind him who he'd helped me become.

"I was so new," I continued, letting the nostalgia creep into my voice. "Three weeks off orientation, and I was convinced I was going to kill someone every shift. Do you remember how I misread that order?

'Nitro sublingual x3' and I gave him all three tablets at once, instead of one tablet every five minutes for fifteen minutes?"

"Yeah," Kellen said quietly.

I closed my eyes, remembering that night with perfect clarity. The patient's blood pressure dropping like a stone, my hands shaking as I realized what I'd done, the absolute terror that I'd just killed someone through sheer incompetence.

"His pressure bottomed out to 70/40," I said. "I thought I was going to watch him die because of my mistake. I was ready to call the code team, call the supervisor, probably call my mother to tell her I was coming home in disgrace."

"Mmmhmm."

"But you just... you stayed calm. Walked me through getting him flat, starting fluids, calling the doc for orders. You didn't panic, didn't make me feel like an idiot. You just fixed it." I paused, remembering the relief when the patient's pressure started climbing back up, when it became clear he was going to be okay. "And then afterward, when I had that complete breakdown in the supply closet..."

I could still picture it: me, sitting on the floor between boxes of gauze and IV flushes, crying so hard I couldn't breathe, thick lines of mucus running down to my chin. I'd been ready to quit nursing right then and there, convinced I wasn't cut out for the responsibility of holding people's lives in my hands.

"You found me in there, snot-crying and hyperventilating," I continued. "Ready to quit nursing forever. And you sat down on that floor with me, used saline wipes to clean my face, and talked me off the ledge."

"Yeah," Kellen said again, but his voice had softened slightly.

I could tell he was remembering, too. The man who'd patiently sat with a terrified new grad, who'd reminded me that everyone made mistakes, that the measure of a nurse wasn't whether you messed up but how you learned from it. The leader who'd seen potential in a scared kid and decided to nurture it instead of crush it.

"You told me that every good nurse has a story like that," I said. "A moment when they realize how much responsibility they're carrying, how thin the line is between helping and hurting. You said the ones who quit after their first big scare were the ones who probably shouldn't have been nurses anyway, but the ones who stayed — who learned and grew and got better — those were the ones who saved lives."

"Mmmhmm."

He was letting me tell the whole story, and I could hear in those quiet affirmations that he knew exactly where this was going. But he was letting me perform this ritual anyway, letting me remind him of the mentor he'd been, the leader who'd shaped not just my career but my entire approach to nursing.

"That's the night I decided I wanted to be the kind of nurse you were," I said. "The kind who stays calm in a crisis, who teaches instead of judges, who sees the person behind the mistake." I took a breath. "That's the night you saved my career, Kellen. And probably my life."

There was a longer pause this time, and when he spoke, his voice carried a weight I recognized. "What do you need, Sophia?"

"It's about Jimmy," I said, my voice shifting from nostalgic to concerned. "He's drowning, Kellen, and I think you're the only one who can pull him out."

I explained the situation as carefully as I could — the breakup with Izzy, Jimmy's transformation into an emotional ghost, the way he was working himself to death rather than dealing with his pain. I told him about watching one of our best nurses turn into a competent machine, technically flawless but completely hollow.

"He's doing exactly what..." I paused before I said "you did", realizing I was treading on dangerous ground. I didn't know the details of whatever had broken Kellen's spirit over the years, but I'd seen enough to recognize the pattern. "He's trying to protect himself by not feeling anything. And it's destroying him."

"And you think I can fix that?" Kellen's voice was back to its usual flat tone, but I could hear something underneath it. Not irritation — consideration.

"I think you can show him what happens when you let the job win," I said honestly. "I think you can tell him what he needs to hear. And maybe..." I took a breath, gambling everything on my read of the man I'd known for over a decade. "Maybe you can remember what it felt like to have something worth fighting for."

The silence stretched so long I wondered if he'd hung up.

"This is a terrible idea," he said finally.

"Probably."

"It could backfire completely."

"Almost certainly."

Another pause, and then something that might have been a sigh. "You know, for a charge nurse who's supposed to be a leader, you're terrible at delegation. Took you fifteen minutes to ask for something I already decided to do fourteen minutes ago."

I felt my face break into a grin. There he was — the gruff, wise-cracking mentor who'd talked a terrified new grad off a ledge all those years ago. Still buried under layers of cynicism and burnout, but still there.

"So you'll do it?"

"I'll do it. But if this goes sideways, I'm blaming you."

"Fair enough. Thank you, Kellen. Really."

"Don't thank me yet," he said, and the line went dead.

I set my phone down and found Jack watching me with a mixture of amusement and concern.

"Please tell me you didn't just manipulate your night shift charge nurse into amateur couples therapy," he said.

"I prefer to think of it as strategic intervention," I replied. "Sometimes people need a push from someone who speaks their language."

"And Kellen speaks Jimmy's language?"

I thought about it for a moment. "Kellen speaks 'damaged healthcare worker who won't let people in.' It's practically his native tongue."

Jack laughed despite himself. "You're either brilliant or completely insane."

"Why can't I be both?" I said, curling up against his side. "Besides, what's the worst that could happen?"

"Famous last words," Jack muttered, but he was smiling.

As we headed to bed, I felt a cautious optimism. Tomorrow, I'd find an excuse to send Jimmy home early, and Kellen would be waiting. The grizzled charge nurse who'd once saved my career was about to work his particular brand of tough-love magic on another lost soul.

Jimmy and Izzy belonged together — I'd seen it in the way they looked at each other, the way they'd both lit up when they talked about their relationship. Sometimes good people just needed someone to remind them what they were fighting for.

And if anyone could cut through Jimmy's self-destructive spiral and make him see sense, it was Kellen. The man might be emotionally distant, but he was also perceptive, honest, and completely immune to manipulation or excuses.

Plus, I had a feeling that underneath his gruff exterior, Kellen was a romantic. You didn't stay married for seventeen years without understanding something about love and sacrifice.

Sometimes love needed a little help from its friends. And sometimes the best help came from the most unexpected sources.

Jimmy didn't know it yet, but his cavalry was coming.

SNEAK PEEK

CODE BLUE HEARTS, BOOK 4: BREAKING POINT

Delaney

The ambulance bay doors had been propped open, and the early afternoon air carried the distant wail of sirens getting inexorably closer. I stood near the triage station Sophia had set up outside, my hands moving in sharp, efficient motions as I double-checked supplies for the third time. Tourniquets. Airway kit. IV start supplies. Everything in perfect order, just like always.

"The chest tube trays are already positioned," I said to no one in particular, my voice clipped and professional. "And respiratory knows to have the vents ready for transport."

Nathan Crawford approached from my left, moving with that particular quiet intensity he got before major trauma cases. But instead of heading to his own station, he stopped directly in front of me.

"Dr. Ward."

I glanced up, then immediately back down at my supplies. "The blood bank confirmed they're thawing our FFP, and surgery's been notified. We should be — "

"Delaney." His voice was quieter now, more personal. When I looked up, he was studying my face with the kind of careful attention that made me want to step back. "Look at me."

"I'm fine, Crawford. We're as ready as we can be." I moved to adjust the position of the trauma board, but Nathan stepped closer, not letting me escape into busy work.

"Look at me," he repeated, and this time there was something in his voice — not command, but the weight of experience — that made me stop moving.

I lifted my chin, meeting his gaze directly. My jaw was set, my expression controlled, but I could see in his eyes that he was reading something I didn't want him to see.

"Nothing in medical school, nothing in residency prepares you for this," he said, his voice low and steady. "You're going to see things that will stay with you forever — there's no avoiding that now."

My mouth tightened. "I can handle — "

"I know you can." Nathan interrupted gently. "That's not what I'm saying." He took a half-step closer, making sure I couldn't look away. "You're going to have to choose who gets care and who doesn't, and some of those choices will haunt you. The kid who looks like your neighbor's son. The mother who's the same age as you. You'll make the right call, and it'll still feel wrong sometimes."

I tried to shrug, to dismiss the gravity in his words. "It's just triage. We do it every day."

"No." Nathan's voice carried the authority of someone who'd been exactly where I was about to go. "This isn't the same, and you know it. When the blood runs out, when the OR's full, when you've got three, four, five red tags and only two trauma bays — that's when it gets real."

The sirens were getting louder now.

Much louder.

My hands had stilled on the equipment, and I could feel the first crack in my armor — a flutter of uncertainty I couldn't quite suppress.

"But here's what I learned in Iraq," he continued, his tone shifting to something almost gentle. "I know you have what it takes to do this, because I've watched you work in our ER. *You have it, Delaney.* I know exactly how scared you are right now, because I've been there. But I also know you can do this.

"I believe in you."

"Nathan — "

"Trust your training, trust your instincts, and when it gets overwhelming — and it will — remember that every life you save matters more than the ones you can't." He reached out and briefly touched my shoulder, a gesture of solidarity. "We're going to get through this together."

For just a moment, my professional mask slipped completely. I felt young suddenly, and scared, and very human. I almost choked out a sob. "What if I freeze? What if I make the wrong call?"

"Then you make the next one," Nathan said simply. "And the one after that. That's all any of us can do."

The sound of an engine straining up the hill cut through our conversation, followed by the metallic smell of diesel exhaust on the wind. We both turned toward the access road, and there it was — the first ambulance, emergency lights painting the sunny afternoon in red and blue, followed by what looked like a police cruiser with someone in the back seat.

The moment crystallized between us: the last few seconds of before, when we were still just colleagues having a conversation instead of trauma workers about to be tested in ways I'd never imagined.

Nathan squeezed my shoulder once more. "You've got this, Doc."

I hadn't asked for reassurance, but I found myself clinging to it anyway. His steadiness made me feel like maybe I could borrow some of that calm, just for a moment.

I straightened, and when I looked at him again, I felt the ice queen snap back into place — but there was something different now. Not just competence, but resolve.

"Yeah," I said quietly, turning toward the approaching sirens. "We do."